KING
COTTON

I am a local author in
Castle Rock, CO. I hope
you enjoy this book! If you
do, please spread the word!

This is the first in a series.

Richard A. Noble

You can see all of them
at www.kingcottonbooks.com.

outskirts
press

Outskirts Press, Inc.
http://www.outskirtspress.com

ISBN: 978-1-9772-6852-5

Outskirts Press and the "OP" logo are trademarks belonging to Outskirts Press, Inc.

PRINTED IN THE UNITED STATES OF AMERICA

PREFACE

$\mathcal{I}$ had several readers of initial drafts of *King Cotton* say that it must have been difficult weaving a story through so many facts, real people, and actual places, dates, and happenings during that impossibly difficult chapter in America's past from April 1861 to April 1865. Truth be told, I found the opposite. I knew the story that I wanted to tell, and the events of the period gave me a framework upon which to build it. Whether or not you will find it entertaining is of course entirely up to you. I can tell you one thing, however, which is that if you read the book, you will learn some history. That was part of my goal, especially for younger readers.

Some of the real-life characters in the book will be familiar to everyone – Abraham Lincoln, Ulysses S. Grant, Robert E. Lee, Mathew Brady, Harriet Tubman, P.T. Barnum, James Wilkes Booth, Allan Pinkerton, and Mary Surratt, for example. Others perhaps less so, such as Kate Warne, Anna Surratt, John Surratt Junior, Chang & Eng Bunker, "Peanut" Burroughs, Rose O'Neal Greenhow, and John Beam. But all existed, as did the songs, guns, and places mentioned herein. The battles and other events (like the recovery of Lee's Special Order 191 and the visit to New York City by the Russian Navy) also really happened. I encourage readers to look things up when in doubt or curious for more. The internet makes doing so about as easy as it can get. But our protagonist, John "Jack" Bailey, is entirely fictitious, as are his father, co-workers Elkins and Dawson, and a few other minor characters. The causes of certain true-life happenings in the book are still debated today, such as who shot Lincoln's hat off outside Soldier's Cottage just a few months before he was assassinated, or how the devastating fire in Columbia, SC really got started. *King Cotton* finally offers some answers on those fronts, although highly speculative ones that involve Bailey.

This book is not meant to be a treatise on the horrors of slavery, although it would be impossible to cover the Civil War without that topic rearing its ugly head. Nor is it meant to be an exhaustive text on all the battles of the Civil War, although the ones that are covered are done so accurately, if briefly. Neither is this book meant to delve into the deep divisions that the country faced at that time and which, sadly, one senses we are experiencing in some ways again today. The newspaper quotes are all accurate, verified through NewsBank, a company that has digitized thousands of newspapers and other primary source materials dating back several hundred years. NewsBank's various databases include some two billion articles and are available in many public and academic libraries around the world.

Photography plays a major role in *King Cotton,* and the Civil War was one of the first conflicts ever covered by that medium. If you've seen even a few photographs from that era, you have almost certainly looked upon the work of Mathew Brady, Alexander Gardner, and/or Timothy O'Sullivan, all of whom are mentioned in the book. I have included some of their photographs herein, courtesy of the Library of Congress and its excellent collections. Again there is much more available on the internet and the same is true of battle and other maps that you might find useful as you follow Bailey's travels. Being conscious of page count, I did not include as much as I could have in terms of either pictures or maps.

What this book is about is one man's (Bailey's) personal journey through a gruesome war as he tries to salvage his business, steer clear of trouble, and avoid responsibility as best he can – all while seeking personal gain and entertainment wherever he can find it. As a result of his experiences, however, a higher set of moral standards and a better appreciation of how others might view the world begin to evolve within him. *King Cotton* is also about an industry and a product that, at the time, countries were willing to fight wars over. Cotton was the oil or rare earth mineral of the day.

Like most authors, I had a lot of help and would like to thank a few people here for exactly that. First and foremost my wife Kim, who was a source of constant encouragement, a proofreader and someone who knew when to leave me to it when I was on a roll. Early readers Ken Aubrey, General Bob Beletic, plus friends Stuart Chinnery and Jeff Topping (both of whom I have had the privilege of knowing for more than 50 years). My sister, another Kim, was also a reader of early drafts who provided very valuable editing and advice, as did my good friend and former colleague in the publishing industry, Lena Huang.

Lastly, many of the places mentioned in the book can be toured today. Battlefields like Gettysburg and buildings like the Peterson House and Ford's Theatre are meticulously maintained by our National Park Service, for example. Certain landmarks still exist but have fallen to other uses, such as the Surratt Boarding House which, the last time I checked, was a Chinese restaurant.

With all that said, I hope you have as much fun reading this book as I did in writing it. Before I started the process I read somewhere that the average novel was 80,000 words. I wondered

how on earth I would ever get there but, next thing I knew, I was at almost 110,000. Although I wrote dozens of business plans and Board decks, hundreds of memos, and thousands of emails during my 44-year career in business, this was my first novel (although some might argue not my first work of fiction). My second novel, a sequel to *King Cotton* with the working title "*Kentucky Gold,*" is in the works. It picks up right where *King Cotton* ends – on 10th Street NW in Washington DC between the Petersen House and Ford's Theatre, minutes after the tragedy of Lincoln being shot and with Bailey frantically fleeing the scene to avoid what he believes could be a date with the hangman.
Enjoy.

Rick Noble
August 2023

FOREWORD

January 30, 1915

*T*his book is best consumed on the heels of a few words of explanation, hence this foreword. I write from the relative safety of what may be the final stop on my life's journey, the Cedar Shores Nursing Home in upstate New York. When I say safety, those of you who have had the ill luck of exposure to nursing homes will know that I cannot possibly be referring to my lodgings. I rather mean safety from my past enemies and acquaintances, all of whom I am hoping by now have either passed on or are past caring. Nevertheless, in an abundance of caution, I am keeping this manuscript under my mattress where I hope it will remain until I myself pass on to a better world. I presume that on that day they will finally change my sheets and, in doing so, find this story.

Some in my position would say they are writing to "set the record straight" (be on alert whenever you hear those words from a politician) or to "fill in some blanks in history". I won't insult you with such claptrap. I am writing primarily to avoid the monotony and constant reminders of the deplorable conditions in which I find myself. Mushy peas and beef not fit for stray dogs, squeaky wicker wheelchairs, starched lace doilies and the ever-present smell of mothballs and aged shut ins. Having seen places like the Florence Stockade as well as Gettysburg and Fredericksburg post battle, I speak with some authority on deplorable conditions. Perhaps I am also indulging myself by reliving old times—good and bad. What I would give to hear the creak of saddle leather once more on a cold fall morning, smell freshly mown hay at dusk on a warm summer's eve in Kentucky, or experience again the yelps and howls of anticipation as opposites approach from either side of a battlefield (or a bedroom, come to that).

It's true there is a nurse or two here that would serve as suitable distraction, but age differences render such dreams as just that. Trust me, I've tried. And while a surprising number of my female fellow lodgers would be more than game, my tastes run a little younger. About a quarter century younger, truth be told. To their credit, however, there are female tenants here ready and willing to do things that would expand the repertoire of a New Orleans bordello tart. And I speak with some authority on that topic as well.

For all my want of something to occupy the days of my twilight, I admit to struggling as to where to begin. In the end I decided to start at the end, mainly because doing so puts the rest of my story in improved context. I'll spare you the customary nonsense about changing names to protect the innocent and the guilty. At my stage in life, I can say that there is nothing to be gained or lost by not offering heartfelt praise where I felt it was due and damning criticism where it was earned—sparing none in the process, least of all myself.

Of course, when I was living them, I didn't know that the four years covered in this book would prove to be such an important period in history. But over the years that followed I jotted down notes documenting my experiences as they came to mind.

Sometimes these recollections are triggered by an event, such as Gavrilo Princip's assassination of Archduke Franz Ferdinand last June, and sometimes they just come to me when I hear a particular word or phrase. In any case, if there are others left on this earth who were present to witness the events I describe herein, I say to hell with the consequences of an occasional embellishment or imperfect memory, and let's raise a glass to old times!

Chapter 1

THE END

Washington, DC, April 14, 1865

*A*s I finished packing the remaining few items I planned to take with me for my elopement with Anna, a rising calamity outside my window became too much to ignore. I made my way across the room and parted the curtains an inch or two to surveil the street below. The pleasant sounds of celebration that had ebbed and flowed in Washington over the past few days had abruptly given way to urgent shouts and a growing sense of foreboding that reminded me of a time in Charleston one spring morning almost exactly four years ago. Recalling where those events had led caused me to shudder. As I strained to see through the dark, I recognized fellow boarder Henry Safford directing a group of men toward the front door of my lodgings. As they moved closer, I realized they were struggling to carry someone. My curiosity turned to panic when I recognized the tall lanky figure that was the focus of their attentions.

Father always took pleasure in reminding me that it was doubtful I would have ever been accepted at Eton, Rugby, or the like, but I possess one skill that I would put up against any of the snoots from those stalwarts of higher learning. With the chips down, my neck on the line and the time to evaluate alternatives short, I am in a league of my own. The interest that this wounded guest would bring upon the Petersen boarding house this night could not help but turn attention my way. Once the inevitable inquiries began, someone would undoubtedly recall seeing me down the street in Peter Taltavull's Star Saloon a short while ago. More digging would place me with Booth on other occasions, as well as with the Surratt's and the rest of the rabble that had almost certainly played some role in what was unfolding in front of me. Just moments ago I had been dreaming of seeing Anna's petticoats swinging on a bedpost, and now it seemed just as likely that we'd be swinging by our necks from the gallows. But with some quick thinking and a little luck, I'd miss that party.

My innocence in any involvement in what had just transpired would matter little in the rush to judgement. Just as easy to build scaffolding for ten as one, many would say. And if casting the net a little too wide resulted in an unjustified hanging or two (especially of a foreigner like me), well what would one or two more wasted lives be in a country that had just squandered hundreds of thousands. I doubt it took me more than a few seconds to process all my options and settle on an old favorite—run.

It's not often that I am regarded as a source of useful advice, but here's some you can take to the bank. When faced with an unexpected need to bolt on short notice, there are four things I have found to be invaluable. A sturdy and nondescript hat (I prefer a cavalry slouch), a coat generously outfitted with pockets, as much coin as you can lay your hands on, and a pistol. I guarantee you will find use for the first three, and I hope for your sake you will not need the last. And while I'm doling out advice, let me say that I prefer the Cooper Pocket Revolver[1]. An entire book could be dedicated to a debate on handguns, but for my money the "ready right now" double action, carry friendly size, and impressive stopping power at close quarters makes the Cooper a sensible choice for almost any occasion. No offence to Samuel Colt of course, God rest his soul. I'd had the good fortune to lighten Sam's wallet in a card game a few years back, and while I would find his Colt Pocket Police Revolver more than adequate in a pinch, personal taste counts a lot when it comes to sidearms.

With a few quick motions I donned my hat and coat, scooped up my cash, tucked a Cooper in my belt and opened the door to the hallway. It took every ounce of restraint I could muster to not take the stairs down three at a time lest I appear to be in full flight, but as I made the landing on the first floor and started toward the door to the street my bad luck continued as I came face-to-face with Mary Todd Lincoln. No one I know would call Mrs. Lincoln handsome, but you can imagine how she looked with her husband lying limp in the arms of several men. Two sons already in the grave (Willie only three years back) and now this. Fortunately, she seemed too distraught to recognize me as she turned to her left and disappeared into the front parlor. As I strode forward toward the front door I could hear a commotion coming from Willie Clarke's bedroom in the back, so I assumed they had taken Lincoln in there. But I never looked back.

In another moment of quick thinking (and to help create plausibility for a hasty exit) I yelled, "Someone fetch Mrs. Lincoln a brandy—Hell, I'll do it". To complete the façade, when my boots

---

1 James Maslin Cooper manufactured the Cooper Pocket Revolver in Pennsylvania from 1850 to 1869. The gun had an octagonal barrel and held five .31 caliber balls. Some 15,000 were manufactured, a small fraction of the more than 300,000 comparable Colt pistols that were manufactured beginning in 1847.

hit 10th Street I immediately crossed toward Ford's Theatre and the Star Saloon, not that I had any intention of entering either ever again. Once south of E Street, I bolted toward Pennsylvania Avenue, my mind racing through the best options for getting out of town.

Chapter 2

A CHANCE ENCOUNTER

Baltimore, MD, February 23, 1861

*A*fter spending the better part of the week doing business in Baltimore, I felt I had earned the luxury of lingering over a late Saturday breakfast in the Barnum Hotel[1] and enjoying a front-to-back reading of the day's papers. The *Baltimore American* was awash in the news of the anticipated arrival of Lincoln's train, which was scheduled to pass through early that afternoon on its way to Washington and the inauguration on March 4. "Mr. Lincoln will remain in the city but two hours. He arrives at one o'clock by the Northern Central railroad—", the *American* reported. It went on to say, prophetically, that "Beyond the people whom curiosity to see Mr. Lincoln may draw to gather we presume his passage through the city will be accomplished quietly—" It would indeed be quieter than anyone imagined.

---

1 Construction on the Barnum Hotel began in 1825 on the corner of Fayette and Calvert Streets in Baltimore. It was torn down in 1890, and over the years its guests included John Quincy Adams and Charles Dickens.

I'm sure I'm not alone when I say that, as a rule, when politicians are about, I usually keep one hand on my wallet and the other ready to thwart unwanted physical advances. But this man Lincoln, despite all the ill will being heaped upon him, seemed different. I decided that I would make my way over to the station to take his measure in person. No doubt my father would want a report anyway, especially as it was beginning to look increasingly like we would need to find creative new ways to sell our product. In fact, our company's survival might well depend on it. When I say our product, I mean cotton. The fact that the Southern states currently satisfied three quarters of the world's seemingly insatiable demand for the stuff gave many in Dixie the confidence that they need not fear a war with the North. Their logic was best articulated by Senator James Henry Hammond of South Carolina when he said, "Without firing a gun, without drawing a sword, should they make war on us we could bring the whole world to our feet. The South is perfectly competent to go on, one, two, or three years without planting a seed of cotton. I believe that if she was to plant but half her cotton, for three years to come, it would be an immense advantage to her—What would happen if no cotton was furnished for three years? I will not stop to depict what everyone can imagine, but this is certain: England would topple headlong and carry the whole civilized world with her, save the South. No, you dare not make war on cotton. No power on earth dares to make war upon it. Cotton is king."

Maybe it was paranoia, but as I swallowed the last of my coffee I couldn't help but think that this logic was deeply flawed. My own opinion was that England and other countries would go to great lengths to find other sources of cotton before becoming embroiled in a U.S. civil war. Being in the business I also knew that warehouses in Europe were bulging with excess inventory and could likely withstand a temporary halt in supply. With hostilities between North and South looking almost certain, a blockade of Southern ports would surely follow, making a stoppage inevitable.

Most of the cotton bound for England, France, and elsewhere in Europe left via Southern ports that included New Orleans, Mobile, Savannah, and Charleston. It was from Charleston that I had been managing my father's cotton business for the past few years. In this capacity I was charged with sourcing and buying the stuff, and ensuring it was loaded onto outbound ships with, using his typically stern words, "the utmost efficiency". Happily, it wasn't a complicated business and I'd become proficient enough to do all this to his satisfaction while leaving myself plenty of time for a decent amount of drinking, womanizing, and gambling. Unfortunately, however, my own view on the slim chances of cotton being king painted a grim outlook for exporters like us. We could all be out of business soon after the first exchange of gunfire. None of these dark thoughts improved my hangover as I plunked down payment for the meal.

I left the hotel and stopped by a gunmaker's shop on Calvert Street to pick up a Cooper revolver I had left with proprietor Alexander McComas[2] for minor repairs. With that retrieved and tucked away in my coat, I walked a quarter mile or so up to East Franklin to the Calvert Street Station where I joined a large group of people bustling with excitement at the prospect of catching a glimpse of the President-elect. Little did I know at the time that some lurking there harbored more sinister intentions. According to the papers, Lincoln was to disembark at Calvert Street Station[3], then make his way by carriage for a mile or so over to Campden

---

2 Born in 1821, Alexander McComas was a prolific gun producer known for winning many craftmanship competitions. He established his shop on Calvert Street in Baltimore in 1843.

3 Calvert Street Station operated in Baltimore from 1858 to 1948, serving passengers on the Northern Central Railway.

Station[4] where he and his family would board another train for the final leg of their journey to Washington. Having worked the docks in Charleston for several years, I'd become a bit of a savant in spotting the ebbs and flows of people within crowds. As I leaned against a wall and studied this one, it became clear that there were several factions mingling about. The majority were there, of course, to witness a piece of history, including layabouts with nothing better to do on a Saturday afternoon. But there was also at least a half dozen gentlemen in the mix who were discretely signaling each other every few minutes. They situated themselves in a way that would enable them to cover the area between the train and the carriages that had been positioned to take the Lincoln party on the short journey over to Campden Station. And there seemed to be another group shadowing this one, which included a woman who appeared to be about my age, in her mid-20's. She seemed to have decided that I was also worthy of her attention.

In different circumstances I might have assumed, or hoped, that the lady's intentions were purely recreational. But before I could fully assess what might be going on, sighs of disappointment rippled through the crowd as it became known that the Lincolns were not on the train. As we were to later learn, Lincoln had already passed through Baltimore hours ago, at 3:30 a.m. at the President Street Station. And while Mrs. Lincoln and the children had been on the train that just pulled in, they had disembarked a few stops back to avoid this mob. Lincoln would later be ridiculed for his caution, with some newspapers even questioning

---

4 The Baltimore and Ohio Railroad began construction on Campden Station in 1856. Better known today for Campden Yards, in the 19th century the area was the scene for several episodes of civil strife, including the Baltimore Riots of 1861 and the Great Railway Strike of 1877.

his masculinity and character. Cartoons, such as *Volck's Passage Through Baltimore* and the *Flight of Abraham* (which appeared in *Harper's Weekly*) provided his detractors with fodder for years to come. Some would even question whether there really was any danger awaiting him in Baltimore that Saturday afternoon, but I am here to tell you that something out of the ordinary was going on in that crowd at Calvert Street Station and, wanting no part of it, I decided not to linger[5].

With people dissipating in every direction, it seemed unlikely that I would be able to secure a carriage, so I decided to again cover the distance back to the Barnum on foot, where I would retrieve my luggage and begin the trip back to Charleston. I'd only made it a couple of blocks before a tap on the shoulder brought me to a halt. Turning around, I came face-to-face with the young woman I had seen watching me just a few minutes ago. Any notion of this being a friendly greeting was dispelled by the presence of the two stout looking gentlemen on either side of her. I also recognized them from the station.

"Mr. Bailey, we would like to speak with you, and we can either do it here or at our offices, your choice."

"How about at my hotel just down the street?" I countered, not liking being outnumbered or the fact that she knew my name. Given the look of her team, I figured that having witnesses close by in the relatively civilized setting of a hotel lobby might be wise.

"Not the Barnum." she responded, "Here, or our offices."

"Well, you three seem to have me at a distinct advantage beyond just numbers. You know both my name and where I am staying. Why don't we talk here, and you begin with an introduction and a reason why I should talk to you at all. You obviously

---

5 The Baltimore Plot was a conspiracy to kill Abraham Lincoln as he passed through that city on his way to Washington and his first inauguration.

aren't with the police, or we'd already be on our way to wherever you chose." I said this with more confidence than I felt, but the Cooper I was touching in my coat pocket was offering some comfort. At the risk of sounding like a braggart, I am quite proficient in talking myself out of difficult situations—a skill well-honed by getting myself into such circumstances with some frequency.

"Fair enough. My name is Kate Warne[6] and I'm with the Pinkerton Detective Agency, as are the two gentlemen beside me and Mr. Harry Davies behind you." So much for my ability to read crowds thinks I, as I'd completely missed this fourth character. His presence off my stern eliminated any possibility of a hasty exit.

"All right then Miss Warne, how can I be of service to you?" I offered.

"You can start by telling us what you were doing at the Calvert Street Station just now." She said as she moved a half step closer.

"Same as everyone else," I answered, "Waiting to catch a glimpse of the President-elect."

"Who were you with?" she asked.

"You were there watching me. Obviously, I wasn't with anyone." I was tempted to add that there certainly were other people at the station that were there working together but just like in a court of law, it's usually best to only answer the question that is asked. Offer up more and it'll end up being a longer discussion than you'd like.

"Do you know James Luckett or Cypriano Ferrandini?"[7] was her next question.

---

6 Kate Warne was born in 1833 in Erin, NY. Widowed at the age of 23, she became the first female detective in the U.S., and worked for the Pinkerton Detective Agency. She is credited with uncovering the Baltimore Plot. Warne died in 1868 at the age of 34 and is buried in the Pinkerton's family plot at Graceland Cemetery in Chicago, IL.
7 Luckett and Ferrandini were alleged conspirators in the Baltimore Plot.

I had a feeling that these folks knew a lot more than they were letting on, so I decided to be straight. "The former is a competitor of mine in the cotton trade, and an ass. The latter is the barber at the Barnum who wears too much eau de cologne, even for a Corsican. I can't wait to hear what those two have in common."

Ignoring the bait, she asked why I had chosen to stay at the Barnum, to which I responded that I always stayed there when I was in Baltimore and was there now as part of a business trip to sell my wares. And, speaking of wares, I was due to catch a train back to Charleston and really needed to be on my way.

"Mr. Bailey, the fact that you are British, and that your name hasn't yet come up in any of our current inquiries is a fortunate thing for you. You should know that the Barnum is a rat's nest of Southern sympathizers and, unless you'd like to have more chats like this one, I'd suggest you consider different accommodations the next time you find yourself in this city."

The feeling that I was about to be dismissed emboldened me sufficiently to say, "I actually would be interested in additional chats with you Miss Warne. Since you seem to be so familiar with hotels in the area, perhaps I will contact you for a recommendation before my next visit. Pick one with a good restaurant and I will treat you to dinner as a show of thanks. Least I can do."

"I assure you, Mr. Bailey, that another meeting with me or anyone else from the Pinkerton Detective Agency is likely not in your best interests," she said as she turned and signaled her entourage to start moving back up Calvert Street toward the station. "And please make certain that you keep your activities confined to commerce. I believe you'll find that politics can be fatal in this country."

In other countries too thinks I, with Anne Boleyn and Spencer Perceval[8] coming to mind. But her questions confirmed that

---

8 Queen Anne Boleyn was executed by order of King Henry VIII in 1533. British Prime Minister Perceval was assassinated in 1812.

there had indeed been something sinister brewing in that crowd. Add that to the fact that Southern cannons had fired upon a Union steamship the prior month, and with Mississippi, Florida, Alabama, Georgia, Louisiana, Texas, and South Carolina having recently seceded from the Union, it seemed almost certain that catastrophe was looming.

With these dark thoughts I started my journey back to Charleston to meet with my father and discuss how we might ensure that our business was positioned to navigate the rough waters ahead.

Chapter 3

THE SEEDS OF AN IDEA

Charleston, South Carolina lies about 600 miles south of Baltimore, and transit between the two requires a hellish combination of horses, carriages, trains, a high tolerance for boredom, often odorous fellow passengers and, in my case at least, a decent supply of whiskey. And on top of all that, in the early 1860's there was a disappointing lack of ladies traveling unescorted along this route, although I planned to remedy that situation once back in Charleston. But as so often happens, setting out on a journey with low expectations can result in pleasant surprises. In this case, chance played a role in providing me with two ideas that would prove essential in saving my business from ruin during the war that was to come. At our stop in Washington, a well-dressed gentleman with an impressive moustache boarded the train and sat in the seat across from me. After exchanging perfunctory nods, I went back to my newspaper, which was filled with criticisms of the "cowardly manner" in which Lincoln had arrived in Washington as well as speculation on the content of his upcoming inauguration speech. An article in the February 23rd issue of *The Evening Post* titled "A Fiendish Plot! Designs Upon

Mr. Lincoln's Life" suggested that "there was a plot to assassinate him while passing through Baltimore, but such stories are not believed." It went on to say that, on the advice of some mysterious third party he had changed plans the night before he was to have arrived in Baltimore and instead took a special train on which he "… wore a Scotch plaid cap and a very long military cloak, so that he was entirely unrecognizable." Once I'd had my fill, I set the paper down and had a quick look around while stealing a swig from the hip flask that typically kept my Cooper company.

"If you don't mind my asking sir, what do you keep in that flask?" asked my traveling companion. Fearing I'd had the bad luck of ending up with a Baptist sitting across from me, I mumbled something about medicinal needs and bursitis.

"Don't misunderstand, my friend", he responded, "I'm not opposed. In fact, I am in the business and simply curious from a professional standpoint." With those words he had my full attention.

"I was in a rush to catch this train out of Baltimore and frankly just purchased whatever the barman at the Barnum was willing to part with. The rest of the bottle is in my luggage, but I think it was Evan Williams," I offered.

"A fine old brand," he opined, "but can I interest you in sampling mine? My name is John Henry Beam[9], although friends call me Jack, and my whiskey is called Early Times."

"Well, that's two things we have in common then," I said, "A keen interest in bourbon and the same given names. My name is John as well, John Bailey, although I too answer to Jack. Let's

---

9 John Henry "Jack" Beam was born in Kentucky in 1839. After apprenticing for his father David, in 1860 he opened his own distillery in Bardstown, KY, called "Early Times". Early Times bourbon is distilled today by the Sazerac Company, which produces other well-known brands, including Buffalo Trace, Pappy Van Winkle, and Blanton's.

have a taste of what you are peddling. I'd be happy to provide an opinion."

Our camaraderie and candor increased as the contents of his bottle diminished. By the time a few hours had passed, we had covered each other's personal histories and our businesses, shared our concerns about the fate of commerce if hostilities worsened, and managed to do it all without revealing our respective political preferences.

"I am confident that I'll be able to sell Early Times to both sides," offered Mr. Beam at one point, "let's face it, there will be plenty of demand driven by both medicinal and recreational purposes. The challenge will be transporting across the lines, but geography presents less of a problem for me than it does you. If conflict comes, I believe that Kentucky will declare neutrality and that I'll be able to move about fairly easily and sell to both sides."

The possibility of serving customers on both sides of the conflict hadn't occurred to me. I'd been wrestling with various idiotic notions ranging from running blockades to simply selling out and going home to Liverpool. In either case, the end result would likely be financial ruin. But selling cotton only to the South seemed a doomed strategy with limited longevity. The South had well under half the population of the North and its economy was overwhelmingly agricultural. The North was far more industrialized, and the fact that more than 95 percent of the country's firearms were currently produced there offered the starkest illustration of that advantage. In my opinion, the odds simply did not favor a Southern victory. But I couldn't help being intrigued that, just like bourbon, there could be interest in my product on both sides. Uniforms and flags would top the list of products needing cotton. After all, pageantry thrives in times of conflict. Logistics would be the issue, not demand.

Beam continued, "Shipping in bulk will also be a problem for you. You can't exactly stash a meaningful amount of cotton in a wagon or two and send your drivers and slaves hundreds of miles North across battle lines to find buyers."

"Obviously," I said, "and, by the way, neither I nor my company owns slaves. Britain abolished such barbarism decades ago."

"But surely your suppliers own them, my friend. Aren't you taking a side in the matter by association?" he replied.

Frankly I had been troubled by this very issue for some time. I usually assuaged my guilt through a selfish combination of pushing it out of my thoughts, reasoning that at least the poor souls were fed, clothed, and domiciled; and choosing to believe that my suppliers treated theirs well. Or similar variations on such nonsense.

"I'm on the side of commerce and Bailey Importers," I offered lamely, "and I have enough to worry about in my own business without trying to manage the affairs of others or correct social injustices."

Our newfound friendship foundering on this uncomfortable moment, we sat in silence for some time. But as the train approached Richmond, Virginia, Beam spoke again as if our last exchange hadn't happened. "It's been a pleasure passing the time with you Mr. Bailey and, again I appreciated your thoughts on my whiskey. I have business in Richmond before I travel back to Kentucky, thus will take my leave of you at the next stop."

"It was a pleasure getting to know you as well Mr. Beam. And it was my very good fortune to happen to sit with a distiller looking to have his product sampled," I said sincerely.

When exchanging addresses he handed me a playing card-sized photograph of himself that included his name, address, and other particulars.

"Look me up if you ever find yourself near Louisville, my friend, and let me know if I can ever be of service to you. It would be an honor to continue our discussion and to commiserate over the effects of politics on our businesses."

"What's this?" I asked looking at the card with genuine curiosity.

"It's a carte de visite,"[10] he responded, "and all the rage in Washington. There are lines of people at Mathew Brady's studio there every day to buy them, although I think Mr. Brady's interests are turning more toward the photographic opportunities that war might bring. He took that photograph of Lincoln at the Cooper Institute in New York a year or so ago you know, and he is in high demand with statesmen and other senior officials. I met him when I was having these cards created and he was quite excited about photographing Lincoln again before the inauguration. He told me he hoped to obtain official permission to document hostilities in the field through photography should war come. Think of how unprecedented that would be! Both sides will be keen to make that happen."

And suddenly the second useful idea to come from my encounter with Mr. Beam began to germinate. The politicians, generals, and captains of industry in any country share many common attributes, and primary among these are an overabundance of self-worth and an utter lack of humility. In other words, the perfect environment in which to sell photography.

"If I may be so bold sir, you could actually be of service to me in a small way right now, Mr. Beam," I said. "I wonder

---

10 The carte de visite was patented in Paris 1854 by André Adolphe-Eugène Disdéri. About the size of a modern-day playing card, they included a small photograph and other information about the subject. Early adopters included Queen Victoria and Napoleon III.

if I could impose upon your generosity to introduce me to Mathew Brady?"[11]

"Of course," responded Beam, "I will write him as soon as I arrive home. What shall I say is the nature of your interest?"

"Please tell him that I am fascinated with photography and that I have some ideas that might be helpful to his business. You can also say that I expect to be in Washington again soon and that I would be grateful for a few minutes of his time," I responded, knowing that few business owners can resist the offer of an idea that might help line their pockets—me included.

"On the topic of introductions, Mr. Bailey, if you are interested, let me also pen you an introduction to a fellow Louisville native and friend of the Beam family, Robert Anderson. Major Anderson was recently put in charge of the federal installations in your hometown, including the Charleston Arsenal, Castle Pinckney and Forts Moultrie and Sumter. Perhaps a good contact to have as you contemplate selling cotton to the Union." He scribbled a note and handed it to me.

Apparently, Beam's knowledge of current events wasn't quite as complete as mine. With Castle Pinckney and Charleston Arsenal having already been surrendered to the South and all Union troops in the area now at Fort Sumter and under siege, Major Anderson wasn't off to an auspicious start. Although it wasn't likely that I could act upon an introduction any time soon, I was in a frame of mind that had me grasping at any straws on offer. I graciously accepted Beam's note.

The remainder of the journey from Richmond down to Charleston was routine. As was my custom, I consumed newspapers that I obtained at almost every stop along the way. In these I

---

11 Born sometime between 1822 and 1824, Brady was a pioneer and innovator in photography. His mobile darkrooms processed thousands of images from the Civil War, bringing the horror of battle to the public in a way that had never before been possible. He died in January of 1896.

read disconcerting articles about gathering war clouds and opinion pieces that were uniformly anti-North and anti-Lincoln, while washing down bad food with the contents of my oft-replenished flask. Under the title "A Confidence Man", *The Richmond Daily Whig* stated, "What a curious man our President-about-to-be is! Up to the time of his reaching Washington, he could not be brought to believe that the country was 'suffering' or that the crisis was anything but 'artificial.' Springfield is blessed with mails, newspapers, and telegraphs, and these have been bur-thened with the evidences of national calamity and disaster, but they have made no impression on the dazed sense and bewildered mind of the man suddenly elevated to the giddy height of the Presidency."

To their credit, many of these Southern papers reprinted the unaltered text of Lincoln's first inaugural address, although I'm not certain how many of their readers were paying attention to the details. In that address he said:

"Apprehension seems to exist among the people of the Southern States that by the accession of a Republican administration their property and their peace and personal security are to be endangered. There has never been any reasonable cause for such apprehension. Indeed, the most ample evidence to the contrary has all the while existed and been open to their inspection. It is found in nearly all the published speeches of him who now addresses you. I do but quote from one of those speeches when I declare that 'I have no purpose, directly or indirectly, to interfere with the institution of slavery in the States where it exists. I believe I have no lawful right to do so, and I have no inclination to do so.'

And '.... there needs to be no bloodshed or violence; and there shall be none, unless it be forced upon the national authority.... there will be no invasion, no using of force against or among the people anywhere.'

In other words, Lincoln had no intention of interfering with slavery in the South, nor would he engage the military to enforce unity unless provoked. While much of that seemed like a genuine attempt at appeasement to me, the opinion pages in these Southern papers suggested that I held a minority point of view. And all the more so the further south I traveled.

Chapter 4

BACK HOME

Charleston – March & April 1861

J arrived home to discover that my father was already in Charleston and close to full blown panic over our prospects should hostilities erupt. Some would later say that the first shots of the Civil War had already been fired two months earlier when cadets from the South Carolina Military Academy shelled the steamship Star of the West as it attempted to reinforce and resupply Fort Sumter. And now our Governor, Francis Wilkinson Pickens, was making ominous demands that the Union surrender that Fort, and it seemed that only a miracle could prevent things from getting far worse, and soon. Against this ominous backdrop, we met for dinner at his hotel, the King's Courtyard Inn.[12]

James Francis Bailey, my father, had built a very successful business in Liverpool importing cotton from the U.S. When I came of age, he dispatched me to Charleston to oversee things for Bailey Importers from this end. I would frankly have preferred to follow some of my friends into higher education, but he claimed

---

12 Built in 1853 by Colonel J. Charles Blum and still operating today.

that I didn't have the character for it. If he had said I was too much of a womanizer, I would have pointed out that the apple doesn't usually fall too far from the tree. If he had said I enjoyed the drink a little too much to have any success with the books I would have, well, I would not have had much of a defense. And I didn't know at the time that those two tendencies were expected of the male student population in any case. At least among the people that you'd want to socialize with. But, as it turned out, Charleston was an assignment I accepted in order to escape both his domineering personality and Émilie, the French trollop he married soon after my mother had passed.

I suspected that Émilie's spending habits might be playing a role in elevating Father's anxiety a notch or two at this moment. I also suspect that the differences in parenting styles between my loving mother and my domineering, self-centered father may be responsible for my issues with authority, but that's a discussion for another time.

"What's the mood up North?" he asked, "Is there any hope that this buffoon Lincoln can or will do anything to settle things down before it is too late?"

"Actually, he's been making some very conciliatory statements" I responded, recalling what I had read in his inaugural address. "That said, many in this part of the country seem to be well past the point of listening. In my opinion, it is indeed already too late."

"Well then, we're finished. A blockade will be one of the Union's first moves. Come the fall harvest, we won't be able to get anything out of Charleston" he observed gloomily. "I'd like to think that the Royal Navy wouldn't stand for it, but my contacts in London believe that Britain will choose to steer clear of this mess."

"I think I may have found an alternative," I offered in a low voice, as I cast a quick glance around the room to ensure that we weren't being overheard. "What if we were to sell our product right here in the U.S.?"

"Don't be a fool," he responded. "With exports halted, the South will be awash in cotton. We'll lose money on every sale. And we'd be competing locally, which we've never done. Our expertise is in exporting to Europe."

"I was actually thinking about selling it up North" I said in an even quieter tone, as I again looked around again to make certain we weren't being overheard.

"Oh, pardon me then," he said sarcastically. "Why didn't I think of that? I'm sure your Confederate friends will provide an escort through the battle lines and the Union will greet you with open purses."

Resisting the temptation of an acerbic response, I said, "Unfortunately, it won't be quite that simple. But I think I may have figured out a way that I can move back and forth across the lines without arousing suspicion. In fact, I could be welcome on both sides if things work out as I suspect." And with that I shared the relevant portions of my conversation on the train with Jack Beam and my theory on how photographers might be able to move unfettered among the troops on both sides to document hostilities for posterity (and vanity).

"Mathew Brady, you say. If memory serves, he made a portrait of the Prince of Wales during his Majesty's visit to New York last year," he said as he was digesting all this. "How, as a cotton trader, do you propose to gain employment from such a man?"

"Mr. Beam knows him and is arranging an introduction," I replied. "Brady is working out of a studio in Washington, and I plan to present myself there as soon as that introduction is made. And, of course, after I have set things up with our suppliers here for the coming harvest."

If he was impressed with my logic, he didn't show it. But a couple more drinks into the evening he seemed to be warming to the idea. No doubt the complete lack of alternatives helped. His one justifiable concern was how we'd manage things in Charleston with me potentially traveling so frequently. With confidence I didn't entirely feel I assured him that Elkins, who had been assisting me here the past couple of years, was up to the task. I'd sort Elkins out later.

"I suppose if we can get enough of the stuff up North, we could start shipping again from New York to Liverpool," he mused, as the whiskey began to reinforce his confidence.

"Probably too complicated," I said, "Better just to sell all we can up there, preferably to a single customer—the government—and avoid drawing too much attention to ourselves."

With him in a calmer state, I turned my attention to convincing him that he should go back to Liverpool as soon as possible. A blockade would trap him in Charleston just as effectively as it would trap our cotton, and the last thing I needed was his first-hand involvement in setting my plan in motion. Happily, he was able to secure a berth on a ship leaving two days later and I saw him off at the docks with promises to keep him informed.

At this time of year, our suppliers were planting, which was traditionally when I liked to visit with them, secure arrangements for the coming harvest and renew bonds over a meal and a drink or three. So, after spending a couple of days spelling things out for Elkins and satisfying my need for some female companionship, I began making the rounds to the plantations with whom we did business. My conversation with Beam had me working harder than usual to ignore the slaves that I saw at each stop, working the fields, serving food and drink, and attending to anything else that required effort. My suppliers were surprised to see me given the looming conflict but were delighted to accept deposits to secure our orders, even though I was able to negotiate these down from typical levels. Being British, they viewed me as a naïve neutral at worst, and a damn sight more desirable buyer at this point than one from New York or Massachusetts. If any of them were concerned on my behalf about a war or blockade, they never mentioned it.

Ten days of this and I was more than ready to get back home to Charleston, where I discovered that an old friend, Stephen Lee, a Charleston native who shared my passion for bourbon and other finer things in life, was in town. Stephen was one of many Confederate officers who had originally attended West Point and served in the U.S. Army but resigned their commissions to join the Confederate States Army (C.S.A.). And so it was that newly minted C.S.A. Captain Stephen D. Lee[13] and I got together a few times over the course of the next couple of weeks. During that time we did our best to ensure that various drinking establishments and bordellos in town had a profitable month. He was a decent and honest sort, but I doubt he mentioned any of our antics when, in 1880, he was being considered for the presidency of Mississippi State University, a position he would go on to hold for almost 20 years.

During one of our excursions in early April we were joined by a couple of his fellow officers, Winder, and Chisolm. I learned that night that they were planning to visit Fort Sumter to demand

---

13 Born in Charleston in 1833, Lee graduated from the United States Military Academy in 1854. He resigned from the Union Army in 1861 and became an aide to Confederate General P.G.T. Beauregard. By late 1862 he had been promoted to Brigadier General. He spent July to October 1863 as a prisoner of war but was released as part of a prisoner exchange. Lee spent much of his wartime service in Tennessee. After the war he briefly served in the Mississippi State Senate before becoming the first President of Mississippi State University in 1880.

a surrender from Beam's friend, Major Anderson.[14] The bourbon caused me to blurt out, "I know Robert Anderson, friend of a friend actually, maybe I can be of some assistance." I'm not sure exactly what I had in mind at that moment, but it seemed like harmless fun to make the offer.

"Anderson and his superiors, all the way up to Lincoln, have refused to comply with our demands, but we know they are running low on provisions" Lee stated. "This meeting will be an ultimatum. Surrender or we bombard the Fort until you either raise a white flag or perish. Maybe you could be useful in trying to make him see sense, Bailey. Official approaches haven't worked; maybe a personal touch would."

"Chesnut would never agree to have a civilian join us, nor would Beauregard, come to that," observed Chisolm. He was referring to Brigadier General P. G. T. Beauregard, another West Pointer that had defected to the C.S.A. and who now found himself in charge of Charleston's defenses. Colonel James Chesnut[15] was one of Beauregard's aides.

"I'll talk to them. If the objective is to get the Union forces out of Fort Sumter[16], what's the harm in trying a personal angle?" was Lee's response. We debated this over another round or two of drinks, but on the morning of April 11, 1861, I found myself in a boat with Chesnut, Lee, Chisolm, and a small crew, making

---

14 Born in Louisville, KY, in 1805, Robert D. Anderson graduated from the United States Military Academy in 1825 was a veteran of the Black Hawk, Second Seminole and Mexican American Wars. He would come to be regarded as a hero for his role as the Union commander of Fort Sumter in 1861. Anderson died in 1871 and is buried at West Point.
15 James Chesnut Jr. was born in Camden, SC, in 1815, the youngest of 14 children. He would later serve as an aide to Confederate President Jefferson Davis.
16 Fort Sumter is located on an artificial island at the entrance to Charleston Harbor. It dates from the War of 1812.

our way across the mile or so of Charleston Harbor from Fort Johnson to Fort Sumter. Although we didn't get eyes on every single one of the hundred or so Union men that were in Fort Sumter at the time, the look of the ones we did see confirmed that they surely were running short of supplies. Hollow-eyed, hungry looks greeted us at every turn as we made our way to a large room located in a part of the Fort not far from the docks. There we were greeted by Union Major Robert Anderson, Captains Abner Doubleday, John Foster and Truman Seymour, and a surgeon with unforgettable whiskers named Samuel Crawford.[17]

Chesnut provided introductions on the Confederate side and, when he got to me, said something to the effect of "—Jack Bailey, who I think you know—" before he continued with the rest. Luckily, my being in the middle of the pack meant that the mildly confused look on Anderson's face as he tried to recall where he knew me from vanished as he focused on the remaining handshakes. Major Anderson reciprocated by introducing the Union contingent.

I read somewhere recently that Doubleday has been credited with inventing baseball, but I can tell you that the man I met that day did not look like he'd ever partaken of any physical activity, let alone created one. For his part, Anderson looked every inch the capable soldier he was reputed to be. The Union had hoped that putting Anderson, a native of Kentucky and someone who had no issue with slavery in charge of a Southern garrison might have bought some goodwill with the locals. If it did, it hadn't been enough to avoid the situation in which we now

17 Samuel W. Crawford was born in Pennsylvania in 1829. Despite his medical training, following the Battle of Fort Sumter Crawford would accept a regular commission and go on to serve in many major engagements, including the Battles of Cedar Mountain, Antietam, Gettysburg, and Five Forks. Crawford reached the rank of Major General and retired from the Army in 1873. He died in 1892.

RICHARD A. NOBLE

found ourselves. Anderson and Doubleday were also West Point grads and both U.S. Artillery veterans. I was to learn later that, in 1839, Anderson had published a manual titled *Instruction for Field Artillery, Horse and Foot.* Whether he might soon be forced to put some of his theories into practice could well hinge on the outcome of this negotiation.

With the pleasantries over, Chesnut got down to business and made the obvious points that Fort Sumter was hopelessly surrounded, heavily outgunned, cut off from supplies, etc. Anderson countered that this was federal property, and he wasn't authorized to surrender it, nor did he intend to. These well-worn arguments were rehashed for some time using different words and phrases until we found ourselves in a lull that otherwise might have been the end of the discussion. That's when I saw my opportunity to pounce.

"If I may be so bold," I offered, "would anyone object to Major Anderson and I conferring in private for a few minutes?" Since both sides had tired of plowing the same ground no one objected, although a look I got from Chesnut would have curdled milk. I followed Anderson, Doubleday and Crawford to another, smaller room, while Foster and Seymour stayed with Chesnut and the others. As soon as we were out of earshot, Anderson turned on me with; "Having had time to give it additional thought Bailey, I've realized that we don't actually know each other, so what's your game?"

"No game at all, sir," I responded, as I produced the letter that Beam had scribbled for me on the train. "I am a friend of John Beam and wanted to take this opportunity to meet you and pass along his best wishes."

After consuming the letter, he looked up and said, "Well, your choice of a place and time to introduce yourself is odd to say the least Bailey. We could certainly use some bourbon here, but I didn't see any in your boat so, I ask again, what is your game?"

Just so I could later say I did, I made another attempt to talk him into a "strategic withdrawal" for the sake of his men, pointed out the futility of his position, prattled on about living to fight another day, etc., but he waved me off and started for the door.

"One last thing, Major Anderson" I said before he got to the door, "When war breaks out, as it surely will, there will be a great need for cotton in the North, and my firm is in a position to deliver."

"Ah, there it is." he sighed, "Commerce. Never a shortage of profiteers when hostilities break out. My compliments, Mr. Bailey, you've crawled out of your counting house earlier than most, it seems."

Before I could offer up what would have admittedly been a lame defense, he was halfway back to Chesnut, Lee, and the rest. I must have struck some small chord with him though, because Anderson never mentioned any details about our conversation to the rest of the group. He even managed to give me a mildly gracious farewell handshake as he promised Chesnut he would continue to consider the terms of standing down. When Lee asked about my tête-à-tête with Anderson during the boat ride back to Fort Johnson, I exaggerated my efforts to appeal to him on a personal level, feigned frustration that I hadn't been more effective—and of course left out the bits about cotton.

Once back at Fort Johnson, Chesnut, Lee, and Chisolm went off to report to Beauregard and I went back to my rooms downtown. The past few weeks had been an exhausting mix of business and pleasure and I needed to get some rest before traveling back to Washington to try my luck with Brady. I learned later that Chesnut and his gaggle made another visit to Fort Sumter later that day, the result of which became obvious to everyone in Charleston at 4:30 a.m. on April 12 when Confederate cannons launched a day and a half artillery barrage aimed at Anderson and his men. Anderson responded in kind but, for all the fireworks and noise, in the end there were surprisingly few casualties. One Confederate soldier died from wounds inflicted by a misfiring cannon and two Union soldiers were killed because of an accident that occurred during the ceremonial 100-gun salute that Beauregard had granted Anderson as part of the terms of surrender—and after the fighting had ceased. As is so often the case in war, needless waste, and damnable chance.

The rude awakening and incessant cannon fire (the Confederacy alone fired 3,000 rounds in 36 hours) was all the encouragement I needed to pack up and begin the journey back to Washington.

Chapter 5

WASHINGTON AND A NEW CAREER

Washington – May & June 1861

*S*etting aside one of the most implausible things I'd ever laid eyes upon, the trip North to Washington was largely uneventful. The papers were filled with news about Fort Sumter and speculation around what would come next. Southerners were both elated and emboldened by their victory in Charleston Harbor. "FORT SUMTER RESTORED!, THE VICTORY COMPLETE!, The Flag is There!" crowed the *Charleston Courier* on April 15, 1861. Virginia seceded from the Union on April 17, joining South Carolina, Mississippi, Alabama, Florida, Georgia, Louisiana, and Texas in the new Confederacy. Arkansas, North Carolina, and Tennessee soon followed. On April 19, Bailey Importer's worst fears were realized when Lincoln ordered a blockade of Southern ports.

The North wasn't immune to war fever either, as evidenced by Robert Anderson being honored by 100,000 people in Union Square Park in New York City a week after he had surrendered Fort Sumter. He was right to hold out down there I suppose—minimal casualties, maximum perception of heroism. He'd go on to take the now-famous 33-star Union flag I had so recently seen flying over Fort Sumter on a very successful recruiting and fund-raising tour across the North—and parlay the whole show into a promotion to Brigadier General.

At a stop in North Carolina, two men boarded my car that were a sight I will never forget (and one that many paid P.T. Barnum to see both before and after the war). Chang & Eng Bunker (or Ham & Egg as I once heard them called) were co-joined twins born in Siam who owned a plantation and slaves in North Carolina. Incredibly, both had their own wives and children. The mind marvels at what the sleeping arrangements must have been. I recognized them because I had read about their agreement with P. T. Barnum to have a wax sculpture of themselves created and put on display at Barnum's American Museum[18] in New York City. Even that knowledge hadn't fully prepared me for seeing them in person. My fellow passengers were equally gobsmacked, although most were polite enough to limit their observations to stolen glances when they felt the Bunkers were not looking. As slaveowners, Chang's and Eng's loyalties were with the South, although in an incredible example of government incompetence, toward the end of the war Eng— and just Eng—would be drafted by the Union Army. False rumors had it that the two were on opposite sides of the conflict, and they thus became a living symbol for the divided nation. But both sympathized with the South, and each had a son that

---

18 P.T. Barnum's American Museum was located at Broadway and Ann Streets in Manhattan. It opened in 1842 following Barnum's purchase of Scudder's American Museum the prior year. He filled it with every curiosity he could get his hands on, including wax figures, exotic animals, performers, midgets, and scientific instruments and appliances of the day. From its opening through 1865, it reportedly saw 38 million visitors – a number great than the entire population of the United States at the time.

would eventually join the Confederate forces by enlisting in the Virginia Calvary.

The Bunkers disembarked in Richmond, which allowed me to focus my attentions on preparing my pitch to Mathew Brady. I'd received a note from Beam in early April informing me that he had sent a letter of introduction to Brady's studio in Washington at 625 Pennsylvania Avenue as promised. I was tempted to stay at the National or Brown's Marble Hotel, both of which were nearby, but they were favorites of Congressmen and the assorted riffraff that politicians tend to attract, neither of which suited my tastes. And the possibility of a challenging financial future made me conscious of the coin required for such establishments, so I settled on more modest accommodations at the Petersen House[19] on 10th Street. The Petersen was only about a half mile from the studio, and it better fit the image I hoped to project with Brady in any case. If Brady happened to share my opinion that no one staying at the National or Brown's ever did an honest day's work, staying at one of them might make it seem odd to him that I was seeking, or even capable of, productive employment. On a pleasant day in mid-May I decided to make a reconnaissance visit to Brady's studio and, in an incredible stroke of luck, not only was he there, but he had just completed that now famous photograph of Lincoln looking very pensive, seated in a chair with his left hand approaching his chin. Brady was escorting Lincoln to the front door, so I planted myself in their path and blurted out, "Mr. Brady, I believe you are in receipt of a letter of introduction from our mutual friend John Beam. My name is Jack Bailey." Then, "It's a very great honor to meet you Mr. President."

"And an honor to meet you as well, my friend. I take it from your accent that you're British. Always a pleasure to welcome

---

19 Built as a boarding house in 1849 by German tailor, William H. Petersen. Maintained since 1993 by the National Park Service.

visitors from across the Atlantic." These were the first words that I heard in person from the President of the United States. "What's the mood in London regarding our political challenges here in America?" he asked. At this point it was unclear whether Britain would recognize the Confederacy, stay out of the conflict or something in between, so he probably welcomed any opportunity to talk with someone who might have an informed opinion on the matter.

"I actually haven't been back home in several years, Mr. President," I offered. "I have been working out of Charleston for my father's cotton importing business. In fact, I just came from there where I had the good fortune of visiting with Major Anderson a few weeks back. We have mutual friends in Kentucky." I didn't think that telling him precisely where Anderson and I met would take the conversation in a constructive direction, but I thought that mentioning a now-famous Union officer might improve the President's view of me.

"Robert's been quite busy of late, as you must surely know," Lincoln responded with his legendary understatement. "It happens that he is also back up here on a tour to raise men and money for the Union. A good man."

"Mr. Bailey," Brady interjected, "my assistant will show you to my offices, and I will come back there as soon as I see the President safely off." I got the sense that he'd have preferred to see me off instead, but my quick connection with Lincoln forced him to make a show of being welcoming. A few minutes later, while I was looking over the work on display in Brady's office, he returned and slammed the door behind him.

"Mr. Bailey, John Beam's letter said you were interested in my business and had some ideas that I might find profitable. I cannot guess what those are, but I assume that they don't include having you accosting my important clients." I suppose he could have said a lot worse, but when someone sees you bond with the President, even in a small way, they tend to proceed cautiously.

"No sir, and I apologize for my outrageously forward behavior. Seeing two famous people together at once and so unexpectedly caused me to momentarily lose all sense of propriety. I hope you'll accept my deepest apologies." When in doubt, you can't go too far wrong with flattery, no matter how feigned. The key is to deliver it with convincing sincerity. Being put on the same level as Lincoln in terms of fame had its intended effect of softening Brady's mood.

"Fair enough, Mr. Bailey, but I am very busy. You've got five minutes."

With that, I launched into a rehearsed monologue on how I thought documenting war through photography was a masterstroke. I babbled on about how, for centuries, the horrors of wars had been witnessed only by the combatants and how he was in a unique position to end that forever. I said something about there being no limit to the demand for such photography, from newspapers to vain leaders on both sides to those following developments from the home front. Thusly wound up, I started heaping it on with phrases like "making history" and "the name Mathew Brady would be known down through the ages." At the end I was worried that I'd gone too far, but the sparkle in his eye told me that he'd likely been harboring similar thoughts. And to hear it all from a third party had him puffed up like a peacock. I concluded with something about it taking more than one man managing things to do it all justice and that was where I could help.

"I couldn't agree with you more, Bailey," he beamed, "although surprisingly few people get it so quickly. What do you know about photography?"

"Truth be told," I replied, "very little. But I do know something about managing laborers and logistics. You will have a lot of equipment to move around, and unless you've got help lined up to support the young whelps I see around this studio, you'll be lucky to get halfway to the action." I'm not sure he had considered that before, but I could see it was concerning him now.

"And what would you do with your cotton business if you were to come and work for me, Mr. Bailey? I can't have you coming and going willy-nilly." A good question which, fortunately, I had anticipated.

"As I'm sure you are aware, sir, Southern ports have been blockaded. This year's cotton has only just been planted so there isn't much to be done at the moment. I can't see a war lasting less than a year, so we won't be able to ship this year's harvest in any case. Thus, I am in the fortunate position of being able to suspend my work in Charleston and be a part of this." For good measure, I exaggerated about the relationships I had with certain C.S.A. officers, which might prove useful to Brady in the field. I disingenuously mentioned Lee's last name, meaning Captain Stephen Lee, knowing full well that Brady would wrongly assume that I meant Robert E. Lee. Though I felt I had made a strong case, Brady asked for the night to think about it and suggested that I return in the morning.

After freshening up back at Petersen's, I walked the half mile or so over to the Willard Hotel[20], an island of civilization in the teeming bog that was Washington in 1861. I'd read that Lincoln had stayed at the Willard until his inauguration and knew that during February it had been the site of the Peace Conference attended by representatives from a couple of dozen states trying to head off the war. In other words, a good place to pick up scuttlebutt that could prove useful in the coming weeks. Being so close

---

20 Located at 1401 Pennsylvania Avenue, two blocks east of the White House, the Willard Hotel's roots go back to six original structures built on that site in 1816, built by Colonel John Tayloe III. Those structures were combined and opened in 1847 as Willard's Hotel. The Willard operates today as the Willard InterContinental Washington.

to national seat of government also meant that public women would be plentiful, and I might just take advantage of that. I didn't know it then but was amused a few years later when the red-light district in Washington came to be known as "Hooker's Division", in a nod to the promiscuity of General Joseph "Fighting Joe" Hooker.

It would be tough to get a table for one on a busy evening with a newly inaugurated President in town, but I tried anyway. As the maître d' was in the process of turning me down and suggesting that I try the Round Robin Bar down the hall instead, I couldn't help but notice P.T. Barnum sitting a few tables into the dining room. I chuckled to myself over the coincidence of just having seen the Bunkers on the train a couple of days prior. The Round Robin was also quite busy, but I did manage to secure the last chair available at the bar. Deciding I needed to celebrate my progress with Brady, I ordered a double whiskey while mulling over the dinner menu. Two sips into my drink, the young man to my left introduced himself as John Surratt, Jr.[21] I reciprocated, at which point he asked if I was a diplomat.

"Good God no," I responded, "what makes you ask?"

"The accent," he said.

Being British and having spent a good amount of time in both the Northern and Southern U.S., I could make a reasonable showing of several accents but, in these troubled times, and especially in Washington, I found it safest to let my Liverpool heritage shine through.

"What is your business then?" he inquired somewhat tactlessly.

"I'm a soon-to-be underemployed cotton exporter, so I am

---

21 John Harrison Surratt Jr. was born in Washington in 1844, one of three children born to John and Mary Surratt. Among other things, his life would include stints as a farmer, schoolteacher, U.S. Postmaster and Lincoln conspirator.

planning to try my hand at photography under Mathew Brady," I offered, "And you?"

"Student at St. Charles College. But also expecting to have to find something else to do because of Lincoln's War," he said in a low voice.

There is never a shortage of opinion in Washington, and that was never truer than in 1861. All sides of the conflict were well represented in this town, including North, South, foreign, business, and religious, so I put it down to youth that Mr. Surratt would clumsily expose his sympathies so soon after meeting a stranger at a bar just steps from the White House. Perhaps he felt safe expressing his views after I had mentioned that I lived in Charleston. What I didn't know at the time was that John Jr. was trying to dig up dirt to earn his bona fides for the Confederate Secret Service, which he would soon join. His brother Isaac had traveled to Texas three days after Lincoln's inauguration and joined the C.S.A., and little brother John, just 17 when we had this conversation, was itching to contribute to the cause. I did my best to minimize the conversation from that point on and hurried through my dinner. That done I scarfed down the last of my second double, paid up and offered a parting handshake and best wishes to Surratt as I pushed my chair back to leave. I left him looking around for his next target.

On my way out through the lobby, I had the pleasant surprise of running into Kate Warne, who was engaged in a conversation with a shabby looking Scot in a bowler hat.

"Miss Warne," I said in greeting, "what unfortunate timing. I just finished dinner, otherwise would have made good on our agreement to dine out the next time I was up in these parts. Perhaps tomorrow night instead?"

"As you well know, Mr. Bailey, we had no such agreement. What I did offer was some advice that you steer clear of politics, and yet here I find you in the very center of one of the most political places in the country." Before I could muster a clever retort, she continued, "May I introduce you to Mr. Allan Pinkerton[22], head of the Pinkerton National Detective Agency."

"And your boss, as I recall from our conversation in Baltimore," I said, although a couple of glances between the two of them suggested to me that they might have something more than just a professional relationship.

She artfully changed the topic by saying, "I thought you were going back to Charleston, Mr. Bailey, what brings you to Washington? A cotton convention perhaps?"

Ignoring the intended slight, I responded innocently, "I did go back to Charleston, but when things got a little frothy in the harbor, I decided I might be safer up North."

"While you aren't far enough North to be entirely clear of trouble Mr. Bailey," said Pinkerton, joining the conversation with his Scottish brogue. "If it's safety you seek, I'd suggest you go back across the Atlantic to your home in Liverpool, assuming I have your accent figured correctly." I've been kicked out of taverns and hotels before, but having it suggested that I leave a country was a new low.

"Does everyone at your Agency offer travel tips?" I asked, emboldened by the bourbon. "Miss Warne was certainly helpful with hotel advice the last time she and I met."

In an attempt to bring the discussion to an end, Miss Warne said, "While I'm sure we'd all enjoy continuing this conversation Mr. Bailey, I regret to have to say that Mr. Pinkerton and I have an appointment that we need to attend to."

---

22 Born in 1819 in Glasgow, Scotland, Pinkerton was a barrel-maker who turned to law enforcement in 1849 when he became the first police detective in Chicago, IL. His home in Dundee, IL, was a stop on The Underground Railroad. The Pinkerton detective agency still exists today, headquartered in Ann Arbor, MI. He died in 1884.

I stifled a comment that was rattling around in my head about what kind of appointment could be taking place at this hour and instead planted my hat on my head, offered up farewells and best wishes, and walked back to Petersen's to sleep off the booze.

Chapter 6

BAILEY THE PHOTOGRAPHER

When I presented myself at the studio the following morning, Brady introduced me to the manager of his Washington studio, Alexander Gardner[23], then ushered us both into his office where he got straight to the point.

"Your observations yesterday made sense, Bailey," said Brady. "Most of my associates are young, and we will certainly need many of them to travel to properly cover the war, not to mention staff this studio and the one in New York. On top of that, some of them will soon either volunteer to join the army or they will be drafted. That'll mean hiring yet more inexperienced people that will need to be managed. If we were to come to some arrangement, I wouldn't expect you to become an expert on photography, but I would expect you to know enough about it to supervise those who are. Additionally, and as you pointed out, having men in the field will require solid logistics and discipline which, given

23 Alexander Gardner was born in Paisley, Scotland in 1821. He started his career as an apprentice jeweler and would later become a newspaper owner and editor. His interest in photography began after seeing some of Mathew Brady's work at the Great Exposition in Hyde Park, London, in 1851. He moved to the U.S. in 1856 and became an assistant to Brady. Gardner died in 1882.

your experience in exporting, I'm sure you must have. When can you start?" And so it was that I agreed to start in two days' time. I needed a day to write to my father and Elkins, work out a longer-term lodging arrangement with Mr. Petersen and attend to a few other mundane details like having clothes laundered. I expected Brady would keep me busy and needed to get these chores out of the way.

I spent the next few weeks in the studio learning the basics of the trade and getting to know Brady, Gardner, and the rest of the crew. As Beam had suggested, the shop was constantly busy with soldiers looking to have carte de visites created to send home. There was also a steady flow of dignitaries, and those that fancied themselves as such, coming by for portraits. The more important of these were usually mollycoddled by Brady himself or, on occasion, Gardner. It became clear to me that while Brady was the idea man and promoter, Gardner was the business mind and coin counter. Being a Scot, he thoroughly enjoyed his role as the latter, even though it contributed to an ever-present tension between him and the more artistic Brady.

I learned a great deal by simply observing, although Brady would periodically spend time educating me on the relevant history and methods around photography. By this time, the industry was well past the old daguerreotype process, which involved lining a copper or brass plate with highly polished silver; exposing it to some combination of halogen, bromine, or chlorine fumes; loading it gingerly into a camera; and then exposing it through a lens for as much as ten minutes. On top of all that, lighting had to be perfect, and subjects needed to remain stock still, otherwise the photograph would be blurred. In sum, a completely unworkable system outside a studio.

Brady was now using a wet plate process that had been invented a few years earlier by one of my countrymen, Frederick Scott Archer. While much less complex than daguerreotype, it still involved coating a plate of glass or metal with chemicals, placing it in a camera, and exposing it to the subject. A distinct advantage to wet plate was that it created a negative that could be used to create copies, while daguerreotype created positives which could not. That said, it became obvious to me why Brady was so concerned about logistics. Even with the simpler wet plate method, taking all the necessary paraphernalia into the field was going to prove to be challenging, particularly with glass involved.

During these weeks Brady made a couple of visits to the White House to press his case for officially documenting the war through photography. He and Lincoln had become somewhat friendly in recent years, to the point where the President had given Brady the chair he had used as a congressman. That very chair was now used for portrait work in the studio, and it provided a prop Brady would use to boast about his relationship with the President.

After one of his White House visits Brady took me aside and said, "Apparently you made an impression on Lincoln when you met him. I mentioned that I had taken you on and he remembered that you knew Robert Anderson."

Now a General, Anderson was still on his recruiting and fundraising tour with the Fort Sumter flag and Lincoln planned to hold a reception for him at the White House. "We've been invited," Brady informed me, "so be prepared in your Sunday best day after tomorrow." Remembering my only previous (and somewhat uncomfortable) meeting with Anderson, my first instinct was to come up with some reason why I couldn't attend. But when Brady added enthusiastically, "This will be an excellent opportunity to promote the studio and add to our military contacts," I knew that he wouldn't have it. Two days later we presented ourselves at the White House and did our best to work the crowd.

The White House in 1860, Courtesy of the Library of Congress, LC-DIG-cwpbh-03295

I tried to steer clear of Anderson, and my heart nearly missed a beat when I saw that Allan Pinkerton was also in attendance, hovering around Lincoln and taking measure of everyone circulating in the crowded rooms. Although I never saw him look my way, I knew instinctively that he had spotted me, and I cursed myself for all the people I had managed to come to the attention of these past four months. The plan I had in mind to quietly sell cotton up North required some delicacy, and here I was drawing scrutiny from all the wrong quarters. I was just about to slink off to another room when Brady appeared at my side and said he wanted to pay our respects to the President in advance of the official festivities. Before I could find a reason to decline, he was steering me by the elbow toward Lincoln and the gaggle around him.

"A pleasure to meet you again, Mr. Bailey," Lincoln said as we approached. "I hear that you've had a career change since we last met."

"Well, sir," I responded, "it seems that circumstances being what they are, the opportunities to ship cotton overseas are severely diminished at the moment. I have been interested in photography for some time and Mr. Brady was gracious enough to offer me a position to assist him while my own business is suspended."

"You'll learn from the best then," he said, then proceeded to introduce me to his wife, Mary Todd, as well as Pinkerton, who had just joined the group and seemed to be staring into my very soul. Mary Todd offered a polite greeting, but her body language suggested she would rather be anywhere else. Pinkerton, on the other hand, was very much in the moment.

"Mr. Bailey and I have met, Mr. President," Pinkerton said. "It seems that, for a Southerner, he spends an inordinate amount of time up North."

"I'm actually British, as you know, Mr. Pinkerton, running an export business out of Charleston. My work takes me to many places—or at least it did."

Thankfully one of Lincoln's assistants interjected just then to say that the President needed to make a few remarks and introduce General Anderson, who would also address the guests. My relief was short-lived however, as Lincoln asked us to join him, Anderson, and Pinkerton in a private room after the ceremony. "With all the attention he is getting, I doubt you have had a chance to say a proper hello to your friend Robert," he said. "Nor is it likely you will unless we can extract you both from this crowd." I suddenly found myself hoping that the speeches would be lengthy enough to allow me to slip away unnoticed. As I turned to slink off to the back of the room, I inadvertently bumped into a distinguished looking woman who was headed the other way, toward Lincoln and Anderson.

"Pardon me ma'am," I offered. "How clumsy of me to not to be paying more attention when I changed direction. Jack Bailey, at your service," I concluded with a bow.

Rose Greenhow, Courtesy of the Library of Congress,
LC-DIG-ppmsca-70284

"No harm done Mr. Bailey," she responded, then introduced herself as Mrs. Rose O'Neal Greenhow.[24] "I don't believe I have ever seen you at one of these soirees. Are you new in Washington?"

"I am indeed ma'am. Newly arrived from Charleston, where I run a cotton exporting business for my father in Liverpool."

"Well, the slight Southern tinge I detected over your charming English accent explains your fine manners, sir," she says. "But

---

24 Rose O'Neal Greenhow was born in Port Tobacco, Maryland in 1813 or 1814. She married Dr. Robert Greenhow Jr. in 1835 and they would have four daughters before his death in 1854. She was a well-known Washington socialite both before and after becoming a widow and would leverage those high-level contacts in her work as a skilled Confederate spy. Rose drowned in 1864 after fleeing a British blockade runner that had run aground near Cape Fear as it was being pursued by a Union gunboat.

surely there isn't much to do in the cotton exporting business these days."

"Sadly, you are correct, so I am taking advantage of this slow period to pursue my interest in photography by assisting Mathew Brady," I responded. Never waste an opportunity to reinforce your cover story.

"I am familiar with Mr. Brady's work. Several of my dearest friends, including President Buchanan[25], and Senator Henry Wilson[26] have sat for portraits with Mr. Brady. John C. Calhoun[27] many years ago too, God rest his soul. Brady does fine work." And thus, with just a few sentences, she deftly let me know that her position in the Washington pecking order was infinitely higher than mine. I remembered seeing a portrait of Calhoun in the studio and thinking at the time that surely such a head is what you'd find under a black plague hood if you'd had the nerve to tear one off someone. Frightening.

"And how will your photography assist the Union Army?" she continued, a barely perceptible edge creeping into her voice. I suddenly felt like I was being interrogated by an expert.

"We aren't setting out to assist the Union, ma'am" I said defensively. "We are hoping to document the conflict through images, for the benefit of all." Mercifully, at this point the formal remarks began, and we both faced forward. I made a mental note to henceforth steer clear of Mrs. Greenhow.

Following the formal remarks, an aide directed Brady and I into a room away from the hubbub, where we found Lincoln, Pinkerton, and Anderson waiting—the latter clearly enjoying his new regimentals.

25 James Buchanan was the 15th President of the United States, serving from 1857 to 1861. He was succeeded by Abraham Lincoln.
26 Born in 1812, Wilson would become the 18th Vice President of the United States, serving under Ulysses S. Grant from 1873 to 1875. He served as a U.S. Senator from Massachusetts from 1855 to 1873.
27 John C. Calhoun was Vice President of the United States from 1825 to 1832.

Pinkerton, Lincoln and McClernand post Antietam, Courtesy of the Library of Congress, LC-DIG-cwpb-04339

"Ah, Mr. Bailey," the President began, "As I mentioned earlier, I was worried that you wouldn't have the opportunity to say hello to your friend Robert with all of the excitement going on outside." Anderson proceeded to dash any hope of my escaping this meeting unscathed by saying he had just been telling the President and Mr. Pinkerton that we had only ever met the once this past April, when I had accompanied the group of traitors sent by Beauregard to demand the surrender of Fort Sumter.

Before the situation could deteriorate, I quickly interjected with; "That's true but, as I said then, I knew Captain Lee and used that and our mutual friendship with John Beam to get myself on that boat with the genuine intent of trying to defuse the situation."

"And to try and sell me cotton or bourbon, I've forgotten which" said Anderson sarcastically. Then he added, "And I have to say that, given your habit of showing up at the most singular of places, I look forward to the possibility of a third meeting, should it ever happen, with genuine anticipation."

"Relax, Mr. Bailey," interrupted Lincoln. "Allan Pinkerton and his Agency have checked your background thoroughly and it seems that you really are just a businessman. That said, we are hoping to convince you to dedicate a small portion of your time to a higher calling. As you have pointed out yourself, your business takes you many places. We would like to take advantage of that fact to help the cause of the Union." With that, Pinkerton laid out a plan for me to become one of his "sources" of information about goings on in the Confederacy. If and when I traveled South, I was to keep my eyes and ears open and periodically check in with his Agency to report anything I'd learned. With my confidence building at the realization that this meeting could have gone a lot worse, I couldn't resist saying; "Maybe Miss Warne and I will finally get that dinner we've been talking about when I make one of those reports."

Ignoring the bait, Pinkerton continued by saying that there would be no compensation involved beyond knowing that I was doing the right thing.

Lincoln added, "Once the war is over and the country is issuing export licenses and considering tariffs, Bailey Importers will of course be remembered fondly." He didn't need to add the obvious—that if I didn't cooperate, we'd be remembered far less fondly. So, there it was. What had already been a risky plan—finding a way to continue to sell cotton to both sides in a civil war—had now been made infinitely more complex with me drafted as a Union spy. Good times.

"Any questions?" asked Lincoln.

"Just two," I said. "Firstly, if I do find myself in the South attempting to return North, what should I say if arrested by the Union Army? Secondly, I'm not sure I will have a cotton business left if this war goes on for very long. I would have a lot more reason to travel South if I had a market for my cotton in the North. Could we also agree to some arrangement whereby my company supplies the Union with cotton?" To which Anderson offered a caustic grunt.

"As to your first question, Mr. Bailey, I will write you a letter that will ensure you will pass unmolested whenever returning to Union territory. I must caution you, however, to keep this letter well hidden. If seen by the wrong eyes, you would have some uncomfortable explaining to do to our Confederate friends. Your second question isn't relevant. I don't expect this war to last more than a few months; certainly, less than a year," was the President's response. In the latter, he was far from alone. As is typically the case at the onset of war, both sides believe it will be short lived, and both are confident they will prevail. The first is rarely the case and the second is true only half the time. But it was using this logic that Lincoln signed up 75,000 new troops to ridiculously short, 90 days enlistments soon after the fall of Fort Sumter.[28]

Only Lincoln and Brady seem pleased with the meeting, which adjourned awkwardly. A few steps outside the White House, Pinkerton caught up with us and said in a tone only a Scot or a Mother Superior could pull off, "Bailey, the next

---

28 To be fair, Lincoln was operating under outdated laws enacted in the 1700's, which limited the number of militiamen the President could call up to 75,000. Such militiamen were also limited to serving only "three months in any one year."

time you carry a gun into the White House or in the presence of the President, I'll see you strip searched and handcuffed." I resisted the temptation to say that I'd been having just such visions about Kate Warne, but instead provided what I hoped came across as a sincere apology. No point in provoking someone who now held considerable influence over my future. I also made a mental note to alter my coat to better hide a weapon, which in turn led to thoughts about what to do with Lincoln's safe passage letter. During the rest of our way back to the studio I received a lecture from Brady about not mixing "my spying business" with our photographic mission, lest I endanger the neutral status he'd convinced himself he had.

Over the remaining weeks we spent in Washington before following the Union Army to Bull Run, I continued to learn what I could about the trade while helping Brady design special carriages in which we could safely transport all our photographic equipment, chemicals, and supplies. These would come to be called "Whatsit Wagons" by the troops, because of their odd, non-military look. I believe that unique appearance, which would come to be familiar to both sides, spared us from the occasional cannonball or grape shot that might have otherwise been directed our way.

On July 4, 1861, 85 years to the day after Congress adopted the Declaration of Independence, Lincoln called for an additional 400,000 men to put down the rebellion. I thought that this part of his speech best captured his thinking: "Our popular Government has often been called an experiment. Two points in it our people have already settled—the successful establishing and the successful administering of it. One still remains—its successful maintenance against a formidable internal attempt to overthrow it. It is now for them to demonstrate to the world that those who can fairly carry an election can also suppress a rebellion; that ballots are the rightful and peaceful successors of bullets, and that when ballots have fairly and constitutionally decided there can be no successful appeal back to bullets—"

Chapter 7

THE FIRST BATTLE OF BULL RUN, JULY 18-21, 1861

*I*f a larger assemblage of naïve people has ever set off anywhere, I'd be surprised, although given human nature, I'm certain there have been other instances. All manner of society was represented among the spectators making their way the 25 miles or so from Washington to the area around Centerville Heights, Virginia, to witness the first major battle of the Civil War. From senators and congressmen to everyday people that included tradesmen, waiters, and newspaper reporters, they came by carriage, wagon, buggy, and horseback. Some brought picnic baskets, champagne, and opera glasses, and a few of the more enterprising souls were selling pies and assorted grub as if at a state fair. Even Union General Irvin McDowell's[29] men conducted themselves like they were out on a Sunday stroll—stopping to pick berries and enjoy shady patches along the way during what

---

29 General Irvin McDowell was born in Columbus, Ohio in 1818. He graduated from the U.S. Military Academy in 1838 and was a classmate of P.G.T. Beauregard. He was blamed for Union defeats at both the 1st and 2nd Battles of Bull Run, and for losses against Confederate General Thomas "Stonewall" Jackson's Valley Campaign of 1862.

were extremely hot and humid days. What we all had in common, and I include myself in this, was a feeling of certainty that the Union troops under McDowell would make short work of the Confederate army led by P. G. T. Beauregard[30], and that we would all be enjoying cocktails in Richmond within days. At this point, Lincoln had been under pressure for months to send the Union Army to Richmond to put down the rebellion once and for all. In addition to demands from Northern newspapers to do so, his 90-day enlistments would soon run out, thus releasing the 75,000 soldiers that had enlisted after the surrender of Fort Sumter. Time was of the essence. For their part, the Confederates figured on stopping the Union Army at Bull Run, or Manassas, as they preferred to call it.

The men in both armies were mostly inexperienced, including the senior officers. McDowell had never led an army in battle, although he and his former U.S. Military Academy classmate Beauregard had both served in logistical roles during the Mexican American War of 1846-1848. But Beauregard was still basking in his victory at Fort Sumter, only three months past. Both men were concerned about Confederate General Joe Johnston's troops in the Shenandoah Valley, but for different reasons. McDowell wanted them held in place and dispatched Union General Robert Patterson to try and do just that, while Beauregard naturally hoped to have Johnston's 9,000 men join him at Bull Run to improve the Confederate's odds. Delays on both sides ultimately resulted in Johnston avoiding Patterson and moving his army to the battlefield by train.

---

30 Pierre Gustave Toutant-Beauregard was born in St. Bernard Parish, Louisiana in 1818. A graduate of the U.S. Military Academy, he served there briefly as Superintendent before resigning that position and his commission once Louisiana seceded from the Union. After serving 23 years in the U.S. Army, he enlisted in the C.S.A. in 1861. He participated in a significant number of Civil War battles, including Fort Sumter, Bull Run, Shiloh, and Fort Wagner. At the war's end he was a breveted Major General. He died in New Orleans in 1893.

Since the details of the first battle of Bull Run have been fully documented in countless other texts, I will spare you the repetition here and stick to my own experiences. I joined the festivities as part of a two-wagon team Brady assembled that included newspapermen Dick McCormick (*New York Evening Post*) and Ned House (*New York Daily Tribune*), sketch artist Al Waud[31], and a few of Brady's young apprentices. I must admit to feeling some sympathy toward Waud at the time, because I believed that photography would soon render his sketch pad and charcoal obsolete. But his employer, the *New York Illustrated News*, and eventually *Harper's Weekly*, would both continue to publish his works for years to come. A Brit like me, Al made for good company on the road as we both enjoyed whiskey and marveling at American's propensity for self-destruction. Now that I think of it, I'm hard pressed to remember any journalist who didn't enjoy the drink.

While our little band of travelers was for the most part as green at warfare as the troops around us, we at least had the option of keeping our distance from the fighting. With all the motion involved in a battle, there wasn't much to be done by photographers in any case. Any request that our subjects remain still for the several minutes required for wet plates to work would have been absurd—and likely met with both derision and musket balls. Thankfully for me, it would be another 30 years before the arrival of moving pictures, finally making it feasible, although not desirable, for photographers to get close to the action to do their work.

We decided to spend the night of July 20 at Centreville and, after leaving our equipment and Whatsit Wagons under the guard

31 Alfred Rudolf Waud was born in London in 1828. During the Civil War he sketched for the *New York Illustrated News* and *Harper's Weekly*. He was present for every major battle involving the Army of the Potomac and his work at Pickett's Charge is believed to be the only rendering done by an eyewitness. He died in Marietta, GA in 1891.

of the apprentices, Waud, McCormick and I set off in search of food and drink. Ever the salesman, Brady decided to make the rounds on his own to visit with senior Army staff in the area. General McDowell had set up shop in Centreville after skirmishing over the past few days with Confederate forces in nearby Blackburn's Ford. He was now planning for the main battle while having his wounded treated in local churches and a hotel. We were fortunate to secure a table in town at the Black Horse Tavern, which was doing brisk business that night serving Union officers.

Once seated and with drinks on order, Waud said, "Well, gents, let us celebrate the beginning of the end this evening. Once the Union deals with these rebels around Bull Run tomorrow, it'll be, as the saying goes, 'On to Richmond' and the ultimate victory."

My battle experiences were confined to arguments with my father and the occasional donnybrook on the docks in Charleston, so this sounded plausible to me. McCormick, on the other hand, was burdened with actual experience in conflict, having covered the Crimean War and its disastrous Charge of the Light Brigade. He'd even published two books on the topic, *A Visit to the Camp Before Sevastopol* and *St. Paul's to St. Sophia*. Not Queen Vicky's[32] or my country's finest hour, to say nothing of the incompetent but impressively whiskered Lord Cardigan[33].

"Never underestimate an army's capacity for overconfidence," McCormick chimed in ominously. "If my experience

---

32 Victoria was born in 1819 and served as Queen of the United Kingdom from 1837 until her death in 1901.
33 James "Jim the Bear" Brudenell, a.k.a. Lord Cardigan, commanded the Light Brigade during the Crimean War, 1853-1856. He was born in 1797 and died in 1868.

is any indication, we may be at this for the next several years". Let's hope not, thinks I, doing a quick mental calculation on the toll that would take on my cotton business. With Southern ports now having been under blockade for three months, trade had ground to a complete halt. Waud and McCormick carried on their debate discreetly so as not to be overheard by the Union officers around us, while I glanced around the room. Sitting a few tables away I noticed Dr. Samuel Crawford, Anderson's surgeon, and witness to my clumsy attempt to intervene for my own profit on the eve of the shelling of Fort Sumter. As luck would have it, he caught my eye and was on his feet before I could blend into my surroundings.

"Bailey, isn't it?" he said when he reached our table. "Last time I saw you, you were escorting Chesnut and his fellow rebels to Fort Sumter to demand our surrender. Switched sides, have we?" Unfortunately, this all came out in a voice loud enough to carry across several tables.

In my defense I offered, "As you'll recall sir, I was only there to support my friend Colonel Anderson and to help avoid bloodshed—a goal which I sadly fell short of," but people around us had already begun taking an interest in our conversation.

"You use the word 'friend' generously, Bailey. As I recall, your only connection to General Anderson was a Kentucky whiskey salesman," he responded, with a nod to Anderson's recent promotion. Before things could deteriorate any further, a red-headed Colonel came up beside Crawford and asked if there was a problem.

"No problem at all Colonel Sherman[34], if you don't mind having Confederate sympathizers among your men the night before battle," Crawford said as he pointed a finger at me.

Sherman fixed a stare at me, but before he had fully decided what to do next, I stood up and said, "Colonel, if you would be kind enough to grant me a private audience, I can assure you that we can clear up this misunderstanding in just a few moments."

"Fair enough" he said, "But let me warn you that if you don't, you'll be finding yourself in irons."

As we started to go outside, he waved off a couple of junior officers who seemed eager to join us. Outside and out of earshot I said, "I'm going to need to dig into a pocket inside my coat to show you a letter from President Lincoln that I'm certain will put your concerns to rest." He nodded his assent, but pointed a pistol at me as he said, "Dig away."

While fumbling with the stitchwork I had used to hide Lincoln's letter and simultaneously trying to avoid revealing the presence of my Cooper, I prattled on nervously about how I was here helping Brady document the battle through photography. After a half minute or so, I was finally able to thrust the paper into his hands. He stole a couple of glances at me as he read, then looked around before handing it back.

"You'd be wise to keep that well-hidden Bailey," he said as he holstered his pistol, "Particularly in these parts. I'll find a discreet way to call off Dr. Crawford, but I suggest you forget about finishing dinner and instead go straight back to your camp."

34 William Tecumseh Sherman was born in Ohio in 1820. He graduated from the United States Military Academy in 1840 and served in the U.S. Army from 1840-1853 and again from 1861 to 1865. Perhaps best known for his "March to the Sea" in 1864, Sherman participated in many Civil War battles including Bull Run, Shiloh, Fort Henry, Fort Donelson, and Vicksburg. He served as Commanding General of the U.S. Army from 1869 to 1883 and died in in New York City in 1891.

Given how many others in the Black Horse had overheard my exchange with Crawford that seemed like good advice, so back to camp I went. A couple of hours later, Waud and McCormick reappeared at the wagons, whereupon I embellished my story about genuinely trying to help Anderson and how Sherman knew that to be true. The combination of my lies and the effects of the whiskey I envied them having in their systems seemed enough to close the matter. We soon turned in ahead of what we all expected would be an eventful day ahead.

Morning came early and abruptly, with Union cannons opening up at just after 5:00 a.m. Shortly thereafter our crew moved southwest toward Blackburn's Ford, where Brady took a few test pictures in advance of the journey we fully expected would take through the battlefield and on to Richmond. We followed Colonel Israel B. Richardson's Fourth Brigade, who had been ordered to engage General James Longstreet's Confederate troops across Blackburn's Ford in an effort to divert attention from the main event—a planned thrust around the Confederate's left flank, led by Union Colonels Hunter and Burnside[35]. In keeping with the picnic-like atmosphere of the past couple of days we joined a gaggle of civilians in the area and settled in to watch the coming action from a safe distance.

At first, all seemed to go well for McDowell's troops. Again, I won't recount details you can read almost anywhere, but from our vantage point you could see a lot of the fighting without having to witness up close what muskets and cannon balls do to flesh and bone. Skirmishes at Blackburn, Mitchell and Ball's Fords, the

35 Ambrose Burnside (1824-1881) graduated from the U.S. Military Academy in 1847. He would eventually attain the rank of Major General in the Union Army and he participated in many Civil War battles including Bull Run, Antietam, Fredericksburg, Spotsylvania, and Cold Harbor. His considerable whiskers inspired the term "sideburns".

Stone Bridge, and other points along this portion of Bull Run did the trick of distracting the Confederates until late morning. Then Hunter and Burnside moved south from Sudley Springs to engage the C.S.A. in the hills around the intersection of the Warrenton Turnpike and Manassas-Sudley Springs Road at what was known locally as the Stone House. Even from several miles away, the noise, smoke, and explosions from this main part of the battle were impressive. Although I didn't say it out loud, I was very happy to be observing events through a spyglass. The wide variety of uniform colors made it difficult at times to know who was on which side. Blue, gray, green, red—all were in use at this early stage of the war on both sides. The C.S.A.'s 7th Georgia and 33rd Virginia regiments predominantly wore blue, for example, while the Union's 8th New York and 2nd Wisconsin wore gray, which lead to confusion among the troops, lost opportunity, and lost lives.

Keen to get closer to the action, Brady moved us and the wagons three miles or so Northwest toward the Stone Bridge on Warrenton Turnpike. Around midday, the fighting became the most intense around Henry Hill, about a mile to the West of our position. We would learn later that the luckless owner of the house atop that hill, 85-year-old widow Judith Carter Henry, had her feet blown off by a Union cannonball intended to drive away Confederate sharpshooters. She would die from her wounds that night, thus becoming the first known civilian casualty of the war. Although her daughter, Ellen, hid in the chimney of the house to escape shrapnel and ball, she was rendered permanently deaf from the relentless artillery fire around her.

Among the scores of people milling about with us east of the Stone Bridge, Ned House spotted one of his colleagues, William Croffut of the *New York Daily Tribune*, who shouted "What news of the battle gentlemen?" He had just come down the Warrenton Turnpike from Centerville with Senator Wilson, one of Rose Greenhow's unwitting sources of intelligence on the Union Army's operational plans. I've wondered more than once how many lives were lost that day because of Wilson's pillow talk. All to be expected I suppose, as his profession seems to attract the vilest of our species.

Although we were already too close to the mayhem for my tastes, Brady responded, "You are looking at the main action Croffut, although we aren't near enough to know much else." Turning his attention to us, he continued, "Bailey, fetch one of the cameras. You and I are going to need to get across the river if we are to do our work properly. The rest of you stay here and keep watch over the wagons. And for God's sake, stay out of the way, we don't need our equipment trampled by this lot."

I'm not sure what Brady was thinking at the time, but I suspect he felt divine protection from the white duster he'd been wearing since McDowell had encouraged the press traveling to Bull Run to "wear a white uniform to indicate the purity of their character." I laughed out loud when I heard that phrase, but Brady took it to heart. And while it was true that we wouldn't be able to effectively photograph anything from this range, the constant motion of the fighting would render a closer position equally useless. Not to mention dangerous. Brady would hear none of it though—he was determined to join the fray.

The back-and-forth, bloody action around Henry Hill would continue throughout the afternoon with positions and cannon repeatedly lost, captured, lost, and recaptured. Several catchphrases were born that day, including the "Rebel Yell." I heard it myself as the Confederates charged down Henry Hill. Fortunately, that blood-curdling, hellish cry was enough to bring Brady to his senses, and he ordered our own little retreat. I was already halfway back to the river before he started after me. The moniker

"Stonewall Jackson"[36] was also born during Bull Run, when Confederate General Barnard Elliot Bee made a complimentary remark on Jackson's actions around Henry Hill. Bee would succumb to his wounds the following morning and would never know that he had coined a nickname that would live on forever.

Among the other casualties at Bull Run was the notion that this would be a short war and a glorious victory for the Union. By 5:00 p.m., McDowell's Army of Northeastern Virginia devolved into full-fledged panic and flight. With all order lost, fleeing federal troops (plus Brady and I) ran headlong into Union reinforcements coming up from the rear. Hundreds of civilian spectators mixed in among us to complete a picture of chaos and rout. Had the Confederates not been so exhausted and disorganized after the long day of battle, they might have chased McDowell and the rest of us all the way back to Washington. Instead, they lobbed shells at the Stone Bridge and up along Warrenton Pike toward Centreville, adding to the panic and revealing the character of many. It quite literally became every man for himself.

Against this onslaught, we were simply unable to protect the Whatsit wagons. Even though somewhat damaged by the time Brady and I returned, we were able to coax them and our terrified horses a mile or two back toward Centreville, before everything came to a halt at an overturned wagon at one of the bridges

---

36 Thomas Jonathan Jackson was born in 1824 and graduated from the U.S. Military Academy in 1846. He would eventually attain the rank of Lieutenant General in the Confederate Army and he participated in many Civil War battles including Bull Run, Winchester, the Seven Days Battles, Cedar Mountain, and Harpers Ferry. He would die in May 1863 as a result of complications from wounds acquired at the Battle of Chancellorsville. In one of the first known examples of forensic ballistics, it was determined that Jackson was struck by a .67 caliber bullet, which was used by Confederate forces. The Union Army was using .58 caliber balls at Chancellorsville.

across Cub Run. As we waited, the mob and the chaos continued to build until the wagon and other debris was cleared. In the gathering darkness our team became separated, and our wagons and equipment were destroyed, along with all the photographs we had taken over the past few days. It was suggested in later years that some of our work from Bull Run survived, but I can tell you that is either wishful thinking or an attempt to increase the value of photographs taken at other times but advertised as Bull Run originals. Brady himself certainly never claimed to have recovered any. Ironically, the only images that survived that excursion were the ones in the minds of witnesses, including Al Waud. In his case, those images were transferred to his sketch pad and then on to the *New York Illustrated News* and *Harper's Weekly*. He and I laughed on more than one occasion afterwards over the sympathy I had expressed on the eve of Bull Run about sketch artists being made redundant by the camera.

Ever the hustler, Brady did have a picture taken of himself the following day, July 22, 1861, back in the Washington studio. Etched on that print is "Brady the Photographer returned from Bull Run." He's in the ridiculous white duster with a sword at his side looking, as someone later said, like a French landscape painter. But I can tell you that he earned every speck of mud on his clothes in that photograph during the previous day and night on the chaotic retreat to the city. As for the sword, I'm not sure he knew one end from the other, but a sympathetic soldier had given it to him in the woods around Centreville the previous night. He must have felt it enhanced the aura of heroism he wished to project.

Brady Returned From Bull Run, Courtesy of the Library of Congress, LC-DIG-ds-13129

Chapter 8

REALITY SETS IN - LATE SUMMER & FALL, 1861

While the astonishing Confederate success at Bull Run shattered any notion of a quick victory by the Union, it also emboldened the South and terrified much of the citizenry in Washington and other areas close to the front lines. Having almost 5,000 Union and Confederate troops and an unknown number of civilians killed, wounded, or captured that day also forever put an end to the picnic-like atmosphere that had proceeded the battle just a few days prior. Among the rumors that fed the heightened anxiety in Washington was one started by none other than General George B. McClellan[37], whom Lincoln had chosen to replace the incompetent McDowell as commander of the Army of the Potomac a few days after Bull Run. "I am

---

37 George B. McClellan was born in 1824 and graduated from the U.S. Military Academy in 1846. He would attain the rank of Major General in the Union Army and he participated in many Civil War battles including the Seven Days Battles and Antietam. McClennan was the Democrat Party's nominee to run against Lincoln in the 1864 presidential election. He served as Governor of New Jersey from 1878 to 1881 and died in 1885.

induced to believe that the enemy has a least 100,000 men in our front," reported "Little Mac" McClellan to his commanding officer, General Winfield Scott. And Washington being Washington, it wasn't long before this grim assessment was known to all, causing many to flee the city.

Our own Alexander Gardner sent his family elsewhere, including a son to boarding school in Emmitsburg, Maryland. Ironically, Emmitsburg is less than ten miles southwest of the horrific battle to come at Gettysburg. Gardner dispatched the rest of his clan to Iowa, but he of course never mentioned these relocations when McClellan presented himself at Brady's studio for portraits in August. Even to the untrained eye, McClellan's arrogance is evident in those sittings, particularly the ones where he has his hand thrust inside his tunic. Those earned him the nickname "Young Napoleon" in some newspapers. Gardner, who was managing the sitting on Brady's behalf, must have made a favorable impression on Little Mac because soon afterwards he was offered a staff position working under Allan Pinkerton in the U.S. Army Corps of Topographical Engineers. His official title would be "Photographer of the Army of the Potomac." Up until then, a small part of me had been struggling for weeks to think of who Gardner reminded me of, and I suddenly realized it was Pinkerton. Similar age, similar accent, and similar irascibility. I didn't mind Gardner all that much, but he went down half a notch in my book by association. Damn Scots.

I thought that Gardner's appointment would infuriate Brady, but I think he may have been relieved to be free of Gardner's frequent lectures on the importance of managing our finances. And while different in many ways, the two shared a common trait of outsized egos, which were struggling to coexist in the same studio. I was concerned that the sudden lack of financial oversight might become a problem for us all, even though Gardner agreed to continue helping part time. That said, I was pleased that his exit would solidify my own position in the management ranks of Brady's staff.

Both the Union and the Confederacy learned much from Bull Run, as did Brady. All spent the next several months preparing for what was clearly going to be a protracted conflict across a wide theatre. Despite greatly superior numbers, McClellan spent those months drilling and parading his troops around without seriously engaging the Confederate Army, much to the frustration of the press, Lincoln, and his own men. His procrastination and timidity would eventually cost McClellan his job but, in the meantime, he was promoted to even higher authority after Winfield Scott retired. At that point Lincoln made McClellan general-in-chief of the Union Army, in addition to his position as commander of the Army of the Potomac. With his characteristic bluster, McClellan reassured Lincoln, "I can do it all."

For our part, and despite the loss of all our equipment and photographs, the episode at Bull Run served to convince Brady more than ever that his vision of photographing the war was sound. That set us off to the White House in yet another attempt to obtain official permission and, we hoped, funding, to document the war through photography. It was a very different White House this time around though, with Lincoln now inundated with advice and opinion from anyone who could fog a mirror. Despite their friendship, Lincoln's exhaustion from all the unsolicited interference caused him to redirect Brady to his Secretary of War, Edwin McMasters Stanton.[38] Brady had previously made several portraits of Stanton and so the two were acquainted. To

---

38 Edwin McMasters Stanton was born in Ohio in 1814. He served as U.S. Attorney General from 1860-1861, and as Secretary of War from 1862 to 1868. Stanton died in 1869 just a few days after having his nomination to the U.S. Supreme Court confirmed.

say that Stanton was a difficult personality would be a gross understatement and, without their prior history, it is likely that we would have never even been granted an audience with him at all, let alone gained official permission to create what Brady called his "War Views." Even so, it was difficult to secure a private meeting with Stanton but, in what turned out to be another stroke of luck, we arrived at his offices to find that Allan Pinkerton had been asked to be Stanton's witness for the meeting.

Following introductions, Pinkerton looked at me and said, "I seem to recall General Anderson saying something during our last meeting at the White House about you having a habit of showing up in the damnedest of places, Bailey. True to form, here you are again."

"Just continuing my work in assisting Mr. Brady, which you will no doubt also recall from that meeting, Allan," I responded. I instantly regretted using his first name, but he seemed unfazed. In fact, I got the sense that he had already done some groundwork with Stanton on our behalf because, after offering up some halfhearted opposition, Stanton agreed to grant Brady and his studio permission to officially document the war. Stanton would not agree to provide us with any funding, however, which again had me wishing that Gardner was still overseeing the studio's books full time. But he did offer us the protection of the Union Intelligence Service under Pinkerton. While Brady was grateful, I strongly suspected that Pinkerton had engineered this "concession" to keep closer tabs on yours truly.

Curiously, Pinkerton never mentioned in front of Stanton that he had already recruited me as a reluctant informant, which was a relief. The fewer people aware of that fact, the better, I thought. I had been hoping that Pinkerton had forgotten about the entire arrangement but knew better when the meeting concluded with him saying, "Brady, if you don't mind, I will drop around to your studio in the next week or two in order to arrange logistics with your man Bailey." Brady's aversion to administrative detail ensured his agreement.

With Brady Studios now officially sanctioned as war photographers, our attentions turned to building new Whatsit wagons, securing additional equipment and supplies and, most importantly, recruiting and training more cameramen for the campaigns that would surely come. Among our new recruits included William Pywell, D.B. Woodbury, J.B. Gibson, and a few others. Perhaps the most prolific among these was T. H. O'Sullivan[39], who would go on to additional fame by taking his talents to the American West after the war.

With Gardner sidetracked in his new role as Photographer of the Army of the Potomac (sometimes I wondered if everyone was working in some capacity for Pinkerton), and Brady's distaste for anything beyond the artistic side of the business, most of the hiring, acquiring, and contracting fell to me. The distraction was welcome, however, since my cotton suppliers to the south were now in the midst of harvest season and would soon be asking Bailey Importers where to ship our orders. If I'd been idle, I'd have had both the time and the inclination to let panic set in. As it was, Elkins and my father had that job covered, although I was keeping both at bay with vague letters of assurance. Amid all this stress, Pinkerton presented himself at the studio one day for our prearranged meeting about security.

"Let's get some lunch Bailey, and we can work out a modus operandi for when your men are back in the field." Knowing that logistics wasn't all we were bound to discuss, I was happy to get clear of the studio and out of earshot of my colleagues.

---

39 Timothy H. Sullivan was born in Ireland in 1840. He started as an apprentice for Brady in New York City, but eventually moved to his Washington Studio to work under Alexander Gardner.

After a short walk, we settled in at the Round Robin Bar at the Willard.

Once seated and after giving lunch orders to our waiter, Pinkerton said, "Here is how this is going to work, Bailey. We'll give you as much advance warning as we can about anticipated battlefield locations and one of my men will accompany any crew you send out to make your photographs. Any Union troops that question you will be handled by my man and, in the remote possibility that you find yourself confronted by Confederates, you will say that my man is part of your crew. Very simple, agreed?"

"Very simple, and yes, agreed," I said. "And will you be my point of contact?"

"Mostly me, yes," he responded, "Although if I am out of town or otherwise unavailable, you should seek out Captain Lafayette Baker on Secretary Stanton's staff. Failing that, please contact Kate Warne. Both are aware of the special status that has been granted to Brady Studios, and of your need for escorts in the field."

Well, now my day just got a little bit brighter. "And how is Miss Warne?" I inquired innocently. "I haven't seen her since I ran into you two in the lobby of this very hotel."

"She is working hard for the cause, Mr. Bailey, which is apparently more than I can say of you. I haven't heard a thing from you since we agreed at our White House meeting that you would use your status as a British cotton trader to keep your eyes and ears open for information that might be helpful to the President."

Trying not to appear defensive I said, "To be fair, that meeting was just a couple of months ago, and all of my time since then has been dedicated to Brady's Studio, including a side trip to Bull Run. I haven't been back south."

"Fair enough," responded Pinkerton, "But I think it's high time we got you into the fight. Now that we have the escort issue settled, shall we move on to more immediate needs?" And with that, my day got a little darker.

"We suspect that a tavern in Maryland about fifteen miles south of here is being used as a meeting place for Confederate spies. I'd like to confirm that, and I can't think of a better way to do it than to have a Southern businessman check in for a stay. What do you think?", he asked.

"I think," I began, "that if your suspicions are correct, without a plausible reason for being there, there is a good chance that I'll end up with a knife between my ribs. I can't very well say that I decided to take a short holiday amid opposing armies."

"We thought of that Mr. Bailey, and the Union has decided to take you up on your offer to buy some cotton. That would give you a reason to meet with one of my people at a discreet location to arrange the sale, shipment details and so on."

"Right—I'm sure these Southern sympathizers would be delighted to have a Union Army supplier enjoy their hospitality" I replied, holding back a more caustic response.

"Thought of that too Bailey, and here's my idea. You'll meet my man at the tavern. You two will argue price but will end up at $65 per bail.[40] The debate should be cordial, but make sure you are overheard."

"But that was the going price last year," I responded. "No one would believe that there wouldn't be some kind of premium to cover the risk of moving a shipment north through the conflict."

"Exactly. That's why you are going to win the argument about payment terms. You'll insist on 100% in advance and, after a suitable period of back and forth, my man will agree."

"And why would you agree to that Pinkerton?"

"Because it will make you appear indifferent to the next part of the plan. To gain favor with these traitors, you are going to

---

40 By 1864, the price of cotton had increased 19-fold from pre-Civil War levels, putting a 500-pound bale at more than $900.

share the shipment details with them so that they have an opportunity to stage an ambush and keep that cotton in the South. So, in their minds, the Confederacy gets both the money and the goods, and you don't care. This will help you earn their trust in a way that may be useful to us in the future." And with that, Pinkerton leaned back in his chair looking quite pleased with himself, although he would have been disappointed to know that he had a bit of soup stuck in his mustache.

I pondered it some, then said, "Sounds a little expensive for the Union to me. You don't get any of the cotton you've paid for?"

Leaning forward again he said, "I'm hoping we can ensure that their ambush isn't successful. Best case, we kill or capture some of them. Worst case, we lose the cotton, but that would be a small price to pay to shut down a nest of spies so close to Washington."

We sat in silence again as I tallied the pluses and minuses from my own selfish perspective. On the plus side, Bailey Importers would have sold some cotton, generated revenue, and saved the business for a time. Father would be pleased, Elkins would remain employed, and I would have Pinkerton off my back for a while. On the minus side, I could end up lying in a ditch in Maryland with a slit throat.

"It would have to be a decent sized sale," I finally said, "Otherwise they'll be suspicious. And I'll need the paperwork signed on the spot that day." Of course, all that mostly helped me, but I didn't say so.

"Agreed and understood," Pinkerton responded. "I'm hoping they search your effects and find that paperwork, as it will add legitimacy to your story. So, make an amateurish attempt to hide it in your room. And, speaking of paperwork and searches, I would strongly recommend that you leave that letter from

Lincoln with me for this trip. Having them find that wouldn't end well."

"True enough," I said, "Although I don't need to trouble you with storing it." The fact is I wasn't sure I would ever see it again if I gave Lincoln's letter over to Pinkerton. And although I was undecided as to whether I'd take it, if I did, I would have to bury it much more carefully in the lining of my coat. The truth was that having that letter with me gave me the same feeling of safety that the Cooper did.

"And where is this tavern exactly?" I asked.

"Surrattsville, Maryland[41]" he answered. "At the intersection of Branch, Piscataway, and Woodyard Roads. The proprietors are John Surratt and his wife Mary."

"Jesus Christ," I blurted. "I met John Surratt at this very bar just before I saw you and Kate in the lobby that night. He seemed awfully young to be a tavern owner."

"That was likely John Jr.," offered Pinkerton. "Senior would have drunk this bar dry if my information is correct. Was the person you met in his teens?"

"He was," I answered. "Said something about going to school at a St. Charles College."

"Definitely Junior then. And did you tell him anything about what you did for a living?" Pinkerton asked anxiously.

"I told him I was in the cotton trade."

"Perfect." Pinkerton responds. "In fact, better than perfect. If Junior happens to be at the tavern when you are, he'll un-wittingly corroborate your story." In that moment, Pinkerton looked as happy as I'd ever seen him. Unfortunately, I didn't share in his elation, although I did manage to talk him into a

41 Now known as Clinton, Maryland. A Surratt House Museum operates today in the building that housed the tavern, at 9110 Brandywine Road, 14 miles southeast of the Petersen House in Washington.

round of double whiskies to seal the deal (not to mention calm my nerves). And I got him to pay for the drinks and the lunch.

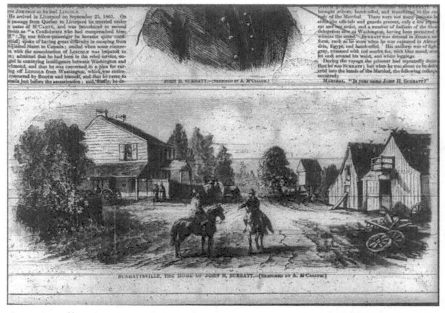

Surrattsville, Courtesy of the Library of Congress, LC-USZ62-54734

Chapter 9

BAILEY THE SPY

Over the next few weeks, I was grateful to be kept busy around the studio which, at least for brief periods of time, kept my mind off the upcoming trip to Surrattsville. In addition to throwing myself into working for Brady, I developed a secondary diversion by becoming a regular at Peter Taltavull's[42] Star Saloon, located across 10th Street from my room at the Petersen House. It was less expensive and more convenient than the Round Robin Bar at the Willard, and I was far less likely to encounter people at the Star like Anderson, Pinkerton, Stanton, Crawford, and the growing list of other characters that I now preferred to avoid.

Brady was not pleased about my having to leave the studio for a few days. I of course kept most of the facts from him, but I did say that the trip was necessary to keep Pinkerton and McClellan happy, knowing that Brady was keen on staying in the Army's good books. I had recently learned that McClellan hired Pinkerton in Chicago four years ago when the former was an executive at the

---

42 Peter Taltavull was born in Spain in 1825. His Star Saloon was situated next door to the right of Ford's Theatre. The Star was demolished in 1930 to make room for a parking lot but was rebuilt in 1967. Today it is used as offices and storage for the Theatre.

Illinois Central Railway. Coincidentally, the legal counsel for that railway at the time was none other than Abraham Lincoln. That shared history helped explain Pinkerton's rise to prominence in Washington and his current stature with the Union Army. It was also another reason to curry his favor (or at least avoid offending him). Everyone in Washington is connected in some way if you dig deep enough. And some combination of cash, sex, or blood is usually the glue. I also pointed out to Brady that Tim O'Sullivan was coming along nicely and that my short absence might be a good way to further test his abilities.

When the day came, I borrowed one of Brady's horses and set off the fifteen miles or so across the Anacostia bridge into Maryland and south to Surratt's Tavern and hotel. The plan was for me to meet there with a Grenville M. Dodge[43] who, in addition to being one of Pinkerton's lackeys and a Colonel in the 4th Iowa Volunteer Infantry Regiment, was also attached to General Montgomery C. Meigs'[44] Quartermaster Corps. All these facts could be confirmed by the rebels and would thus add to the legitimacy of my story, should they care to check.

And so it was that by mid-afternoon I found myself at the tavern, and I didn't have to wait long for Dodge to appear. Our timing was good in that the place wasn't overly crowded, so anyone could have overheard our discussion if they'd had a mind to. And I suspect that our stern looking, 40-something server was trying

43 Grenville M. Dodge was born in 1831. He would serve as U.S. Grant's intelligence chief in the Western Theatre during the Civil War and would rise to the rank of Major General. From 1867 to 1869, Dodge would represent Iowa's 5th District in the U.S. House of Representatives. He died in 1916.

44 Montgomery C. Meigs was born in Georgia in 1816. He graduated from the U.S. Military Academy in 1836 and served in the U.S. Army from then until 1882, attaining the rank of Brevet Major General. He died in 1892 and is buried in Arlington National Cemetery.

to do just that. She seemed to be quite enthusiastic about tidying up the areas close to our corner table.

Just as Pinkerton had advised, we argued over price, but ended up at $65 per bale, payable in gold. At one point, I felt that Dodge may have been hinting at a higher price with me kicking back the difference to him, but I am probably wrong. More likely it was a test set up by Pinkerton to trap me. That said, given Dodge's ability to consume alcohol at a heroic rate and this possible attempt at skimming, I wasn't surprised when I read of his 1867 election to Congress, where such skills are common.

Following Pinkerton's plan, Dodge put up a good show of resistance, but eventually agreed to full payment up front. We signed two copies of the paperwork, agreed to meet again soon to discuss delivery logistics and ordered another round to celebrate the deal. While Dodge's impressive stamina with the bottle enabled him to excuse himself and ride off upright shortly thereafter, I decided to linger and nurse my last glass of bourbon. I hadn't been sitting there for more than five minutes, when in walked John Jr. He did a brief double-take and then walked straight over to my table.

"I remember you" he said, pointing in my direction. "We met in the bar at the Willard a few months ago. You are a Brit in the cotton trade, am I right?"

"Right on both counts" I responded. "Good memory. And you were a student, as I recall, although I apologize that I've forgotten your name. I'll blame the drink for that."

"John Surratt," he said, puffing his chest out just a little. "My family owns this building and tavern. This town is named after us."

"It's a beautiful spot" I offered sincerely. "And very conveniently located. You must get a lot of trade passing through this intersection."

Just as he was about to respond, the humorless looking server came up and said, "I must go out for an hour or so. You and your sister will need to watch things."

"Okay," he replied. "But let me first introduce you to a nice British gentleman that I met in Washington a few months back." Then, turning to me he said, "Mr. Bailey, as I recall."

"Jack Bailey," I said as I rose and bowed.

"Mr. Bailey, this is my mother, Mary[45], although I'm guessing you have seen her here all afternoon" said John Junior.

Maintaining her stern look, Mary said, "Nice gentlemen don't sell supplies to the North." With that, she turned on her heels and left.

"I apologize, Mr. Bailey. I hope you take no offense. What say I join you for a drink on the house to make amends?"

Even with a few bourbons on board, I sensed that the entire exchange had been somewhat staged. Between Mary's swipe at the Union and Jr.'s comments at the Willard about Lincoln's war, they had made their allegiances clear. I think they had decided to test mine. Had I known what this free drink would spawn, I might have made my excuses, walked briskly to the door, and bolted back to Washington. Sadly, however, one of my many flaws is an inability to refuse a free drink.

As John Jr. pulled out the chair Dodge had been using and started to sit down, he called out over his shoulder, "Anna!"

Once seated, he continued, "Again, I am sorry if my mother offended you in any way, Mr. Bailey. Talking politics in a tavern is best avoided." Then, ignoring his own advice, he asked if I was indeed selling something to "that Union man."

"Just cotton," I replied.

---

45 Mary Surratt was born Mary Elizabeth Jenkins in Maryland 1820 or 1823. She married John H. Surratt in 1840 and had three children (Isaac in 1841, Elizabeth Suzanna "Anna" in 1843 and John Jr. in 1844). She would be hung in July 1865 for her role in Lincoln's assassination, to be known forever as the first woman executed by the U.S. government.

"A dangerous thing to be doing in these parts, Mr. Bailey. Although this state hasn't seceded from the Union, there are many here that believe it should. If you must, sir, you'd be better off holding such meetings in Washington."

"Well, there are many up there that see things the other way around. They would prefer that the Union didn't line the pockets of the South through trade," I said, trying to avoid an escalation. "And it is cotton, after all, not gunpowder or firearms." And then the floor seemed to fall away. The woman I assumed to be Anna presented herself at our table to ask what we were drinking. I was instantly and totally smitten.

"Anna, this is Mr. Bailey. Mr. Bailey, this is my sister Anna Surratt." While she might have been able to replicate her mother's stern looks if she'd had a mind to, the big eyes and charmingly pert mouth were irresistible. Miss Warne moved down a notch or two in my private ledger.

"A pleasure to meet you, Miss Surratt. I'll have another bourbon if you don't mind," I said, ratcheting up the accent. In my experience one's odds with a woman improve measurably with an accent (or a uniform, come to that).

"Same," said Junior dismissively. I tried to keep my eyes on John as Anna retreated to the bar, but it was an effort.

"More harmless than guns that's true, Mr. Bailey," Surratt said, bringing us back on topic, "but I would still recommend that you be more discreet in these parts in terms of whom you are seen trading with."

His voice had gone up a note or two, so I countered with, "My bigger enemy would be bankruptcy John, if I may be so bold as to use your given name. And, as I see it, accepting a sale that will support my suppliers and their families in South Carolina isn't something I could pass up in these times."

That logic stumped him for a while, although he continued to

probe with questions and comments that I knew were designed to figure out where my loyalties lay. All that aside, he wasn't bad company
though, and I accepted his offer of a second free drink as we continued the conversation. My concerns about having one too many were
trumped by my desire to steal a few more glances Anna's way. It may
have been the drink or, more likely it was wishful thinking, but I swear
she took another look at me once or twice. It was likely part of their
plan but, along with offering me a bite to eat, John suggested I stay in
one of their rooms for the night. By this time there is no way I could
have sat astride a horse for the fifteen-mile journey back to Washington
in any case, so it was either a room here or a night on the road under
the stars. I accepted and, after stowing my gear, excused myself for a
walk and some fresh air before bed.

When I returned to my room, I smiled to myself when I saw that
the small black thread that I had used to seal a dresser drawer was now
on the floor. I had fastened Dodge's paperwork under that drawer and
was now confident it had been read by my hosts. I had to hand it to
Pinkerton. His ability to predict human behavior was impressive. I'd
have to remember that. Before turning in I jammed the one chair in the
room under the doorknob and placed my Cooper on the nightstand.

Although I didn't feel much like eating the next morning, the
chance to interact again with Anna as she served me breakfast was
worth the possibility of depositing that meal in a ditch as I rode back
to Washington. I saw John Jr. briefly that morning as well, and he
thanked me again for yesterday's conversation. It was probably my
imagination, but I'm certain that I felt Mary's eyes boring into the
back of my head as I rode away from the tavern and turned my horse
north up Branch Road toward Washington.

Chapter 10

THE BAIT IS TAKEN

I hadn't been in Brady's studio for more than a couple of hours the day after my return when Pinkerton appeared and suggested we take a walk. I'm sure he had already debriefed Dodge, but he wanted to hear my version of events, which I provided. The fact that I enjoyed a few drinks and dinner with John Junior was news to him, since all that occurred after Dodge left. I left out any mention of my infatuation with Anna but did confess to being served by both her and Mary. I also offered that John Jr. in particular seemed to be directing the conversation in a way to test my allegiances and that I had been careful but Southward leaning.

"This is all excellent Bailey," he beamed. "I had very much hoped that we would be able to penetrate that traitor's nest and it seems like you are well on your way. Was there anyone else around the tavern that caught your attention?"

"There were others, yes, but no one that seemed to interact with the Surratt clan in any way other than what you would expect from ordinary patrons. Maybe I should go back, saying I need to scout out the final leg of the shipping route we'll use," I suggested, with Anna top of mind.

"Not yet," Pinkerton said. "I'm guessing that young John will be in touch with some suggestions. He is trying hard to work his way into the Confederate spy networks, and he may see a successful hijacking of this cotton as his ticket. If so, he'll want to have a hand in the arrangements. Let's give him a couple of weeks to make a move. I assume you'll need that time to get the order together anyway." And, with that, he tipped his peculiar hat and turned northwest up Pennsylvania Avenue in the direction of the White House.

I didn't need to wait two weeks to hear from Surratt. A few days after my stroll with Pinkerton, I ventured into the Star Saloon after a full day at the studio, and there he was.

"Greetings, Jack!" he beamed. Then he introduced the young lady seated with him as a Miss Antonia Ford[46].

Recovering from my surprise, I couldn't help but say, "What a strange coincidence meeting you here."

"Not a coincidence, I must confess," he said in a hushed tone, while glancing around at the other patrons. I noticed he had chosen a table in a corner which, while not private, was more secluded than any other in the room. "I am not completely without contacts here in Washington. I made a few inquiries and discovered that you are staying across the street and that you have a habit of coming in here most nights. I was actually hoping to meet you." Before I could ask why, he launched into a series of harmless questions to soften me up, including inquiring about my trip back to Washington from Surrattsville, the photography business, England's view of the conflict, and so on. Only after the third round of drinks arrived at the table did he get down to business.

46 Antonia Ford was born in 1838 in Fairfax Court House Virginia. Her father Edward was a merchant and secessionist, no doubt influencing Antonia's decision to spy for the Confederacy. She died in Washington in 1871.

"Jack, after our conversation back in Surrattsville it seemed to me that although you are English and, as you've pointed out, first and foremost loyal to your business, I just couldn't help but think that your heart is in the South."

"My home is certainly in the South, John, as you know. As is my business," I responded noncommittally.

"I have an idea on how you can support both your home and your business, if I may be so bold," he said. "You mentioned that you have been paid in full for that cotton you sold the Union. Let's imagine that it didn't make it all the way North. There would be no harm to you, and it would bring much good to the South."

"I actually don't recall saying that I had been paid in full, but I do remember having one or two bourbons too many that evening, so perhaps I did," I said, not wanting him to think I knew that they had found and read the paperwork in my room. "And how exactly could failing to deliver the cotton help me or Bailey Importers?"

"Oh, you will make all the arrangements to deliver it in good faith, my friend. But due to circumstances beyond your control, it won't get into Union hands" he said. "All you need to do is tell me the timing and I will take care of the rest."

"I see. You'll need to know where as well, or does your talent for making inquiries also extend to shipping routes?" I said, playing along.

"We have a suggestion in that regard, Mr. Bailey," said Miss Ford, breaking the silence she had maintained since being introduced. Surratt gave her a sidelong glance that suggested he would prefer to be the one in control of the conversation, but he let it go. "We think that Port Tobacco should be where you commit delivery to the Union. They control Port Tobacco and so shouldn't object. You get it to Norfolk by rail and arrange for a ship to take it the final 150 miles up the Chesapeake and into the Potomac. The Confederacy controls Norfolk, so we can take over from there."

After pondering this in silence for a few moments, I said, "That shipment will have to leave Norfolk bound for Port Tobacco, or I will be suspected of fraud. And when it, as you say, doesn't make it into Union hands, the cause will have to clearly implicate the Confederacy and not me."

"Of course," responded Surratt, reinserting himself into the conversation. "All of that would be arranged."

"And I will need to travel to Port Tobacco to meet with receivers and warehouse people. I have no experience or contacts there," I said as I glanced around to be doubly sure that we weren't being overheard.

"Of course, Mr. Bailey," said Miss Ford. "We will provide you with some names to make it easy."

More silence. "I could hang for this," I observed somberly.

"We all could," agreed Surratt. "But, to the bold goes the booty, if you'll allow me to paraphrase a proverb."

"I'll need to think about this John. It's a very big risk."

"Let's meet here again in two days Jack. I'm sure you'll come to the right decision," he said as he and Miss Ford stood to leave. "And the tab is already paid," he added, as if that minor gesture would influence my thinking.

I stopped by Pinkerton's offices the next day and, much to my delight, he was in and meeting with Kate Warne. He asked me into his office and invited her to stay, so they both received a report on my encounter with Surratt and Ford.

"Another job well done it seems Bailey," Pinkerton said after I finished my summary. "And Port Tobacco makes sense given Miss Ford's recent visit to Rose Greenhow's home. It's Greenhow's birthplace. I am sure that she is well connected there."

Astounded, I asked, "What does Rose Greenhow have to do with any of this?"

"She's a traitor, Bailey. And a strumpet, peddling her charms for information to assist the Confederacy." I remembered this conversation sometime later when I read that Rose herself described her spying methods by saying, "I employed every capacity with which God has endowed me—" From what I had seen, God had been generous in those endowments.

Pinkerton continued, "Among her unwitting sources is that idiot senator from Massachusetts, Harry Wilson. We believe that is how Beauregard came to possess advance warning of McDowell's plans before Bull Run, which was a major contributor to that humiliation. We have her under house arrest here in Washington. I allow visitors, only because seeing who comes by is quite informative," he concluded with a smug look.

"Good God, I met her at that White House fête for General Anderson a few months ago. She was within a few feet of the President!" I exclaimed using my best patriotic voice, but privately fearing for my own skin in retrospect.

"She's a spy, not an assassin Mr. Bailey," said Kate. "And a mother. No woman is going to book a trip to the gallows and orphan her children by attacking the President in the White House." I could think of one or two that might but held my tongue.

Still somewhat shocked, I did manage to say, "Pinkerton, I lately find myself thinking that I'm in a play but am the only actor that hasn't been given a script. It would be helpful to know some of these things if I am going to continue working for you."

"It would be most decidedly unhelpful if you willingly or unwittingly share information that you don't need to have with the wrong people," he responded. "We would be putting ourselves and our people at grave and unnecessary risk. I compartmentalize for that very reason. Look, let's get back to the task at hand," he continued. "When you see Surratt tomorrow, I want you to agree to Port Tobacco. Insist on going there yourself to make the arrangements for offloading and warehousing and we'll see what cockroaches come into the light to help you."

And I'll stop by Anna's tavern both ways I thought to myself, but I said, "You'll need to talk to Brady for me. He wasn't pleased with the time off I needed for my last excursion, and he's going to be even more agitated if he thinks this is going to keep happening. And, while I'm at it, I have another request. Since this town is apparently teeming with Southern spies, and you won't tell me who they are, I can't continue meeting with you in public. It would only be a matter of time before it's noticed."

"Fair enough," he conceded. "Let's make Miss Warne your primary contact for the time being. Having spent most of the past few months in Cincinnati with McClellan's Ohio division, she's not well known here in Washington. Worst case, you could explain contact with her as a necessary part of your work with Brady." I smiled at the prospect of having to meet Kate, which earned me yet another one of Pinkerton's Scottish headmaster glares.

"And one more thing," he added, probably recalling my outburst about Greenhow, "I have one of my agents, Lafayette Baker[47], camped out with a couple of hundred Union soldiers near Surrattsville. He's keeping an eye on the Surratt's and other rebel sympathizers in the area. He has made some arrests, but he knows what side you are on and will steer clear. In an emergency, go to him for help." I just stared at him.

---

47 Lafayette C. Baker was born in 1826. During the Civil War he spied for General Winfield Scott and, from 1862 to 1863 served as the Provost Marshall of Washington, heading up the National Detective Police Department. Known for his lack of regard for constitutional rights and severe interrogation methods, he was eventually demoted. Baker published a book titled *A History of the Secret Service* in 1867 and died in Philadelphia the following year.

The following evening, I visited the Star as usual. Surratt wasn't there when I arrived but came in a half hour or so later. I suspect he had been lurking somewhere on 10th Street to see if anyone was following me or with me but, if so, he never said. Since all the tables were occupied, we shuffled down to the less populated end of the bar and ordered drinks. After a moment or two of small talk I got right into it with, "Port Tobacco is workable, John, but to keep up appearances, I need to make a show of being personally engaged in the process. As we agreed the other day, I'll need to go there to arrange offloading and storage. I'll need those contacts you promised, and I'll need to have the usual deposit against their fees waived. I'm taking enough of a risk; I'm not going out of pocket for this."

"I expected all that, Jack, and it's no problem," he agreed. "And I also expect that you will want to be present on the day of delivery, which is fine too. Just stay out of the way. And, by the way, we could arrange to have you hog-tied when the time comes, to reinforce your story once your buyers realize they've been duped."

"That won't be necessary, I'm sure. But how in the hell do you intend to pull this off in the middle of a town occupied by Union troops?"

"It's best that you don't know the details Jack," he said, sounding a lot like Pinkerton. "Suffice it to say that the Union may control the town, but we control the docks. They are two different things." That was certainly the case in Charleston, I knew from hard experience. He continued, "I hope you will visit the Tavern on your way back and forth, Jack. It's about midway, after all." Damn right I will, I thought to myself, but showed no enthusiasm in agreeing. No point in revealing my interest in seeing his sister. We decided that my visit would take place the following week, but I didn't bother to inform Kate in advance, I think in part to feel I still had some control and partly due to paranoia about being watched here in town by Surratt's lot. Who knew that Washington was such a rat's nest outside of Congress? By this time, I found myself imagining cloaks swishing in every doorway.

Chapter 11

BACK TO SURRATTSVILLE
AND BEYOND

*P*inkerton must have made good on his promise to have a chat with Brady, because I didn't get the customary resistance when I asked for another few days off. I borrowed the same horse and set off again for Surratt's Tavern, where I planned to stay the night before proceeding on to Port Tobacco. Mail had been banned between the North and South since August, so Pinkerton had sent one of his lackeys across the river into Virginia to post my instructions to Elkins in which I asked him to send our shipment by rail to Norfolk and have it deposited in a warehouse near the docks. In the letter, I assured Elkins that I would organize things from there, since he had no need to know about Port Tobacco or the rest.

John Jr. must have told the family something about our arrangement because I received a decidedly warmer welcome from both Mary and Anna this time around. While it was the latter that interested me the most, the softer version of Mary at times reminded me of my own mother. Iron fist in a velvet glove, rabid guardian of the family, and willing to endure an impossible husband to make it all work. In the Surratt's case, John Sr. was a raging alcoholic, which Pinkerton had alluded to at the Willard, and which I soon witnessed for myself. Like most of his kind, the arc of Senior's typical day went from sullen to exceedingly friendly to boorish to comatose. I don't imagine that owning a tavern and its inventory helped, and the effect on profits must have been monstrous. Mary did her best to keep her husband away from the paying customers and at one point she went so far as to offer me an apology for his behavior. I hinted that my mother had endured similar burdens, although I failed to mention that in the Bailey household the issue had been women more so than whiskey. My words were heartfelt, and I think that exchange further enhanced my position with the Surratt matriarch.

Before dinner that night, John Jr. and I were joined by Frank Stringfellow[48], a wisp of a lad with a psychotic stare who couldn't have tipped the scale at more than 100 pounds. He spent most of the evening complaining about being turned down for service by various units of the Confederate Army, including the Little Fork Rangers, the Prince William County Troops, and the Goochland County Dragons. I'm not sure I would have admitted to such a string of rejections, but I had to give him credit for his tenacity. I would learn later that he had wormed his way into the C.S.A. by "capturing" three Confederate soldiers then presenting them to their commanding officer as prisoners. By the end of the war, Frank would have a $10,000 bounty on his head—the highest for any of his ilk. What he lacked in size he made up for in zeal, so I made a mental note to report him to Kate.

---

48 Benjamin Franklin Stringfellow was born in 1840. Repeatedly turned down by the Confederate Army for health reasons, he would eventually be admitted as a Captain in the 4th Virginia Cavalry. In addition to spying, he served under J.E.B. Stuart in battles that included Seven Pines and Cold Harbor. Stringfellow died in Virginia in 1913.

After a few drinks, John Jr. and Frank excused themselves with vague references to another meeting. Shortly after they left, and much to my surprise, Mary invited me to dine with her in the family kitchen while Anna was asked to mind the bar. Following the customary pleasantries and a couple of polite questions about my trip to Port Tobacco, Mary leaned in and said, "Jack, you have been of great service to my family and to the Confederacy these past few weeks, but I was wondering if I could impose upon you for another favor." Although I felt a sudden surge of anxiety, what choice did I have at this point other than to reply, "Of course ma'am, I would be happy to help out if I can." It also wasn't lost on me that Mary must know a lot more about my dealings with her son than she had previously let on.

"Very much appreciated," she said, "and I hope you will find that this won't be anything more than a minor inconvenience. Anna has been attending Saint Mary's Female Institution in Bryantown, and she needs to return there to finish up. While a person wouldn't normally pass through Bryantown on the way to Port Tobacco from here, it isn't all that far out of the way." My anxiety was instantly replaced with excitement, although I tried very hard to look indifferent. "My son cannot get away from his business at the moment, I need to mind the tavern and, well, you've seen for yourself that we can't ask my husband for anything, so I was hoping that you might escort Anna back there on your way to your meetings."

I'd escort her anywhere, I thought to myself, but instead offered, "No trouble at all Mrs. Surratt, I would be delighted to be of service. As you say, it isn't all that far out of my way."

"Of course, in normal times Anna might have made the trip herself," Mary continued, "but with soldiers and who knows what riffraff wandering about these days I would feel much better if she had a gentleman looking out for her."

If you are looking for a gentleman, I'm not sure I'm your man I thought to myself, but I instead responded, "You are right to be cautious given the times, ma'am. Don't give it another thought." I was in fact giving the situation enough thought for the both of us, to the point that I had trouble focusing on the rest of the conversation.

Following an after-dinner stroll on my own around the property, I passed Anna on the narrow staircase on the way up to my room. As I tipped my hat and excused myself, she leaned in, whispered some thanks for assisting her brother and planted a soft kiss on my cheek. Although a late-night visit from her was probably a longshot, I did not put the chair against my door that night, just in case. The Cooper, however, spent the night in its customary position on the nightstand.

The following morning I was up early and enjoying the breakfast Mary had cooked and served when John Jr. sat down at my table.

"I hear you have been asked to make a stop on your way to Port Tobacco, Jack," he began in a tone that was all business.

"No need for thanks," I said, trying to steer the conversation in a friendlier direction. "Your Mother did more than enough of that yesterday. I'm happy to help, and it's not an imposition in the least."

"You are very gracious, but that wasn't what I was thinking. You seem honorable, sir, but with Anna being my sister, I feel compelled to—"

I cut him off with, "John, you don't need to say it. I understand completely. You don't need to worry about her. It's just a few hours on the road, and I'll see her there safely. In my business I've learned to handle myself," at which point I put the Cooper on the table for emphasis.

"Others aren't all that I am worried about," he said, although his tone had relaxed slightly.

"As I said, I understand. She's your only sister. If you aren't comfortable, I will find a reason to tell your mother I can't do it," I offered, knowing that his alternatives were limited and that this was closed business in the eyes of his mother. That completely took the wind from his sails, and he went in a different direction with, "I was going to offer you a firearm, but see that you have that covered. You should know that Anna carries a pepperbox derringer[49] and is quite skilled in its use."

I wasn't certain if he meant that as a further warning to me, or if he was informing me that I could count on Anna's assistance should we encounter trouble on the road, but decided that the sooner we got off this topic the better. Fortunately, at that moment both Mary and Anna joined us, and the talk turned to the day's logistics. The family had decided that they would prefer not to part with a horse and Mary wondered if I would object to hitching mine to a buggy. I assured them that this was no problem and explained that my horse had experience being hitched to Brady's Whatsit wagons. John was aware of my side business assisting Brady, although I had to offer a brief explanation to Mary and Anna. As usual, my story was that the slowing of the cotton business had allowed me to temporarily pursue my passion for photography. That tale seemed to successfully satisfy the Surratt's just as it had anyone else I'd seen the need to mention it to.

It took John and I a half hour to hitch the horse and pack my saddlebags, Anna's luggage, and the food and water Mary had prepared for our journey. Mary thanked me again, hugged Anna and went back inside to serve a customer. John offered a steely-eyed glance and handshake to me and a hug for Anna, then we

---

49 A pepperbox is a multi-barrel gun with roots going back to the 15th century. It became popular in America around 1830 and was built by multiple manufacturers in various calibers. Some included a retractable knife blade.

were on our way. We rode the first mile or so in silence, which I broke by asking Anna about her studies. She described them un-enthusiastically and offered that at least she was nearly finished. She said that she was anxious to get back to support her family in these difficult times.

"I think that experience is a much better teacher than most of my instructors have been" she said at one point, "and with the state of the country at the moment, we are all surely about to have a great many new experiences in the near future." I caught myself before blurting out "let's hope," although not meaning it in the context of the war.

"You must have already seen so much of the world, Mr. Bailey," she continued. "Born in a foreign country, managing your own export business, taking photographs of battles and great people, living in the deep south. What's it all been like? You must feel like you've already lived many lives!"

"Many of the people we photograph aren't as great as they'd have you believe, Miss Surratt" I said. "And that has certainly been enlightening for me. As for the rest, I hadn't really thought about it all in quite the way you describe it, but I suppose it has indeed been an education. I can tell you though that people are very similar no matter where they live. Most simply want to pro-vide for themselves and their families, go about their lives without interference from their neighbors or the government, and be able to make their own choices and find happiness."

"Well I envy you in any case, Mr. Bailey" she said. "I'm 18 years old and have only ever seen Washington and our little piece of Maryland. I imagine that I am destined to lead a very ordinary life and won't see a tenth of the things that you already have." I hope not, I thought to myself, as the rabble working round the Liverpool docks, Charleston's bordellos, and the recent carnage at Bull Run all came to mind. Although neither of us knew it at the time, she was destined to live a life that was anything but ordinary. In fact, the very route we were traveling this day would soon play a role in history that would implicate the Surratt's in a way that would shape the remainder of her life, and not for the better.

The getting-to-know you banter continued, with me playing up the British accent for good measure. By the time we stopped for a rest and to feed and water the horse and ourselves we had established a certain comfort and ease in our short relationship that I'd never felt before with anyone. I liked her. I liked talking to her, and I liked listening to her, and I dare say that she seemed to feel the same way. At one point she said, "I think that taking me so many miles out of your way entitles you to call me Anna." To which I naturally responded, "Only if you agree to call me Jack."

The rest of the journey to Bryantown went by far too quickly and, when we arrived at Saint Mary's, I found myself tarrying over the simple tasks of unhitching the horse, stowing away the buggy and unpacking the bags. A formidable looking woman rejected my offer to help Anna up to her room with her luggage, so our goodbye was stilted and formal. I recall hoping at the time that our sudden return to the use of "Miss Surratt" and "Mr. Bailey" was simply for the benefit of the flinty headmistress who was blocking me from the door of Saint Mary's, and that it was not permanent.

The dozen or so miles from Bryantown to Port Tobacco were dreary in contrast to the first part of the journey. I checked in at the Brawner Hotel[50] that evening with plans to seek out Junior's local contacts the following morning. Even though the town was occupied by Union troops, Pinkerton had warned me that the place

---

50 There is a marker near the site of the Brawner Hotel today that reads, "In this center of Confederate activity, at the Brawner Hotel, Detective Captain William Williams unsuccessfully offered Thomas Jones $100,000 reward for information that would lead to the capture of John Wilkes Booth."

was likely teeming with people sympathetic to the Confederacy. I had assumed as much, otherwise Surratt wouldn't have suggested it as my delivery point. But with so many Union troops around I couldn't help but wonder what brazen plan Surratt had to make off with all those bales of cotton from right under their noses.

The following day, my meetings with the warehousing contacts went far more efficiently than I expected, which suggested to me that Surratt had done some advance work. That troubled me on some level, although it enabled me to finish up early and make my way back to Surrattsville where I planned to spend the night before returning to Washington. The full 35 miles back to the Petersen from Port Tobacco would have been too much for my horse to handle in a single day in any case, and I felt compelled to report (and take credit for) the safe delivery of Anna to Saint Mary's.

Surratt's Tavern seemed colorless that evening without the presence of Anna, although there was no shortage of drama as John Sr. was well into an impressive binge. Mary did her best to contain him while simultaneously serving guests. For his part, John Jr. was huddled with a dubious looking group of accomplices that included the diminutive Stringfellow. I tried to avoid the lot of them but appreciated Mary's gracious thanks for my successful transport of Anna to Bryantown. That night, the door to my room was once again held firmly shut with a chair.

Chapter 12

BUSINESS IN NORFOLK

I rose early the next morning and set off immediately for Washington and the studio, arriving around midday. I went back to work with a renewed sense of vigor, in part because I needed to get my mind off Anna, but also wanting to prove my worth to Brady lest he start thinking he could get along without me. On the ride back from Surrattsville I had decided that I should travel down to Norfolk to make a show of supervising the transfer of my cotton onto the ship bound for Port Tobacco. Maybe I was just getting paranoid, but I had concluded that my being there would be interpreted by both sides that I was pulling for their cause. I had fallen into a dangerous game that I was making even riskier by getting close to the Surratt's. I couldn't have Pinkerton wondering where my loyalties might lie, and I certainly couldn't have the Surratt's doubting my commitment. The business with Rose Greenhow had also made me realize that there were probably players in this game that I was not even aware of. I decided that I had been far too cavalier to this point and promised myself to henceforth manage appearances (and my tongue) more tightly. In any case, a trip to Norfolk was going to require more time away from the studio.

A few days after my return from Surrattsville I met with Kate in a lowbrow tavern west of the White House and away from my usual haunts. I've long since forgotten the name of it, but there was no shortage of these establishments in Washington in 1862, and they were well-suited to my desire to keep a low profile when meeting with Pinkerton or his people. A journalist from my home country had called Washington, "A great, scrambling, slack-baked embryo of a city basking in the sun like an alligator on the mud-bank of a bayou in July." Charles Dickens more graciously called it, "A city of magnificent intentions," and the unfinished Capital Dome, visible from almost everywhere in the city, provided a fitting metaphor of just that. For my money though, the abundance of venues where you could get reasonably priced bourbon and hold clandestine meetings was a major asset of Washington in the 1860s.

I gave Kate a not-so-fulsome account of my trip to Port Tobacco, leaving out the bits about the side trip to Bryantown and my growing friendship with a certain Surratt. I provided her names and addresses of the contacts I had made in Port Tobacco, the plan to move the cotton there by boat and my observations on Stringfellow and the two Johns. She offered no comment about my plan to be in Norfolk for the transfer but asked a few questions and took notes on it all. I realized after we parted that, with Anna on my mind, for the first time ever I hadn't made any suggestive remarks to Miss Warne. I wondered afterwards if that had been a mistake. Pinkerton and his people seemed to be able to sense even the slightest shift in the wind, and I worried that the absence of my customary repartee might have put her on alert. If so, the damage was done, and I consoled myself with the knowledge that at least I was starting to be a little more self-aware.

Although I'm sure it didn't seem so to those on the front lines, in looking back there wasn't much in the way of serious fighting in the months following Bull Run in July of 1861. Early in the New Year, however, there were several notable wartime events both on the battlefield and elsewhere that included General Ulysses S. Grant's[51] victories at Fort Henry and Fort Donelson, Jeff Davis's inauguration as President of the Confederate States, and selfishly, my trip to Norfolk.

Grant's success at those two forts in Tennessee served to not only give the North a welcome victory, but they would launch him on his way to much greater prominence in the months and years to come. They also very likely helped keep Britain and other European countries from formally recognizing the South, which would have been problematic for the Union to say the least. Charles Francis Adams, the U.S. Minister to Great Britain, may have said it best when he wrote, "I feel that one clear victory at home might save us a foreign war." The victories at Fort Henry and Fort Donelson may well have done exactly that.

Grant had taken Fort Henry in two hours, then immediately marched 12 miles east to Fort Donelson where he had ridden among his troops to rally them in the face of an attempted rebel escape to Nashville. After three days of fighting, Confederate General Simon Bolivar Buckner[52], command-

---

51 Hiram Ulysses Grant was born in Ohio in 1822. He graduated from the U.S. Military Academy in 1843 and, because of his Civil War successes, served as Commanding General of the U.S. Army from 1864 to 1869. He became the 18th President of the United States in 1869, serving until 1877. He died of throat cancer in 1885. Grant has been pictured on the U.S. $50 bill since 1913, as well as on the 1922 one-dollar gold piece, 1922 silver half dollar and 1890 five cent stamp.
52 Simon Bolivar Buckner was born in Kentucky in 1914. A graduate of the U.S. Military Academy, he rose to the rank of Lieutenant General in the C.S.A. In addition to Fort Donelson, Buckner saw action at Perryville and Chickamauga. He served as Governor of Kentucky from 1887 to 1891 and died there in 1914.

er of Fort Donelson, asked for terms of surrender. Grant earned his nickname "Unconditional Surrender Grant" that day when he responded, "No terms except an unconditional and immediate surrender can be accepted. I propose to move immediately upon your works." Ironically, and again like so many others in this war, Grant and Buckner had at one time served together. When Grant was going through hard times after the Mexican American War, Buckner had come to his assistance financially. Now he found himself once again contributing to Grant's success by way of surrendering thousands of Confederate troops, horses, weapons, and other spoils of war. I've wondered more than once if Buckner noted the irony and regretted his previous philanthropy.

Brady was disappointed that we had not been in place to document this action in Tennessee, and his frustrations grew every time the press published illustrated works of those battles by my friend Al Waud and his contemporaries. I tried to console him by pointing out that, with the distances involved, even with advance warning there is no way we could have arrived in time. In the end, the effect was to have him redouble our efforts to maintain sufficient Whatsit wagons and crews prepositioned in the field for the battles that were expected to come.

In mid-February, I set out across the Long Bridge from Washington to Alexandria to begin the journey south to Norfolk. Among my personal effects were papers showing that I ran a business in Charleston, South Carolina. I stowed them in a manner to ensure that they were readily available to prying eyes. More discreetly, I also carried the Cooper and, sewn very deeply inside the lining of the back of my coat, the letter from Lincoln. As always, I hoped to have no use for either of these last two items but couldn't imagine not having them close by. Most of the 200-mile trek south could be covered by rail, although engine trouble outside Richmond, Virginia, forced me to have to have to unexpectedly spend the night there. I decided to book into the relatively new Spotswood Hotel at 8ᵗʰ & Main. I had heard that the Spotswood[53] was a five-story luxury marvel but, more importantly, had been used by Jefferson Davis[54] while his White House of the Confederacy was being completed. In keeping with my decision to be more thoughtful about my actions, I figured it might be best to hide in plain sight. What Union spy in his right mind would check into Jeff Davis's former residence?

It wasn't the Willard, but the Spotswood had a passable bar that served decent food and carried an impressive selection of liquor. I chuckled to myself when I ordered a double Early Times and thought about my old friend John Beam. Had it really only been a year since we had shared that rail car and swapped stories most of the way from Baltimore to right here in Richmond?

I had picked up a newspaper at the front desk and learned that Davis was to be officially inaugurated tomorrow, just a few blocks away, in a ceremony marking the transition from a provisional to a permanent government. The February 21ˢᵗ edition of Richmond's Daily Dispatch reported that, "Tomorrow the permanent Government of the Confederacy will be organized by inauguration of the President. The Permanent Congress has already been in session for three days and has given indication of a purpose to act with energy." It went on, "If a people as numerous

53 The Spotswood Hotel opened in January 1861 on the corner of 8ᵗʰ and Main Streets. Confederate President Jefferson Davis held his first meetings in Richmond there, and the hotel also served as a place where relatives would come for information on rebel soldiers. It was destroyed in a fire in 1870 that claimed eight lives.
54 Jefferson Davis was born in Kentucky in 1808. He graduated from the U.S. Military Academy and served in the U.S. Army from 1825 to 1835 and again from 1846 to 1847. In addition to being the only person to serve as President of the Confederate States, Davis was a U.S. Senator for Mississippi from 1857-1861 and the U.S. Secretary of War from 1853 to 1857. He died in 1889 in New Orleans, LA.

as those of the Southern States desire to be free, they cannot be subjugated by any power on earth. The thing is an impossibility. All depends upon the spirit and temper of the people; for, even if their Government should prove incompetent, it would not destroy the vitality or repair the recuperative energies of a people determined to be free. Again we say that all depends on the people. If they will not be subjugated they cannot be subjugated." It got more confrontational from there, causing me to think that if these words truly reflected public opinion in the Confederacy, this country was in for a long fight.

The fact that the inauguration date, February 22, 1862, was also George Washington's birthday was no doubt intentional. Since I was already going to arrive in Norfolk later than planned, I decided to stay in Richmond a few extra hours to attend. No matter which way the war went, this was bound to be considered a historic event. The weather that day was miserable, but not so bad as to keep thousands of spectators away, including yours truly. As I set out, my mood matched the weather following the news that Willie Lincoln, the third son of Abe and Mary, had passed away two days ago in the White House of typhoid fever. As if all that Lincoln was already dealing with wasn't enough.

I'm not generally fond of pomp and pageantry but must admit that it can be amusing at times. You can tell a lot about people by the way they conduct themselves at self-aggrandizing ceremonies and, as a result, I learned something about President Davis that day. What I already knew was that he had graduated from West Point in 1828, 23rd out of a class of 33 cadets, and that his major mark of distinction there was being involved in the Eggnog Riot of Christmas 1826. Texas Governor Sam Houston had described Davis as "cold as a lizard and as ambitious as Lucifer." He began his climb up the ranks of society in 1835 by marrying Sarah Taylor, the daughter of his commanding officer. Sadly, Sarah died of yellow fever just three months after the wedding. Ten years later, in 1845, Jeff was at it again when he married 18-year-old Varina Howell, 18 years his junior and granddaughter of New Jersey Governor Richard Howell. I know you are probably thinking that Anna was also 18 when I took a fancy to her, but I was 24. An 18-year age difference is an entirely different matter than one of just six years.

The first thing that struck me was the fact that Davis (looking every bit as flinty as he had in the portrait Brady had taken of him in 1859) was escorted to the platform by black footmen, all of whom were dressed in black. Some would later say that the somber appearance of the procession and the weather portended the fate of the Confederacy, but the benefit of hindsight makes such observations easy. While Lincoln's inaugural address had contained olive branches directed toward the South, Davis did not reciprocate. Phrases like "the malignity and barbarity of the Northern States in the prosecution of the existing war" left no doubt as to his thinking. He painted a picture of the Union as "Bastilles filled with prisoners, arrested without civil process or indictment duly found; the writ of habeas corpus suspended by Executive order—elections held under threats of a military power; civil officers, peaceful citizens, and gentlewomen incarcerated for opinion's sake." I assume he had Rose Greenhow in mind when he mentioned "incarcerated gentlewomen", but we'll never know. He was certainly correct that Lincoln had suspended habeas corpus in Maryland and portions of some other states in May of 1861, but I knew firsthand what a rat's nest of Southern sympathizers and spies Maryland had become and could therefore understand why Abe would feel the need.

Like all leaders, regardless of political stripe, Davis prattled on about being a defender of freedom and having the confidence in his people to endure temporary hardships to forge a better world.

I must credit him for acknowledging the Confederacy's recent defeats at Fort Henry and Fort Donelson, as he said during one crescendo of his speech: "After a series of successes and victories, which covered our arms with glory, we have recently met with serious disasters. But in the heart of a people resolved to be free these disasters tend but to stimulate to increased resistance."

As I reflected on it all and contrasted it with words I had read from Lincoln's addresses, it struck me again that I didn't really have a horse in this race other than my own interests. Yes, like most thinking people I abhorred slavery but, truth be told, I was a selfish bastard that cared more about my business and personal entertainment than I did about this conflict and what it might bring for millions of people. I saw blockades, battles, and spies as obstacles interfering with my personal success, not in the context of any higher purpose. It was an epiphany. On some level though, I found myself envying the people in this crowd who were so keen to support what they perceived as a fundamental battle for right over wrong. The people gathered at Calvert Street Station in Baltimore almost exactly a year ago had emitted a similar sense of hope and excitement as they waited to catch a glimpse of their new President on his way to his own inauguration in Washington. I now had friends on both sides of this conflict, and I suddenly had an entirely new empathy for what they felt and how they viewed their world.

Before my thoughts could fully coalesce, however, I began to take notice of the profile of a person a few rows in front of me as he periodically turned to survey the crowd. He was dressed in a Confederate Major's uniform but, as I focused more intently, there was no question in my mind that it was Allan Pinkerton, head of the Union Intelligence Service. General Anderson had accused me of "turning up in the damnedest of places," but this trumped all.

After Davis wound down and the crowd began to disperse, I

positioned myself such that Pinkerton would have to pass me on his way out. Allan is nothing if not calm under fire, I'll give him that. When our eyes met, he only showed a split second of surprise before coming right up to me with his hand out.

"Mr. Bailey, what an unexpected pleasure," he began. I was too dumbfounded to say anything straight away, so he filled the silence with, "Let me spare you having to tax your memory. I am Major E. J. Allen[55]. We met at a function a few months ago, but I'm sure you must have met a lot of people on that occasion."

Recovering as best I could I said, "That's right Major. I seem to recall that you had a beautiful female companion on your arm that day, so I will use the fact that I found her so distracting as an excuse for my clumsy failure to recall your name." I'm certain that he caught the opaque reference to Kate Warne because there was a slight edge in his reply of

"Don't give it another thought." Only someone who knew him would have noticed the disapproving look.

"Let me buy you a drink by way of apology," I offered. I had a score of questions I wanted to ask him in private, starting with the uniform. "Besides, I would love the opportunity to show my support for our men in arms, even in such an insignificant way."

"Unfortunately, I have other obligations, Mr. Bailey. Perhaps another time," he replied in the same tone. "Next time, perhaps." And with that, he melted into a group of other grey uniforms, leaving me standing alone and confused. I went back to the Spotswood, checked out, made my way to the station, and boarded a train that would take me the remaining 100 miles of my journey down to Norfolk. I found lodgings late that evening near the Norfolk

---

55 Allan Pinkerton was known to work undercover in the South, where he posed as a Confederate soldier – Major E.J. Allen, a rank that was senior enough to allow him to move about freely, but not too senior to attract unwanted attention.

harbor, too exhausted to do anything but bed down for the night.

Feeling refreshed after a good night's sleep and a hearty breakfast, I made my way to the warehouse where Elkins had arranged to store the shipment of cotton. Having arrived a day late, I was only mildly concerned when I learned that the cotton bales had already been moved down to the piers and so I proceeded there. John Jr. had helped arrange this last leg of the shipment's journey and I cursed myself for not demanding to know more about the specifics. During the course of my meandering around the docks I caught sight of what had been the USS Merrimack, a steam frigate that had been scuttled by the Union in April 1861 but raised and restored by the Confederacy as an ironclad. Rechristened after that refit as the CSS Virginia[56], the result was something to behold to those of us accustomed to wooden ships and stately sails. I had read about the Union's use of ironclads in the capture of Fort Henry, but this was my first sighting of such a beast.

The Virginia sat low in the water, sinister and shark-like, but at the same time looking barely seaworthy. I found myself wishing that I had one of Brady's cameras so I could take a photograph for Pinkerton's files but, in the end, it wouldn't have been much use. The Virginia was destined to see action in less than a fortnight during the Battle of Hampton Roads just offshore from Norfolk. During that engagement she rammed and sank the USS Cumberland, thereby demonstrating the futility of wooden ships against iron. But the next day she would engage the USS Monitor, a Yankee ironclad recently arrived at the Union's Fort Monroe, across the harbor. There was no clear victor in that first showdown of ironclads despite both ships coming under heavy fire from one another, often at point blank range. How Brady

---

56 The CSS Virginia was the Confederacy's first ironclad warship. She was 275 feet long, carried just over 300 officers and men and travelled at 5-6 knots (6-9 miles per hour).

would have loved to have captured all of that with his cameras but, once again, it was left to the illustrators to help us imagine what the combatants witnessed that day. The CSS Virginia's short life would end less than three months later, on May 11, 1862, when she was scuttled to prevent her from falling into the hands of the Union troops advancing on Norfolk.

My search of the port eventually took me to a pier where I could see scores of bales of cotton on the docks, the remnants of a larger load that apparently had already been moved onboard a boat nearby. I had no way of knowing if it was mine, so made a mental note to tell Elkins to start stenciling "Bailey Importers" onto the bales of future shipments, something I had noticed our competitors doing during my last visit to the Charleston docks. I was partway up the boat's gangplank when I was stopped by a sailor whose enormous frame blocked my way. He pointed a bale hook he was carrying at my neck and said, "We are fully crewed son, no need for help, so you can turn your ass around and get out from underfoot."

"This is my shipment," I responded with a certainty I didn't feel, "and I would very much like to inspect it. May I have a word with your captain?"

"You'll be inspecting the bottom of the harbor if you don't get off this boat right now," he growled in return.

"It's okay Gus," said a familiar voice behind him, and I looked over Gus's massive shoulder to see John Surratt Jr. "Let him come up," he added.

Even though Gus moved to one side, it was still a tight squeeze to get past him. At close quarters the smell of his sweat and breath would have knocked a vulture off a manure wagon. When I reached John, he took me aside by the elbow and asked what the hell I was doing here.

"Just making sure the goods are in order and well on their

way, John," I assured him.

"You should have told me you were coming here. I was expecting to see you in Port Tobacco," he responded. "I'll show you around and you can see for yourself that all is in order before you leave. We are casting off soon."

"I could use a ride back north," I said. "If you don't mind, I'll just tag along."

"This isn't a pleasure boat," said someone behind me. "And although it's a porous one, we plan to run a blockade as we pass Fort Monroe. I don't need excess cargo aboard, including sightseers." John introduced me to the source of these remarks, Captain James Nickels, then suggested that we take our discussion to the captain's quarters.

After John explained who I was, Nickels relaxed somewhat and invited us to sit down as he poured a round of drinks. He outlined his plan to get underway soon after dark and run out to Chesapeake Bay as quickly as possible. I offered that I weighed less than a third of a bale of cotton, which would hardly tip the balance and slow the ship down. "And besides," I continued, "I could use a ride up to Port Tobacco and promise to make myself useful both there and along the way."

"Port Tobacco?" he exclaimed before John cut him off with a hard look and said, "It will be fine, Captain Nickels, I will take full responsibility for him, and there will be a little extra in it for you."

"Let me start making myself useful right now" I said as I reached under my coat. Both Surratt and Nickels stiffened, then relaxed when they saw me pull out my flask and start to refill their glasses. Just then Stringfellow stuck his head in and said, "All loaded and ready to go, gentlemen." He looked at me with mild surprise, and I couldn't resist giving him a wink.

"Jack, let's enjoy a smoke on deck with this drink," said John, as he moved to usher me outside. "I just have a couple of things to do but will meet you at the stern so we can watch Norfolk fade away as we set sail."

I found my way to the ship's stern and had worked through a good bit of my cigar before Surratt appeared. As I offered him one, he said, "Sorry about the Captain. Nickels is jumpy about sailing past Fort Monroe and he doesn't like surprises."

"Understood, and no harm done" I responded. "And I appreciate the ride back north, thank you." What I really appreciated more than anything was the fact that my intended route from Port Tobacco to Washington was going to be by way of Bryantown, but of course I didn't mention that.

We both remained silent as our boat sailed passed the naval yards and we got a closer look at the CSS Virginia. I broke the silence with, "I'll bet that monstrosity has something to say about the blockade."

"We'll soon see, I'm sure," he responded. "The Union also has ironclads. I think the days of wooden ships are numbered."

We were a couple of hundred yards offshore facing each other along the rail and making more small talk when John looked over my shoulder and started to say something about sincerely appreciating my help when two huge paws grabbed my shoulders, and I found myself launched over the rail. I hit the cold water cursing and when I broke the surface, I saw Surratt and his ape Gus looking down on me from the back of the boat as it continued on its way.

"No hard feelings Jack. You are still always welcome in Surrattsville!" John yelled. What I was feeling was rage, and I dug into my coat for the Cooper. I'm not sure what I was thinking as the chances of hitting him as he faded away were zero. More importantly, putting a .31 caliber ball or two into him, or even trying to, might diminish my chances with his sister. I never got the chance in any case, as the hammer caught on my coat and the gun sank down to the bottom of the entrance of Willoughby Bay where it likely remains today.

I'm a decent swimmer, but fully clothed and in the cold tidal waters of February it took every ounce of concentration I had to swim back to the pier. At one point, I tried to remove my coat and pants, but they clung stubbornly to me, and the effort was just too taxing. I did manage to get my boots off, but otherwise arrived intact back at the pier. I couldn't see a way out of the water and was just starting to panic when I heard a voice yell, "Jack, over here." I then noticed a crude ladder that ran down one of the pilings and a man most of the way down it toward the water. When I reached it, a hand appeared out of the darkness, and I could just make out the insignia of a Confederate Major. Major E. J. Allen, as it turned out. I resisted the temptation to pull him in and instead accepted his help up to the pier. We sat in silence for some time as I spat up water and recovered from near exhaustion.

"I take it there's been a falling out," Pinkerton said sarcastically, "if you'll pardon the pun."

"Not in the mood Allan," I responded breathlessly. "Although it's nice to finally see that you have a sense of humor."

"About the name, Jack. If you encounter me in Confederate territory, please pretend not to know me unless I approach you. And for God's sake don't say a name until I use one, which will likely be Major E. J. Allen, but not necessarily. Same goes for Kate. If you see her down here, ignore her unless she approaches you. And she'll undoubtedly also be using an alias," he said, ignoring my compliment.

"You send Kate down here?" I asked incredulously.

"She can handle herself," he responded. "And what better cover than a woman. We also sometimes travel as husband and wife."

"I'll bet you do," I said. "And speaking of travel, you better get some of your people going to Port Tobacco if you want to see who tries to abscond with that cotton."

"I doubt very much that shipment is going to Port Tobacco Jack," he replied. "In fact, I doubt it ever was. Why go to the effort of stealing it from a Union controlled port, when you can simply point the boat in a friendlier direction?"

"Good God," I said. "Why on earth didn't you say something to me? You might have saved me the time and expense of a trip there!"

"The Confederates had to believe that you had their best interests at heart. I suspect that would have been more difficult if I had shared my suspicions with you," he said.

I pondered that for a minute and decided to let it go, since my last encounter with Anna wouldn't have happened without that visit to Port Tobacco. I finally said, "So you've lost both the shipment and your money which, by the way, I am not paying back. I delivered."

"I'm not asking you for the money, Jack. We had an agreement, and I will stick to it."

"Being new to Washington, I guess I'm just not accustomed to such a cavalier attitude toward waste," I said.

"Actually, the Union has received quite a lot from that investment, Jack, with more to come. I've confirmed that the Surratt's are, at the very least, Southern sympathizers and maybe worse. I have the names of the people in Port Tobacco that you met and a few more from my visit here," he continued. "Knowing who they are will save money and lives in the future."

"On that topic," I added, "that fanatic Stringfellow was on the boat with Junior. I told Kate about him a few weeks ago."

"Indeed, I saw him, but thanks," the 'Major' responded. With that he stood up and offered a hand to help me up. "You still in one piece?"

"I lost my pistol and boots out there," I replied with a nod toward the water, "and I'm quite sure that my cheroots are ruined. I probably left some pride in the water as well but, other than all that, I'll be fine."

"Let me walk you back to wherever you are staying, and I'll leave you to it then. The police might ask some inconvenient questions if they find you walking around soaking wet, bootless, and alone."

"So, there is no personal escort back to Washington for me then, Major?" I chided.

"I know you know the way, Bailey. And the less we are seen together the better," he said. I had to agree.

Just as we started to walk, cannon fire erupted from the direction of Fort Monroe, and I wondered if Surratt may be getting shot at after all. And with something larger than a pistol. Pinkerton and I glanced in the direction of the sounds but couldn't see much through the stacked cargo and infrastructure on the pier.

A short time later we parted with a handshake outside my lodgings. Once upstairs I was delighted to find that my flask had survived the evening swim. I wiped off the salt water and put it to immediate use.

Chapter 13

UP AND BACK

*W*hen I reported back to the studio a few days later, I half expected Brady to give me grief about my absence, but instead found him in high spirits. Like everyone in gossipy Washington, he had heard that the Union Army was about to launch two campaigns. The first was to begin on March 7, 1862, when McClellan would send a portion of his Army of the Potomac to Centerville, Manassas, and Bull Run. There they planned to again confront the rebels under Confederate General Joseph Johnston[57]. Johnston and his troops had wintered in the area after their victory the previous July, a Union humiliation that I had witnessed with my own eyes. Brady was particularly excited to have his men revisit the scene where we had been unable to retain any photographic record of this first major battle of the war. He had already assigned Tim O'Sullivan to the Shenandoah

---

57 General Joseph E. Johnston was born in Virginia in 1807. He graduated from the U.S. Military Academy with Robert E. Lee in 1829. He served in the U.S. Army from 1829 to 1861 before resigning to join the C.S.A. Johnston saw action in many Civil War battles, including Bull Run, the Peninsular Campaign, and Vicksburg. He represented Virginia in the U.S. House of Representatives from 1879 to 1881. Johnston died in Washington in 1891.

Valley region, which included Warrenton, north to Harpers Ferry, Maryland, and south to Culpeper, Virginia. He teamed James Gibson and George Barnard with O'Sullivan for the studio's return to Bull Run although, it turned out that they would find no fighting to photograph there. They did, however, bring back dozens of photographs of last year's battlefield, including Beauregard's headquarters, fortifications around Manassas and images of the famous Stone Bridge, which I had crossed with Brady at the height of the chaotic Union retreat. Embarrassingly for McClellan, our men also took photographs of what would come to be known as "Quaker Guns," or logs painted black to look like cannons. As one writer opined, the Union had "been humbugged by the rebels" and McClellan, who had a growing reputation for finding any excuse not to fight, reportedly received an earful from Lincoln on the matter.

The second phase of McClellan's plan, the "Peninsular Campaign," was far more ambitious. It involved sending several hundred vessels 200 miles south down the Potomac, into Chesapeake Bay and on to Fort Monroe. From there, his army was to fight their way up the peninsula through Williamsburg and on to the Confederate Capitol of Richmond. Brady asked me to help organize the logistics for our participation in this action. Given the sheer scale of it, we decided to deploy two teams of photographers to maximize coverage. Brady and David Woodbury would lead one, and James Gibson and John Wood the other. My job would be to ensure that everyone was kept supplied and to facilitate communication between the teams. As Brady put it, he wanted the photographers to worry about taking photographs and me to worry about everything else. Our preparations over the past few months meant that we had all the necessary equipment ready to go in the future. Unfortunately, with my recent absences, I couldn't find a defendable excuse to stay in

Stone Bridge, Courtesy of the Library of Congress, LC-DIG-cwbp-00953

Washington, and I didn't want to jeopardize my position with Brady by not riding along in support. While Brady may have been disappointed by the fact that the rebel withdrawal from Bull Run meant no pictures of the aftermath of any great battle, I had other concerns. If Johnston had withdrawn south, it likely meant he was on his way to protect Richmond, the very place we were headed with McClellan. I didn't mention to Brady that I had just been to both Richmond and Norfolk, and I shuddered when I recalled how close I had come to being on the receiving end of Fort Monroe's cannon fire. Amid our final preparations I sent word to Pinkerton's office that I needed to meet him, and I suggested a date, time, and another seedy tavern west of the White House. I already had two bourbons on board when Kate came in with Harry Davies, who I had last seen on my walk from Calvert Street Station back to the Barnum Hotel in Baltimore a year ago. I suspect he had a gun pointed at my back that day and he didn't look much friendlier on this occasion. She sat down at the table right beside me with Harry across and said, "Before you get the wrong idea Jack, like you, I don't like having my back to the door."

"Understood," I responded, "but I think I'll still pretend that you sat beside me for other reasons."

"Glad to see that the swim you took in Norfolk didn't wash away your sense of humor," she whispered. "Speaking of which, I have a gift for you from Major Allen." At that point, Davies slid a box across the table toward me. I probably would have recognized it for what it was before seeing the label, but the name Cooper Firearms Manufacturing Co. etched across the top eliminated any doubt.

"Well, I have to say that I am genuinely touched, Kate," I said, meaning it. But before she could think I was getting too sentimental, I added, "I hope to be equally thoughtful when I get you two a wedding gift."

"What the hell are you talking about," she snapped. "Allan is married."

"Sorry, I didn't know that" I said. "I swear he was just telling me how you two sometimes travel together as husband and wife."

She glanced around to make sure we were out of earshot, then hissed, "For undercover work, as you well know."

"Right. Sorry," I said. Deciding that a change in topic might be wise, I launched into a description of Brady's plan to accompany McClellan's men to Fort Monroe with me along for the ride. I asked her if she could tell me anything about what we should expect to encounter there, and she said that she couldn't. Not won't, but can't, she assured me, as they really didn't have much in the way of intelligence. The hope was that Johnston and his 50,000 or so strong Confederate Army of Northern Virginia would have their hands full countering McClellan's thrust to Bull Run and that the route up the peninsula to Richmond might be undefended. We'd soon find out. She also said that Pinkerton would assign an agent to be with us from Fort Monroe and all the way up to Richmond. With that she excused herself and, with Davies in tow, left me to make my way back to the Petersen. Once in my room, I opened the Cooper box and chuckled when I saw cheroots packed in amongst the powder and balls. I suppose I must be a little sentimental after all, since I decided to carry this pistol instead of the replacement I had bought just a few days earlier. I would ask my landlord, William Petersen, to hold onto that one. A tailor by trade, I had employed Petersen's services to add various pockets and hiding places to my coat, and we had become friendly enough for me to get away with minor impositions like firearm storage. After depositing the cheroots in the pocket of that coat, I bedded down for the night.

The flotilla that McClellan had assembled for the trip down river from Alexandria, Virginia, to Fort Monroe was a sight to behold. More than 120,000 men, 15,000 horses and some 1,000 wagons (including Brady's two Whatsits) were packed onto hundreds of vessels. By this time news of the CSS Virginia's defeat of the USS Cumberland and other Union ships in the Battle of Hampton Roads had reached us. The Union's answer to the ironclad Virginia, the USS Monitor, had joined the fight late, but the result was a standoff. The fact that the CSS Virginia was still lurking in the waters ahead was more than a little disconcerting to those of us who found ourselves on this wooden armada. As we sailed south to Fort Monroe, in addition to worrying about the Virginia, I found myself peering down the many inlets and creeks along the way wondering if Surratt had ventured into any of them with my cotton, or if he'd gone south from Norfolk toward the Carolinas. Ideally, the Union cannons had cut short his plans the night he set sail. If so, I owed him a favor for sending me overboard.

Once we arrived at Fort Monroe, the process of unloading so many men, horses, and materiel was daunting. Since we weren't officially part of the Army, I focused on keeping Brady, our crews, and Whatsit wagons out of their way. We camped outside the Fort, which was near Hampton, Virginia, a town that was no stranger to both conflict and slavery. In the early 1600's, some of my British countrymen had landed here and traded some of the first slaves to be brought to America. During the war of 1812, the English pillaged Hampton before heading north to burn Washington. And less than a year before our arrival, three slaves had presented themselves to General Benjamin Butler at Fort Monroe. Butler famously declared them to be the "contraband of war," which eliminated any legal need to return them to their owners. This notion of slaves as contraband spread across the Union and resulted in thousands more of them presenting themselves at Fort Monroe. They would soon call it "Fort Freedom." It struck me as ironic that here was yet another army in Hampton intent on marching to Richmond and burning another capitol.

During the couple of days we were camped here, George Curtis presented himself to me as Pinkerton's representative and our liaison to the Union Army. What I didn't know at the time was that Curtis was also used and trusted by the Confederates as a merchant of non-human contraband, including ammunition and quinine. He was acquainted with Confederate Generals A.

P. Hill[58] and John B. Magruder[59], at times carrying dispatches for the latter. He claimed to faithfully copy these for Pinkerton, but I've found that people working both sides make a lot of claims. I should know. In any event, as the army was preparing to march north, Brady talked McClellan and ten of his general officers into posing for a photograph in front of a brick wall on one side of Fort Monroe. While their stances varied, McClellan chose to stand with his right hand thrust into his coat, with cap and sword hanging on his left. I couldn't help but notice that, at five foot eight, he appeared to be the shortest of the lot and I wondered if that fact influenced his decision to strike another Napoleonic pose.

Our march up the peninsula started on April 4; a beautiful sunny spring morning that soon turned dismal. The combination of torrential rain, countless wagon wheels and thousands of horse's hooves churned the red soil beneath us into a muddy paste. Being lighter and fitted with larger wheels than those found on the typical army wagon, we fared better than most. But just north of a town called Big Bethel our progress was halted by a burning bridge, set alight by retreating Confederates. We were all forced to spend a miserable night in wet clothing waiting for the bridge to be repaired.

A day later, the Union Army's IV Corps, led by General Erasmus Keyes, encountered the enemy in force at Lee's Mill on the Warwick River west of Yorktown. Across that river awaited

58 Ambrose Powell Hill Jr. was born in Virginia in 1825. Hill entered the U.S. Military Academy in 1842 and one of his classmates was Stonewall Jackson. Hill had to repeat his third year due to a medical furlough for gonorrhea, thus graduated in 1847 along with Ambrose Burnside. He saw much action in the Civil War, including both Battles of Bull Run, the Peninsular Campaign, Cedar Mountain, Antietam, Fredericksburg, Gettysburg, and Cold Harbor. He died in April 1865 at the Third Battle of Petersburg.
59 John Bankhead Magruder was born in Virginia in 1807. He graduated from the U.S. Military Academy in 1830 and saw action in the U.S. Civil War in the Peninsular Campaign and the Battle of Galveston. He died in Texas in 1871.

Confederate General Magruder, who would once again "humbug the Union" into believing that the rebel forces were much larger than they were. He did so by marching some of his troops in patterns that gave the impression that thousands of reinforcements were arriving. He also spread out his artillery and fired at us sporadically, giving the illusion that he had many more guns than he did. And all this again brought out the trait in McClellan that so infuriated Lincoln—procrastination. I admit to being fooled by the rebel's antics myself. And with last year's flight from Bull Run still fresh in my mind, I made certain that Brady's team was ready to skedaddle back south on very short notice. But while keeping a watchful eye on the Confederate lines and enjoying a drink and cigar, I received an education on battlefield deception from George Curtis.

"Magruder is no doubt up to some of his crafty tricks again," he observed as we discussed the day's events.

"Tricks?" I asked. "Surely he is just softening us up before sending all those men our way?"

"I know Magruder and have a pretty good idea what he's got," he says. "He'll be puffing himself up like a pigeon to hold us in place until help arrives."

"Good God man, if you are certain that's true, why don't you take it to McClellan?" I asked.

"Have done," he said. "Or at least Pinkerton has. McClellan won't listen to anything that doesn't support his desire to proceed with extreme caution. The troops on both sides appreciate the delays though, even if Lincoln doesn't."

When I asked how he knew all this is when he told me about his role as a merchant of contraband and occasional messenger for Magruder. It struck me yet again how many people Pinkerton must have on this chessboard. Oddly, part of me may have been disappointed to realize that I was likely just one small cog in his intelligence machine.

"Speaking of contraband, Curtis, has Magruder or any of your friends on the other side ever expressed an interest in cotton?" I asked hopefully.

"Not to me, but perhaps that's because they think of me in terms of other materiel," he offered. "Why do you ask?" At this point I told him about my cotton business and vaguely hinted at how Pinkerton had used a shipment to flush out Southern spies and sympathizers.

"Makes sense," he says. "I'll keep it in mind. Maintaining my access to Magruder and other senior C.S.A. officers has had its advantages. The Union certainly thinks it's worth providing them with the occasional shipment of ammunition." Ever mindful of selling cotton, I gave him one of my carte de visites and suggested that he contact me if he ever saw an opportunity.

Over the next few days, reports reached us regarding the Battle of Shiloh, which took place on April 6 and 7, hundreds of miles to our west in Tennessee. Grant had again emerged victorious, although the appalling number of casualties—more than 20,000 dead, wounded or missing including both sides—reinforced McClellan's inclination to procrastinate. He decided to put Yorktown under siege rather than attack the rebel lines across the Warwick River. I decided to move our wagons toward Yorktown and McClellan's base believing that we might be safer there, but that would turn out not to be the case. One day McClellan came near our position while giving the French Prince de Joinville, François d'Orléans[60], a personal tour of our lines. While near us they peered across the river using field glasses, which attracted rebel artillery. One cannonball whistled over our heads and

---

60 François-Ferdinand-Philippe-Louis-Marie d'Orléans was born in France in 1818, the third son of King Louis Philippe. In 1843 he married Princess Francisca of Brazil, daughter of Brazilian Emperor Pedro I. He died in France in 1900.

another other exploded nearby. Brady was unfazed, and he and Woodbury would soon take photographs of the prince and his hangers-on as they ate dinner on camp stools.

Unfortunately, I had the misfortune of being struck by some shrapnel from that second cannonball, although my wounds were so minor that I didn't realize I'd been hit until Gibson asked if I was in pain. Even small head wounds tend to bleed profusely and, once they got going, the nicks on mine were no exception. Brady suggested I go back a few hundred feet to where we had passed a surgeon's station, and he asked one of his apprentices to accompany me. As we approached, a young lad rushed forward with a bandage and directed me to a chair. Once seated, he started cleaning me up then did an examination to locate any hidden cuts by foraging through my hair. Something seemed odd, and I couldn't put my finger on it until *she* inadvertently brushed her chest against the side of my head. Damned if it wasn't a woman in disguise. I immediately understood why a woman wouldn't want to be identified as such here in the field surrounded by thousands of men, so I kept quiet. As she was finishing up and when everyone was out of earshot, I said, "Thank you, miss, you really seem to know what you are doing. I'm grateful."

She sensed my certainty, which I believe is why she didn't deny it. Instead, she looked around quickly to make certain we weren't being overheard. Then she said, "Listen, it would be very difficult—"

But I cut her off with, "I completely understand. Your secret is safe with me." Then added, "Interesting accent you have, by the way. I don't recognize it."

She looked around again before sticking out her hand

Federal Battery #4, Courtesy of the Library of Congress, LC-USZ62-68172

and saying, "Emma Edmonds.[61] I'm originally from New Brunswick."

"Canada? Well, that explains it." I felt I should repay her for her assistance by putting a quick end to the discomfort I'd so clearly created, so I stood up quickly and started to move

---

61 Sarah Emma Edmonds was born in New Brunswick, Canada, in 1841. She joined the 2nd Michigan Volunteer Infantry in 1861 using the alias Franklin Flint Thompson. She served as a field nurse at both Battles of Bull Run, the Peninsular Campaign, Antietam, and Fredericksburg. Edmonds documented her exploits in a memoir titled *Unsexed: Or, The Female Soldier*, which she dedicated to "the sick and wounded soldiers of the Army of the Potomac." She died in Texas in 1898. In 1992 Edmonds was inducted into the Michigan Women's Hall of Fame.

off. "Thank you again, sir. Much obliged," I said loudly.

Fortunately, the remainder of April was not nearly as exciting. We settled into a routine of taking pictures on the sunny days and playing cards, smoking, and drinking on the cloudy ones. Thus, as luck would have it, I was present for the taking of some of Brady's more famous early Civil War photographs, including "Battery Number One," "Confederate Water Battery," and "Federal Battery #4". The enormous 13-inch mortars pictured in the latter were the size of an elephant's torso and, when fired, sounded like the very gates of Hell were being torn open. The one thing that McClellan was confident in was his artillery, and he moved it up toward the lines as fast as he could. The rebels also had great respect for these guns, which caused them to quietly begin retreating toward Richmond in early May. Despite being informed of this retreat by escaped slaves, McClellan refused to believe it until it was confirmed on May 4 by way of a Union observation balloon[62]. I mentioned to Brady at the time that placing a camera in one of these balloons would offer an incredible opportunity for photographs from the air, although we agreed that it be too unstable to be practical. What pictures we could create from a bird's eye though! Unfortunate that it would never happen.

Emboldened by the knowledge that the Confederate positions had in fact been abandoned, McClellan ordered his forces to pursue them toward Williamsburg. A day and a half later the Union columns reached Fort Magruder and found that the rebels were

62 Both sides used balloons during the Civil War and the Union had a dedicated Balloon Corp. A civilian, Thaddeus Lowe, was named Chief Aeronaut of the Union Army in the summer of 1861. Early in the war Lowe had balloons tethered along the Potomac as an early warning system to detect any armies that might be approaching.

dug in with heavy guns and rifle pits, determined to make a stand. This was Brady's and my closest exposure to heavy fighting since Bull Run. But, again, since the details of this battle are so widely available, I'll spare you the details. Suffice it to say that after one day of fierce fighting, the rebels continued their withdrawal toward Williamsburg. I got our teams working quickly at the now abandoned Fort Magruder before the burial parties arrived. The scene was horrific, with bodies and limbs strewn everywhere. We were taking pictures as fast as we could, but our pace slowed significantly when a Union officer warned that live shells had been buried by the retreating rebel forces. Pressure would cause these traps to explode, killing or maiming anyone in the vicinity.

I'd now seen enough of the aftermath of these battles to know that I had no desire to be in the middle of one when the lead was flying. I know that my colleagues felt the same way, and we moved in respectful silence when we eventually followed the Union advance toward Williamsburg. Recalling what had happened to our photographic plates during Bull Run in 1861, Brady decided when we reached Williamsburg I should take what had been created thus far back down to Fort Monroe for safekeeping. Curtis agreed to stay behind and watch out for the crews, so I loaded up what we had and set off to the Fort. When I arrived on May 7, I was surprised to learn that Lincoln had landed there the previous day with Secretary of War Stanton and Treasury Secretary Chase[63]. This wasn't

---

63 Salmon Portland Chase was born in New Hampshire in 1808. He graduated from Dartmouth in 1826 and, over the course of his career was the Governor of Ohio, a U.S. Senator representing Ohio, and the U.S. Secretary of the Treasury. In 1860 he sought the Republican nomination to run as President but lost out to Lincoln. Chase was nominated by Lincoln on December 6, 1864, to replace Roger B. Taney as Chief Justice of the U.S. Supreme Court and he was confirmed by the Senate that same day. He held that position until his death in 1873.

the only time Lincoln would put himself within sight of the enemy, and I had to admire his courage.

As luck would have it, I happened to be inside the Fort when Lincoln was circulating among the troops in one of his frequent efforts to boost morale. He'd aged considerably since the last time I saw him, no doubt a result of both the war and Willie's passing just three months earlier.

"Jack Bailey, if memory serves," he said in a tired voice as he came upon me. "I suspect that you and Brady have had plenty to photograph of late."

"We have indeed sir," I responded. "And no doubt more to come with the army still working its way toward Richmond."

"Let's hope they get there," he sighed. "McClellan says he is too busy to see me, and I am not certain whether to interpret that as good news or bad."

"I've just come from the lines, Mr. President, and can attest to the Union Army being very busy. The rebels too, come to that."

He steered me aside and out of earshot of others and said, "I've decided to make the Confederates even busier. I have ordered a bombardment of their batteries in Norfolk to commence tomorrow. I am told that you were there recently and wondered if you could tell us anything that might be helpful."

"It was a very short visit, sir, most of it at night. And I spent much of it on the piers. Other than seeing the CSS Virginia docked, I can't think of anything in particular that you would find useful."

"I hear that you spent a little time in the water as well Bailey," he said with a chuckle. "But, no matter, I suspect the rebel troops there dispersed when they saw our 100,000 men sail into this fort. In any case, Stanton and I intend to see for ourselves after we soften things up with artillery."

"You are going over there personally?" I asked incredulously.

"Surely you can't be serious?"

"And why not, son? I can't let you folks have all the fun."

"The Confederate troops may have dispersed, but one determined man with a rifle can do a lot of damage. With all due respect, sir, why not leave it to your men to sort things out?"

"I'm going," he said in a tone that made it clear that there was no room for debate. "And I would be grateful if you would come along."

After cursing myself silently for being in a position to be going back to Norfolk, I said, "Can I make one suggestion, sir? Please wear a different hat. The rebels will spot that stovepipe a mile away."

"And so will our men, Bailey. That's the point."

I don't know whether he wasn't thinking clearly because of Willie's passing, or if he was out to give McClellan an example of what pushing forward looked like, or if he was just plain reckless. Probably some combination of the three. In any case, my mouth had just earned me another cruise on the waters of Hampton Roads. As it turned out, the Confederates had abandoned Norfolk and by May 10 it was completely occupied by Union troops under the command of General Wool. I can't recall a time when a Commander in Chief was so involved and in such proximity to a military operation but am certain that Lincoln's actions were noted by both Union and Confederate forces, and by McClellan. The fall of Norfolk also meant that the CSS Virginia was now without a port and so, with a hull too deep to make her way up the James River to Richmond, she was scuttled on May 11. Good riddance to her, in my opinion.

With the excitement over in Norfolk and the initial batch of photographic plates on their way back to the Washington studio, I set out to find Brady and the rest of our lot back up the peninsula. They had decided in Williamsburg to split the teams

Entered according to Act of Congress in the year 1865, by LEVY & COHEN, in the Clerk's Office, of the District Court, for the Eastern District of Pennsylvania.

Drewry's Bluff, Courtesy of the Library of Congress, LC-DIG-ds-05470

up, so I reunited with Brady and Woodbury on May 15 near Drewry's Bluff[64] where a small fleet of Union boats would soon test the defenses of this outpost less than ten miles downriver of Richmond. The Union fleet, led by Commander John Rodgers, included the USS Monitor, USS Galena, USS Port Royal, and USS Naugatuck. For three hours, the Confederates poured everything from cannonballs to musket shot down on the flotilla. As some of our photographs show, the rebels' position on the high ground surrounding this narrow, obstacle-strewn section of the James River made it impossible for the Union to advance. Rodgers later suggested to McClellan that even though trying to get past the rebel cannons by boat was futile, it would be possible to land troops short of Drewry's Bluff where they could surprise the Confederates and advance on to Richmond. He was ignored.

64 Located in Virginia just 10 miles south of Richmond, Drewry's Bluff rises some ninety feet above the water at a bend in the James River, providing commanding views and an excellent defensive position.

At White House Landing, Courtesy of the Library of Congress, LC-DIG-ppmsca-33375

Confederate Generals Magruder, Longstreet, D. H. Hill, Early, Pickett, and the rest were by now all under the command of General Joseph E. Johnston, who had come south from Manassas. Overly cautious like McClellan, Johnston consolidated his force of about 60,000 men from Drewry's Bluff out to the east and north along the Chickahominy River, where they burned all the bridges and settled into defensive positions. McClellan positioned his 105,000 men up the Pamunkey River further to the east and north of the Chickahominy. He hunkered down believing that the Union forces were outnumbered two to one based on an erroneous assessment of the rebel's strength he'd received from Pinkerton. Thinking back, I wondered if George Curtis was the source of this bad intelligence, as he would often leave us for a day or two without explanation.

Brady soon sent me afield again to locate Wood and Gibson to make sure they had what they needed. From Williamsburg, they had set out for Cumberland Landing on the Pamunkey River, although I eventually found them about six miles east of that at White House Landing, a Union supply base also on the Pamunkey. There is a photograph called "At White House Landing" that shows a group of men, including me, by the bridge on the river. One of our development tents is visible on the lower left.

Throughout the last week of May, there were minor skirmishes along the lines before two larger engagements eventually erupted at Hanover Court House and Fair Oaks. These two actions resulted in a total of 11,000 or so casualties counting both sides, with almost 1,800 dead. Most notable among the wounded was General Johnston himself, who was evacuated to Richmond and replaced briefly as commander of the Army of Northern Virginia by Confederate General G. W. Smith. Unimpressed with Smith, Jeff Davis replaced him after just a day or two with Robert E. Lee, a man whom we would soon all come to know better. Just prior to the battle of Fair Oaks, an aide-de-camp of Johnston's was captured by Union troops, and he ended up being one of two subjects in a Brady photograph that would grow in historical significance. The aide-de-camp was one Lieutenant James Barroll Washington, a great-great-grandnephew of George Washington and former West Point classmate of George Armstrong Custer. Custer is the other subject in the photograph. Being 30 miles away on the Pamunkey River I missed these two battles and the taking of that photograph, but I'd soon meet the flamboyant Custer in any case. Like tens of thousands of men on both sides, I was thankful that throughout most of June the action was again limited to minor skirmishes.

McClellan spent most of that month engaged in his customary lollygagging, while Lee took advantage of the calm to build up his defenses around Richmond. With not much to do and the temperatures, humidity, and quantity of insects all on the rise, I decided to pack up the photographs we had created over the past six weeks and take them back to Washington. I had just set out to reunite with Brady's crew and add their photographs to the collection when major fighting erupted south and east of Richmond in what would become collectively known as the Seven Days Battles. The names are all familiar now—Oak Grove, Mechanicsville, Savage's Station, White Oak Swamp, Malvern Hill, and so on. Approximately 36,000 killed, wounded, captured, or missing counting both sides. I saw only a small fraction of it and am at a loss to find words that sufficiently describe the carnage. As we learned at Fort Magruder, seeing the dead and maimed up close offers a different kind of perspective than reading the numbers in a newspaper. The pain these men endured and the anguish that was to come for their loved ones was unimaginable. The lucky ones were killed in an instant. The unlucky died slowly and painfully

Savage's Station, Courtesy of the Library of Congress, LC-DIG-cwpb-01063

or lost limbs and lived. How the survivors went back into battle after witnessing such savagery remains a mystery to me.

On June 28, Gibson took another now famous photograph the day after the fighting at Savage's Station and which was published in *Harper's* that November. With a ladder in the foreground for perspective, the photograph captures much of the fenced yard of a farmhouse and multiple tents in the distant background. The yard is almost completely covered in the bodies of Union wounded, although what is visible is but a fraction of the 2,500 men that would be abandoned there a day later when the Union withdrew. Several Union surgeons volunteered to stay along with the wounded, and all soon became prisoners of war, destined to be subject to the abhorrent conditions of Confederate hospitals and prisons. I prayed that my friend Emma Edmonds wasn't among them, although I would come to experience some of that rebel hospitality myself soon enough. Not that the Union's prisons were much better.

At this point I had certainly had my fill of it all, as had Brady. On July 1 we made our way to Harrison's Landing on the James River, seven miles south of Malvern Hill. We secured space on one of the boats heading back up to Alexandria and sailed back to Washington and the studio with a treasure trove of photographs, including a fresh set from the Seven Days Battles.

Chapter 14

ANTIETAM

oon after arriving back in Washington, we sold copies of the aforementioned photographs in both the Washington and New York studios for $0.75 or $1.00, depending on the print. With no financial support from the government and Brady spending money like a drunken sailor, sales of these "War Views," as Brady called them, were a godsend for financing our activities. At this stage in the war we had more than thirty bases of operations across several states, all of which had to supplied with plates, cameras, chemicals, men, horses, and food. Brady boasted about having "men in all parts of the army, like a great newspaper," and he wasn't far off the truth. In addition to his desire to be ready anywhere hostilities might erupt, we were now facing competition from several other photographers, including Anthony & Company and Armstead & White. This development drove Brady all the harder to continue investing in our preparedness.

Logistics for our bases mostly fell to me and having spent much of the past couple of months in Virginia meant that I had a lot of catching up to do. I spent most of July and August engaged in exactly that and, as a result, missed the action at Cedar Mountain in early August and Manassas (the Second Battle of

Bull Run) later that month. Tim O'Sullivan, who had been assigned to the Shenandoah Valley, covered these with assistance
from Barnard, Gibson, and Brady himself.

Tired of McClellan's procrastinating, Lincoln put Major
General John Pope[65] in charge of the Union Army of Virginia
in late June. It was Pope that presided over the two Union losses
at Cedar Mountain and Manassas. Although he certainly didn't
need any assistance in proving his incompetence, Pope had the
misfortune of facing Robert E. Lee in these battles at a time
when Lee was beginning to hit his stride as commander of the
Army of Northern Virginia. Lincoln would soon dismiss Pope
as he had so many others. One of Pope's former subordinates,
Brigadier General Alpheus Williams, would write: "His pompous orders ... greatly disgusted his army from the first. When a
general boasts that he will look only on the backs of his enemies,
that he takes no care for lines of retreat or bases of supplies; when,
in short, from a snug hotel in Washington he issues after-dinner
orders to gratify public taste and his own self-esteem, anyone may
confidently look for results such as have followed the bungling
management of his last campaign .... Suffice it to say that more
insolence, superciliousness, ignorance, and pretentiousness were
never combined in one man. It can with truth be said of him that
he had not a friend in his command from the smallest drummer
boy to the highest general officer. All hated him."

I could think of a few other examples of such loathsome
traits existing in others (Lord Cardigan comes to mind again),
but Pope's losses were in some measure Brady's gain as another

65 John Pope was born in Kentucky in 1822. He graduated from the U.S.
Military Academy in 1842 and saw action in the Civil War at the Battles
of Island Number Ten, Rappahannock, and the Second Bull Run. His
father was a Federal judge and a friend of Abraham Lincoln's. One of
Pope's cousins married Mary Todd Lincoln's sister. Pope died in Ohio in
1892.

collection of War Views was created, including one of an almost completely demolished Henry House atop Henry Hill where only the remnants of the chimney remained standing. Seeing that photograph I couldn't help but recall that a year earlier I had seen that same house shelled by Union artillery. I have marveled more than once in my life about how, even in this vast expanse of a world we live in, violence seems to repeatedly visit certain small points on the map.

On August 30, the Union army retreated to Centerville and east toward Washington, just as it had done the previous year. Along with the troops rode O'Sullivan, Brady, and the rest of our crew, exhausted from their activities over the past month. Those two Confederate victories emboldened Lee to take the fight into enemy territory and so, on September 3, he moved his army north into Maryland where it captured the city of Frederick. The Baltimore Riots of 1861 (the center of which occurred near the President and Campden Street Stations where I first met Kate)[66] and the large number of Southern sympathizers in the state had Lee assuming that he would be welcomed by the locals. But by 1862, public opinion in Maryland had shifted toward the Union, and it was the Union Army of the Potomac that would receive the warmer reception. Exasperated with Pope, Lincoln put McClellan back in charge. On September 9, Alexander Gardner, Brady's former colleague and now head of Pinkerton's U.S. Army Corps of Topographical Engineers, sent a telegram from McClellan's

---

66 On April 19, 1861, one week after Fort Sumter was shelled, Southern sympathizers clashed with Massachusetts and Pennsylvania militiamen who were on their way to Washington. The Baltimore Riot, also known as the Pratt Street Riots or Pratt Street Massacre, saw 4 soldiers killed and 36 wounded. On the other side, 12 civilians were killed, and hundreds were reportedly wounded in what is acknowledged as the first bloodshed of the Civil War. That said, two Union soldiers died in accidents at the surrender ceremony at Fort Sumter the prior week.

headquarters back to the Washington Studio hinting that significant action might be imminent. That news caused Brady to send a team into Maryland and, since I had not been in the field for some time, yours truly was tasked with leading it.

I decided to take James Gibson, now a veteran of these excursions, and put him in charge of one of the crews. I then created another using men from one of our bases south of Frederick. We set out on September 10 and soon caught up with McClellan's army and Gardner. Gardner told us that Lee was somehow keeping the location of his main force a mystery, so McClellan planned to advance on Frederick to find them. I also learned from Gardner that Pinkerton was traveling with McClellan, so I made a mental note to steer clear of headquarters. On September 12, Lee's forces were finally heard from when Stonewall Jackson began an assault on Harpers Ferry, a town well known to them both. In October 1859, then Colonel Robert E. Lee oversaw the retaking of the arsenal there after it had been occupied by John Brown[67] and twenty-one of his followers as they attempted to instigate a national slave revolt. Jackson happened to be among the troops guarding Brown and the six others that were captured when the arsenal was retaken. Brown and his six companions would be hung. Ten others had died during Lee's assault, but the remaining five of Brown's original band of twenty-two revolutionaries escaped.

I left Gibson and his men with Gardner so I could form up the second crew from our station just south of Frederick. None of this new team had the experience of Gibson, Wood, or

---

67 John Brown was born in Connecticut in 1800. His grandfather, Captain Owen Brown, died in the Revolutionary War in September 1776. John Brown was hanged in December 1859 for organizing an attempted slave revolt that he planned to launch with a raid on Harpers Ferry, Virginia in October 1859.

O'Sullivan, all of whom had either been at Bull Run or in the Peninsular Campaign, so I decided to have them spend some time in the field to get comfortable with moving and using the equipment. When I learned that troops under Confederate General D. H. Hill had abandoned their position at a farm about three miles south of Frederick, we moved there in the hope of finding something worthy of our cameras. While the crew was setting up I was wandering around the site when, around 11:00 a.m., I came across an envelope in the tall grass. When I opened it I was delighted to find three cigars wrapped in a piece of paper that I very nearly discarded before realizing that it was a letter. The word "Confidential" across the top caught my eye, and when it continued "Special Orders, No. 191, Hdqrs. Army of Northern Virginia, September 9, 1862[68]" I knew I was onto something. The text included detailed plans, movements, and dates for all of Lee's army. My first thought was that this must be a prank or perhaps an elaborate Confederate ruse. They seemed to be skilled at deception, with the Quaker Guns at Bull Run and Magruder's circular marches west of Yorktown coming to mind. But after reading it a third time, it simply made too much sense to be false. The bits about taking Harpers Ferry we knew were already underway, for example. Now convinced of its authenticity, all that remained for me was to figure out how I could profit from its discovery.

I decided that there was no way I could avoid turning it over to the Union troops on the scene. Before doing that, however, I spread it out against the side of our Whatsit wagon and had the crew take a photograph. That done, I gave the original over to Corporal Barton W. Mitchell of the 27th Indiana Volunteers and

---

68 Also known as the Lost Order or the Lost Dispatch, Special Order 191 contained troop movement orders from Robert E. Lee. Copies remain available for viewing to this day.

asked him to sign a receipt I had drafted. If this was authentic, there were bound to be questions around who did what when, and I wanted to be seen as extraordinarily cooperative. I chose a Corporal in the hope that it would take more time to move up the chain of command, perhaps giving me the opportunity to break the news before anyone else. I tucked the cigars into my pocket, took the photographic plate, and left my crew with instructions to catch up with me later as I rode off hard toward McClellan's headquarters. Given this turn of events, I now actually hoped to see Pinkerton.

"Well, well, if it isn't Jack Bailey," said Pinkerton when I found him outside McClelland's command tent.

"No time for our customary repartee, Allan," I responded. "You are going to want to have one of Gardner's men develop this plate straight away." While that was happening, I explained what I'd found and recounted as many of the details as I could remember. Partway through my report he sent for McClellan, who came in just as the developed photograph arrived from Gardner. After a debate about authenticity, which covered the same ground I had done in my head when I first set eyes on the document, McClellan, Pinkerton, and the rest of the senior staff grew increasingly excited. A Colonel Colgrove soon barged into the meeting with the original copy of the order and offered that an aide could confirm that the signature of Robert H. Chilton on it was authentic, since this aide had done banking business with Chilton before the war. This news ended any doubt about the order being genuine, and it sent McClellan and his men scurrying to their maps.

"Well Bailey," Allan said after the others had moved off, "you've outdone yourself. This discovery may well turn the tide of Lee's move into Maryland. My congratulations. I will see that the President is informed of the service you have done for the Union. This might get you a medal."

"Not to seem unappreciative," I responded, "but there is something I would find much more practical than a medal. Another order for cotton, for example. It's obvious that this war isn't ending anytime soon, and my business continues to be at risk. Surely the Army has a legitimate need for cotton but, if it doesn't, allowing safe passage of some shipments to Europe would suffice."

"That seems a reasonable request Jack, and I'll pass it along to the President." With that, Pinkerton moved to join the general staff gathered around their maps planning their next move on Lee. And that move was to come just a few days later, on September 17, 1862, at Sharpsburg and Antietam Creek. With more than 22,000 dead, wounded or missing on both sides, it remains the bloodiest day in American history.

News of potential action so close to Washington encouraged Brady and O'Sullivan to join us, and they arrived in Frederick on September 16. We all set out for McClellan's headquarters early on the morning of the 17. Somewhere south of Keedysville, we could hear the unmistakable sounds of a major battle a few miles to our west, but our meanderings unwittingly landed us on the front lines. Just as a Union soldier directed us back toward where he thought McClellan was positioned, shells began bursting all around us. By the grace of God, we were able to move the Whatsit wagons away from the action before any damage was done, although it took all my willpower not to bolt alone to safer ground. In the end, we found McClellan and his staff at Pry House which, situated on a hilltop a couple of miles northeast of Sharpsburg, afforded a remarkable view of most of the battlefield.

Miller's Cornfield, Dunker Church, the Sunken Road, Burnside Bridge—the names of these actions within the larger battle will forever be etched on the pages of American history. We took a great many photographs that day that have become famous in their own right, including "Battle Smoke," which turned out to be the only picture of fighting during the entire war. "What the Tide of Battle Left" is an iconic shot of a dozen or so dead Confederate soldiers on the Sunken Road, with the debris of war scattered around them. With Dunker Church in the background, another entry shows both Union and Confederate dead in the same frame, along with a broken artillery caisson and a dead horse. I had wondered after the Peninsular Campaign whether I would become numb to such scenes and, in a way, was relieved that I hadn't.

Gardner and Brady were prolific in the weeks that followed Antietam, including during Lincoln's visit to the area in early October. One photograph taken in front of a tent shows Lincoln with Pinkerton on his right and General McClernand on his left, all standing. Only Pinkerton is looking at the camera and, perhaps emulating McClellan's signature look, both he and McClernand have their right hands thrust into their coats. In another photograph in front of that same tent, Pinkerton sits on his horse, left hand holding the reins, right arm dangling down, and cigar stuck firmly in his teeth. My favorite, however, was a photograph taken at Grove Farm that includes Lincoln, "Little Mac" McClellan and fourteen of his senior staff. Custer[69] can be seen standing apart from the rest on the right, wearing one of his flamboyant hats. Getting a collection of such men to stand still long enough for a photograph was an impressive feat, although I suppose egos played a role.

A few days after the battle when it became clear that Lee was withdrawing back across the Potomac into Virginia, Brady asked me

---

69 George Armstrong Custer was born in Ohio in 1839. He graduated from the U.S. Military Academy in 1861, after accumulating a record 726 demerits. He saw much action in the Civil War at Antietam, Chancellorsville, Gettysburg, Petersburg, and Appomattox, to name a few. He died in 1876 at the Battle of Little Bighorn.

to take the photographs we had created to that point back to the studio while he and some of the others stayed on. More than happy to oblige, I set out with one of the wagons and a couple of assistants and we made our way the fifty or so miles south back to Washington.

With Brady still in the field, at the end of September I happened to be enjoying dinner and drinks in the Star when, much to my astonishment, Anna Surratt walked in and joined me at my table in the back corner. I must admit that my travels to Virginia and Maryland these past few months had caused Anna to fade some from my memory but seeing her now instantly brought back every ounce of my infatuation. My chair scraped the floor loudly as I quickly rose to greet her.

Dunker Church, Courtesy of the Library of Congress, LC-DIG-cwpbh-03384

"My God, Anna, what are you doing here?" I exclaimed.

"I hope you aren't disappointed to have me interrupt your dinner, Jack," she replied.

"Absolutely not," I said. "I'm delighted. Just very surprised.

I assume that your brother must have told you about this place, but I never expected to see you here."

"John would have preferred to come," she offered, "but the federals seem to be very interested in his activities lately, so he thought it best not to be in Washington. Also, my father passed away last month, and John is needed at the Tavern. With my father gone, he is now the man of the house in addition to being the postmaster in Surrattsville."

I offered condolences about her father and tactfully asked all of the questions one normally asks in such circumstances. Although she was circumspect, I gathered that Senior essentially drank himself to death. Despite the beastly behavior I had witnessed from her father, she seemed genuinely saddened by his passing. What I was more interested in hearing about, however, was John Jr. I had to assume from her earlier comments that he had not been blown out of the waters around Norfolk after all.

"Anyway," she said at one point, "with my father passed, we have found our finances to be in a challenging condition." No doubt, thinks I, as she carried on with, "Mother owns a townhouse a few blocks from here on H Street and I am visiting to collect rent from our tenants."

"So, you expect to be here in Washington from time to time then?" I asked hopefully.

"John and I will share those duties but, yes," she responded.

"I suppose you are staying there at the moment?" I asked.

"No," she said. "I'm staying across the street at the Petersen. The rooms at our townhouse are all occupied."

"What a coincidence," I say, trying not to appear too enthusiastic. "That's where I am boarding. What room are you in?"

"The same one you are, I hope," she offered quietly, while looking me straight in the eye. "And if I may be so bold."

"What are friends for, if not to offer hospitality during

difficult times?" I said, staring back. "But the Petersen is no place for a lady. I'll check us into the Willard." The Petersen really was no place to entertain, and the walls weren't thick enough for the hospitality I had in mind. On top of that, I had no interest in subjecting myself to the cold shoulder that Mrs. Petersen would show me for weeks if I were to bring a female companion to my room.

Like most men, given a choice and the opportunity to frolic with the opposite sex I'd choose age and experience, but there is something to be said for youthful enthusiasm. I confirmed as much that night.

Chapter 15

A NEW DEAL FOR BRADY IMPORTERS

*I*n the end, we enjoyed two nights at the Willard, which included a dinner at the Round Robin Bar. Anna was amused by the fact that I had first met her brother there fifteen months ago. But as soon as her September rents were collected, and we'd both made effusive promises to stay in touch, she traveled back to Surrattsville.

With Brady still in the field through most of October, I continued to do what was necessary to ensure that our bases were well-provisioned and that sufficient copies of our photographs from Antietam were available for sale in both the Washington and New York studios. One of those bases, located by a Union signal station near Fairview, Maryland, was destroyed by Confederate General J.E.B. Stuart's[70] calvary during a raid he led across the

---

70 James Ewell Brown Stuart was born in Virginia in 1836. He graduated from the U.S. Military Academy in 1854. Robert E. Lee was superintendent of the Academy at the time, and Stuart became a friend of the Lee family. He saw much action in the Civil War including at Bull Run, Fredericksburg, Chancellorsville, and Gettysburg. Stuart died in 1864 from wounds received in action at the Battle of Yellow Tavern in the Overland Campaign.

Potomac that month. While we only lost some equipment and supplies there, these raids and McClellan's resistance to pursuing Stuart and Lee's army into Virginia finally cost him his job for good. In early November, Lincoln appointed a reluctant General Ambrose Burnside to the position of commander of the Army of the Potomac despite signs that he wasn't up to the job either.

Burnside had been assigned the southernmost portion of McClellan's army at Antietam and had distinguished himself on September 17, 1862, by ignoring opportunities to send his 12,000 troops across some shallow sections of the Antietam Creek that were out of range of rebel fire. He instead chose to focus his attentions on a bridge that would become a slaughter-house and make "Burnside Bridge" synonymous with futility, stupidity, and stubbornness. Perhaps grandiose whiskers are a sign of military incompetence, as Burnside and Lord Cardigan shared both traits. It was only Burnside, however, who would receive eternal credit for his facial hair when "sideburns" became a common descriptor of the style of whiskers that both he and Cardigan favored.

Brady returned to Washington in November and spent most of the month preparing for his next foray into the field. The midterm elections on November 4 saw Lincoln's Republicans lose 22 seats to the Democrats. The Emancipation Proclamation, which had been issued on September 22 but would not come into effect until January 1, 1863, likely had an impact on voters. It read, in part, "That on the first day of January, in the year of our Lord, one thousand eight hundred and sixty-three, all persons held as slaves within any State or designated part of a State, the people whereof shall then be in rebellion against the United States, shall be then, thenceforward, and forever free; and the Executive Government of the United States, including the military and naval authority thereof, will recognize and maintain the freedom of such persons, and will do no act or acts to repress such person ... in any efforts they may make for their actual freedom".

Despite the disappointing election results, Lincoln held a reception in the White House that month to which Brady and I were invited. It was a subdued affair, with Mary Todd still in a deep depression from Willie's passing earlier in the year. That tragedy, the mixed results of the war to date, and a looming winter campaign intensified the gloom of the election results. I may have been the only person there to have come away happy from the occasion, as my stumbling across Special Order 191 in Frederick and my shameless self-promotion of it paid off in a big way.

"Hello Bailey," Pinkerton offered in greeting soon after my arrival. "If you have a few moments, the President would like to see you in private this evening in order to officially thank you for your contributions to the war effort."

"That would be an honor Allan," I said, as if there was a choice in the matter. And so, forty-five minutes or so later I found myself in Lincoln's office with Pinkerton, Lincoln, Major Montgomery Meigs (the army's Quartermaster) and an underling or two. All of us seemed relieved to be away from the crowd at the reception.

"Mr. Bailey," Lincoln said after introducing me to Meigs, "Allan has told me about the great service you did for the Union before Antietam. I'm sure you are aware of the fact that the information you uncovered did a great service to the army and may have prevented a catastrophe in Maryland."

"I was fortunate to have come across those orders, Mr. President, and only did what I know that any of us would do in such a situation."

"Well, you were clever enough to recognize valuable intelligence when you saw it, and you apparently knew exactly what to do with it," he said. "And for that, we are very grateful. Allan also tells me that you would appreciate some quiet help for your export business more than a medal or formal recognition for your actions."

"Actually sir, official recognition might be a real problem for me given some of the work that Allan asks me to do from time to time," I said, trying to sound modest (and to overstate my importance). "It's the last thing I would like."

"It seems we are aligned then, Mr. Bailey. As it happens, we are very much in need of cotton now that it seems the war will drag on longer than we'd hoped. I will give you two facts to illustrate what I mean. Firstly, before this war began cotton was responsible for nearly 60 percent of all U.S. exports. Our blockage of Southern ports has created a very significant revenue problem. Secondly, and as you know, we have a need for the stuff here in the North, both for the products it is used to make and the employment it creates. Did you know that 75 percent of New England's 4.5 million spindles now sit idle due to a lack of cotton? The effects on the economy and employment have been disastrous."

I'm sure it didn't help election results there either I thought, but instead I said, "I wasn't aware of those precise numbers, sir, but I can see that the lack of supply must be creating all sorts of problems."

"Problems you can help with, Mr. Bailey," he observed. "As you can imagine, Southern plantations are not keen to sell their product to Northern buyers, despite their badly needing revenue. In addition, the Confederate Congress and several states have tried to force cotton growers to switch to corn, wheat, potatoes, and other such crops, to help alleviate their food shortages. One southern newspaper has gone so far as to suggest that growers who continued to produce cotton be hung as traitors." Now that I hadn't heard but would write Elkins about it tomorrow.

"Bailey, we believe that many plantations will continue to produce cotton anyway because that's all they know. And we think that they will be willing to sell to British buyers, which is where you come in," he concluded.

"That all makes sense, Mr. President, but with the blockade I also think that they'll wonder how Bailey Importers would get its shipments to England," I offered. "Without a credible story, they'll be suspicious."

Meigs chimed in with, "Likely true, Mr. Bailey. But we have a plan that we believe will provide you with that credibility. We propose that you purchase as much cotton as you can from your suppliers. Tell them that you will use your men to move it to Charleston, from where the bales will be sent by rail to Atlanta, Columbia, Charlotte, and so on, so long as they believe that its ultimate destination is within the Confederacy. But before these shipments get to Charleston, we will divert them to Port Royal, which the Union controls. With the cotton then on Union ships, the blockade will not be an issue. And your suppliers will be none the wiser."

I thought about all that for a moment or two then, worried about my own neck, said, "My involvement in this cannot go beyond this room. If news got to my suppliers, I'd be out of business. And if the Confederacy found out, I have no doubt that I'd be hung at their first opportunity."

"Jack," said Pinkerton, "we have plenty of incentive to keep this quiet. We want the cotton for a start, and you are our best hope to get it. What else concerns you?"

"I'm going to assume the price will be as it was the last time," I said.

"It is," said Meigs, "except that we'll be paying to get it to port, so this trade will be more profitable for you. Pinkerton's men, posing as yours, will collect the cotton from the plantations, so your only expense is paying your suppliers."

"Can any of the product be sent to England?" I asked, thinking that my father would welcome an opportunity to mark it up outrageously over there given the tight supplies. Such a development would also keep him out of my hair.

"We'll think about that but, for the moment, the US Army is your sole customer. We may decide to use some of it in international trade for war materiel," Meigs said.

"If that's the case, can Bailey Importers in Liverpool help facilitate?" I pushed.

"Assuming we need an intermediary, we'll consider it," he said. In government speak, "we'll consider it" is a solid "no," by the way.

Other issues came to mind as the plan took root in my head. "My man in Charleston, Elkins, could be a problem," I said. "We've never had any serious discussions on politics, but he's a southerner."

"What if you met him in the company of a certain Confederate Colonel, Jack?" asked Pinkerton. "One that is buying cotton on behalf of the C.S.A. Quartermaster?"

"That could work," I agreed. "He's certainly too timid to do any serious checking."

"Have him come up to Virginia next month and we'll meet," Pinkerton said without a thought for any plans I might have. "Is there anything else we are not considering?"

"With inventories relatively high at the moment, I think we should plan for a steady flow of cotton versus one big shipment," I offered. "I assume you don't have an unlimited number of men in that area in any case, Allan, so many smaller shipments might be more easily managed than a big one or two."

"We plan to set up a bogus C.S.A. camp on the Combahee River and will have our men deliver the cotton there, Jack," said Pinkerton. "From there, we can send it by boat down to Port Royal, where it will be loaded onto Union ships and sent north."

"So, in the off-chance your men are followed, it will look like a legitimate delivery to a Confederate way station," I said, warming to the idea. "And the plantation owners are likely to be so enamored with the revenue that they won't be inclined to look beyond the façade in any case."

"Exactly. It's settled then," said Lincoln. "When can you start?"

"We'll need to meet with Elkins, as agreed," I offered. "Since the war has disrupted the normal flow of things, I suspect that most of the plantations still have inventory on hand from last fall's harvest. Once Elkins can make the rounds, we should be able to start shipping right away. Maybe January?"

"I can have the phony depot set up on the Combahee by then," offered Allan. "Jack, let's have your man meet us in Ashland, Virginia in mid-December. We can settle on the exact details later. Do you know it?"

"Birthplace of Henry Clay, just north of Richmond. I've passed through it on trains, once quite recently, as you well know," I added with a touch of sarcasm.

"Right," he said, ignoring my dig. "Far enough from Richmond for you and 'Major Allen' to attract too much scrutiny, yet close enough to leave a favorable impression on your man Elkins."

"Now I just need to get Brady on board with another of my absences," I sighed.

"Go fetch him in here, Mr. Bailey," said Lincoln. "I suspect I can get him to ask you to go to Virginia."

Once Brady had joined us and been sworn to secrecy, Lincoln told him that Burnside was gathering his troops in force in Falmouth, and that the plan was to confront Lee's army in Fredericksburg, then move down to Richmond. After expressing his gratitude for this information, Brady turned to me and asked that I make arrangements for another expedition that would include him and Tim O'Sullivan as the lead photographers. Given the potential for significant fighting in Fredericksburg and the possibility of moving on to Richmond, he was anxious to put our best in the field. And so, just as Lincoln predicted, it ended up being Brady's idea that I go to Virginia in December 1862. I swear the President winked at me when Brady suggested I join this expedition.

Chapter 16

FREDERICKSBURG

On December 2, Brady, O'Sullivan, yours truly, and a handful of assistants and Whatsit wagons boarded an army transport and sailed down the Potomac to Aquia Landing, Virginia. This route was becoming all too familiar to me. If we had kept sailing for another hour, we'd have passed Port Tobacco, only 20 miles from Aquia Landing as the crow flies. And if we'd have kept on going further south, we would have found ourselves in Chesapeake Bay and could have gone on to Fort Monroe. Thankfully we were not going that far south on this day, but I had other reasons to be anxious. From Aquia Landing we took a train a dozen miles or so inland to Falmouth, just north of Fredericksburg, where we disembarked and moved our men and equipment into a log hut we had been assigned by the army. On December 7, Pinkerton came calling and asked Brady if he could borrow me for a couple of days. Soon thereafter I found myself in a Union wagon with him and a driver, heading for yet another train that would take us south to Ashland, Virginia, and a meeting with Elkins. I had notified Elkins of the location and approximate date of this meeting by mail, but not enough time had passed for me to receive a reply. I was relieved to see him when we arrived at Slash Cottage in Ashland. Oddly named, Slash Cottage was a collection of more than a dozen buildings that had served as a mineral springs resort in more peaceful times. The town of Ashland had been used in the early stages of the war as a training ground for Confederate calvary but, with that cavalry now deployed, it was now home mostly to refugees and a smattering of Confederate troops. Since Pinkerton had transformed himself into Major E. J. Allen on the train down, we didn't attract any unwanted attention.

After I'd introduced "Major Allen" to Elkins and established his bona fides as working in the Confederate Quartermaster Corp, the three of us settled in for dinner. Elkins surprised me with some insightful questions, including asking why the C.S.A. didn't simply buy cotton directly from the plantations. Pinkerton had clearly anticipated this and said that his team didn't have the time or resources to go plantation to plantation to negotiate purchases, nor did they have the know-how on pricing or quality that we surely had. He was equally deft at answering Elkins' other inquiries and, by the end of dinner, had won him over. After drinks and a cigar Pinkerton retired, leaving me to finalize things with Elkins.

"Jack," Elkins said at one point, "is Major Allen aware of your employment with Mathew Brady?"

"Of course he is, Elkins," I replied confidently. Then, without providing specifics, I hinted that I was leveraging my position with Brady to supply Major Allen with information that he might find useful. All of that was all true, of course, if you substitute Major Allen for Allan Pinkerton and Union for Confederacy, but I wasn't about to burden Elkins with such details. In the end, he seemed suitably impressed and said as much as we ended the evening with another bourbon and a toast to more orders for Bailey Importers.

The train back up to Falmouth provided an opportunity to get to know Pinkerton better on a personal level. Normally tight lipped, I think my assistance at Antietam and the fact that we were both immigrants from the U.K. may have put him at ease. In any case, I learned that he was 43 years old and had emigrated to the U.S. from Scotland in 1842. A cooper by trade, he became Chicago's first police detective in 1849 after playing a role in the arrest of counterfeiters he'd encountered in the woods while looking for timber for his barrel making. It was while investigating train robberies in the 1850's that he first met McClellan and Lincoln. At the time, McClellan and Lincoln both worked for the Illinois Central Railroad, the former as chief engineer and the latter periodically providing legal representation. Those prior relationships helped Pinkerton achieve his current status within the U.S. Army and Lincoln's administration. When he mentioned his wife, I resisted the temptation to recount how I'd teased Kate about getting a wedding present for the two of them. I reciprocated with some basic facts on my own history but got the sense that none of it was news to Pinkerton. Whatever the case, I felt that we had made some progress in our relationship and hoped to leverage that into more business for Bailey Importers. We parted company in Falmouth, and I returned to the cabin and Brady's team.

With temperatures hovering around zero, Brady and O'Sullivan had discovered that the process of using our collodion[71] coated wet plates had to be stretched to an hour instead of the usual few minutes. While the reduced need for urgency in developing photographs was on some level a welcome change, it did not compensate for the discomforts of having to work bare handed in such frigid conditions. But none of that had stopped

71 A viscous and flammable combination of nitrocellulose, ether, and alcohol.

them both from taking photographs around the Union camp when the light was favorable. December 11 did not start out as one of those days, although the mist and fog that was present in the early morning hours provided cover to the Union forces building the pontoon bridges that Burnside's men intended to use to cross the Rappahannock River into Fredericksburg. Amid the sounds of hammering and cursing that accompanies such work, we set up a large Anthony camera near a destroyed railway bridge and waited for the sun. Unbeknownst to us, Confederate sharpshooters and a light cannon situated in a mill directly across the river also awaited that first light. As soon as the fog began to clear, rifle shots came raining down upon us. A cannonball overturned the camera and sent us and our horses scattering for cover. Once we were out of range, the rebels concentrated their fire on the unlucky engineers still trying to complete the pontoon bridges. For the next three hours, both sides traded bullets and ball until Union General "Fighting Joe" Hooker sent a volunteer force across the river in boats to try and push the Confederate snipers back into town and out of range of the river. All we could do was watch and listen as these volunteers from the 17th Michigan and 19th Massachusetts bravely forded the Rappahannock under fire, then fought street by street in Fredericksburg.

The fighting subsided as darkness fell, but the success of the volunteers allowed for the completion of the pontoon bridges the next morning and enabled the Union Army to cross in force. Perhaps it was the miserable weather, maybe it was anger over the withering sniper fire they had endured the previous day, or maybe it was just the booze, but the most egregious acts of looting seen to that point in the war took place on December 12 in Fredericksburg. Stately old homes were ransacked and torched, kegs of wine and bottles of liquor were either consumed on the spot or emptied into the streets, windows were broken, heirloom furniture smashed—an appalling show of barbarism by Union troops unfolded before our eyes and camera lenses. Sadly, this would not be the war's last display of men at their worst.

We crossed the Rappahannock and brought a Whatsit wagon into town as soon as it was cleared of rebel troops. Brady's photographs such as "Effects of the Bombardment on Fredericksburg" and "Battlefield of Fredericksburg" provide some notion of what we came across there although, as good as they are, these pictures don't capture the devastation in quite the same way my eyes did. We camped in the streets that night among the Union troops, all of us anxious about what tomorrow would bring. With campfires forbidden due to the proximity of the rebels, I can't recall ever being colder, before, or since. The following morning brought more fog, and, with the light insufficient to take photographs, we decided to retreat to the rooftop of a house on the edge of town that provided a view of the northern end of the battlefield. Burnside had assigned the areas south of Fredericksburg to Generals Reynolds, Meade, Gibbons, and Doubleday and, while we couldn't see the action down that way, we could hear it in the distance. Within our view, a few hundred yards across the fields in front of us and to the west of Fredericksburg, the ground rises into a series of hills collectively known as Mayre's Heights. On this day, December 13, 1862, those picturesque fields became slaughterhouses. By the time it was all over, Burnside had sent seven Union divisions at Generals Lee and Longstreet[72], one at a time, in fourteen individual assaults. All failed and, in the end, Union casualties were eightfold that of the rebels. A stone

---

72 James Longstreet was born in North Carolina in 1821. He graduated from the U.S. Military Academy in 1842 and, during his time there befriended John Pope, William Rosecrans, and Ulysses S. Grant. His Civil War action reads like a comprehensive list of every major battle, including Bull Run, Seven Pines, Seven Days Battles, Fredericksburg, Gettysburg, Chickamauga, Chattanooga, and the Knoxville and Appomattox Campaigns. After the war, he would briefly serve as the U.S. Minister to the Ottoman Empire in 1880 and 1881. Longstreet died in 1904.

wall and sunken road near the peak of the Heights offered excellent cover and a perfect view for Confederate snipers and artillery who poured deadly fire down onto the advancing Union troops, repelling them every time.

We watched in stunned silence and, not for the first time, I was grateful that the ceaseless motion on the field of battle rendered our cameras useless. Had it not, Brady's bravery, or foolishness if you prefer, would likely have had him ordering us into the middle of the carnage. While darkness brought an end to the gunfire, the horror went on as wounded and dying Union troops cried out for help throughout the night. The following morning, we watched as a Confederate sergeant walked unmolested among the Union wounded handing out canteens of water. While no ceasefire had been called, Union soldiers realized what he was doing, and he was left unmolested. That sergeant, Richard Rowland Kirkland, was to meet his end nine months later at Chickamauga after surviving this battle and several others, including the First Bull Run, Antietam, Chancellorsville, and Gettysburg.

After his own generals had talked some sense into him later that afternoon, Burnside contacted Lee and the two agreed to a truce to collect the dead and wounded. During this ceasefire Brady's team took to the fields and we once again captured some gruesome images documenting the aftermath of battle. That night both sides witnessed a stunning display of the northern lights—a rare sight this far south. On the morning of the 15th, we packed our gear and retreated across the river along with a bloodied Union Army. Burnside had been planning to spend the winter in Falmouth, although following a failed attempt to outflank Lee in late January in a campaign known as the Mud March, Lincoln dismissed him and put Joe Hooker in command of the Army of the Potomac.

The final tally of casualties over those few days in mid-December, counting both sides, was about 18,000 men, 2,000 of which had been killed. Although the South was jubilant, Lee was more circumspect, writing: "At Fredericksburg we gained a battle, inflicting very severe loss on the enemy in men and material; our people were greatly elated—I was much depressed. We had really accomplished nothing; we had not gained a foot of ground, and I knew the enemy could easily replace the men he had lost, and the loss of material was, if anything, rather beneficial to him, as it gave an opportunity to contractors to make money." I took offense to the bit about contractors, likely because his words came uncomfortably close to the truth. Up north the public's mood was soured yet again by the news of another Confederate victory. During a visit to the White House, Pennsylvania Governor Andrew Curtin, reporting on his recent visit to Fredericksburg told the President, "It was not a battle, it was butchery." Lincoln himself would later write, "If there is a worse place than hell, I am in it." He was of course referring to the war but could just have easily been commenting on the cold, muddy conditions of Washington that winter.

In the December 16, 1862, edition of the *National Republican*, under a title "What Should be Done," that newspaper stated that "While our brave men are fighting and falling at Fredericksburg in defense of the Union, Washington is crowded with shoulder straps and private soldiers who appear fully able to do duty. There is something wrong somewhere, and the remedy should be applied at once ... Let every man and officer who is capable of doing duty be sent to the front at once. Hotels and houses of ill-fame may lose by this order, but the country will gain discipline—let us have discipline in the army."

I should point out that my memory isn't good enough to have remembered that word for word. Kate Warne had saved that issue of the paper for me because of the article that appeared right above that one. It described a debate in the Senate about whether to eliminate taxes and duty on Surat cotton from India. While I am usually not one to support government meddling, I have been known to temporarily abandon that opinion when it might positively affect me or my business. I found myself hoping that they would raise taxes on Indian cotton, not eliminate them. Higher taxes and duties on imports would of course make my product all the more attractive.

Chapter 17

NEW YORK CITY

*A*lthough Brady's activities in the field were largely put on hold during the winter and spring of 1863, there was no shortage of drama during those months. The year started with Lincoln's Emancipation Proclamation, which enraged most in the South, even though a preliminary proclamation had been issued the previous September. Others in Dixie, however, thought the Proclamation an advantage in that it might stoke pro-slavery sentiment and assist the C.S.A.'s recruiting efforts. In Robert E. Lee's opinion, a recruiting boost was necessary to counter what he felt would be a surge of freed slaves joining the ranks of the Union Army. General Grant agreed with the latter, later writing Lincoln that arming the freed slaves was "…the heavyest (sic) blow yet to the Confederacy…" For the moment, however, the actual impact to the 3.5 million slaves in the country was limited mostly to those being held as "contraband," although there is no doubt that Lincoln's Proclamation served to boost the hopes of all that were aware of it.

Closer to home was the decision by Alex Gardner to leave Brady and establish his own photography business just a block or two away at 7th & D Streets in Washington. While he had been given the position of Photographer of the Army of the Potomac in the fall of 1861, Gardner had, until now, been assisting Brady part time. He had been especially helpful with the finances even in that limited role and would be missed as a counterbalance to Brady's tendency to spend extravagantly. Worse, Gardner took his son, James, with him. O'Sullivan, Gibson, and Barnard soon followed, severely depleting Brady's ranks. He also helped himself to all our negatives from 1862. Oddly, Brady seemed quite indifferent to it all. I would have been livid. I suppose the magnitude of these defections probably said something about Brady's relationship with his staff, but I must admit to being unaware of any morale issues, probably because Brady's management style was well down the list of things I cared about. Selling cotton, Anna, various other forms of personal entertainment and avoiding physical harm topped my priorities at that moment.

Around this time Gardner secured a new Federal appointment as the official photographer of the Army Secret Service where he, among other things, was responsible for the distribution of maps and diagrams. Although I wasn't given credit, I would be flattered to think that he stole my idea of photographing original documents, as I had done with Lee's "Special Order 191" just prior to Antietam. Eliminating the old process of hand copying maps and orders saved a great deal of time and ensured that everyone up and down the chain of command was looking at the same information. I had to credit him for another clever idea though, which was to take photographs of groups of men in Union Army camps, which the Army then used to identify spies. I was asked on occasion to study some of these works for any Confederate faces I might recognize from my visits to Surrattsville, Port Tobacco, Richmond, and the like. Every time I did, I reminded myself to avoid getting in front of any camera.

Speaking of Anna, while we had been corresponding these past several months, I was delighted to learn that she was planning a visit to Washington in late January to conduct business at her mother's boarding house. In anticipation of reviving the magic of our last visit, I booked a room at the Willard and suggested that we meet for dinner at the Round Robin Bar the evening of her arrival. While I hadn't mentioned the room to her, I liked my chances when I saw her walk in carrying a carpet bag large enough to hold a few days' worth of clothing and toiletries.

"Jack, it's so nice to see you after these few months. At times it has seemed like years," she said. "I apologize for not being more available, but Mother and I have been struggling to maintain the tavern and the other properties in Surrattsville. It's been so hard with Father gone and my brothers busy with their responsibilities." Given where we were sitting, I was grateful that she was vague about "their responsibilities".

Probably easier on them all with John Sr. gone I also thought, but instead said, "I can only imagine. You must let me know if there is anything I can do to help." I admit to feeling some relief at her apology, as I had been prepared to make my own excuses for not having made more of an effort to see her over the past four months. Truth was, I was happy to let her take the blame. "Please, sit down and allow me to take your bag. I hope my choice of location for dinner meets with your approval."

"It does indeed. I have very fond memories of our last time here," she responded in a tone that confirmed there wouldn't be a problem convincing her to join me in the room I'd booked upstairs. We spent the next two hours enjoying dinner and filling in the details of our respective activities since last September. As she'd done in her letters, she spoke of the financial hardships her family faced trying to operate their tavern, hotel, and farmland in these tumultuous times. She reminded me that her brother John had been appointed postmaster in Surrattsville the previous fall and said that the family would truly be in dire straits without the income it provided. She was, however, worried about his position given "John's sympathies," although he had avoided the fate of some of his peers in the area. Many of them had been dismissed for disloyalty by my old friend (and Pinkerton flunky) Lafayette Baker. I made a mental note to say something to Allan about leaving Junior alone so as not to cut off this potential source of intelligence.

"Speaking of John," she said at one point, "he still feels terrible about having you pushed off that boat in Norfolk. He told me all about it and how you had been there to help, but that he thought it best for your own safety to remove you from the situation."

My safety be damned, I thought. More likely he wanted to be able to claim all the credit for himself when he arrived at wherever he was going with all that cotton. In any case, and not wanting to spoil my chances for later this evening, I graciously responded with, "I suppose I owe him thanks then, if he believed he was taking me out of harm's way."

"Well, he feels that he owes you the thanks," she said, "and he asked me to give you this to help make amends." And with that she reached into her carpet bag and slid a familiar-looking box across the table. "He says it's your preferred model."

My first thoughts included "just what I need, another Cooper" and "Petersen is going to think I'm building an arsenal in his boarding house," but I'll be damned if I didn't almost choke up when I took out the gun and read the inscription that appeared on both sides of the barrel. "King Cotton" it read. There is no way that John had the imagination or sentimentality to have even thought of such a thing, so I knew it was her doing.

"This is very touching Anna," I said sincerely. "But while he may have purchased the gun, I suspect the inscription was your idea. Very creative." The blush on her face confirmed it was true. As I put the pistol back in the box, I continued, "I very much appreciate your thoughtfulness and will cherish this gift forever." I went on to mumble something about showing her my own creative side upstairs, summoned our waiter, and requested the check.

My jovial mood soured when we passed Allan Pinkerton in the lobby on our way up to the room. He never looked our way, but I knew instinctively that the bastard had not only seen us, but that he knew who Anna was (or would make it his business to know). I cursed myself again for my carelessness and bad luck but said nothing to Anna. After calming down some, I realized I should be grateful that he hadn't confronted me right there and then, although I also knew that I would hear about this later. Once upstairs though, Anna helped push all my concerns to the side, at least for the next couple of days.

Brady being short staffed elevated my position and influence with him and enabled me to exert more control over my responsibilities and whereabouts. In his last few letters, my father had been suggesting that we meet in New York City and, being out of excuses to avoid him, I decided to use that leverage to suggest I accompany Brady to New York City. The papers had been full of news on the upcoming wedding of Charles Stratton (a.k.a. "General Tom Thumb") and Lavinia Warren, two of several midgets in the employ of P.T. Barnum. The wedding was to take place on February 10, 1863, at Grace Church, which happened to be across the street from Brady's New York studio. The best man was going to be another of Barnum's little people, George Washington Morrison Nutt, a.k.a. "Commodore Nutt" or "the $30,000 Nutt." Thirty thousand dollars was the alleged value of his first contract with Barnum. Lavinia's diminutive sister Minnie would serve as bridesmaid. Such a spectacle was simply too much for Brady to ignore, so we set off by train to New York City in late January to join the fun.

Although Brady was quite skilled at it, P.T. Barnum was in a category by himself when it came to self-promotion. The two were acquainted, so we enjoyed special status in photographing the couple and in creating carte de visites for the celebrities, socialites, elite, and other hangers-on that wanted a piece of the action surrounding the wedding. A reception was held at the Metropolitan Hotel and guests included the incompetent and disgraced General Burnside along with an impressive representation of New York society, including the wives of John Jacob Astor and William Vanderbilt. Tickets cost $75 apiece, so I was happy to be allowed in for free as part of the "staff." In a stunning example of Barnum's braggadocio, he claimed to have turned away 6,000 people that wished to attend. If my math is correct, that would have been a highly improbable $450,000 in ticket sales, although no one called him out on it. At one point I introduced myself to Chang & Eng Bunker, the Siamese twins I had seen on one of my train trips from Charleston to Washington. They were among a contingent of acts present from Barnum's American Museum, but for my money they were the most unique. I found myself again wondering how things worked in the bedroom with their wives but, fortunately, was one or two bourbons short of having the courage to ask. The bride and groom left the next day for a honeymoon in Washington, where they enjoyed another, somewhat smaller reception at the White House hosted by President and Mrs. Lincoln.

A day or two after the nuptials I met up with my father at "The Old House at Home," an ale house on 7th Street, just a few blocks from Brady's Studio. The Old House at Home had been established by a John McSorley a decade earlier and I picked it in part to tweak the old man, who wasn't fond of the Irish. With only two beers on offer—McSorley's Light and McSorley's Dark, along with several Irish whiskies—he'd be forced to consume an Irish product. Despite this petty attempt to annoy him, he showed up in an uncharacteristically good mood.

"I have to admit it, my boy," he began after we'd found a table, "I had my doubts about your ability to find a market for our cotton during this war but, against all odds, you've done it."

Unable to recall the last time he'd offered me a compliment, I struggled to respond. In the end I said, "No shortage of luck involved in all that, father. Every day has its risks, but we seem to be off to a respectable start in getting product up North. Hopefully, Elkins doesn't get too curious as to where these latest shipments are headed."

"He should be more curious about where his compensation would come from if we had no business," was his predictable response.

"I agree," I said, "but it's a little more complicated than that with the politics involved. Elkins is a Southerner, born and bred, and with emotions running so high, I'm not sure what he would do if he knew we were shipping to the Union. It's best for all if he doesn't find out."

"I've been meeting with some brokers here in New York and discovered that we could sell as much cotton as we can get up here for almost twenty times the prices we were getting two or three years ago." He responded. "As you know, half of all the factories in Britain are involved in cotton production. The country has worked through the surplus it held at the start of the war and those factories are now operating at a third of their capacity. The situation is dire—but one of incredible opportunity for us. Some cotton gets through courtesy of the blockade runners, but it isn't nearly enough. You need to get as much of it as possible up to New York or other friendly ports. We'll make a fortune."

"Father, again, it isn't that simple. The license I have is to supply the Union. I've suggested to them that we would be willing to move higher quantities, and of course paying for that right, but they aren't interested. Besides, we've just begun. Maybe if we demonstrate that we can meet their demand over the next few months we can ask again, but it's too soon."

To my horror, he suggested that he "will go back to Washington with me and talk sense into them" and "even meet with President Lincoln" if that will help.

"Help," I said? "If you wanted to bugger up the entire works, what you are suggesting would be an excellent way to do it. I cannot, quite literally, provide you with any details on how this all works without compromising everything. Even your meetings with brokers here in New York put me at risk. You need to stop, go back to Liverpool, be grateful for the business and income we are getting and stay out of things at this end. There is a war going on here for God's sake, and anyone caught on the wrong side of things ... well, you know how that works."

And so it went for the next hour, although it took a threat from me to simply walk away from it all before father relented. He accused me of being overly dramatic when I suggested his interference could cost me my life, and I blamed Émilie's trinket budget as the root cause of his desperation. If I burned some bridges permanently, so be it. In the end I promised to keep pressing my contacts to allow us to ship more cotton North than the Union needed so we could send that surplus to Liverpool, but I also swore that I would abandon my post if he insisted on getting more involved or, God forbid, showed up in Washington. Hopefully none of the other patrons of The Old House at Home were all that interested in our conversation, although our occasionally raised voices did earn us a disapproving glance or two from the bartender.

With that business concluded, I took a train back to Washington and my home at the Petersen Boarding House.

Chapter 18

ANOTHER DEBATE

I'd only been back in the studio a day or two when, as I'd feared, Pinkerton appeared wanting to discuss my presence at the Willard with Anna Surratt. He suggested we go for another of our walks, although there was no offer of lunch or cocktails this time around.

"Bailey, I'm going to assume that you had temporarily taken leave of your senses when I saw you at the Willard with Miss Surratt and that I won't see you in her company again," he said once we were out on the street. He could have made some amusing reference about my actions to be guided by the wrong organ or some such, but the humorless Scot simply wasn't capable of such levity. I tried to make up for his lost opportunity with, "I seem to recall you wanting me to 'penetrate' that nest of sympathizers not that long ago, Allan." But to that he spun around and let me have it.

"Listen Bailey," he said, "between that indiscretion, your presence at Calvert Street Station awaiting Lincoln, your boat ride to Fort Sumter, your visits to Surrattsville and Port Tobacco, your attendance at Jeff Davis's inauguration and another boat ride in Norfolk, I have ample reason to wonder about your true loyalties."

"Jesus Christ Pinkerton, most of those times I was in those places at your request. What the hell are you accusing me of? Disloyalty? You must be joking! I've put myself in very real danger more than once for you."

"I'm not accusing you of anything just yet, but you must admit that you always seem to be on the fence. Yes, you've done what I have asked on occasion, and brought us information from time to time, but beyond your business and your personal entertainment, I'm not sure you are truly committed to anything."

Well, he had me there, damn his instincts. The one time I was truly committed to anything, my mother, it was taken away and replaced with a French floozy. Perhaps I had some deeply rooted fear of commitment lest it end again in disappointment. Don't commit and you don't get hurt, or some such. But before I could reflect on it any further, he continued with, "It's time you chose a side Bailey. And I mean choose right now," at which point he nodded toward two thugs who had been hovering off our port side for the past several minutes.

"Fair enough, Allan. What is it you want from me? A sworn oath?"

"I may eventually need something formal like that Bailey but, for the moment, convince me here. Just you and me." Although it wasn't just him and me.

"I've probably had this all percolating in my mind for some time anyway, Allan, but let me say this. It's true that in some sense I've just been going along for the ride. Trying to sell cotton to save my business, enjoying some personal activities along the way, and hoping to stay in one piece. I'm from another country, and I first saw this war as none of my affair, but rather as an impediment to my personal enrichment. My adopted home here and my company are in the South, and I have many friends there. On the other hand, I think Jeff Davis is an ass, even measured against the low bar of politics. But there are plenty of buffoons in the North as well, with McClellan, Burnside, McDowell, and Senator Harry Wilson coming immediately to mind. Give me a few minutes, and I'll come up with more. I wouldn't follow those cretins anywhere."

"Can't argue with any of that, Bailey. What's your point?" he pressed.

"I'm with the Union, Allan. And its slavery that tips the balance. I've seen it up close and ignored it every time, much to my own shame. The notion that rights or opportunity should be based on skin color is absurd. Americans need to look no further than their own Bill of Rights for the answers. I saw the joy in black faces here and in New York after Lincoln's Proclamation. And I've contrasted that with the sorrow and hopelessness in faces on cotton plantations in the South. Places that make my business possible, I'm embarrassed to admit. I get it. Sign me up."

He stared into my eyes for what seemed like a very long time while we stood on that muddy street with his attack dogs lingering nearby waiting for a signal. At last, he dropped his shoulders ever so slightly and said, "Okay, Bailey. I'm going to continue to take a chance on you, but don't think for a moment that you are entirely off the hook. You of all people know what damage Rose Greenhow did as a result of her pillow-talk with Senator Wilson."

"I doubt that many people ever are entirely off the hook with you Allan, but I understand. I am going to continue to see Anna, though. It's not long since she's been just an innocent student, and now she is working full time just keeping her mother's business afloat. I've never heard a single word from her about politics. I'll grant you that her brothers are a problem, but surely the best way to keep an eye on them and their associates is for me to maintain a connection to the family. You have my word that I will let you know if I become aware of any plans they might hatch to harm the Union's cause—our cause, I should say. And speaking of such, I was happy to hear that your man Lafayette Baker left John Jr. alone when he recently fired several other Maryland postmasters. We'd be foolish to cut off a source of valuable intelligence."

Another long pause, then Pinkerton extended his hand. We probably should have aired this laundry some time ago, but it needed a catalyst and my tryst with Anna had provided it. I wouldn't have admitted it to Pinkerton, but this discussion really was the impetus for me finally coming off the North versus South fence, even in my own mind. I may have done so at some point later but will never know. Perhaps it was my imagination, or maybe it was just surviving this confrontation with Pinkerton, but I felt a little lighter walking back to the studio, unburdened from a weight that I didn't fully realize I'd been carrying.

Chapter 19

BACK INTO THE FRAY

I made good on my vow to continue seeing Anna and did so several times that spring. I also accompanied Brady on a return visit to Fredericksburg in April, during which he took photographs of that ruined town in part to train some of the recruits we had brought on board to replace the defections we'd suffered in January. One of these photographs was of Confederate troops sitting on the wrecked Mayo's Bridge across the Rappahannock River, which some say is the only one in existence that shows a close-up view of rebel forces. Just a stone's throw away, they taunted us with, "Before you get to Richmond, you have a long street to travel, a big hill to climb and a stone wall to get over," referencing Confederate Generals James Longstreet, A. P. Hill, and Stonewall Jackson. At least some in the military have a sense of humor, I thought, even if one must go down into the ranks to find it. The photograph also showed that not every building in Fredericksburg was destroyed, despite the best efforts of drunken Union troops late last year. I didn't stay with Brady very long though, as he wanted me back in the Washington studio given our thinned-out management ranks.

A subject of frequent discussion in Washington at that time were the "bread riots" taking place in many cities across the Confederacy. Inflation and shortages had caused prices to spike, and the situation was exacerbated by the migration of people into cities. Richmond's population had almost tripled to 100,000 since 1860. Supply lines had been disrupted and foraging armies often scarfed up whatever crops and meat products might have otherwise been available. Despite the Confederacy's best efforts to suppress this news, it was reported that more than 5,000 people had looted shops in Richmond in early April, causing the mayor to read the Riot Act and call out the militia. Life in Washington wasn't easy, but up to this point at least, we had not seen anything like that.

On one of Anna's visits to the city, she insisted on seeing one of her fellow Marylanders perform in "Richard III," an actor named John Wilkes Booth[73]. I didn't frequent the theatre, but after she expressed interest, I began to pay more attention to the advertisements. Some declared Booth "The Pride of the American People" and "A Star of the First Magnitude." I figured this was just Barnum-like puffery, but independent critics were similarly unreserved in their praise. One in the *National Republican* claimed that Booth "took the hearts of the audience by storm." Another in the *Intelligencer* wrote that he played "from the soul, and his soul was inspired by genius." I suppose his good looks didn't hurt, although I was unimpressed when Anna commented on that aspect of his charm during the performance we attended. That night I did my best to ensure that her thoughts were diverted away from Booth.

Spring also saw the return of major engagements between

---

73 John Wilkes Booth was born into a theatrical family in 1838 in Bel Air, Maryland. His father, Junius Brutus Booth was a Shakespearean actor, and two of his siblings, Edwin, and Junius Brutus Jr., were also actors. Booth died of a gunshot wound on April 26, 1865, in Port Royal, Virginia, twelve days after he shot Lincoln.

John Wilkes Booth (by Gardner),
Courtesy of the Library of Congress,
LC-DIG-ppmsca-19233

the Union and Confederate armies. Late April and early May brought the Battle of Chancellorsville, about ten miles west of Fredericksburg, Virginia. Due to our personnel challenges Brady was not present but, happily, neither was Gardner's team. Military photographer Captain A. J. Reynolds did manage to create some haunting images, however, including an iconic one of the lane behind the stone wall atop Mayre's Heights, shown littered with corpses and abandoned rifles.

Hooker began this campaign by moving the bulk of his army from Fredericksburg along the Rappahannock River toward Chancellorsville. The small force he left at Fredericksburg under Union General John Sedgwick would soon advance upon and defeat the contingent Lee had left to defend Mayre's Heights, but the main event was yet another defeat for the North. Later dubbed "Lee's perfect battle," it proved a showcase for his ability to read the field, split his army at just the right time and take advantage of poor decision making by timid Union army leadership. Lincoln was beside himself and was quoted as saying (among other things), "My God! My God! What will the country say?" The South had mixed feelings, as their joy over Lee's victory was tempered by the death of Stonewall Jackson. Jackson had been struck by friendly fire, resulting in the need to amputate an arm. He died a week later from his wounds, joining more than 3,200 other soldiers on both sides who also lost their lives. Another 27,000 were wounded, captured, or went missing, making this battle one of the highest butcher's bills in the war. Again, I'll spare you any further detail, other than to say that novelist Stephen Crane provides an excellent picture into the horror of battle using Chancellorsville as his canvas in his 1895 work *The Red Badge of Courage*. We didn't know it at the time, but the seeds for a turning of the tides were planted a week later about 1,000 miles Southwest of Chancellorsville in Vicksburg, Mississippi. On May 18, 1863, Ulysses S. Grant began a siege there that would last until early July and end coincident with the Battle of Gettysburg. It also meant that the Union had taken control of the Mississippi River, and they would hold it for the remainder of the war.

Back in Washington, I had my own challenges to deal with, which began with a visit by Pinkerton and Kate Warne to Brady's studio and an invitation to join them for lunch. Up to this point, I had noticed that when a meal or drinks were on offer, meetings with Pinkerton tended to be nothing to worry about, but today would see that pattern broken. We settled in at the Round Robin, where the waiter greeting me by name elicited a smirk from Kate as Pinkerton got down to business.

"Jack, we've had some disturbing news regarding our shipments of cotton out of Port Royal. It seems that your man Elkins has become suspicious about that cotton's true destination. He's asking questions and has been spotted more than once following our men to our pier on the Combahee River."

That certainly was disturbing, but our plan was complicated, and I'd had concerns about Elkins from the beginning. Unfortunately, I hadn't been able to come up with anything better.

Basically, Elkins was to have visited our suppliers and introduced them to a couple of our "employees," who were actually Union men dressed as Confederate junior officers. These imposters would then periodically show up at the plantations with men and wagons and take the cotton bales down to a station on the river, where it would be loaded onto boats and taken to Beaufort or Port Royal. There, it was loaded onto larger, seagoing vessels and sent north. The plan depended on Elkins remaining in Charleston after those initial introductions were made, and on the chaotic situation in the lowlands north and west of Port Royal. The Union controlled that city and port and, since there was only a token Confederate presence in the surrounding rural areas, things had worked exactly as planned for several months now. Any suspicions our suppliers may have had were abated by the incoming revenue they were receiving, and I had hoped the same would be true for Elkins.

"Elkins was supposed to stay out of things once the routine was established," I said to give myself time to think. I knew that if Pinkerton decided that Elkins was an unsolvable problem, he'd end up as alligator food in the swamps around the Combahee.

"We know that, Jack, but he's apparently had other ideas. Have you heard from him?" asked Kate.

"I have not," I said, "but mail has been spotty of late, as I'm sure you are aware."

"We are willing to deal with this," Pinkerton said ominously, "but if Elkins is made to disappear, I worry that your suppliers may find out, creating new risks."

I could see where this was headed and decided to offer up another option. "Allan, why don't I go down there, find out what Elkins knows or doesn't know, and we can take it from there. If he is just suspicious, perhaps I can talk him down."

"I'm willing to give you a little time for that, Jack," he responded, "but we've come to rely on that cotton, and I can't have any disruptions. While we could make do without your cotton, you aren't our only supplier. News of this being a deception could cause all the plantations and the C.S.A. to shut things down. Worse than that, I've got men down there wearing the wrong uniforms who would be hung on the spot as spies."

"I'll leave for Charleston tomorrow," I said reluctantly. I hadn't been back for some time now, and the thought of traveling along those 600 miles in time of war held no appeal. In addition, I had fallen into a comfortable routine with Anna, plus I knew that Brady would not be pleased at my taking a couple of weeks or more away from the business just as we were getting back on our feet.

The rest of our conversation was all about how I would keep Pinkerton informed. As usual, he had a contact on the scene that I could use both for that and for assistance, if I needed it. Colonel James Montgomery[74] was my man. He was commander of the 2nd South Carolina, a regiment made up of former slaves. I sincerely hoped to never need his help.

---

74 James Montgomery was born in Ohio in 1814. He was a staunch abolitionist, Jayhawker, and supporter of John Brown. He died in Kansas in 1871.

Chapter 20

THE COMBAHEE

*a*s I've previously noted, the trip from Washington to Charleston was always taxing, but it was particularly difficult this time around. I let my Southern accent dominate and had carte de visites with my Charleston address at the ready, since many of my fellow travelers were Confederate soldiers. Several days, many poor meals and two bottles of Early Times later (don't judge, I shared with seat mates), I arrived home in Charleston on a late May afternoon. I went straight to the office of Bailey Importers and was relieved to find Elkins at his desk. I had hired another man at the start of the war, Frank Dawson, to help Elkins out when it became clear that I would be spending considerable time up north. He was also there. Almost 50, Dawson was reliable, apolitical, and too old to be called up for service, so he had seemed the perfect fit.

"Great to see you, Jack!" Elkins exclaimed, sounding sincere. "You should have let me know you were coming!"

"I would have," I said, "but, as you know, the mail can't be relied upon. How are things? You should know that my father is pleased, and the shipments seem to be getting out as planned."

"About that, Jack," he said, looking more serious. "I have some concerns about where that cotton is really going. I followed a couple of shipments at a distance and swear I saw some Union uniforms among the men loading at the piers on the Combahee River. I'm not certain that Major Allen has been completely forthright with us."

"Followed them?" I said, feigning surprise. "That's a dangerous risk, Elkins, with soldiers from both sides milling around the swamps, not to mention the wildlife. What the hell were you thinking?"

"Some of the chatter among Allen's men picking up the bales at our suppliers sounded odd. I had assumed that this cotton was going to the blockade runners and generating cash for the Confederacy. I was proud of that. Many of the weapons our troops used at Shiloh were purchased from Britain with cotton that was run past the blockades."

I didn't know that, but it gave me an idea to discuss with Pinkerton next time I saw his ruddy face. I responded opaquely with, "Raising money was the whole idea, Elkins. And clearly it must be working."

"But what if the cotton is getting into Union hands? Let me take you out there to see for yourself Jack. If everything is as intended, I will sleep easier. If it isn't, I'm sure we'll both want to know."

As if the trip down from Washington hadn't been risky enough, now Elkins was proposing that we go sneaking around the bayou. For a moment, Pinkerton's solution for Elkins seemed appealing, but I'd known the man for years and couldn't bring myself to approve his assassination. I agreed to travel with him the next day. It was about 50 miles out to the area where the cotton was being loaded, mostly along roads I had traveled many times in the past. Elkins assured me that he had been unmolested on recent trips, although we both carried sidearms and knives.

The morning of May 30, 1863, we mounted up and headed west toward Parkers Ferry, where we planned to spend the night

before moving on to the Combahee. There were several plantations in the area and Elkins and I were both known in these parts.
The first leg of the trip was uneventful, but we had another 20
miles to go the following day, so got an early start on the 31st on
our way to the pier. I wasn't sure what I planned to do, especially
if we did see men in Union uniforms loading our cotton onto
their boats. These shipments were happening with some regular-
ity, so the odds of witnessing something were high. I was hoping
Pinkerton had had the sense to order the Union sailors to stow
their uniforms, but of course had no way of knowing whether
he'd had the chance. If he had, I thought it would be an easy discussion with Elkins and that I could bluster my way through it all
and save his hide in the process.

Soon after we passed through the town of Wiggins and got
close to the river, we tied up the horses and walked toward an
area near Fields Point. Elkins said he had found a spot there
that offered a decent view of the pier. None of this ground was
much higher than sea level, but Elkins' perch was on a slight rise
canopied in tupelo, bald cypress, and Spanish moss, allowing us
to watch from cover. We laid on our bellies and, trying not to
think about snakes and other deadly vermin, surveilled the pier
through our spy glasses. Sure enough, there was a contingent of
Confederate soldiers, or at least men dressed as such, lounging
around and on some cotton bales. There wasn't a boat at the pier,
but one was approaching and several of the men moved out to
receive it.

"I told you, Jack, look at that," said Elkins, as he gestured
toward the incoming craft. I fixed my spy glass on the boat and
to my horror saw that, while they weren't wearing uniforms, several of the sailors wore either Union kepis or sailor caps. Idiots,
I thought, although old habits die hard. Nevertheless, I silently
cursed Pinkerton for the oversight, but said, "We're in the back

of beyond here, Elkins, they are probably forced to wear whatever they can lay their hands on. I don't see any uniforms, do you?"

"If it was just one, I might agree Jack, but there are several. And I saw the same the other times I was here. I think we should report this to the C.S.A."

Before I could come up with a response, a voice behind us said. "Several what, gentlemen?" and we turned to see four Confederate soldiers standing behind us, guns drawn.

"Thank God," says Elkins. "Several Union caps among the sailors on that boat. We suspect that they are taking our cotton to the enemy. Now that you are here, we can do something about it. We need to speak to your commanding officer as soon as possible."

"We might be able to arrange that," one of them said. "But first, we'll need you to hand over your weapons and tell us how that is 'your' cotton."

As we turned over our pistols and knives, Elkins prattled on about who we are and how we are selling cotton to Major E. J. Allen of the Confederate Army, but that we now fear it might be getting to the Yankees, etc.

"That's an interesting, if far-fetched story, Mr. Elkins," responded the one that had thus far done all the talking on their side. As he rummaged through our pockets he found my carte de visites, which at least validated some of the story. But they all remained alert. He instructed one of his companions to tear apart our coats. He apologized, explaining that there had been spies in the area and that they have been found to carry orders, maps and other information hidden in linings. I fought hard to keep my breakfast down as I remembered that Lincoln's letter was sewn into mine. I racked my brain to come up with some kind of plausible explanation, but there simply wasn't one. Inevitably, the letter was pulled from my coat and handed to the man in charge.

He glanced at both sides, then looked at me and said, "That's odd. Why would you carry a blank sheet of paper so meticulously sewn into your coat lining?"

I remembered my "swim" off Norfolk and was suddenly grateful for Surratt having me pushed into the harbor. The water must have washed away all the ink, so John Jr. had indeed taken me out of harm's way, but in a manner neither of us could have imagined.

"You'd have to ask my tailor, sir," I responded. "As you can see, I had him install some extra pockets and he must have done it then. He's a bit of an odd duck, truth be told, but for the most part does fine work."

He got back to the business at hand with, "Well gentlemen, you'll be sorry to hear that your suspicions are correct. Those are Union sailors accepting your cotton from other Union soldiers dressed as Confederates. Unfortunately for you, we are also with the Union, and are going to have to place you under arrest. You'll be sent downriver to Port Royal and … " Before he could finish, Elkins was on his feet brandishing a derringer he'd pulled from his boot. What he expected to do with a two-shot handgun against four armed men only he could say, but he never got the chance. A moment later he was lying dead on the ground beside me.

I looked wide-eyed at the man that had done all the talking and spewed, "What you read on my carte de visites is true. I'm Jack Bailey, a cotton dealer based in Charleston, but I also work for Allan Pinkerton. We arranged these shipments together, but my local man Elkins here has loyalties that lie elsewhere. Or had. He had become suspicious, so I came down here from Washington on Pinkerton's orders to sort things out. My contact here is Colonel James Montgomery. If you could take me to him, I guarantee that he will corroborate all this."

"You are either the fastest thinker I've ever met, Mr. Bailey, or what you say is true. I suppose I have got nothing to lose by taking you to him, and plenty to lose if we hang you here and it turns out that you were telling the truth. Get up, let's go."

"What about Elkins," I asked sheepishly.

"The gators will have all that cleared up by morning, Bailey. It's too hot to carry him out, and one can't make a hole in this soggy ground to bury a body. Let's go."

The way this man spoke told me that he was an officer disguised as an enlisted man, and I directed my questions to him as we made our way to the pier. He was largely unresponsive, and I figured he would stay that way until he had confirmed my status. I eventually gave up and focused my full attention on swatting insects and keeping my eyes peeled for snakes, alligators, and whatever else lurked in this hellhole. One of the men was sent off to collect our horses, leaving the rest of us to stumble and curse our way through the bog.

When we arrived at the dock, it was clear that my captor was the ranking officer among the entire group, including the half dozen or so sailors from the boat now mingling with the ten men on shore. I still hadn't been given the courtesy of any introductions and doubted I would be before we met Montgomery. Darkness was falling, and, despite the boat being almost fully loaded, he ordered that we spend the night here. I would have preferred to get out onto the water, but the plan was to sail downstream to Port Royal the next morning, Monday, June 1. To get off the ground and away from reptiles, we bedded down in the empty cotton wagons, with two-man shifts standing two-hour watches throughout the night. One man seemed to have been assigned the task of sitting on a large leather satchel sitting in the corner of one of the wagons, but I didn't give that much thought at the time. Even though both my hands and feet were bound, I consoled myself with the fact that it was better than sleeping in the streets of Fredericksburg in December. At the risk of stating the obvious,

I'd have preferred a bed at the Willard with Anna. And if she had been tied up, so much the better.

First light comes early at that time of year in that part of the world, so after what seemed like no time at all, we were up milling around, once again enthusiastically cursing the insects. I was surprised to see that most of the soldiers had changed into Union uniforms. After being given water and something to eat, I was being bound again when a shot rang out and the man that was tying me up dropped to the ground. Another shot felled a man on the other side of the wagon, then a cacophony of gunfire was my cue to drop to the ground and lie face down and stock still until silence was restored. I soon heard footsteps moving around the camp and the sickening sound of bayonets finishing off a couple of poor souls before a kick in the ribs turned me over. I found myself staring up at a C.S.A. Captain.

"It seems this is your lucky day, son," he said. "Carter, come untie this one. Looks like he's a prisoner. Boy, what's your story?"

When making something up, it's always wise to include as much truth as possible. In this case, it wasn't hard, and the carte de visites that one of the Confederates found offered corroborating evidence. I basically told Elkins' version of events and said we had come here to confirm our suspicions when we were taken captive. I concluded by saying Elkins had been shot by these brutes when he had pulled a gun they hadn't found on him.

"And why do you suppose they didn't shoot you while they were at it, Mr. Bailey?", the Captain asked.

"Probably because I truly am the supplier of their cotton. I imagine they wanted to check with higher ups," I speculated. This was also mostly true. "They planned to sail down to Port Royal this morning to do just that and to deliver these bales," I added.

That got them discussing what to do with the boat and the cotton. Some of the men were set on torching the lot, but the

Captain seemed to be thinking that it might have some value to the Confederacy. He sent a couple of men north to the town of Green Pond to get a more senior opinion and put the others to work dragging bodies into the woods. It was then I noticed that the number of dead seemed to fall short of the sixteen men I had counted earlier. No doubt some had run off into the heavy foliage during the confusion and were putting some distance between themselves and this lot. The Captain came up again and offered a canteen they'd taken from one of the dead Union soldiers.

"Based on the inscription, I assume this must be yours as well," he said as he handed me my Cooper. I thanked him as I glanced down and ran my finger along "King Cotton." It felt good to have her back in my belt.

Once the camp was cleaned up a couple of fires were lit, and the smell of food cooking made me realize how hungry I was. Like the Union soldiers they had just killed or driven off, this group consisted mostly of young men just trying to survive each day. They bantered among themselves, complained about the swamp, and mostly left me alone. There were twenty of them, including the Captain. The two that had been sent off to find out what was to be done with the boat and shipment had not reappeared by nightfall, so we again posted sentries and took to the wagons to sleep. In the early hours of the morning, the sentries roused us just us shots began to ring out. Two boats had appeared around the bend in the river, and one was in the process of offloading troops. I was over the edge of the wagon and, after grabbing the reins of one of the horses, into the woods in an instant. It looked to me like this camp was about to change hands for the third time in less than two days. I had no desire to linger and, assuming I even survived the fight now raging, risk that my convoluted story would save my neck a third time. With the darkness and unfamiliar terrain, I had little choice but to strike out north, following the river. It wasn't long before my progress took me out of range of the sound of the gunfire, but I kept moving in case soldiers from either army were following this same route.

Shortly after sunrise, I could hear a boat making its way up-river, so I moved a little deeper into the woods while maintaining a sightline to the water. As it caught up, I knelt and watched as not one, but two gunboats moved past my position. Incredibly, the majority of the men on board appeared to be freed slaves in Union uniforms. The boats were moving carefully, staying alert for Confederate guns on shore. I moved a few yards further in-land for cover, but with all the twists and turns in the river was able to keep pace by maintaining more of a straight line. Surely these men were going to land upriver somewhere and, once they did, I planned to surrender to them and ask to be taken to Montgomery. Sure enough, a short time later one of the boats anchored off a plantation I had just gone around—the Nichols Plantation I would later discover. The Union troops disembarked and started to lay waste to buildings with such rabid intensity that I decided to keep moving along with the second boat. That second gunboat soon came to a halt at a pontoon bridge span-ning the Combahee, where more troops disembarked and began exchanging fire with a smattering of Confederates who they soon drove off. Again, these black Union troops started to lay waste to another plantation with a vengeance.

I dismounted and decided to bide my time until their fury had run its course. With the pontoon bridge blocking any further progress upriver, this last gunboat wasn't going anywhere anyway. Through my spy glass, I could see a couple of officers on board, and I planned to surrender to them if they came ashore. As I hid behind the tall roots of a bald cypress, I suddenly heard a commo-tion in the trees off to my right. I hunkered down further until I realized that a woman must be involved in some kind of struggle, so I cautiously crept toward the sound. In a small clearing I came upon two men who were clearly intent on raping a diminutive black woman. Glancing back and seeing that no one else from the ship or plantation was nearby, I stepped into the clearing and cleared my throat. All three looked toward me, and I recognized the two men as being from the group of Union soldiers that had kept me prisoner two nights ago.

"Just in time, Bailey," said one. "You'll get your turn in a few minutes." He then turned his attentions back to the woman he had pinned to the ground.

Back in my room at the Petersen, I sometimes did an exercise to see how quickly I could pull a Cooper from various locations in my clothing. While boredom played a role in this little game, I also felt there might be a time when getting it clear and ready to discharge in just a few seconds might have some value. This seemed to be one of those times. I didn't much care if these cretins were Union or Confederate, and my first bullet went into the center of the chest of the man waiting his turn. The second went into the forehead of his friend who had turned away from the woman toward me as he heard the first shot. My third went again into the chest of the first man, still writhing on the ground. People say it's a difficult business shooting another man, especially your first. This wasn't my first. A few years ago as I was leaving a tavern on the Charleston docks in the wee hours one morning, I had put down a man who was intent on assaulting and robbing me. These two hadn't given me much choice either and I had my doubts that reasoning would have worked, not that I tried. Some men just need to be stopped and some of those can only be stopped one way. All that said, if it had to happen, I preferred this to having to shoot young men on the battlefield whose only offense was answering the call of their cause.

After a few seconds of silence, the woman looked up at me and, seemingly without fear, said, "Too impatient to wait for your turn mister?"

"No ma'am. I mean no, I don't mean you any harm ma'am. It's just, well, it obviously wasn't right. You should go back to your plantation. I need to get out of here." I turned to go and came face-to-face with three black Union soldiers, all with their bayonet fitted rifles leveled at me.

"You go back to the boat Moses," one said. "We'll finish up here."

"This man just saved my life, Sam. Lower your guns. Mister Bailey was it?" she asked, turning to me.

"Yes, Jack Bailey," I responded.

"Well, thank you, Mister Bailey, I am certainly glad that you happened along."

"You are welcome ma'am. Now, as I mentioned, I must be going. I'm hoping to speak with an officer from that boat over there. I need to find a Colonel James Montgomery of the 2nd Carolina."

"We are the 2nd Carolina sir, and I am working for the Colonel," she said as she gestured toward the chaos and flames coming from the plantation buildings. "My name is Harriet Tubman[75]. I scout for Colonel Montgomery. We are here freeing slaves and killing Confederates." If this was her work, I have to say that both she and her men seemed to have a real zest for it.

---

75 Harriet Tubman was born into slavery as Araminta Ross in Maryland in 1822. She was an abolitionist and, during the Civil War, a nurse, scout, and spy for the Union Army. Among her many accomplishments was to rescue and free scores of slaves using the Underground Railroad. She and her brothers Ben and Henry escaped slavery themselves in September 1849. In 1858 Tubman met and aided John Brown in his plans for a slave revolt. She was also known by the nicknames "Minty" and "Moses". Tubman died in 1913. The U.S. Treasury plans to honor her by placing her portrait on the $20 bill by 2030.

"Well I'll be damned," I blurted out with more surprise than I'd intended. "I'd be very grateful if you could take me to him," I said. "It's a long story, but I've also been working down here for the Union. The Colonel is aware of my activities."

With that, she picked herself up and all five feet of her stood tall in front of me. "Follow me," she commanded as she set out toward the gunboat. It was then I noticed the leather satchel I'd seen the other night in a wagon now lying on the ground a few feet away. I picked it up as I followed Tubman out of the clearing and toward the boat.

Harriet Tubman in 1868, Courtesy of the Library of Congress, LC-DIG-ppmsca-54230

Chapter 21

BACK NORTH

*W*e boarded that boat, the USS John Adams[76], a few minutes later. I followed Tubman as she pushed her way
through the throng that was moving about the decks loading
rice, potatoes, and other items they had just liberated from the
plantation. She gave me a quick introduction to Montgomery,
then immediately excused herself and went back the way we'd just
come. Fortunately, Montgomery had indeed heard of me from
Pinkerton, although he expressed surprise that our first meeting
would be here, miles up the Combahee, and via an introduction
from Harriet Tubman.

"Bailey, I will have to speak with you later. As you can see, at
the moment I have men on shore, Confederates sending the occasional shell our way, slaves to liberate and plantations to burn.
As soon as we mop up, we'll turn back down river toward Port
Royal. You are welcome to stay on board for the trip, and we'll

---

76 Originally built in 1799, the USS John Adams saw service in the War of 1812,
the Mexican-American War, and the Civil War, including the Raid on Combahee
Ferry. She was 139 feet long, designed to be crewed by 220 officers and men, and
heavily armed with two dozen twelve-pound guns and a half-dozen twenty-four
pounders. The USS John Adams was decommissioned in September 1865.

have time to talk then. Feel free to make yourself at home, but I'd be grateful if you would help stow some of this produce and organize the placement of these freed slaves. There will be a lot of them, and we need to be mindful of weight distribution." With that, he made off toward another part of the boat.

Indeed, there were a lot of them, with more arriving at the shore every minute. I heard somewhere later that a total of more than 700 made the return trip on these boats following what would collectively come to be called "The Raid on Combahee Ferry." These slaves had not been aware of the Emancipation Proclamation, and I'm not sure how many would have been so eager to join us had Tubman not been there to speak with them. The sight of so many of their kind in Union Army uniforms likely also helped. Their wariness turned to unbridled excitement once they understood what was happening. I enlisted a few to help explain the importance of spreading out evenly on the boat, and they did so willingly both here and on the USS Harriet A. Weed, which had just joined us on this part of the river. Sporadic gunfire and the smell of burning buildings ensured that everyone worked with a sense of urgency. A short time later some of Montgomery's men set fire to the pontoon bridge before we turned our bows south and set off back downriver.

Once we were well underway Montgomery sent for me, and I found him sitting at a small table in the Captain's quarters. I must have looked longingly at the bottle of bourbon that was open on his desk, as he started off by offering me a drink. We clinked glasses and sat down for a chat, which he began with, "Let me first thank you for getting Moses out of danger, Bailey. Apparently, your timing couldn't have been better."

"Moses?" I asked. Then remembered that one of the colored soldiers had called her that. "Ah, right. Miss Tubman. Well, I only did what anyone would have done."

"We both know that isn't true, Bailey. It must have been difficult. She says you knew them."

Now this could be a problem. They were Union soldiers, although they weren't dressed the part. And they had called me by name. I hoped he hadn't seen the bodies, as they might have been his men, which would have been awkward even if they were about to commit a crime. I decided to offer up the least amount of information possible and said, "I'd met them locally. As I'm sure Pinkerton told you, my office is in Charleston." Both sentences were true, although I was lying by omission and was relieved when he moved on.

"I assume the cotton on that boat we passed at Fields Point is yours then?" he asked.

"It was mine but belongs to the Union now."

"Well we would have taken it in any case. It's on its way back downriver even as we speak. Why on earth were you out here in the first place? Is it customary for the head merchant to make deliveries?" he asked.

"Not usually," I said. "My man Elkins had concerns about where our shipments were actually ending up, so we came out here to have a look."

"I'm sorry, I didn't realize you had someone with you. I'll have one of my men find him and invite him to join us."

"He didn't make it," I responded truthfully but, again, vaguely. "Shot in one of the skirmishes."

"I'm sorry for your loss then," he offered. "Here's to him," and we took another sip. "What are your plans now?" he continued.

I frankly hadn't had time to give this much thought, but it was an excellent question. I quickly decided that my main priorities were to get back to Washington to both talk to Pinkerton and resume my duties with Brady. I also needed to let Dawson know that he was now running the show down here for Bailey

Importers. In a way this was better than having Elkins in the equation. Dawson was far less likely to care where the cotton was going so long as he was getting paid. He also knew our suppliers and they knew him, so we should be able to carry on as usual. I would write and let him know that Elkins had been shot by Union soldiers while I had made a narrow escape. News of this raid would no doubt make its way to Charleston in any case, so the story would fit.

"I need to get word to my people in Charleston about Elkins and then, with any luck, find a ship that is going up to Washington," I answered.

"I can help on both counts," Montgomery offered. "We occasionally slip people in and out of Charleston and there are ships going up the coast all the time. Write a letter to your people and I will see that it is delivered. I will also arrange passage north for you when we get back to Port Royal."

Suddenly the bourbon tasted a lot better. A commotion on deck brought our meeting to an end as we joined up with a third boat in Montgomery's expedition, the USS Sentinel. The Sentinel had run aground off St. Helena Sound the previous night but was afloat once again. All three boats turned to starboard and steamed west toward Brickyard Landing. From there we would turn south to Beaufort and, ultimately, Port Royal. The entire journey from the pontoon bridge upriver was only about 40 miles, and I enjoyed every minute of it. At one point I found someone willing to part with a cheroot, and I enjoyed it along with another glass of bourbon as I stood on deck listening to scores of newly freed slaves sing some of the most enchanting music I have ever heard. I'd been cursing the heat these past few days, but the light breeze coming off the water and the sight of Spanish moss-covered Cypress along both shores made for an idyllic scene. I thought that the only thing that might have improved it all would have been to have Anna standing along the ship's rail with me until I picked up the satchel I'd liberated from the Union thugs. I undid the straps, peered inside, and looked upon what must have been at least $50,000 in a variety of denominations of Confederate bills. I nonchalantly closed it up, and thereafter never let the thing out of my sight.

Chapter 22

SAILING NORTH

The journey back up to Washington wasn't quite as pleasant as my trip down the Combahee. While it would have been about 600 miles over land, by ship we were forced to take a less direct route in order to stay out of range of cannon on the shores of the Carolinas and Virginia. And an open sea is something entirely different from the inland cruise I had just been on, although once we turned into Chesapeake Bay and passed Norfolk, I was back in calmer waters and familiar territory. When we passed Chapel Point on the Potomac, beyond which lay Port Tobacco, I had a fleeting thought about requesting to be put ashore so I could go see Anna, but quickly came to my senses. A few hours later I was back in Washington, where the humidity made it feel like I had never left South Carolina. We docked on an early afternoon in mid-June and, despite the warm weather, instead of going back to the studio I stopped and bought a coat to replace the one that lay shredded in the swamps of South Carolina. I left it with Petersen so he could install the customary array of hidden pockets before going over to the Star for an early dinner and a couple of drinks. I was greatly looking forward to spending a night on dry land and in my own bed and turned in early so as to be rested and ready for Brady the following morning.

The next day I found Brady in good spirits with high anticipation, as the opportunity for more battlefield photography was
imminent. General Lee had his Army of Northern Virginia on
the march north toward Pennsylvania in the rebel's second major
effort to take war into Union territory. From June 13 to 15, the
Union and Confederate armies clashed once again in and around
Winchester, Virginia, a town 75 miles northwest of Washington
that would change hands more than forty times during the war.
Brady was planning to set off to visit the New York studio, and he
asked that I take a crew north to follow the action. He had heard
that Gardner was already on the move, so it was decided that I
would take a team that included David Woodbury and Anthony
Berger to follow Hooker's army and ensure that the competition
didn't have the field to itself. If any major action materialized,
Brady would join us from New York. He set off the next day
leaving me to oversee our final preparations, and it wasn't long
before I received a visit from Pinkerton. With Brady gone, we sat
down in his office and Pinkerton began with, "When you decide
to come off a fence, Bailey, apparently you do so in no uncertain
terms."

"What do you mean?" I asked.

"Elkins dispatched, a shipment saved, Harriet Tubman rescued from thugs, plantations looted and torched ..."

"Wait a minute, Allan," I interrupted. "I'm not responsible for
any arson or looting, and I had no choice but to shoot ..."

"Relax, Jack. You did good work," he said, breaking into a
smile. "Colonel Montgomery was very complimentary." Happily,
he didn't ask for details about the men I'd shot, but I quickly
changed the topic in any case.

"One thing I learned down there Allan, although you likely
already know, is that there is apparently some successful blockade
running going on, and it's helping the Confederacy buy arms."

"It's a big ocean, Jack, and we only have so many ships to patrol the coast," he acknowledged. "I wish it weren't the case."

"It seems that my home country is responsible for many of these purchases." I continued. "I know from my father that three quarters of Britain's spindles are now idle due to a lack of cotton. It's no wonder people are willing to go to great lengths to get the stuff."

"No doubt, but we are doing all we can," he replied.

"Maybe not," I said. "What if the Union starts offering significant quantities of cotton to Britain? You could do so at lower prices since you don't have the risk and expense of running blockades. We could simply increase what is coming down your Combahee route and offer the excess to Britain. That would undercut the blockade runners and keep the money out of the hands of the Confederacy."

"Well that would also work out well for you, wouldn't it Jack?" he observed sarcastically.

"It would work out well for the Union, that's for certain. You'd generate some revenue for the North by taking it away from the Confederacy."

I could tell by the thirty seconds of silence and twinkle forming in his beady eyes that I'd set him to thinking. I didn't want to get ahead of myself but couldn't help but feel I might have just made another major sale for Bailey Importers. Father would be pleased and Émilie likely more so, not that I gave a damn about her. Finally, Pinkerton said, "That idea may have some merit, Jack. Let me discuss it with the President." A cynical person would have thought he wanted to figure out how to take all the credit (and perhaps a percentage) before raising it with Lincoln, but I didn't give a damn about that either. What I did care about was the cash coming my way. And if the Union bit on this, there would be plenty of that to go around.

He moved on to the real reason he had come, which was to question me about sentiments in the South. I confirmed that there seemed to be food shortages, but we knew that from the Bread Riots. I said that spirits generally seemed high, as was confidence in Robert E. Lee. While it's true you can always find a variety of opinions, I spoke with many people and witnessed much during my journey down to Charleston and, as a result, was confident in my assessment.

"By the way, Allan," I said at one point. "I found this during my travels," and handed him the satchel. I'd thought long and hard about what to do with this money and eventually decided that, knowing Pinkerton, there was a good chance he already knew about it. Better to have the Union pay me for my cotton above-board, I decided, than risk imprisonment for possession of rebel currency. He looked inside, extracted, and inspected a couple of the bills and then said, "It's Samuel Upham's work." I'd heard of Upham. A publisher in Philadelphia. Early in the war he put his skills to work creating mock Confederate currency that, among other things, depicted Jefferson Davis's head on a donkey's body. Apparently, he'd moved on to produce more legitimate fakes.

"Just between us, Bailey," he continued, "We've been moving a lot of this stuff into the South."

"If you are planning to pay my suppliers with this garbage," I said angrily, "you'll risk the entire operation and my reputation. Not to mention the fact that my man Dawson could end up with his throat slit. What the hell are you thinking?"

"Of course, we aren't going to jeopardize those supplies with counterfeit currency, Jack," he claimed. "We get it into circulation in less obvious ways. An abundance of money like this in an economy has great utility in creating both inflation and confusion. But you have my word that we won't use it with your suppliers." That calmed me down somewhat, as did the realization that the act of turning in this worthless paper had given me the highest possible value from it.

Pinkerton asked a few more questions, took notes and, when he rose to leave, expressed the opinion that there might soon be some major action north of Washington. I let him know that we intended to follow Hooker's Army so as to be in position and thanked him for the confirmation. He paused at the door on the way out and seemed about to ask something else, but then thought better of it. I'd have bet a cotton shipment that the subject was going to be Anna Surratt.

A few days later I set off with Woodbury, Berger, and a few apprentices north toward Hooker's position. Elements of Lee's army had moved through Maryland and were crossing over into Pennsylvania, causing significant anxiety in Philadelphia and as far north as New York City. But, as it turned out, both armies were destined to meet just a few miles across the Maryland and Pennsylvania border in a town called Gettysburg. As we traveled with the Union Army through Emmitsburg, Maryland toward Gettysburg I wondered if Alexander Gardner would also come this way. He had sent his young son to boarding school here nearly two years ago to get him away from Washington and out of harm's way. I'm sure he was now having regrets about that idea.

At some point during our journey, Lincoln accepted Hooker's[77] resignation and replaced him with General George Meade. While throwing Hooker overboard was, in my opinion, the right thing, I thought Meade a curious choice to replace

---

77 Joseph "Fighting Joe" Hooker was born in Massachusetts in 1814. He graduated from the U.S. Military Academy in 1837. Hooker's nickname came about because of a typesetting error in a newspaper, and his career was somewhat tainted by his defeat by Robert E. Lee at Chancellorsville in May of 1863. Although in and out of favor, he also saw action at Williamsburg, Antietam, Fredericksburg, Chattanooga, Atlanta, and Lookout Mountain. Hooker died in 1879.

him given that he was outranked by several other active Union Generals at the time, including Hancock, Reynolds, Sedgwick, and Slocum. Obviously Lincoln had more first-hand knowledge than I did, so I figured he must know what he was doing. But, for my money, Grant would have been the best choice. I admit that saying so now seems like a cheap observation in hindsight, but he seemed to me the only one of the bunch that was consistently willing to take the fight to the enemy. In any case it was a moot point, as Grant currently had his hands full a thousand miles away in Vicksburg, Tennessee.

Chapter 23

GETTYSBURG

With a steady flow of Bailey cotton now going to the Union and the potential of much more to come, it would be fair to ask why I should bother to continue to work for Brady. God knows this job had exposed me to significant danger at Bull Run, Antietam, Fredericksburg, and the like. And on top of that were Pinkerton-inflicted risks in Port Tobacco, Norfolk, and along the Combahee, to name a few. So, I spent considerable time on this journey to Pennsylvania asking myself that very question, eventually concluding that I must. My association with Brady had provided exposure to Pinkerton, Army Quartermaster Meigs, and others that had made these sales possible. Given his friendship with Lincoln, leaving Brady in the lurch might jeopardize these high-level relationships, and I worried that the recent defections of Gardner, O'Sullivan, and the others might make him even more inclined to be vindictive should I resign. Unlike Brady, I didn't believe that we were on some holy mission that made us immune to any danger, but the job did provide me legitimate cover at times. And with that cover came the ability to move around with the appearance of neutral purpose, which was especially important in my relationship with Anna. And what would I do if I did leave? Going back to Charleston didn't seem wise, and I certainly had no interest in Liverpool. After weighing the pros and cons of it all, I decided that my best course was to stick things out. I vowed to try to keep myself further away from these battles, which would be easier on this particular trip with Brady in New York. To that end, when it became clear that a major clash was about to occur near Gettysburg, I set up camp with my crew a couple of miles south of town to the east of the Emmitsburg Road at a place called Round Top. I figured we would be well clear of danger here, and the elevation provided a good view north to observe the action. Once the battle was over, we would be in a perfect position to move in promptly, do our work and get out. There was no way now to get word to Brady in New York, which suited me just fine. He could get his information from the papers and make his own decision as to whether he should join us. That first day of battle, July 1, 1863, saw only portions of both armies engage. After clashes to the west and northwest of Gettysburg, the Union was driven back through town and up onto the now famous Cemetery Hill. Unfortunately, the worst was to come on July 2 and 3.

I have found myself in some unusual places over the years, but an army encampment on the eve of battle is truly unique. I decided to take one of our horses and ride a little farther north toward town to see if I could pick up any scuttlebutt on what tomorrow might bring. Top of mind of course was whether our position on Round Top was sufficiently out of harm's way. The landscape in front of me was dotted with white tents and fires, and the smell of cooking was everywhere. Music filled the air, coming from fiddles, fifes, harmonicas, banjos, and guitars. Old classics such as *Nearer My God to Thee* and *Nelly Bly* were common, as were the newer songs such as *Battle Hymn of the Republic*. Both sides had their favorites, such as *Dixie* in the South and *John Brown's Body* in the North. Some were played by both sides, like *Home, Sweet Home,* and *Maryland My Maryland,* but I found them all moving, especially on a night like this. I think it was Robert E. Lee himself that said, "I don't think we could have an army without music." I was certainly happy to hear it—especially when I was well clear of the front lines.

I moved slowly among the troops, often walking my horse when moving through an area that was particularly crowded. Overhearing conversations told me that most of the men felt fear. Many were now veterans of this conflict and all too aware of what was in store. As always though, a group this size is guaranteed to contain a few unbalanced minds. Some of these fools seemed eager for action, although I was certain they would have a different view by this time tomorrow, if they even survived. At one point, I noticed Abner Doubleday[78] speaking with a few men around a fire close to a large tent. I'd last seen him at Fort Sumter when he was a Captain under Robert Anderson. His uniform told me that he was now a Lieutenant General and, when our eyes met, a look of recognition slowly crept across his face.

"Hey, sir," he said, pointing accusingly at my chest. "I know you," he added as he closed the ten feet between us. Talking quickly, I gave him the same story I told Dr. Samuel Crawford when he confronted me in Centerville. Friend of a friend of Anderson's—just trying to avoid bloodshed—not actually working with Chesnut's detachment of rebels demanding their surrender—etc. I no longer had the benefit of showing Lincoln's letter, so instead leaned in and, under my breath, said something about working for Allan Pinkerton.

---

78 Abner Doubleday was born in New York in 1836. He graduated from the U.S. Military Academy in 1842 and his classmates included Rosecrans and Longstreet. Known for firing the first shot of the Civil War at Fort Sumter, Doubleday also distinguished himself at Gettysburg. Although falsely credited for inventing baseball, he did patent a system used for San Francisco's iconic cable cars. Doubleday died in 1893.

"Maybe I should keep you here until I can confirm that," he said suspiciously.

"Obviously that would be your decision," I answered with more confidence than I felt. "And, when you speak with him, would you mind telling him that detaining me is the reason Mathew Brady's team will be unavailable for photography here?"

"We can sort all that out right now," he said, staring intently into my eyes. "I just saw Pinkerton an hour ago over in General Reynolds headquarters, not far from here."

"How fortunate," I said, "Would you mind if we went to him right now?" And with that request his interest in me subsided. I never found out if Pinkerton was in fact with Reynolds, but the crafty Doubleday had apparently decided I was telling the truth based on my eagerness to go meet him. I'm sure that he would have just as quickly decided to hang me right there if I had instead tried to bolt. I decided not to press my luck further and excused myself to rejoin my crew on Round Top.

The following morning, July 2, began quietly. Reinforcements for both armies were continuing to arrive on the field. We could see movement among the Union forces along Cemetery Ridge, and by the Confederates north and to our left. We watched as Union General Sickle moved his men off the Ridge and to the southwest into areas we now know as the Peach Orchard, Rose Woods, and Devil's Den. He got ahead of himself in the process, and Meade was forced to send 20,000 men to support him. By mid-afternoon, Longstreet's Confederate artillery opened fire and I watched in horror as the ensuing battle suddenly was raging just a few hundred yards in front of us. It was then that I decided that we would retreat, but we could see that Emmitsburg Road, which we had used to come from Washington, was teeming with Confederate soldiers. I became worried that they might circle around us to the south to move up Taneytown Road and attack

Meade from the rear, but thankfully they never did. The threat was enough to keep us in place, though, but I feared the worst as we watched Union Colonel Strong Vincent's men repeatedly thwart rebel attacks on Little Round Top, just a stone's throw in front of us. At the point when I wasn't sure how much more his men could have taken, they were reinforced by an artillery battery and men from the 140th New York. A bayonet charge by the Union's 20th Maine against Hood's Confederates put an end to the action on Little Round Top, but not soon enough to prevent a brutal slaughter. Among the casualties there and on Cemetery Ridge was General Sickle himself, who had to have a leg amputated after being struck by a cannonball.

Darkness brought relief for my group, but not for the thousands that lay wounded on the battlefield, many crying out for help. The mood among the Union troops around us had changed markedly from the previous night. While the fear remained, the music was all but gone and what we did hear was melancholy. Cooking fires were less prevalent, and men mostly sat or lay around exhausted. I thought again about trying to get word to Brady, but eventually decided that the newspaper dispatches going out from here to Philadelphia and New York would be timelier than anything I could manage. After talking to my crew about the possibility of moving our equipment east to Taneytown Road and heading south, we agreed that doing so in the dark would be foolish. In addition, we still had concerns about Confederates moving that way to attack Mead's forces from behind. It all added up to a sleepless night, during which I again asked myself whether staying with Brady was the right course of action.

The fighting would rage again on July 3, although we didn't know at the time that this would be the final day of the Battle of Gettysburg. The main action started late with what would be the largest exchange of artillery fire in the war. More than 150 Confederate guns and 80 Union cannon exchanged fire for two hours beginning at about 1:00 p.m. Most of the fire was concentrated around Cemetery Ridge, about two miles in front of us. The center of that ridge was the focus of Pickett's Charge when more than 12,000 of his men advanced toward the Union lines. Given the distances involved, we could see explosions, smoke, and the general movement of men, but were spared witnessing the gruesome hand-to-hand combat, where men were eventually reduced to using bayonets, rocks, and their bare hands. Many others have found better words to describe this carnage so I will not even try. As always, individual tragedy is lost in the overall tally of 35,000 dead or wounded, counting both sides. Equine losses were also horrific. I read somewhere that 5,000 horses were killed at Gettysburg, and many of their carcasses would later be burned in pyres. Thousands of fallen men had to be buried quickly so as not to be exposed to the early summer heat. In addition to all that, this town of just over 2,000 people was now also home to 14,000 Union wounded and 8,000 Confederate prisoners. When I hear someone who hasn't been witness to carnage like that seen at Gettysburg, Antietam, or Fredericksburg complain about calamity or misfortune, you'll understand my lack of compassion.

I will mention one individual casualty, however, but only because he became a subject of one of O'Sullivan's photographs and a Union hero after the battle. John L. Burns, a 69-year-old veteran of the War of 1812 served as constable in Gettysburg and was jailed by the Confederates when they occupied the town in late June. Released when the rebels retreated, he in turn arrested some of their stragglers. On July 1, he traded his antique flintlock rifle for a wounded soldier's modern Enfield, then presented himself for duty to Major Chamberlain's 150th Pennsylvania Infantry. While serving as a sniper in McPherson Woods, he reportedly shot a Confederate officer off his horse. Later wounded and once again arrested by the rebels, he managed to convince them he was a noncombatant out looking for help for his ailing wife. Upon being treated by Confederate surgeons he was released and eventually made his way back to his house in Gettysburg. A few months later he would take a stroll through town with President Lincoln, who was there to deliver his Gettysburg Address.

On July 4, heavy rain and exhaustion among both armies put an end to any serious fighting, and Lee began his retreat on July 5. Gettysburg was considered a resounding Union victory, and the surrender of Vicksburg, Tennessee that same day added to the feeling that the tide was finally turning in favor of the North. With the benefit of hindsight, Pickett's[79] furthest penetration up Cemetery Ridge on July 3 would become known as the "high water mark of the Confederacy."

We finally heard from Brady through a newspaperman who gave us a letter that was brought in from New York by one of his runners. In that letter, Brady asked that Woodbury and Berger not take any photographs. He ordered that we instead spend our time scouting for suitable vistas and gathering eyewitness accounts to the fighting so as to be ready when he arrived. I was furious. There was no end to the subject matter all around us and, while it was happening slowly, every passing day meant more evidence of battle was cleaned up and more bodies buried. Not that I took any joy from photographing such, but Gardner and his team had arrived and were now doing just that. Was Brady really that petty that he was willing

---

79 George Edward Pickett was born in Richmond, Virginia in 1825. He graduated from the U.S. Military Academy in 1846, last in his class. Wounded in the Peninsular Campaign, Pickett also saw action at Fredericksburg, Five Forks and of course at Gettysburg with "Pickett's Charge" up Cemetery Hill. He died in 1875.

to let others beat us to the punch just so he could take credit for all our photographs? I held no animosity toward Gardner, as he was just a businessman going about his business. In fact, I enjoyed being around both him and O'Sullivan, but it was galling to see them to be the first to get battlefield photographs in Gettysburg. That said, I ended up sharing a few drinks with them the evening of July 5, shortly after they had arrived. We avoided any talk of business, but I did learn that they had indeed come up via Emmitsburg, where they had been only briefly detained by retreating Confederate troops. Maybe photographers did enjoy a special status after all, I recall thinking. But I reminded myself that flying bullets and grape shot made no such distinction.

My opinion of Gardner, Gibson, and O'Sullivan changed dramatically the following day, after I happened upon them near Devil's Den. Following Brady's instructions, I split up our team and sent them on reconnaissance trips around Gettysburg in search of promising locations to photograph once he arrived. We wrote locations on slips of paper, then drew them to determine our individual assignments. Woodbury ended up going to Seminary Ridge, Berger to Cemetery Ridge, and I to Rose Woods, the Peach Orchard, and Devil's Den, which were the closest to, and just to the northeast of our camp. I happened upon Gardner and his men taking a photograph of a Confederate soldier lying dead beside his rifle in Devil's Den and, after exchanging greetings, I moved on to Rose Woods and the Peach Orchard, thinking I would circle back through Devil's Den on my way back to camp. When I did that, I came across Gardner's team again, this time farther up the hill toward Little Round Top. I went over to them to suggest that we get together for a few drinks again that evening but, while we were chatting,

I couldn't help but notice that they were photographing the very same corpse and rifle. Both had been repositioned in a crevasse near a stone wall, more than 100 feet from where I had previously seen them. They had moved and posed the corpse in a way that suggested he was a rebel sharpshooter shot dead in his nest. I'm sure he must have noticed the look of comprehension start to creep across my face, because Gardner abruptly took me by the elbow and guided me away. While doing so he jabbered on about how busy they would be that evening developing their plates, and that he didn't want to distract his team with another night of drinking. As I rode back into our camp, the significance of what I had just seen fully dawned on me. Those of us photographing these

Gettysburg Sharpshooter, Courtesy of the Library of Congress, LC-DIG-ppmsca-33066

war scenes were coming to be regarded with some reverence as trusted chroniclers of history in a way that had never been possible. If word got out that photographs had been faked, we would lose all credibility with the public. Worse, I could see how staged photographs could be used to mold public perceptions. String up corpses from one army and claim they had been tortured and hung by the other, for example, and watch enlistments and enthusiasm for retribution soar. I knew that half of what I read in the newspapers was clap-trap usually written in a way to advance someone's agenda but, like many, I had assumed that photographs didn't lie. I couldn't believe that these men that I thought I knew as pro-fessionals would stoop to theatrics at a level that would make P. T. Barnum proud. I decided to keep my mouth shut for the moment, figuring that I would find a use for the information at some point down the road.

Brady arrived in Gettysburg a few days later, complaining that while the trains were running from New York to Harrisburg, the tracks from Harrisburg on down had been commandeered by the military to transport the wounded. He was, therefore, left no choice but to come the final 40 miles south by wagon and thus arrived looking even more disheveled than usual. He also brought some disturbing news of unrest in New York City. Residents there were angered by what they perceived as an over-representation of New Yorkers among the casualties at Gettysburg. An upcom-ing draft lottery was also very unpopular, as was the fact that a $300 "commutation fee" could entitle a person to have someone else serve in their place. That was a price far beyond the reach of the typical $2 a day laborer so, in practice, it was an option only available to the wealthy. Brady left the city just prior to the infa-mous Draft Riots, which, with more than 100 people killed, were the worst in American history. But his absence was a bit of a lost opportunity, as it was largely left to sketch artists to create images of the unrest. In the end, Brady did take some three dozen highly acclaimed photographs around Gettysburg, and I must hand it to him for one clever twist. He appeared in most of these, often as just a small feature in the distance. But by doing so, he eliminated any possibility of someone else taking credit for his work. I guess he did learn something from Gardner's defection after all. Once he became fully engaged, I didn't see any reason to stay in the field, and Brady was happy to have me go back and manage the Washington studio. Looking back on their respective works, Gardner became known for the iconic Gettysburg photographs of dead soldiers and horses, while Brady was credited with depictions of the fields of battle. I knew that we could have done both and was sorry we hadn't, but such is the lot of a subordinate.

Chapter 24

A VISIT TO THE QUARTERMASTER

I had a little over a week on my own in the studio before Brady returned from Gettysburg and, among other things, I took advantage of it to enjoy an unexpected visit by Anna. As was our custom, I booked a room at the Willard to spare her (and me) the judgmental stares we would have received from the Petersen's and their guests at the boarding house. The most worthwhile meeting I had during that time, however, was with Brigadier General Montgomery C. Meigs, Quartermaster of the Union Army. A few days after returning from Gettysburg, I received a note from Pinkerton's office requesting that I present myself at Meigs' office in the War Department on Pennsylvania Avenue between 17th & 18th Streets. When I arrived at the appointed hour, I was delighted to see Kate Warne waiting in Meigs' outer office and even more delighted that there was no sign of Pinkerton. She and I had just managed to exchange greetings before being ushered in to see Meigs and

his second-in-command, Colonel Charles Thomas[80]. I had
met both Meigs and Thomas at the White House the previous
fall when the plan to acquire cotton for the Union was initially
hatched, so the introductions were brief. Kate got things started by addressing Meigs and Thomas with, "Gentlemen, Allan
Pinkerton sends his regrets for not being able to attend today, but
he knew that you were keen to meet as soon as possible. I am here
on his behalf and in support Mr. Bailey here."

"We appreciate that, Miss Warne," began Meigs. "I wanted to
have this meeting now, since I will be traveling for the next few
months. I asked Colonel Thomas to join us because he will be acting for me here in Washington while I am in the field." Turning
to me, he continued, "Mr. Bailey, I'll get straight to the point.
You have been supplying the Union with cotton from various
plantations in South Carolina just as we agreed a few months ago.
We have been attempting to do the same with other wholesalers,
but so far your methods and route have been the most successful.
Pinkerton believes that we should be procuring as much cotton
as we can and selling what we don't need ourselves to Britain and
France. He thinks, and I tend to agree, that doing so might cause
buyers in those countries to stop trading with the blockade runners, which would in turn deprive the rebels of some income."

I figured that Pinkerton would claim this idea as his own but
held my tongue. I also sensed Kate was relieved when she realized
that I wasn't going to say anything to the contrary or try to take
any credit. I'd get my revenge when it came time to discuss price.

---

80 Charles Thomas was born in Philadelphia in 1797. He joined the
U.S. Army Ordinance Department in 1819, beginning a long career of
military service. At the outset of the Civil War, Thomas was head of the
Quartermaster Department's Inventory and Accounts Office as well as
the Philadelphia Quartermaster Depot. He would eventually be breveted
a Major General in recognition of his service. Thomas died in 1878 and
Meigs was one of his pallbearers.

"Yes, General," I said compliantly. "I also think that offering Britain (screw the French, I figured) legitimately sourced cotton at prices below what the blockade runners are demanding would be guaranteed to hurt the rebels." Although I was aware that Meigs was born in Georgia, I knew that he despised the Confederacy and had no doubt he'd be all in on this plan if he felt it would hurt them.

"How much more can you get us?" Thomas asked, joining the conversation.

"I'll need to have my man in Charleston make the rounds," I responded. "At the moment, we are buying about half what we normally would, so I have to assume that we could at least double what we are sending you today."

"We'll take all you can get us," Meigs responded. "Why don't you see what that might be, then you can negotiate pricing with Colonel Thomas. We would expect discounts at higher volumes, of course."

"Fair enough," I said. But since I knew that time kills deals, I added, "In order to get started right away, why don't we agree now that for anything we ship above the current volume and up to double that, we'll give you at a 10 percent discount?" To create a heightened sense of urgency, I added, "I'm sure you are also aware that Egypt's cotton[81] shipments to Britain have doubled since the start of the war, so time is of the essence. I hear that the Egyptian cotton is of good quality as well, not to mention that it's a shorter trip from Port Alexandria, Egypt, to Britain than it is from here." All of this was true, but I could see that the doubling

---

81 Although cotton in Egypt dates to 2500 BC, during the U.S. Civil War production there increased five-fold to 250 million pounds a year. By the end of the 19th century, more than 90% of Egypt's export revenues were derived from cotton. Their product is still known for quality to this day and the term Egyptian Cotton™ is trademarked.

of the volume coming from Egypt was news to these gentlemen. While Egyptian cotton could reduce the blockade-running revenue going to the Confederacy, it would also deprive the Union of what might become a material source of income.

"Say 15 percent and were done," Meigs responded quickly, his black eyes boring into me from under his extraordinarily bushy eyebrows.

"Agreed," I said, "On two conditions. One, the current arrangement where Pinkerton's men disguised as rebels pay for the cotton and take delivery at the plantations stands. Two, none of my suppliers get paid in counterfeit currency."

"What are you talking about? Why on earth would we do that?" Thomas asked. "If discovered, it would kill off the supply."

"Exactly," I answered. "But let's just say I've seen the stuff floating around down there. A lot of it."

"Ah," said Meigs, "no doubt some of Upham's handiwork. You know what the Union is trying to accomplish with that, right Bailey?"

"I understand," I said. "And it makes perfect sense, but you keep it away from this arrangement. Someday this war will end, and so will my business if I get a reputation for paying suppliers with worthless paper."

"Seems like we are agreed on all points then," Meigs replied. "Come back and see Colonel Thomas once you know the total volume you will be able to supply. You and he can negotiate a price for anything above and beyond what we've discussed. Miss Warne, I am going to assume that your people in South Carolina can handle the extra volume?" After Kate said she would make certain they could, Meigs stood up with an abruptness that signaled the meeting was over. I tried not to show too much excitement but smiled broadly at a wall on the way out when I knew that none of them could see my face. Once outside, I invited Kate to lunch and was surprised when she accepted.

"Congratulations, Jack," she said once we had been seated at a tavern not far from Meigs' office. "And thank you for your continued support of the cause. Allan told me about your excursion down to South Carolina. He's almost convinced that you are 100 percent Union at this point."

"Where is Allan, by the way?" I asked. "Not that I am complaining, but I expected that he would have been at that meeting just now."

"You've been around us long enough now, Jack, to know that I won't answer that question," she said in response.

"Right. And what do you mean 'almost 100 percent'? After what I've been through for him, I am almost insulted by that," I replied a little testily.

"Easy Jack, no need to get riled. It's your close relationship with the Surratt clan that still bothers him. You know what we've been through with Rose Greenhow, Antonia Ford, and their like," she said. "Attractive women using their charms to extract information for the Confederacy. You must admit that he has seen enough precedent to justify his concerns."

"I have a close relationship with just one Surratt, as you know. And I am fully aware of the political leanings of the rest of them. Allan has on occasion encouraged me to engage with them all for his purposes, as I would assume you know," I said, still hot under the collar.

"I do know. And how is Anna?" she asked.

"You've been around me long enough to know that I won't answer that question," I said, and, after a brief silence, we both chuckled.

Our food arrived and once the server retreated she broke the silence with, "Well, I figure it must be going well with her since you haven't flirted with me for several months now."

"I'm flattered that you are keeping track, Kate," I said, meaning it.

"Trust me, I'm not," she said a little more seriously. "Just be careful, Jack. Things would get ugly if Allan ever thought you might be working both sides. Very ugly. Even if you were only helping the rebels unwittingly."

"Message received," I responded.

The remainder of our lunch discussion was quite enjoyable. We talked some about my time on the Combahee and, like Pinkerton, she had questions about the general mood in the South. She also asked what that part of the country was like, and I described the bayous, plantations, weather, and so on, all of which seemed to be of genuine interest to her. In other circumstances, I might have suggested sarcastically that I take her on vacation there at some point but, given her earlier remarks, decided to hold my tongue. She carried on with similar questions about Britain and, before I knew it, a couple of hours had passed. When we finally left, she asked that I keep Pinkerton or her informed regarding the volume and pricing I would propose to Colonel Thomas but allowed that I could deal with him directly.

Walking back to the studio, I couldn't help but reflect on my first meeting with Kate Warne in Baltimore just over two years ago and how far the country had come off the rails since. Setting aside a few close calls in terms of my personal safety though, I had no complaints.

Chapter 25

THE RUSSIANS

*T*hrough an exchange of letters with Dawson I learned that it wasn't going to be possible to do much better than double the amount of cotton we had been sending down the Combahee prior to my last meeting with Meigs and Thomas. A combination of labor shortages caused by newly emboldened slaves fleeing, farmers switching from cotton to food crops and some plantations being torched (which I had witnessed first-hand), meant that the overall supply was not what it had been in 1860. I was somewhat relieved at this, truth be told, as I had been concerned that buying too much beyond our pre-war volumes might raise eyebrows among my suppliers. I certainly didn't want any of them poking into things the way Elkins had done. And, despite Kate's assurances to Meigs, I also had my doubts about the Union's ability to handle much more while maintaining the ruse of being Southern buyers. In any case, I informed Thomas and Pinkerton that we could double our quantities, stuck to my guns on the 15 percent discount and instructed Dawson to buy as much as he could get his hands on.

While returning from Thomas' office after informing him of all this, my route took me past Alexander Gardner's Gallery at 7th and D Streets, just a stone's throw from Brady's. Passersby couldn't resist the inviting signs on both sides of the building which shouted, "Views of the War," "Stereographs," and "Hallotypes." His shop was above a book and stationery store, the name of which I've long forgotten, and I decided to ascend the stairs to see what he had on offer. He was doing a decent trade that day, which enabled me to blend in with the crowd as I walked around examining his wares. He had a good number of works from Gettysburg on display, including the one of the Confederate soldier lying on his back in the crevasse. He had labeled it "The Home of a Rebel Sharpshooter." While I was taking a close look, Gardner came up behind me and said, "You must admit that this particular image does a tremendous job of sweeping the viewer into the drama and agony of conflict on a very personal level."

"That it does, Alex," I agreed. "I also have to say that I hope no one notices that the rifle is standard issue and not a Whitworth[82] or the like, which is what one would actually expect to find on a sniper." That caused him to get very close to the photograph and scrutinize it in a way that I doubt he had done until just now.

"You are just saying that as a competitor," he said, stepping back. "And besides, the Whitworth is a British gun. What would it be doing in the hands of a Confederate soldier?"

"I'm impressed that you would know it's British, Alex," I said. "In fact, Queen Vicky herself fired one during an opening

82 The Whitworth, considered the world's first sniper rifle, was a single shot .451 caliber muzzle loader, introduced in 1857 and manufactured through 1865. More than 13,000 were built. Shortly after berating his staff for taking cover from Confederate snipers that were more than 500 yards away ("They couldn't hit an elephant at that distance") Major General John Sedgwick would take a Whitworth round to the head and become one of the most senior Union officers killed in the Civil War. He died on May 9, 1864, at the Battle of Spotsylvania Court House.

ceremony for the new target range at Wimbledon a few years ago. They are supposedly accurate up to 800 yards and the rebels love them enough to risk running blockades to get them. If you are going to stage a photograph Alex, you really should do your homework. Given the number of people that will view this image, I can guarantee you that I won't be the only one that notices the rifle. At least you've had the good sense to place the other photograph of this same poor fallen soul and his gun on the opposite side of your shop." I was referring to a photograph he had titled "A Sharpshooter's Last Sleep," which we both knew was of the same dead soldier and the same rifle. It had been taken a few hours before this one and a hundred feet away, which I knew for fact since I had been there on both occasions. By this point in the conversation his face had turned a remarkable shade of crimson but, knowing I had witnessed it all, he had the good sense not to challenge my accusations.

Looking around conspiratorially, then leaning in closer, he said quietly, "Listen Jack, I think our job as photographers is to give the public a firsthand look at the horrors of war. Perhaps by doing so, in some small way we can contribute to the prevention of such conflict in the future. Is it really such a bad thing if we use a little artistic license to advance that cause?"

"I'm all for trying to end such insanity," I replied, "but where do you draw the line? Who decides the limits? What's to stop anyone from creating false images to incite violence instead of ending it?" Now I'll admit that I'm not qualified to take the high ground on any issue, but I was still angry about his leaving Brady and taking O'Sullivan, Gibson, and others with him. Not to mention helping himself to all last year's negatives. Whatever my motivation, I'd decided to make him sweat.

In a desperate attempt to win me over, he tried a different approach by saying, "If you make any allegations about this Jack, it'll hurt everyone in this business, including you and Brady."

"As you know, I'm not in this business Alex. I've joined it temporarily. But I do know that in my chosen industry of selling cotton, short shipping, delivering inferior quality, not paying vendors, or any number of other frauds would see me bankrupt at best, or earn me a bullet or knife at worst." Yes, I was getting wound up and pouring it on. But here's a tip if you ever find yourself in a similar situation. Take your victim right to the edge, then let them off the hook. You'll be surprised at what you can extract from them down the road.

"All that said, Alex," I continued with that strategy in mind, "I am going to keep my mouth shut. You and O'Sullivan have been good friends and colleagues, after all. And you've caught me in a charitable mood." With that, I abruptly turned and headed back down the stairs and into the street. I'd be surprised if Gardner didn't lose some sleep over the next few weeks, but I know he didn't learn a damn thing. A few months later when he returned to Gettysburg to hear Lincoln's address, he claimed he found the rifle in those photographs still in the crevasse. With the number of burial parties, gawkers, and souvenir hunters going over that area after the battle, the odds of that rifle still being there four days, let alone four months later, were the square root of zero. Hearing Gardner say that it had been finally caused me to say something to Brady about the entire incident, but I found myself shocked at his cavalier response. I had expected him to be incensed, but his dismissiveness caused me to wonder if he hadn't done something similar at some point. I never did witness anything of the sort with Brady or any of his teams but, for the record, I was not present at all his photo taking.

The remainder of the summer was reasonably quiet. Brady had decided to stay close to home and focus on selling the images we had taken over the past year, including those at Fredericksburg and Gettysburg. Following Lee's defeat at the latter, I read that he had submitted his resignation to Jeff Davis, only to have it declined. That was bad news for the Union, as Lee had proven to be the most competent commander the rebels had fielded thus far. And his successes were not over. He certainly put McClellan, Burnside, and most of the Union lot to shame.

While there were no major engagements during August, I took a personal interest in the Union bombardment of Fort Sumter that began on the 17th and would carry on for the remainder of the year. It had been more than two years since I had stood on that rock in Charleston Harbor, just a few miles away from Bailey Importers' offices. I wondered what was going through Dawson's mind as he heard the cannon fire in the distance every day. Farther west, on August 21, a Confederate guerilla force led by William Quantrill[83] conducted a raid into Lawrence, Kansas. They proceeded to slaughter more than 150 men and boys, most of whom were unarmed. I only mention this because the bloodthirsty James brothers, Frank, and Jesse, were with Quantrill at the time, and I would have the misfortune of getting to know them both years later. The raid was the Confederate's retribution for attacks that abolitionist Kansas "Jayhawkers" or "Red Legs" had been making upon towns like Osceola in Western Missouri for years. John Brown himself had been involved in these border wars (on the Jayhawker side) during the late 1850's, before leading his own raid on Harpers Ferry and hanging for it in late 1859.

Major action returned in September, with the Battle of

---

83 William Clark Quantrill was born in Ohio in 1837. After a brief career as a schoolteacher, in 1860 he joined a band of ruffians who earned a living stealing cattle and capturing runaway slaves. By late 1861 he had formed his own group of men that would come to include the James brothers, Cole Younger and Bloody Bill Anderson, all accomplished Confederate guerillas, and murderers. Although Lee surrendered to Grant on April 9, 1865, Quantrill was still fighting a month later when he was mortally wounded in Kentucky. He died in Louisville, Kentucky, on June 6, 1865.

Chickamauga taking place in northern Georgia on the 19th and 20th. As it was with the Lawrence Massacre, that fight was largely left to sketch artists to create imagery for a news-hungry public. Being 600 miles southwest of Washington, Chickamauga was too distant a slog for us to have sent any photographers there even if Brady had been up for it. Had we been present, we would only have witnessed more of the same in my ever more calloused opinion of battle scenes. The twisted bodies and dead horses were losing their shock value, but we'd certainly have seen plenty more there. Almost 35,000 killed, captured, wounded, or missing on both sides, which was 28 percent of the combined forces on the field of 125,000. What drives men into battle when they know that one in four of them will fall? While the casualty count at Gettysburg was higher than it was at Chickamauga, it was only because the number of combatants was also greater. The casualty rate was about the same in both engagements, so by this point in the war the men on both sides had a good idea of what awaited them when they rose to meet their enemy. While Chickamauga was considered a tactical victory for the Confederates, ten of their Generals were either killed or wounded, and Union forces managed to retreat unmolested to Chattanooga, Tennessee.

Staying in Washington that summer had other benefits for me, despite the oppressive heat and humidity. I managed to see Anna on a couple of occasions, and she stayed with me at the National Hotel at 6th and Pennsylvania on both occasions. I had temporarily moved to the National to escape the noise and filth emanating from a construction site across 10th Street from my room at the Petersen House. The First Baptist Church of Washington had been acquired by John T. Ford in 1861 and converted into a theatre called Ford's Athenaeum. The Athenaeum had burned down the following year and Ford was in the process of rebuilding. He planned to reopen in November as Ford's Theatre and, judging from the long, noisy hours his workmen were putting in, they must have been behind schedule.

I was getting a little stir crazy by October though and managed to convince Brady to allow me to join him on a trip to New York City. My father had written a few weeks before saying that he planned to come to Washington and, given his prior comments about wanting to meet our Union buyers, I thought it wise to intercept him in New York City. Brady's objective was to take photographs of the visiting Russian Navy[84]. Several of their ships had begun arriving in September, led by the frigates Alexander Nevski and the *Peresviet*. Within three weeks, they had been joined by the *Variag*, *Vitiaz*, *Almaz* and *Osliaba*. New Yorkers and the North in general viewed their visit as a nod of support for the Union, coming from a country that was having its own issues with rebels in Poland. Britain and France had sided with the Poles in the conflict and were horrified when the Russians were so warmly welcomed in New York. U.S. Secretary of the Navy Gideon Wells wrote his Russian counterpart, "The Department is so much gratified to learn that a squadron of Russian war vessels is at present off the harbor of New York, with the intention, it is supposed, of visiting that city. The presence in our waters of a squadron belonging to His Imperial Majesty's Navy cannot but be a source of pleasure and happiness to our countrymen. I beg that you will make known to the Admiral in command that the facilities of the Brooklyn navy yard are at his disposal for any repairs that the vessels of his squadron need, and that any other required assistance will be gladly extended."

The Russians were welcomed by every level of New York society and feted with dances, receptions, and even a parade down

84 Russia's "Atlantic Squadron" arrived in New York City beginning on September 24, 1863, and they remained for a couple of months.

Broadway where women swooned over their impressive uniforms. At one point early in the visit, the band on the Nevski answered the cheers of New Yorkers with an awkward rendition of "Yankee Doodle," although their bumbling was ignored by onlookers who just appreciated they had made the effort. Brady managed to get quite a few excellent images, both on and off the ships. The size and majesty of the Nevski in particular was striking. A reporter from *Harper's Weekly* (which published several artist's rendering of the ships and related festivities), said when speaking of the Nevski, "A lady with the most immaculate skirts and kid gloves can move anywhere, on deck or below, without danger of soiling either, so perfectly clean everything about the ship is kept." While standing on her impressive decks I found myself thinking about the rebel submarine CSS Hunley, which had sunk on October 15th for the second time in her short existence. This time she took her inventor, Horace Lawson Hunley, down with her. I couldn't help but wonder why anyone would think that these absurd little vessels would ever amount to anything but curiosities. While the CSS Hunley would be raised again to fight another day, Hunley himself would of course not.

I had two meetings with my father during this visit to New York, both of which were exasperating. Although initially grateful to get back to our pre-war sales levels, he hadn't stayed satisfied for long. He spoke incessantly about the insatiable demand for cotton in Britain and worried that Egyptian cotton would come to be permanently accepted as a viable alternative. He said we could sell far more than we were, and just couldn't get it through his head that a shortage of supply from the plantations was the problem, not a lack of desire by me or the Union to expand our volumes. The more my father prattled on, the more relieved I was that I had met him here and he had not come all the way down to Washington. On October 3, Lincoln had issued a proclamation declaring that the last Thursday in November would henceforth be a day of national thanksgiving, but my personal thanksgiving had come early. The mess that my father would have made meeting with Meigs or Thomas or, God forbid, Pinkerton, caused me to shudder.

The rest of my time in the city was less trying, although my liver took a beating. Good God those Russians can drink. At first, I figured their vodka mustn't be as intoxicating as American whiskey, but when the *Nevski's* Captain, Mikhail Yakovlevich Federovsky, insisted I try it, then challenged me to keep up with him, I was able to put that theory to rest. It was a fortunate thing that Czar Alexander II's name was pronounceable, as the bulk of the formal toasts were to him. Had we been toasting the Captain, I'm sure that most Anglo tongues would have been hopelessly tied even before the first drink. With a few vodkas on board, I just took to calling him Captain Mike and he didn't seem to mind. Toward the end of the month, I decided I'd had enough and took the train back down to Washington while Brady remained to work in the New York studio.

Chapter 26

THE FIRST SIGN OF TROUBLE

*B*ack in Washington, I was relieved when I saw that the work on Ford's Theatre was complete. The absence of construction noise on 10ᵗʰ Street made the Petersen House livable again. Nevertheless, I moved over to the Willard for a couple of nights after Anna obtained tickets to see a play called "The Marble Heart". We saw it together at Ford's on their opening night, November 9, 1863. She arrived in the city on the 8ᵗʰ, and so began an unusual couple of evenings that would mark the beginning of a particularly difficult period in our relationship.

We were walking through the lobby of the Willard on our way to the Round Robin for dinner early in the evening of the 8ᵗʰ when we ran into Jack Beam. He seemed genuinely happy to see me and, after introducing him to Anna, he insisted that we join him in the dining room.

"I'm being hosted by Major Joseph Willard," Beam informed us before taking us to his table. "He runs this hotel with his brother Henry, and, fortunately for me, they enjoy my Early Times bourbon. And they buy a lot of it."

"Well then, you'll be happy to hear that I have been doing my part to deplete their inventory over the past couple of years,"

I said, which earned a chuckle from him. When we arrived at his table, I did a double take when I saw that Major Willard's other dinner guest was Antonia Ford. I had last seen Miss Ford with John Surratt Junior two years ago in a more modest setting at the Star Saloon. Her words then plus Pinkerton's accusations made it clear that she was a Confederate spy. I vaguely recalled reading something recently about her arrest this past spring for involvement in Confederate Colonel John Mosby's capture of dozens of Union soldiers and horses. She'd been arrested in Fairfax, Virginia, with thousands of dollars in Confederate currency found in her house, along with a letter from Confederate General J. E. B. Stuart anointing her an aid-de-camp, or some such. The whole episode had only stuck in my mind because it was reported that when he learned that one of the Union soldiers captured by Mosby was General Edwin Stoughton[85], Lincoln remarked that while a General could easily be replaced, "those horses cost $125 apiece!"

As we took our seats, Anna whispered in my ear, "Don't say anything. Pretend you've never met her." That was the first time I realized that Anna must be more involved in her brother's activities than she let on. Beam spent the next few minutes recounting to everyone how he and I first met on a train just before the war began, which gave me a few moments to gather my thoughts. He asked if his introduction to Mathew Brady had ever come to anything, and I was able to prattle on about my adventures with him and how we had been able to chronicle some important moments of the war through photography. By this point I thought I was in

85 Edwin H. Stoughton was born in Chester, Vermont in 1838. He graduated from the U.S. Military Academy in 1859. Stoughton was reportedly disliked by his men and ridiculed over his capture by Mosby. Although he saw action in the Peninsular Campaign, his appointment as a Brigadier General was never confirmed, and he resigned from the U.S. Army in 1863. He died of tuberculosis in 1868.

Ford's Theatre, Courtesy of the Library of Congress, LC-DIG-ppmsca-23872

the clear, but he then asked about my cotton business. Before I could say anything, I received a gentle kick in the shins under the table from Anna. Of course she and Miss Ford knew about the delivery to Norfolk, and I'm sure she didn't want that mentioned. Although unlikely, it was possible that Willard knew about my current arrangement with the Union and I in turn wanted no mention of that. What I did want was to drop the topic as soon as possible and so, hoping to close it off, said, "It's been tough with the war and blockades, so that's all been pretty much on hold for the moment."

"Sorry to hear that, Bailey," said Beam. "The war has been tough in my business as well, although I am very fortunate to have kept good customers like the Willard Hotel. With the blockade down south, I would have thought you could take advantage of your being in Washington to sell cotton up here." I ignored this and hoped I would make everyone else forget it by asking him if, speaking of commodities, he was having any trouble sourcing corn, rye, and barley. That led to a brief discussion about the current state of farming, during which Anna and Miss Ford excused themselves to go to the ladies' room. As soon as they were out of earshot, Willard launched into a bizarre monologue about how Antonia had seen the light and sworn an oath to the Union. I must have looked a little puzzled because he concluded with, "I only bring all that up in case you'd seen her mentioned in the papers." I lied saying I hadn't, mumbled something trite about her seeming to be nice, and managed to resist making a petty comment about what looked to me like a 20-year age difference between the two of them. I was relieved when dinner ended, and we started excusing ourselves although, given my druthers, I would have loved to have had a drink or three alone with Beam in the Round Robin. When we got to our room, it was clear that Beam's remark about selling cotton in Washington had not gone unnoticed by Anna. She asked some pointed questions, and I responded by reminding her that I had indeed sold cotton to the Union with the full knowledge that it would be hijacked by the Confederacy. I also mentioned that I was currently selling to the Confederate Army, leaving out the key detail that it was actually to men dressed in Confederate uniforms. It would have been extremely unlikely that she would be able to dig into that, but I figured I would say something, just in case. I thought I put her suspicions to rest, but apparently I wasn't convincing enough to avoid a lonely night on the opposite side of the bed. She had warmed up some by the next day, although we regressed again that evening at Ford's Theatre.

During the intermission as we were admiring the venue from our seats, we both happened to look up to our right toward the presidential box. Lincoln was seated there with Mary Todd's sister. He happened to look our way at the same moment and gave me a wave and a nod. Anna immediately turned on me and hissed, "Don't tell me you know that Illinois Ape?[86]"

"What? No, not really. Why would you say that?" I said defensively.

"Because he just waved at you!" she said.

"He's a politician," I replied. "They always wave in everyone's general direction hoping that people will feel a connection they'll remember at the ballot box. It's standard practice."

"He was looking right at you," she countered. And the fact that most of the people around us had left their seats during the intermission to use the restroom or congregate in the lobby didn't help my argument.

"He's been by Brady's studio a few times to have his portrait taken," I said. "We've had a lot of politicians and generals come in for the same. I'm sure he recalls seeing me there." She may have bought that had the seeds of doubt not been planted by Beam the previous night, but I'll never know. I did know that I had a great deal of repair work ahead of me with her, but it couldn't begin with her in this frame of mind. Maybe she was doing it to get back at me, but my mood darkened over the remainder of the play as she made what I thought was an inappropriate number of comments about how handsome and elegant the lead actor was. He was John Wilkes Booth, whom we had seen perform earlier this year in Richard III. I made a mental note to avoid any of his performances in the future. We didn't talk much that night or the next morning before she left to return to Surrattsville.

---

86 The "Illinois Ape", "Stinkin' Lincoln", and "The Abolition Emperor" were examples of nicknames used by Lincoln detractors. Supporters preferred monikers such as "Honest Abe" and "The Sage of Springfield."

That next day I happened to mention the Ford's Theatre encounter with Lincoln to Brady, which prompted him to invite me to accompany him to Gettysburg on November 18 to witness the dedication of a cemetery the following day. Pennsylvania Governor Andrew Curtin had arranged that 17 acres be purchased there for a military cemetery where some 7,500 soldiers would be buried. Lincoln was invited to attend and "set apart these grounds to their sacred use by a few appropriate remarks." Brady had been vexed when Lincoln recently visited Alex Gardner's studio for a couple of portrait sessions, so perhaps he thought that having the two of us there might improve his odds of rekindling their friendship. Whatever Brady's logic, the net of it all meant me traveling with him and a couple apprentices to Gettysburg. We set up a camera on the morning of the 19th, but with more than 100,000 people in attendance, we faced the same problem we had when attempting to photograph battles. At any given moment, a significant percentage of the subjects were in motion, which resulted in blurry images. In the end, we made one somewhat workable photograph in which a hatless Lincoln is visible on the podium a few hours before he was to make his speech. Maybe it was his distance from the camera, or perhaps confusion around the fellow in the stovepipe hat to Lincoln's left that obviously isn't him but, whatever the case, I am surprised that no one has yet spotted him in that image. Despite what you might hear to the contrary, there is in fact a photograph of Lincoln at Gettysburg on the day of his address.

The formal program began with a band playing "Homage d'uns Heros," followed by a prayer from Reverend Thomas Stockton. Another band then played "Old Hundred", which was followed by a grueling, two-hour monologue delivered by Edward Everett. Everett was a politician, educator, pastor, and diplomat and none of these vocations is known for brevity, but this was a test of everyone's patience. When he finally wound down, a choir sang the hymn "Consecration Chant" just before Lincoln was introduced. The President began his now famous remarks: "Four score and seven years ago our fathers brought forth on this Continent a new nation, conceived in liberty, and dedicated to the proposition that all men are created equal…," but that was all I heard before Brady began whispering in my ear. In his defense, he probably thought that we were at the beginning of another two-hour marathon, but he chose that moment to point out that Gardner and his crew were standing fifty feet away and he made a couple of brief, uncharacteristically disparaging remarks about Gardner that were variations on "trying to steal Lincoln from us like he had stolen O'Sullivan and the rest." But his babbling was enough that I missed the remainder of Lincoln's speech. After just two hundred and seventy-one words contained in ten sentences, it was over. There were then a few moments of utter silence followed by scattered applause that detractors say reflected the audience's disappointment and disapproval. Supporters would counter that listeners were just showing reverence and respect, but I think that both sides had it wrong. Judging from those around me, people were simply caught off guard that it was all over in two minutes, especially on the heels of Everett's rambling. The *Daily National Republican* reprinted the entirety of Lincoln's speech on page 2 of its November 20, 1863, edition. The text was interspersed with five mentions of applause plus one of "long continued applause" at its conclusion. That may have been a little generous, but I will say that although the speech has since become known as one of the greatest ever, it admittedly didn't seem so at the time. I'll add that Lincoln did not look well that day, so Brady and I decided that trying to get to see him would be a lost cause. We packed up and took the train the 80 miles back down to Washington that evening.

During the couple of weeks before and after my excursion to Gettysburg, battle lines were again being drawn in the vicinity of Chattanooga, Tennessee. General Grant, freshly promoted to lead all Union forces in the West, was preparing to avenge Union General Rosecrans' defeat in the Battle of Chickamauga during September and break Rosecrans' besieged forces out of Chattanooga. Typical of the action-oriented Grant, he relieved Rosecrans of command of the Army of the Cumberland when he learned that he was planning to withdraw from this strategically important city just 120 miles north of Atlanta. Rosecrans' replacement, Major General George Thomas, vowed to "hold the town till we starve." Fortunately for Thomas and his men, Grant's forces opened a supply line (dubbed the "Cracker Line"), which prevented their starvation from being necessary. Following a series of skirmishes and maneuvers in late October and early November, the opposing armies under Grant and Confederate General Braxton Bragg got down to serious business from November 23 to 25, 1863.

Monday, November 23 proved an easy victory for the Union, as 14,000 of Thomas's men overwhelmed 600 or so Confederates at Orchard Knob, just west of Chattanooga. On the 24th, Union General Joe Hooker gave Grant a second day of victory at Lookout Mountain, just southeast of Chattanooga. From there Hooker would drive east to form up alongside the rest of the Union army facing Bragg's army on Missionary Ridge, where most of the action would occur on November 25. Years later I visited both Missionary Ridge and Lookout Mountain and it wasn't until then that I could fully appreciate what stunning victories these were for the Union. From the latter, they say you can see seven states: Tennessee, Kentucky, North and South Carolina, Virginia, Georgia, and Alabama. That will tell you all you need to know about the advantages the rebels had in terms of elevation.

Fighting one's way across open fields is one thing, but doing the same up steep inclines is entirely another.

These three days gave Lincoln a very special day on November 26, 1863, the first federally recognized Thanksgiving. But in pursuit of retreating Confederates on Friday the 27th, the Union army was halted by Confederate General Patrick Cleburne's forces about 14 miles southwest of Missionary Ridge at Ringgold Gap, Georgia, thus ending Grant's otherwise successful Chattanooga campaign. Although none of Brady's men had been there to see any of it, we would soon meet Grant in the Washington Studio.

Chapter 27

EARLY 1864

*T*he approach of Christmas and the New Year brought a sense of melancholy to soldiers on both sides of the war as their thoughts turned to family and what they were missing at home. I must admit to feeling a sense of sadness myself, although certainly not because I longed to be with family. Three letters to Anna in December and early January had all gone unanswered. Holiday decorations around Washington and the traditional appearance of Thomas Nast's Christmas drawings in *Harper's Weekly* had likely influenced my decision to reach out to her for the first time since that uncomfortable evening at the grand reopening of Ford's Theatre in early November. I hoped that she was simply too distracted trying to salvage the Surratt family's beleaguered finances to respond but feared that her growing Southern sympathies had caused her to have second thoughts about our relationship. I was proud of myself for not turning to copious amounts of bourbon and frequent visits to houses of ill repute as I normally might have when feeling such stress.

Things began to pick up at the studio on Friday, January 8, however, when Lincoln visited and had four photographs taken by Brady himself. With the President's two sittings at Gardner's studio during the latter half of 1863 still fresh in his mind, Brady couldn't have been happier. He observed that this was surely a sign that Lincoln had come back into the fold, but I suspected that the fact that 1864 was an election year had Lincoln looking to be photographed at any time and by anyone he could. A month later, on February 9, Lincoln was back, and he sat for several photos that were taken by Anthony Berger. Mrs. Lincoln and son, Tad, joined us part-way through the sitting, and their presence made possible one of the two very memorable photographs from that day. The first was an unusually informal shot of Lincoln seated in a chair with Tad standing beside him and to his left. Both are looking down at a book that is open on Lincoln's lap, and Lincoln is wearing a pair of small reading glasses. The second was a profile that I doubt that any of us thought at the time would amount to much. Then in 1866 it appeared on the 15-cent stamp, and I recognized it again last year on the new 1909 penny. I've lost track of Berger, but, wherever he is, I hope he knows that his work from that day has been reproduced millions of times.

The excitement continued on March 8 when Brady and I joined a large contingent of well-wishers at the train station who had come to welcome Ulysses S. Grant, "the hero of the Mississippi and Lookout Mountain," to Washington. Grant had been summoned to the White House to be promoted to Lieutenant General and commander of all the Union's armies. By this time, Brady had made sure that the seemingly unending flow of new Union generals all came through his studio for portraits, and he wasted no time in proposing the same to Grant. He and I were among the first to shake Grant's hand when he got off the train, and Brady was quick to both invite him to come by for photographs and to recommend that he stay at the Willard Hotel. I heard a day or two later that when Grant and his 14-year-old son checked in there they were cheered heartily by Army officers in the lobby. He only stayed in town for a few days before he traveled west again to meet with Sherman and plan the Union's next moves. General Sherman had been serving under Grant prior to Shiloh in 1862 and was now promoted to Grant's former position of commander of the Army of the Tennessee. I, of course, met Sherman as a Colonel just prior to Bull Run in 1861, when he rescued me from Dr. Samuel Crawford in a tavern in the Black Horse Tavern in Centerville. Crawford had recognized me from my visit to Fort Sumter a day before it was shelled by the rebels, and he was loudly accusing me of being a traitor in front of dozens of Union officers. In an effort to make conversation, I told Grant that story when we were taking his portraits, but I could tell by the look on Brady's face that he disapproved. He started to scold me for it after Grant left but backed down when I asked him how developing a personal relationship with the new head of all the armies of the Union could hurt us.

Grant being at the Willard rekindled thoughts about Anna that I had been suppressing since the beginning of the year. Looking for a distraction, I enthusiastically agreed to travel to Virginia in mid-May on Brady's behalf with Alexander Gardner's brother James and military photographer A. J.

Lincoln and Tad, Courtesy of the Library of Congress, LC-USZ62-8117

Russell. We hadn't been in the field for months, and our competitors Tim O'Sullivan and Alex Gardner were gaining some notoriety with recent photographs of 50,000 Union soldiers and their gear crossing the Rapidan River in Virginia. Those troops were destined for the Battle of the Wilderness (May 5 to 7) and the Battle of Spotsylvania Courthouse (May 9 to 21), neither of which would be visited by Alex Gardner or Brady photographers. James Gardner, Russell, a couple of assistants, and I hitched a ride on a Union supply boat and sailed once again down the Potomac along a route that was identical to the one I had taken in December 1862 on my way to Fredericksburg. On this occasion, we sailed to Potomac Creek and offloaded on the south shore at a landing called Belle Plain.

Belle Plain was a bustling terminus, with an endless stream of supplies coming down from the north and equally robust traffic, primarily comprised of Union wounded and Confederate prisoners, heading back upriver. We stayed for a couple of days and took pictures of the docks, soldiers, prisoners, camps, and the like, before moving on to revisit Fredericksburg. There we took more photographs of the old battlefields of 1862 and 1863, as well as various images of prisoners and burial parties. With reports of heavy fighting still raging in nearby Spotsylvania and much farther south in Louisiana's Red River Campaign, I was grateful to have found plenty to keep us credibly occupied in safer territory. I stuck to that strategy by moving our team down the Rappahannock River to a staging area called Port Royal, even as our competitors O'Sullivan followed the vanguard of Grant's army south toward Richmond. I'd enjoyed some good fortune at Port Royal, South Carolina, almost exactly a year prior, which was part of the appeal of going to its namesake in Virginia. That said, its main attraction in my mind was the fact that it was 50 miles north of Richmond, Grant's advance, and an abundance of flying lead. Booth would also pass this way in less than a year, but that's another story.

After frittering away as much time as I could making images here, we set off south again to White House Landing, where we had taken pictures during the Peninsular Campaign in May of 1862. During that campaign Robert E. Lee's wife, Mary Anna Custis Lee, had become trapped at White House Landing behind Union lines. Learning this, Union General George McClellan had graciously provided her safe passage out. Mary married her now famous husband in 1831, but she held some notoriety in her own right as the daughter of George Washington Parke Custis, a grandson (through her first marriage) to Martha Washington. As we were camped here, I again found myself thinking about all the interconnections and coincidences that seemed to arise at every turn in this war. I was also thinking that my choice of coming to this location was a fortuitous one, because horrific fighting raged just 20 miles to the west at Cold Harbor. At the risk of being labeled (correctly) a self-serving cynic, there really was no point in going toward battle motion in Cold Harbor that we couldn't photograph. And nor were we likely to come across any carnage there that would be unique to anything we hadn't already documented. The fact that we were safely out of range here was just a bonus. And, speaking of carnage, between Cold Harbor, Spotsylvania, and the Battle of the Wilderness (collectively known as the "Overland Campaign"), almost 90,000 casualties, including 10,000 dead, would be added to the grim tally from the war to date.

We took several panoramic photographs in and around White House Landing, including many of Confederate prisoners. Brady joined us on June 10 and, to his credit, redirected our efforts toward more individual and group portraits, none more iconic than the one of Grant leaning against a tree in front of his command tent. I enjoyed being around Grant, and not because of his alleged love of the bottle. I saw him drink on occasion, but never witnessed any of the excessiveness that he has been accused of more than once. He just seemed at ease around people from every level, from enlisted men to the President. Although brutally determined, he didn't take himself too seriously and was easy to talk to. Maybe his prior business failures and, until recently, lackluster career had removed the arrogance that plagued some of his predecessors (and the current generals, come to that).

After we took the tree photograph, he approached me and said,

"By the way, Bailey, I told Sherman that we'd met, and we shared a chuckle over your encounter in Centerville. I'd love to see that letter from the President that you showed to him then."

"And I would love to show it to you, sir," I responded, "except it was washed clean during an unplanned swim I took off Norfolk in the winter of 1862. Good thing too, as it turned out, otherwise it might have been discovered when I was stripped searched along the Combahee a year ago." As always, a little truth seasoned with some key omissions had its intended effect.

"This just gets more and more interesting, Bailey," he said. "Sounds like you should write a book. Pinkerton told me that you were an interesting character. Please, do tell!"

Fortunately, one of Grant's aides came over at that moment and insisted he go back into the headquarters tent for a meeting, otherwise I might have revealed information that was best kept to myself. I'd like to think that our connection had played a role when Grant named Brady the official photographer of his command but, truth be told, Brady's own talents and the connections he had cultivated with Lincoln, Pinkerton, Burnside, and the like should get full credit. We took other photographs during this time of General Meade, Winfield Scott Hancock, Assistant Secretary of war Charles Dana, and so on, but we probably spent the most time with General Ambrose Burnside. Brady was well acquainted with Burnside from Bull Run, Antietam, and Tom Thumb's wedding, and they enjoyed a camaraderie that was sufficient to allow Brady to insert himself into a couple of the photographs we took of him. What struck me about most of the images we took of all these men at that time though, was the contrast between their arrogant poses and the thousands that lay dead, dying, or wounded from the Overland campaign of the past few weeks. How they reconciled such madness escaped me. After a couple of days of this, we followed the Union army south another 50 miles to Weyanoke Point, where we took photographs of Union troops crossing the James River to the south and observed O'Sullivan and his crew doing the same. In fact, we ended up traveling with O'Sullivan and his team for 20 miles west toward Petersburg, where Grant's army was attempting to cut off the supply lines heading north from there to Richmond. Lee's "Dimmock Line" defensive works there put a stop to their plans, however, and both sides settled in for what would become a 10-month siege.

With Brady remaining in the field, it made little sense for me to linger and so, following the pattern we had established on earlier occasions, I eagerly accepted his request that I make my way back to Washington with the work we had completed over the past few weeks. Truth was, I had decided somewhere along the way to take the bull by the horns, write Anna and tell her I was coming her way on business in the hope she would agree to see me. I figured I would go back to Washington, deposit our plates, then proceed down to Surrattsville even if I didn't hear back from her. Showing up unannounced would be rude, but I wasn't going to be discouraged by silence. While I was packing, Brady and our competitor O'Sullivan were both setting up to take photographs of the imminent hanging of a black Union soldier, William Johnson. Johnson had been convicted of assaulting a white women at New Kent Courthouse earlier in the month, and the Union had decided to make a statement for all to see. The gallows was set up so it could be seen from the Confederate lines, and a good number of Union calvary and infantry were assembled as witnesses. In spite of a Confederate artillery shell landing at almost the exact moment Johnson dropped, we managed to get a photograph of him swinging. But that perfectly timed shell killed an unfortunate 24-year-old, Sergeant Major George Polley. Ironically, Polley's regiment's term of enlistment had ended the previous day, and they were set to head home to Massachusetts. As I said after Fort Sumter, needless waste, and damnable chance. I, on the other hand, was able to head home in one piece. At Weyanoke Point, I hitched a ride on a boat with the help of a note from Grant and again traveled the familiar waters of the Chesapeake and Potomac between Norfolk and Washington.

Although I didn't know it at the time, at some point during our journey across those waters we passed the USS Baltimore heading south. On board that steamer were President Lincoln and his son Tad. Their destination was City Point, Virginia, at the junction of the James and Appomattox rivers, where Lincoln planned to meet with Grant and make a quick, morale boosting visit with the troops. Although he was just a few miles away at his Field Quarters near Petersburg at the time, Brady never saw Lincoln or took any photographs of the event. A shame, as I read later that Lincoln took a highly emotional ride among black troops there, with tears shed on both sides. Brady and the team arrived in City Point after Lincoln's departure, and they managed to get several photographs of Grant and his staff. Brady appears off to the left in one of them, with eleven of Grant's staff in front of a cabin. In it, and perhaps in a nod to Lincoln, Brady is wearing a stovepipe hat instead of his customary straw.

As luck would have it, on my way back up the Potomac we put in at Fort Foote, Maryland, before proceeding the remaining 15 miles to Washington. I was tempted to disembark right then and there and make my way the ten miles east to Surrattsville, but the lack of a horse and the fragile photographic plates I was responsible for returning to the studio dictated otherwise. Instead, the brief stop gave me the opportunity to post another letter to Anna.

Chapter 28

A Close Call

*A*s I was making this journey back up to Washington, General Robert E. Lee had ordered his "Bad Old Man", Confederate General Jubal Early[87], to take his army up the Shenandoah Valley, harass any Union troops he found there and threaten cities along the way. The hope was that such an action would compel Grant to reduce the forces he currently had laying siege to Petersburg and Richmond. Although we didn't know it at the time, this was to be the Confederacy's final foray into Union territory, and the first time any enemy force had entered Washington since the British had done so during the War of 1812. It would also be the first of three occasions when Lincoln would attract rebel gunfire in the coming nine months. I'm embarrassed to say now that in two of those instances, my gun was involved.

---

87 Jubal Anderson Early was born in Virginia in 1816. He graduated from the U.S. Military Academy in 1837 and resigned the U.S. Army in 1861 to join the C.S.A., where he would eventually attain the rank of Lieutenant General. Early saw much action in the Civil War, including the First Bull Run, Williamsburg, Malvern Hill, Antietam, Fredericksburg, Chancellorsville, Gettysburg, and the Overland Campaign. His other nicknames included "Old Jube" and "Old Jubilee". Early died in 1894.

The heat and humidity in Washington during July of 1864 was brutal. I spent the first week of that month supervising the reproduction and pricing of the photographs I had brought back from Belle Plain, Fredericksburg, Port Royal, and so on, and arranging to have copies displayed and available for sale in both the Washington and New York studios. On Friday, July 4, I wandered over to the South Grounds of the White House to watch Lincoln play host at a picnic for Black schools and churches and other religious groups. It was a nice show of tolerance and inclusion, although I recall that *Harper's* illustration of the event only depicted white faces.

Early the following week I had just settled in to order dinner at the Star, when in walked John Surratt Jr. He sat down at my table and said, "Evening, Jack. I received your letter and, since I was in town anyway, decided to respond in person."

"You mean the letter I sent to Anna?" I asked.

"Well, yes," he answered. "Being a postmaster has its advantages."

"I take it she hasn't read it then?" I asked testily.

"No, she hasn't. The fact is Jack, she's very upset with you, and it's only been recently that she has seemed to be in better spirits. I thought it best to spare her a relapse," he said.

"Last time I checked John, interfering with the U.S. mail was a felony," I observed.

"Probably the least of my crimes of late," he responded. "But, since finding myself the man of the house, I feel responsible for the happiness of my sister and mother. Fact is, Anna believes that you may be a traitor to our cause."

"Based on what?" I asked. Make sure you know what you are up against before putting together your denials, I always say.

"Based on your cozy relationship with that swine Lincoln," he hissed.

"Peter Taltavull," I said.

"What does he have to do with anything?" Surratt asked.

"He waved at you when you came in. And you waved back, tipped your hat, and smiled."

"So what," he said. "He owns this place, I've been here several times before and have exchanged words with him, which you have witnessed."

"I try to avoid talking politics in saloons," I said, "but I know Peter well enough to be fairly certain that he'll be voting Republican this November. He supports Lincoln."

"What's your point?" Surratt responded.

"My point," I said, "is that Anna saw Lincoln wave to me at Ford's Theatre, and I nodded back. I met him on more than one occasion when he came into Brady's studio for portraits. Same with Grant, McClellan, and a few others. None of that makes me a Unionist. And I suspect that Anna's concerns are based entirely on that exchange of waves between Lincoln and I at Ford's last November. And, by the way, Brady has also done portraits of Jefferson Davis," I tossed in for good measure. I didn't point out that the Davis work was done before the war, when he was a senator. And long before I joined Brady's team.

"Entirely different," Surratt responded, although I sensed some of the wind had leaked out of his sails.

"I think it's exactly the same, but why don't we order some food and drink, and you can explain to me why you believe that it isn't," I invited.

Surratt changed the topic for a time, no doubt to give himself time to think about how to defend his position. But, in the end, he couldn't. Late in the conversation though he said, "Okay Jack, I see your point. But why don't you accompany me on an errand here in Washington later this week to prove your allegiance?"

"If this is about another cotton shipment, I am currently selling everything I can get my hands on to the Confederacy. We deliver it all down on the Combahee," I said. I doubted that he had the connections to check but, if he did, this story would hold. We were, in fact, delivering to men in Confederate uniforms.

"Nothing to do with cotton," he answered. "But, if you help me out, I promise to pass your letter on to Anna along with my support of you."

I didn't like the sound of that, but love will make you accept risks that you likely wouldn't otherwise take. Besides, this "errand," as John called it, was here in Washington, not Port Tobacco, Norfolk, or the like. How bad could it be? We agreed to meet again on Friday, July 11 at the main gates of the Prospect Hill Cemetery[88], just a couple of miles northeast of the Petersen House.

As the week progressed, concerns in the city regarding General Early's advances toward us were beginning to evolve into mild panic. Early's army had battled Union troops at Harpers Ferry and Maryland Heights at the start of the month and he had gone on to extort money from the residents of Hagerstown and Frederick in exchange for agreeing not to ransack their towns. Frederick lay only 50 miles north of Washington, and reports suggested that Early's army was now moving in our direction. Although Grant sent two divisions up from Virginia to help reinforce the city, by any definition, it remained only lightly defended.

In describing the situation in Washington, journalist Noah Brooks wrote, "The city is in a ferment; men are marching to and fro; ablebodied citizens are gobbled up and put in the District militia; refugees come flying in from the country, bringing their household goods with them; nobody is permitted to go out on the Maryland roads without a pass, and at every turn an inquiring newspaper

88 The German Evangelical Church Society bought the land and established Prospect Hill Cemetery (also known as the German Cemetery) for Concordia Church in 1858. It sits on high ground with views of the U.S. Capitol and the Washington Monument.

correspondent is met by some valiant in shoulder straps, pompous and big with importance, in the rear of all danger, with 'By what authority are you here, sir?'" As to the able-bodied citizens being gobbled up for militia, I heard later that even Quartermaster Meigs took charge of an "emergency division" of the army, that was comprised largely of federal employees. Given these ad hoc and desperate recruiting efforts, I decided that it was probably safer that I be on the move in any case.

When I met Surratt on the morning of the 11th, I was packing two concealed Coopers, along with my flask, spy glass, some jerked beef, and a respectable supply of cheroots. As we set out from the Prospect Hill Cemetery heading north, it soon became clear why Surratt was so keen to have me along. As Brooks had pointed out, there was no shortage of Union troops moving about, and we were asked for identification more than once. On each of these occasions my carte de visites was sufficient to allow us to continue and for Surratt to avoid questioning, even though we were not carrying any photographic equipment. I'm not sure what he or I would have said had John Jr. been asked for identification, but I suppose I would have said "he's with me" and hoped for the best. I was just glad it never came to that. Surratt deflected my occasional questions about where we were going, but I was relieved when we swung east and away from Lincoln's Cottage on the grounds of the Old Soldiers Home[89]. We also stayed east of Forts Totten and Slocum, although once north of those we veered northwest toward Piney Branch Road and Fort Stevens. In retelling this now it sounds like we were covering a lot of ground, but

---

89 Old Soldier's Home was established in 1851 in part with the $150,000 paid to General Winfield Scott by the Mexican Government for his agreeing not to sack Mexico City in the Mexican-American War, 1846 to 1848. In addition to Scott, other notables serving in that War included Robert E. Lee, Ulysses S. Grant, and Jefferson Davis.

it was less than three miles from Prospect Hill Cemetery to Fort Totten and only another two from there to Fort Stevens. And these "forts" were better described as earthwork fortifications, typically containing a dozen or so cannons behind thick, high walls. Forts Totten, Slocum, and Stevens were three of seventy or so such installations encircling Washington at the time.

After crossing Piney Branch Road, we began to hear the unmistakable sounds of skirmishing as Confederate troops worked their way south from Silver Springs, Maryland, which lay about two miles north of Fort Stevens. After crossing Seventh Street Road heading west toward the Georgetown Pike, we were confronted by forward units of Early's troops. Seeing Surratt's confident demeanor, I resisted the temptation to turn and bolt south. Not that I would have gotten far since a few members of one of Brigadier General John McCausland's Virginia Cavalry Regiments had already come up behind us. As he presented paperwork that he pulled from under his saddle blanket, Surratt demanded to be taken to McCausland's commanding officer, Major General Robert Ransom[90]. While we were being taken to Ransom, I moved up alongside Surratt's horse and quietly asked him what the hell he would have done if we'd been searched back in Washington by Union troops, and they had discovered whatever it was that he had just handed these men. I imagined it was some kind of letter like the one Lincoln had given me, but never saw it. He brushed me off by saying it was a moot point since it hadn't been found, and that he was confident that I would have talked us out of trouble if it had been. Given my fatigue from the

90 Robert Ransom Jr. was born in North Carolina in 1828. He graduated from the U.S. Military Academy in 1850 and resigned his Captain's commission in the U.S. Army in 1861 to join the C.S.A., where he would eventually attain the rank of Major General. Ransom participated in Civil War battles at Harpers Ferry, Antietam, and Fredericksburg. He died in 1892.

heat and humidity and the hundreds of Confederate soldiers now moving around us, I decided to drop the subject and fall back into line.

After going a quarter mile or so north toward Silver Spring, we came upon a heavier concentration of cavalry units and Ransom's makeshift headquarters. A senior officer walked out to greet us and was given Surratt's letter by one of our escorts. "Which one of you is John Surratt," he asked after reading it.

"That'd be me," John responded.

"And who might this be then?" the officer asked, pointing at me.

"Jack Bailey," answered Surratt, before I could say anything. "He's also my escort though the Union's troops and, if he had his way, my future brother-in-law." This last bit was a real surprise. I took it as an indication that I might have passed whatever test Surratt had put me through in his mind but, more importantly, it seemed to elevate my stature with the rebels. I doubt that this rabble would have had any trouble stringing up someone they thought was a Unionist, especially one found in their camp. Surratt was invited over to an area under some trees where a group of officers were conferring, while I was told to cool my heels nearby. I made sure that my horse (again borrowed from Brady) got some water, then settled in under a tree and lit a cheroot. Sometime later Surratt came back and told me that his job was done, but that we had been invited to observe the festivities that were about to unfold.

"What festivities?" I asked, though it was all too obvious that the citizens of Washington were about to have their worst fears realized—a Confederate attack on the capitol. Even from our position, the unfinished Capitol Dome was visible to the south.

"The C.S.A. is about to enter Washington and give that bastard Lincoln his due," responded Surratt. "I just delivered General

Ransom my verbal assessment on the pathetic state of the city's defenses. That drunkard Grant has all his men down in Virginia and that mistake is about to cost him dearly."

I'd guessed as much about Surratt's mission when he was walking over to meet Ransom and his staff. What neither of us knew though was that reinforcements sent by Grant had already begun to arrive at the Sixth Street docks in Washington, less than ten miles to our south, where they would soon be greeted by Lincoln himself. Surratt continued to prattle on about justice finally having its day, all the while twirling one or the other side of his lengthy moustache. One of Ransom's men eventually came over and invited us to join them for a meal and we gladly accepted.

On most of the occasions that I have found myself among men about to go into battle, the fear is palpable. Some cope through excessive chatter, others with silent thought and prayer and some through music. This camp was different. Perhaps they were emboldened by the liquor they had liberated in Silver Spring and points farther north over the few days, or maybe they were intoxicated by their recent raids on Harpers Ferry, Hagerstown, and Frederick. But I suspect it was mostly the fact that these men knew that Washington was vulnerable, and they could sense that an enormous victory was within their grasp. Whatever the case, almost everyone around us was in high spirits. As Surratt made small talk with several of the junior officers on Ransom's staff, he would introduce me as "a cotton trader from Charleston, who is also working as a photographer for the famous Mathew Brady." That would inevitably trigger a litany of questions about how the cameras worked, what famous people I had met, and so on. Naturally I embellished and used facts such as President Davis being photographed by Brady to imply that I was a Confederate. I also mentioned that I had been in Richmond for Davis's inauguration, vaguely conflating that story with the one about the photograph. At one point, I felt some anxiety when I imagined a scenario whereby Pinkerton had a spy among this group but was able to calm myself by thinking it was a longshot. Nevertheless, I subsequently toned things down just to be cautious.

A vigorous exchange of artillery began late in the afternoon as Early moved to soften up the Union defenses. The Confederate cannon fire was answered by the Union from Fort Stevens to our front, Fort Slocum to our left and Fort DeRussy to our right. I'd have been happy to stay where we were and watch, but Surratt insisted on moving a little closer to the action. We eventually settled into a wooded area several hundred yards north of Fort Stevens along with a handful of Confederate snipers. I smiled to myself when I noticed that many of them carried Whitworth rifles, the weapon I had schooled Gardner on while chiding him about his bogus picture from Gettysburg. Then I realized that the Fort was well within the 800-yard effective range of these guns and found myself hoping that heads were being kept low downrange. As the snipers occasionally plinked away, Surratt and I took turns on my flask and enjoyed a cheroot. At one point a sharpshooter yelled "Jesus Christ, it's Lincoln!" which sent me fumbling for the spy glass in my saddlebag. Sure enough, looking over one of the parapets in Fort Stevens was a tall figure in a dark suit and stovepipe hat.

"It's got to be a mannequin," I yelled, hoping to quell their interest. "He can't be that stupid. Don't waste your ammunition." Unfortunately, I knew all too well that Lincoln was reckless enough to be doing exactly what they hoped he was doing. I'd seen him in action sailing into Norfolk during the Peninsular Campaign two years ago. Sensing an opportunity to further ingratiate myself with Surratt though, I rose from our cover and fired off three or four shots from my Cooper toward the Fort.

"You idiot," Surratt shouted, "He's way out of range of that pistol! You are just going to send him running for cover!"

"As if these sharpshooters haven't been firing that way all afternoon," I pointed out. "But you're right. He's out of my range. Sorry, I couldn't control my excitement."

"I'd have thought you'd have known how to use that thing a little more effectively, Jack," Surratt said more quietly.

"I think that the two Union soldiers rotting in the ground on a plantation near the Combahee would tell you that I know how to use it well enough," I said in another attempt to establish my bona fides in Surratt's mind.

He looked at me with mild surprise, then we both turned our attentions back toward the ramparts of Fort Stevens as the snipers around us let loose with a vengeance. The stovepipe hat quickly disappeared and that proved to be the high-water mark for our excitement that day. We could soon see what looked like a significant number of Union reinforcements arriving. When it became clear that Early was not going to order a full attack, Surratt said he was going to go back over to Ransom's camp to see what he could find out. I stayed put, although at one point engaged in a discussion with a couple of the sharpshooters, one of whom allowed me to examine his Whitworth up close.

Surratt eventually returned and reported that Early had decided to attack the following morning, July 12. We decided to hunker down for the night with the sharpshooters, with whom we shared a meal as well as drinks and smokes. I would have preferred to make my way back to my lodgings at the Petersen but decided that traveling into the city after dark and emerging from the Confederate lines was a bad idea. Even if I'd have swung way around to the east, it would have been a risky move. Surratt, on the other hand, could barely contain his excitement and was convinced we would be in the city tomorrow anyway.

"Hey, Jack, let's dine at the Star tomorrow night. We'll see what Taltavull thinks about Lincoln with Washington in Confederate hands," he said at one point.

Not wanting to rain on his parade I responded, "To hell with the Star, let's eat at the Round Robin where we first met. From there we can watch the White House burn as we toast General Early with some Early Times bourbon." I was of course laying it on thickly for personal reasons, but Surratt lapped it up. Late in the evening, with our bellies full and several drinks on board, I said, "John, I really would like to see Anna to try and clear up our misunderstanding. I've never quite felt the same way for anyone else," but he cut me off with "Of course Jack. You've proven your worth today. I can't make any promises, but I will show her your letter and put in a kind word."

First light brought the familiar sounds of thousands of soldiers stirring and preparing for a day of fighting. The mood on the Confederate side remained confident and, even in the unrelenting heat, there was much jocularity among the men around us. My spy glass survey of the fortifications to our front confirmed that the Union lines had been reinforced, and I suspect that Early had come to the same conclusion since no attack was ordered. The skirmishing and exchange of fire from a distance continued, increasingly testing Surratt's patience.

"What the hell are we waiting for," Surratt said at one point. "I told him that the city is probably as lightly defended as we'll ever see it. These delays are doing nothing more than giving the enemy time to reinforce. Let's go, for Christ's sake!"

By sheer coincidence, Frank Stringfellow, now with the 4th Virginia Cavalry under Brigadier General William Terry, found us that afternoon when he was delivering a message to Ransom. He and Surratt wound each other up even further over Early's reluctance to attack. Of course, I was perfectly happy lounging in the grass among the trees, but I periodically tossed enthusiastic comments their way for show. At one point, I again considered bolting east and circling around the Union fortifications and making my way back into the city, but that would have scotched everything with John and, by extension, Anna. Better to wait and be separated from these two lunatics in the confusion of a battle, and I planned to do exactly that if a charge was called. Thankfully, Stringfellow eventually had to return to his unit, so Surratt and I were again alone amongst the snipers. In the late afternoon one of them called out, "By God, he's back!"

I grabbed my spy glass and, sure enough, a tall, bearded figure in a stovepipe hat was again peering over the ramparts at Fort Stevens. There was no question that this was an actual man, not a mannequin, and I cursed Lincoln for a fool under my breath. Even if it wasn't him, I couldn't see what was to be gained by putting a surrogate at risk. I would later learn that it was indeed the President himself and that one of the shots directed at him had struck a surgeon in the leg. Lincoln disappeared immediately after that near miss, but the sharpshooters continued to plug away enthusiastically. When darkness fell, we were informed that Early had decided that his forces were not sufficient to enter Washington. The Union kept reinforcing all day, and he'd had reports about troops on the move toward us from the west. His new plan was to withdraw north under the cover of darkness. After much debate, Surratt and I decided that our own withdrawal would be to the east to avoid the Union's forces between us and Washington. His circuitous route back to Surrattsville would be about 30 miles. We split up around Bladensburg, with me turning back southwest toward the city and him continuing east for a few miles before making his own turn south toward his home. When we parted, I reminded him of his promise to speak with Anna and he said he would see me again soon in Washington. He seemed sincere about talking to Anna, which had me riding tall in the saddle. I must have traveled at least 15 miles on my way to the Petersen House that day but was never stopped. Apparently, most of the Union's regular forces were pursuing Early to the north, and the militia that had been called up temporarily for the city's defense were already heading home too exhausted and relieved to care about a lone rider that looked like one of them.

Chapter 29

A SECOND CLOSE CALL

*O*ver the last half of July, my excitement at the prospect of reconciliation with Anna began to fade. I hadn't heard anything from her or her brother since he and I went our separate ways at Bladensburg, and I found myself wondering if he had just used me to secure safe passage through Washington on July 11. Then I would remember that I had conducted myself convincingly by taking potshots at Lincoln and champing at the bit to join a Confederate attack on the city and my hopes rose. War news suggested that Early's retreat westward from Fort Stevens had taken him to battles in Berryville then Kernstown, just south of Winchester, Virginia. Down south, my old friend General Sherman began his assault on Atlanta, which evolved into a siege after the Battle of Peachtree Creek. Atlanta was a vital rail hub and so, with his army outgunned by Sherman, Confederate General John

Bell Hood[91] was forced to set up a defensive position around the city. Farther north, Grant's forces remained deadlocked with Lee's around Petersburg, thus continuing to threaten the Confederate capitol of Richmond. Despite Early's success at Kernstown, these sieges of important Southern cities and Admiral Farragut's victory in the Battle of Mobile Bay, Alabama, in early August had the Union beginning to sense that a victory in this war might actually be possible.

I don't recall the exact date in August, but one afternoon I found John Surratt browsing around Brady's studio. Part of me suspected that he was just confirming that I actually worked there, but I put that all aside when he told me that he'd talked to Anna, delivered my letter, and that she was willing to see me. Better yet, she was at that moment in the townhouse her mother owned a few blocks away on H Street. He said he had an errand to run but would come back in a couple of hours and take me there if I wished. I of course agreed, and soon found myself riding alongside him on one of Brady's horses, anxious to see Anna for the first time in many months.

The townhouse[92] was four stories high, with a kitchen and dining room on the ground level. We found Anna on the second floor, where she was at work cleaning and, as I would soon discover, preparing for her, Mary and John Jr., to move in on November 1.

---

91 John Bell Hood was born in Kentucky in 1831. He graduated from the U.S. Military Academy in 1853 after coming close to being expelled due to demerit points (he received 192, eight short of the allowed limit). He resigned his First Lieutenant's commission in the U.S. Army in 1861 to join the C.S.A., where he would eventually attain the rank of Lieutenant General. Hood participated in many Civil War battles, including the Peninsular Campaign, Seven Days Battles, Antietam, Fredericksburg, Gettysburg, and Chickamauga. He died in 1879.
92 Built on a 29x100 foot lot in 1843 and purchased by John Surratt Sr. in 1853, the townhouse operates today as a restaurant at 604 H Street N.W. in Washington's Chinatown district.

Apparently the third and fourth floors, which I never visited, each had three rooms. Some of these were occupied by tenants, and one was a servant's quarters. Our meeting was awkward at first, although after some small talk John was gracious enough to excuse himself. He suggested that we have dinner at a tavern down the road in an hour and, before I could say anything, Anna agreed. They had obviously preplanned this as a way to cut things off if the reunion went badly, but I didn't mind. If that's what it took to make sure she was comfortable, so be it. As John left, we followed him as far as the kitchen, where Anna made the two of us some tea.

"It's so nice to see you, Anna," I said as soon as John was out of earshot. "It's been far too long. I am sorry that I offended you, and truly hope that I can redeem myself." Take the blame straight away in situations like this, whether or not you deserve it. As often as not a tactical surrender can better position you for a strategic victory.

"I was just feeling so confused, Jack," she replied. "In the beginning, I thought this war would be settled quickly. Now it's dragged on for what seems like forever, and I know people on both sides that have been killed or badly wounded. My family all feel strongly that the Confederacy is on the right side of the fight, and I just don't want to create more problems for them." Her voice quivered, but she never broke down.

"I can imagine that if I was a Union soldier it would create enormous problems with your family," I responded. "But I'm not. I'm a cotton trader that has supplied and continues to supply cotton to the Confederacy. I temporarily work for a photographer that has taken pictures of Jefferson Davis and Confederate troops at Fredericksburg and offers them for sale in his Washington and New York Studios. I personally attended Davis's inauguration in Richmond. And I was with your brother and Confederate cavalry as we fought a few miles north of here at Fort Stevens." All true on the face of it of course, but not quite so innocent if you peeled back a layer or two. My goals today did not include complete transparency.

"I'm sorry, Jack. It's just that some of the things Mr. Beam said at the Willard that night and then Lincoln seeming to be so familiar with you at the theatre … I just didn't know what to think." When a pretty woman says she's sorry, I'm always quick to move in and offer a selfless, comforting hug, as I did on this occasion. The rest of our conversation included more apologies going in both directions, as well as promises to not allow such pettiness to get in the way of our relationship in the future. Just as I was trying to figure out a way to get Anna back upstairs, John returned to escort us to dinner.

We made our way east on H Street and settled in at a modest establishment, the name of which I've forgotten. Over dinner and drinks, I inquired as to why Mary had decided to move into the city. Although the question caused them to exchange a knowing glance, Anna explained that times being what they were, their mother had decided that they needed to generate additional income by leasing out the tavern and hotel in Surrattsville. Even with her, Anna, and John at the townhouse, they still had space for rent-paying tenants there as well. It all made sense for them, but my selfish mind quickly turned to the difficulties it would present in seeing Anna in private going forward. Her occasional visits to the city had been the perfect cover, but her being here full-time would present logistical challenges for our trysts. I decided to worry about that later and instead focused on the decent food, whiskey, and small talk at hand. John was on his best behavior, and the fact that we'd accumulated some shared history over the past few years gave us a few things to laugh about. I've certainly had worse evenings and the mood was such that when John suggested we ride around town and enjoy a smoke after dropping Anna back at the townhouse, I was happy to agree.

With Anna safely home, John suggested that we ride up toward Prospect Hill Cemetery as we had done a few weeks ago. We covered the couple of miles to there in what seemed like no time, as we continued the pleasant conversation we had started at dinner. Before I knew it, we had gone another couple of miles and found ourselves at the road leading to President Lincoln's cottage. Surratt cursed that he couldn't get his cheroot relit, so he dismounted and moved in amongst the trees just off the road. When he called out for me to join him, I suggested that we go somewhere else, but he ignored me and asked for a light. Hoping that getting his smoke restarted would get him moving again, I also moved into the trees and dismounted to help him out. That done I suggested we get started back south toward the city, but he sat down and started to talk about Anna. Always interested in that topic, I sat down beside him and pulled out my flask. Much to my delight, he said he was very pleased that Anna and I had seemed to patch up our differences and he looked forward to seeing me around more often now that they would all be living in Washington. He shared a few funny stories about Anna growing up and at one point mentioned that he heard she had arranged to have the Cooper he'd given me engraved.

"She did indeed," I said. "And very cleverly, I might add."

"You can't say that and not let me see it," he said, smiling. The mood being what it was, I foolishly broke two cardinal rules of gun handling. One, never disarm yourself unless you have absolutely no choice. Two, never hand a loaded firearm to someone you don't trust completely. Like an idiot, I proudly passed him the Cooper and lit a match so he could read the inscription in the darkness.

"King Cotton," he said laughing. "Very clever indeed." He then ignored my subtle gesture to take it back and instead let it bob around in his hand as he told some story about a time he'd fired the new Henry 16 shot, .44 caliber repeating rifle that a few Union troops had been using. I feigned interest but was feeling increasingly agitated—and naked—without my pistol. Just as I was about to get more insistent in asking for it back, the sound of a horse coming along the road to our left got our attention. By this point, my eyes had become accustomed to the darkness, and in the moonlight, I was horrified to see the silhouette of an exceptionally tall man wearing a stovepipe hat sitting astride his horse and coming our way. Just as I realized who it was, Surratt stood up, took aim, and fired. As Lincoln's hat flew off his head, he kicked his horse and fled up the road in full gallop. In one motion, Surratt tossed me my pistol and remounted before setting off in the opposite direction. After quickly doing the math on which way to go, I followed him back south toward the city, although never caught up. After returning the horse to the stables Brady used, I made my way back to the Petersen House where, after a couple of healthy swigs from my flask, I bedded down for the night praying that the darkness had eliminated any possibility of being recognized.

I decided to lay low for the rest of the month and kept a close eye on the newspapers for any mention of Lincoln being shot at near his cottage hideaway on the grounds of Soldier's Home. Apparently, Lincoln played the story down, although I read years later that he did report the incident to his friend Ward Hill Lamon, albeit in a casual manner. Lamon wrote in his book *Recollections of Abraham Lincoln* that the President told him, "*Last night, about 11 o'clock, I went out to the Soldiers' Home alone, riding Old Abe, as you call him [a horse he delighted in riding], and when I arrived at the foot of the hill on the road leading to the entrance of the Home grounds, I was jogging along at a slow gait, immersed in deep thought, contemplating what was next to happen in the unsettled state of affairs, when suddenly I was aroused ... by the report of a rifle, and seemingly the gunner was not fifty yards from where my contemplations ended and my accelerated transit began. My erratic namesake, with little warning, gave proof of decided dissatisfaction at the racket, and with one reckless bound he unceremoniously separated me from my eight-dollar plug-hat, with which I parted company without any assent, expressed or implied, upon my part. At breakneck speed we soon arrived in a haven of safety. Meanwhile I was left in doubt whether death was more desirable from being thrown from a runaway federal horse, or as the tragic result of a rifle-ball fired by a disloyal bushwhacker in the middle of the night ... I can't bring myself to believe that any one has shot or will deliberately shoot at me with the purpose of killing me; although I must acknowledge that I heard this fellow's bullet whistle at an uncomfortably short distance from these headquarters of mine. I have about concluded that the shot was the result of accident. It may be that someone on his return from a day's hunt, regardless of the course of his discharge, fired off his gun as a precautionary measure of safety to his family after reaching his house."*

I could have told him that it was neither an accident nor a rifle, and the distance was more like 25 yards. But, for obvious reasons, I chose not to. I did marvel, however, at the thought that a President, especially one so despised by a significant percentage of the populous, was allowed to travel openly and alone along a road he was known to frequent. And after dark, no less. I would have gambled the entire proceeds of my next cotton shipment that Presidential transport going forward would be in covered carriages but didn't want to reveal any interest in such matters by placing such a bet.

Chapter 30

MORE SALES

By the beginning of September 1864, Sherman's efforts around Atlanta finally paid off and the city was officially surrendered to him on September 2. In addition to being a major strategic victory, Atlanta's fall proved to be a morale boost to the North and, by extension, to Lincoln's reelection campaign. Lincoln's Democrat opponent was none other than General George B. McClellan, veteran of the Peninsular Campaign and Antietam, as well as the subject of many Brady photographs. True to form, McClennan ran on a confusing platform, advocating continuing the war and restoration of the Union, while simultaneously proposing negotiation with the Confederacy for peace. He did not support the abolition of slavery despite the fact that his party's official platform did. Among other things, Confederate General Hood's retreat from Atlanta and his destruction of significant Confederate military supplies during the process had the average Union voter wondering why the North would bother to negotiate with a weakened enemy. Atlanta was an important railway hub, and its lines were now in the hands of the Union. The fact that some of those lines ran northwest through Tennessee and Kentucky were suddenly of great interest to Lincoln, Quartermaster Meigs and, soon enough, me.

In 1860, textile mills around New England consumed more than 280 million pounds of cotton per year and employed tens of thousands of people. The steep drop in the cotton supply caused by the war contributed to a 75 percent decline in this industry and the jobs associated with it. Lincoln had figured out that the liberation of the railway lines coming out of Atlanta gave him an opportunity to restore both supply to those mills and the hopes of the voters that worked in them. Thus, the seemingly unconnected combination of 1864 being an election year and the sudden availability of rail lines out of Atlanta resulted in my being summoned once again to Meigs office in the War Department. The presence of Pinkerton and Kate Warne at the meeting told me that the Union took this project seriously, and it was Pinkerton himself that kicked things off.

"It's been a while, Jack," he said. I couldn't tell if he was being sarcastic or not since I hadn't checked in recently. I did have material intelligence that I could have passed along of course, but most of it involved my pistol being fired at Lincoln on two separate occasions. I didn't see any upside in recounting those moments.

"I've been busy, Allan. Down in Belle Plain, Cold Harbor, Weyanoke Point and the like with Grant, as I'm sure you know. After that, like everyone else in town, I was getting ready to fend off Early a few months ago. And, through it all, I've been making sure that your cotton continues to be sent to the Combahee." All true of course but lacking some important facts that might have landed me in the Old Capitol Prison or worse.

"It's those shipments that we want to talk about today," Meigs chimed in. "We are handling about as much as we can along the Combahee River. But the taking of Atlanta gives us an opportunity to supplement that if you can procure more cotton."

I knew through recent correspondence with Frank Dawson that we now could in fact acquire additional supplies. The ever-rising prices of cotton had caused many of the plantations to hoard their inventory in the hopes of getting more for it later. That, combined with declining demand from a fading Confederacy had created a modest glut.

"Your timing is excellent," I said. "My man in Charleston tells me that, for a variety of reasons, we can now get our hands on more. What did you have in mind?"

"Very simple," Meigs replied. "We'll take as much of it from you as you can get to Atlanta."

Pinkerton added, "The situation in Georgia east of Atlanta is chaotic, but we hold the city. We suggest you ship it by rail out of Charleston with paperwork showing it is going to Columbia, South Carolina, so as not to arouse suspicions with the Confederates. We'll divert the shipments around Orangeburg and send them west through Augusta to Atlanta. From there, we'll forward the cotton into Kentucky, then on to New England. We may only get away with it a few times, so we want as much as you can ship on each run."

"The fact is, we would like to tell the mills in New England as soon as possible that help is on the way," Kate added. It was at this moment I made the connection between this cotton and New England voters.

"Tell them it's coming," I said. "I'll send word to my people that we'll continue with the current quantities going to the Combahee, but that we need as many additional bales as we can manage sent to Charleston by rail. Let's talk price." I knew what we were paying the plantations now and believed that we could expect the same, or maybe better prices, given higher quantities. The debate ended up centering on what moment the Union was deemed to have accepted a shipment, which would determine when and if I was paid. Their opening position was Nashville and mine was Orangeburg, South Carolina. It was clear they wanted me to have some incentive to ensure that the hijackings were successful, which I understood. I eventually argued that Atlanta achieved that and reduced the risk I had in the journey from Atlanta to Nashville, which was completely out of my control. We finally came to an agreement on designating Atlanta as our free on-board point. Bailey Importers would need to take the risk of transport to there from Charleston but given the opportunity for increased sales, I decided it was worth it. I was certain my father would agree but, with any luck, by the time I received his opinion we would have made at least one successful delivery.

I left the War Department with Kate and Pinkerton, who suggested we get something to eat. Halfway through lunch, Pinkerton surprised me with, "Jack, I'd like to talk about participating financially in this new arrangement."

"A kickback?" I blurted out incredulously. "I didn't have you down for that sort of thing, Allan. But hell, I wouldn't have this opportunity without you, so I get it." The look in his eye and color of his face above his beard instantly told me I'd overstepped.

"How dare you suggest such a thing, you bleeder," he roared. I also got a glare from Kate.

"Good Lord, I'm sorry, Allan," I offered. "I have obviously completely misread the situation. It's just that I figured this was a military contract and you are a government employee after all, and…." but let my voice trail off as I realized I was just digging myself in deeper.

Pinkerton slammed his fist on the table, which attracted glances from people around us. Noticing the attention, he lowered his voice and said, "I was simply going to suggest that it seems to me that you may require more capital to get this going than you are accustomed to putting up. I was going to offer some of my own funds. If you agree, I propose that I invest at the price you are paying the plantations and that I get paid, as you do, at the price you receive from the Union."

I could have pointed out that even though the Union wouldn't be out of pocket, this was still a significant conflict of interest, but I instead replied, "Again Allan, please accept my deepest apologies. Inexcusable, especially given how long I've known you. I guess I've grown too accustomed to dealing with the grifters on the Charleston docks and elsewhere in this business. That said, it was an outrageous assumption to have made."

After about a half minute of silence, he said, "I am not asking to be treated any differently than you or your other investors."

Although we didn't have other investors, I said, "And now I really do understand. And, you are right. The capital we will require for this is likely to go above what we are accustomed to needing. It's really quite thoughtful of you to offer." Might as well pour it on thickly. The more I thought about it, the more I realized that having Pinkerton in the game could prove to be very beneficial. I added, "Kate, when I ask our attorney to draw up the paperwork for this, should I ask him to prepare some for you?"

"Thank you, Jack," she said. "I'm not really in a position to participate, but I appreciate the offer." She looked like what she really appreciated was the fact that Pinkerton and I hadn't just come to blows. We spent the remainder of lunch discussing the size of Pinkerton's investment and other deal terms, but it was all fairly straightforward. Again, I hadn't consulted my father on this, but planned to tell him that the extra orders wouldn't have been possible without taking Allan on as a very minor partner in the deal. Greasing palms was right up his alley, so I knew he would understand.

As it turned out, the timing of all of this turned out to be fortuitous. When I arrived back in the studio, Brady asked me into his office where he launched into a monologue about how my assistance over the past few years had been so important to his success and how my steady hand at managing his people had made so much possible and so on. With the war apparently winding down, he planned to spend less time in the field and, when he did send people out, I'd trained them well and they could now manage just fine, etc. After less than a minute into his rambling, it was obvious to me where he was headed, although I was surprised when he only asked me to go on half pay. I assumed he was cutting ties completely but suspect that he still wanted a little adult supervision around. Even though I feigned disappointment, it suited my needs perfectly. The new arrangements I'd just struck with Meigs and Pinkerton would require more of my attentions, and the prospect of Anna moving into Washington at the beginning of October already had me thinking about how to spend more time with her. But staying connected to Brady, even in a lesser way, would give me the plausible cover and access I had come to enjoy.

During the remainder of the month of September, I had an attorney draw up papers memorializing the arrangement that Pinkerton and I had agreed to. I also sent a long letter to my father containing the good news of these new shipments and hinted that the arrangement with Allan had been a necessary concession to get the deal done. I traveled down to Surrattsville at one point, ostensibly to court Anna and offer my assistance with the Surratt's upcoming move into the city, but also to telegraph instructions to Dawson and to see where I stood with John. I couldn't decide if the incident outside Lincoln's cottage was an attempt to frame me for attempted murder, or if he had simply assumed I would be up for it given my shooting at Lincoln as he manned the ramparts at Fort Stevens. I decided to handle it by waiting for Surratt to make the first move, which he did as soon as we had a private moment.

His version of events was that it was a lucky coincidence that we encountered the President that night and he actually apologized for "acting spontaneously." I didn't buy any of it. I am certain he was expecting Lincoln to happen by, since it was common knowledge that he moved his family up that way during the hot summer months to escape the heat and humidity in the city. But I will never know if he was trying to frame me or if he simply assumed I would approve of his actions. Relieved that he was playing things casually though, I took the conversation in another direction by commenting how extraordinary it was that the incident was being taken so lightly. While Lincoln spoke of it to his friends, it was never given the press coverage one would expect of an attempted assassination of a President.

Chapter 31

JULIUS CAESAR

I visited Surrattsville a couple more times during the month of October, continuing my courtship of Anna and, truth be told, of Mary. As one would expect, Mary was protective of her children and none more so than Anna. By offering my assistance with the move and by lending a sympathetic ear to her business difficulties, I built upon the trust I had gained from her by escorting Anna back to school a few years ago. Despite owning the tavern, hotel, stable, general store, granary, gristmill, and seemingly half the town, Mary's financial problems continued to mount. While the war and related labor shortages were partly to blame, I suspect that John Sr. had overpaid for some of these properties and mismanaged them while he was still alive. It was all good news to me, however, as my making myself useful continued to elevate my standing with Mary. I was even so bold as to ask if I could receive mail and telegraphs at their hotel, since I needed to correspond with Dawson about our new orders. I was reasonably certain that John Jr. would read these, which presented another opportunity to endear myself to the family by waxing on about how these shipments would assist the Confederacy. I doubt Dawson would have cared either way and he was probably puzzled by my zeal, but he cared too much about the bonuses I'd promised him to make a fuss.

During one of my visits, I arrived to find John, Mary, Anna, and a John Lloyd all seated around a table at the tavern deep in conversation. It was clear that they were discussing some bad news and when I sat down and asked, John shoved a newspaper across to me and pointed to an article. I had been less diligent about scouring the papers for news on the attempted assassination of Lincoln of late, so had missed this piece he was showing me about Rose O'Neal Greenhow. I, of course, had met Mrs. Greenhow at a White House reception a few years back and knew from Pinkerton that at one point she had been imprisoned as a Confederate spy. I recalled that she had been released from the Old Capitol Prison in 1862 on the condition that she remain in the South, and she and her daughter were subsequently shipped off to Fort Monroe, Virginia. From there she made her way to Richmond, where she was given a hero's welcome and was eventually asked by Jeff Davis to travel to Europe to promote the Confederacy. She had been traveling back to North Carolina on a British blockade runner which, on October 1, had run aground off Wilmington while being pursued by a Union gunship. The rowboat she used to flee had capsized and, weighed down by more than $2,000 worth of gold that was sewn in her clothing, she drowned. The Surratt's were mourning her passing in a way that suggested they knew her, but I thought it best I didn't mention that we'd met. I did make a good show of expressing sympathy for Rose's daughter, however, then turned my attentions to Lloyd.

John M. Lloyd[93], I would learn, was an ex-Washington police officer, bricklayer, and Southern sympathizer who had relocated

---

93 John M. Lloyd was born in Maryland in 1835. Over the course of his career, he was a bricklayer, police officer and construction contractor. Before leasing the Surratt properties, he was one of the first officers hired by the Washington Police Department. His testimony was important in convicting Mary Surratt as a Lincoln conspirator.

to the area. I got all this from him over the next few hours as he accompanied me on my rounds around Mary's holdings as I continued to try and make myself useful. He enjoyed my cheroots and flask, with the latter helping to make our conversation more enlightening. I had at first been concerned that he might have his eye on Anna, but soon realized that he was more interested in Mary's properties than anything else. He asked me at one point if I thought Mary would consider leasing him some of them, and I promised that I would make some inquiries and let him know.

The war continued to occasionally rear its ugly head during October with relatively small encounters at Saltville, Virginia (a Confederate victory), Tom's Brook, Virginia (a Union victory) and the Second Battle of Fair Oaks (a Confederate victory), although the combatants would undoubtedly curse me for labeling them small. My friend, Al Waud, did some sketching at Fair Oaks, but none of these battles was on the scale of a Gettysburg or Antietam and thus were not of interest to Brady. I had hoped that my reduced time at the studio would increase my quality time with Anna, if you get my drift, even though I knew I would be heavily chaperoned in Surrattsville. To my great disappointment, things didn't improve in November when she and John moved into the Washington townhouse. John wouldn't think twice about taking a shot at the President, but he wouldn't stand for anyone touching his sister, including me. I told Mary about John Lloyd's interest in leasing some of her properties, and their discussions led to an agreement whereby Lloyd would be leasing all of Mary's holdings in Surrattsville. As a result, Mary would be moving to Washington on December 1, thus making it even more difficult for me to see Anna alone.

Al Waud at Gettysburg, Courtesy of The Library of Congress, LC-DIG-cwbp-00074

To say that Lincoln's resounding victory in the election on November 8 furthered soured John's temperament would be an extreme understatement. Given McClellan's incompetence and recent Union victories in the deep south, I can't imagine how he expected otherwise, but I suppose folks believe what they want to believe. It's also difficult for zealots to consider other points of view, but the net result of it all had me searching frantically for ideas on how to get Anna out of town and alone. Salvation came through a notice in the papers about a "one night only" performance of Julius Caesar at the Winter Garden Theatre in New York City starring Junius, Edwin, and John Wilkes Booth. Proceeds from the performance were to be used to build a statue of William Shakespeare in a new "Central Park" in New York[94],

94 The 18-foot stature is still located in the Mall and Literary Walk just south of Bethesda Terrace in New York City's Central Park.

and the tickets were outrageously priced at $5 each. Despite that, and the fact that I didn't like the way Anna had admired John Wilkes' looks during past encounters, I saw this as my opportunity. Brady had been complaining about a shortage of staff in the New York studio, so I graciously offered to travel there to sort things out. When I suggested the trip to Anna, I probably should have been offended at how quickly she accepted after the mention of Booth, but the prospect of a couple of nights with her blinded me. For the family's benefit, she came up with an excuse to travel on her own to New York City to visit one of former classmates from the Saint Mary's Female Institution in Bryantown. She naturally didn't mention the fact that I was to be in New York City at the same time, and so all the pieces fell nicely into place.

I noticed in the press coverage of the play that, in addition to his playing the role of Brutus, Edwin Booth co-managed the Winter Garden Theatre with his brother-in-law. In an outrageous overstepping of my authority, I wrote to Edwin on Brady's letterhead. I signed my own name but suggested that "Lincoln's Photographer" might be in New York on Friday, November 25 and I wanted to purchase seats for him "in an area of the theatre worthy for someone of Mathew Brady's stature." Feeling flush from the prospect of Bailey Cotton's impending increase in business, I enclosed $20—$10 for two tickets and a $10 donation toward the Shakespeare statue. The tickets arrived a week later, along with a note inviting Mr. Brady and his guest backstage following the performance. I was certain that the Booth's would be disappointed when yours truly appeared instead of Mathew Brady, but I would deal with that at the time. Anna would be thrilled. Like politicians, actors loved the camera, which is why the tickets weren't a surprise, but the post-show invitation was a bonus. By the time they realized they weren't going to see a Brady camera, I would have impressed Anna to no end. I immediately sent a letter to the Metropolitan Hotel requesting that they book me a room for three nights, beginning on November 24. I was familiar with the Metropolitan having been a guest of P.T. Barnum's at reception there following the wedding of "General Tom Thumb" and Lavinia Warren. I knew that it was just a few blocks south of the Winter Garden, with both on Broadway. I also knew that the Metropolitan was large enough that we wouldn't draw much scrutiny from the staff or other guests.

Ten days before the play, on November 15, General William T. Sherman began his now famous (or infamous if you're a Southerner) march to the sea. We didn't hear much news of it in Washington right away, as he had convinced Grant and Lincoln to allow him to conduct the campaign without supply lines. The lines of communication, while not cut, were therefore also less reliable than normal. The plan was for Sherman's troops to live off the land, foraging what they needed to survive along the way. They were instructed to destroy military targets, industry, and any civilian property that might assist the rebel's ability to wage war. Sections 4, 5 and 6 of his *Special Field Orders No. 120* said it all:

"4. The army will forage liberally on the country during the march. To this end, each brigade commander will organize a good and sufficient foraging party, under the command of one or more discreet officers, who will gather, near the route traveled, corn or forage of any kind, meat of any kind, vegetables, cornmeal, or whatever is needed by the command, aiming at all times to keep in the wagons at least ten days' provisions for his command, and three days' forage. Soldiers must not enter the dwellings of the inhabitants, or commit any trespass; but, during a halt or camp, they may be permitted to gather turnips, potatoes, and other vegetables, and to drive in stock in sight of their camp. To regular foraging-parties must be entrusted the gathering of provisions and forage, at any distance from the road traveled.

5. To corps commanders alone is entrusted the power to destroy mills, houses, cotton-gins, etc.; and for them this general principle is laid down:

> In districts and neighborhoods where the army is unmolested, no destruction of each property should be permitted; but should guerrillas or bushwhackers molest our march, or should the inhabitants burn bridges, obstruct roads, or otherwise manifest local hostility, then army commanders should order and enforce a devastation more or less relentless, according to the measure of such hostility. The army will forage liberally on the country during the march. To this end, each brigade commander will organize a good and sufficient foraging party, under the command of one or more discreet officers, who will gather, near the route traveled, corn or forage of any kind, meat of any kind, vegetables, cornmeal, or whatever is needed by the command, aiming at all times to keep in the wagons at least ten days' provisions for his command, and three days' forage. Soldiers must not enter the dwellings of the inhabitants, or commit any trespass; but, during a halt or camp, they may be permitted to gather turnips, potatoes, and other vegetables, and to drive in stock in sight of their camp. To regular foraging-parties must be entrusted the gathering of provisions and forage, at any distance from the road traveled.

6. To corps commanders alone is entrusted the power to destroy mills, houses, cotton-gins, etc.; and for them this general principle is laid down:

> In districts and neighborhoods where the army is unmolested, no destruction of each property should be permitted; but should guerrillas or bushwhackers molest our

march, or should the inhabitants burn bridges, obstruct roads, or otherwise manifest local hostility, then army commanders should order and enforce a devastation more or less relentless, according to the measure of such hostility.

Had I seen this order at the time, I would have been terrified for the shipments of cotton I had coming out of Charleston. But, as it happened, the route his men marched was south toward Savannah, Georgia, 100 miles south of Charleston. While Sherman's army might have encountered the trains with my cotton as they approached Atlanta from Augusta, I would have told myself that they would be flying Union flags along that section of the journey and therefore would pass unmolested. But I was blissfully unaware of any of these developments as I looked forward to my trip to New York with Anna. We took a train from Washington up to New York City on Thursday, November 24, covering the 225 or so miles relatively painlessly. After a nice dinner in the Metropolitan Hotel's dining room, we retired upstairs to satisfy a different sort of hunger.

The next morning, I encouraged Anna to visit the fashionable shops below the hotel. I then walked the half mile or so north on Broadway to Brady's studio and spent a few hours cracking the whip with the staff and interviewing a couple of prospective new employees. Boring work, it's true, but it had given me an excuse to be in the city and was going to enable me to charge Brady for some of my expenses for this trip. I made it back to the Metropolitan in time for lunch with Anna, after which we took a stroll before dressing for the theatre.

Suitably attired, we made our way up Broadway and stopped in at the bar of the Lafarge House hotel for a cocktail before proceeding next door to the Winter Garden Theatre. I must confess to only having glanced at the seat numbers on the tickets until that moment and was therefore pleasantly surprised to be escorted to the second-row middle. Anna was beside herself with excitement and the packed house was bristling with anticipation. At the appointed hour, the curtain rose and three members of the most prominent acting family in America proceeded to ply their trade. John Wilkes played Marc Antony, Edwin was Brutus and Junius played Cassius. With the benefit of hindsight, it would have been more poetic had John Wilkes played Brutus, Caesar's assassin, but I doubt that even he knew his destiny at the time. At the start of Act Two, a loud clanging of fire bells got everyone's attention. Apparently a fire had broken out at the Lafarge House next door and only quick thinking by Edwin, who interrupted the play to assure everyone that there was no danger to the theatre, prevented what might have been a disastrous stampede to the exits. How he would know that there wasn't any danger is a mystery to me, but his confidence, and that of a certain Judge McClunn, who rose from his seat in the audience to add some reassuring words, calmed nerves and enabled the play to continue.

The excitement of the fire was mostly forgotten by the time the audience took to their feet to offer hearty applause during the curtain call. With that over, I directed Anna forward, swimming upstream against the people heading back toward the exits.

"Where are we going? I think we leave that way," she said, pointing toward the rear.

"You'll see," I said, as we climbed the stairs stage left. I presented Edwin Booth's letter to a man standing by the end of the curtain and he pointed us toward a door at the back of the stage. Through that, we joined a group of three dozen or so people, who were mingling about with the cast enjoying drinks and hors d'oeuvres. For some reason it struck me that the actors were chatting in the same animated way you would see among the survivors of a battle. Anna's eyes grew to the size of banjos, and she squeezed my arm in appreciation. She was off like a racehorse when she spotted John Wilkes in a small group toward the back, but I figured I would deal with that later. In the meantime, I thought that I should seek out Edwin to head off any problems I may have created by being here in place of Brady.

"Mr. Booth," I said when I found him. "Jack Bailey. We corresponded about the possibility of Mathew Brady attending this special performance, but he unfortunately could not get away from Washington. I didn't want to waste the tickets, so decided to come instead."

"Well, he may end up regretting missing some unique excitement here in New York, Mr. Bailey," Edwin responded.

"I agree," I said. "The play was excellent."

"I meant the arson," he replied. "I've just heard that the fire next door at the Lafarge was just one of many started in hotels up and down Broadway. Some are suggesting it's the work of the rebels."

"The South was right to attack New York City," observed John Wilkes, who had come up beside us to "meet Anna's date."

Edwin, a fan of Lincoln and supporter of the Union, was not having it. The two launched into a heated argument that caused many of the guests to migrate to other parts of the room. "You're never welcome in my house again," Edwin said at one point. I was happy to take it as my cue to escort Anna back to our hotel and away from John Wilkes. Despite his outburst (or maybe because of it), she was clearly smitten, while I thought he had all the earmarks of a skilled rake. Two good reasons to leave.

When we arrived back at the Metropolitan, we learned that it had also been the target of arson. It seemed like there had indeed been a coordinated effort to set fire to the city, although at this point it was difficult to separate facts from speculation. I wasn't going to let that spoil the evening, however, and after a couple of drinks with her at the bar, we went up to our room and I took advantage of the fact that Anna was still euphoric over the terrific seats, the play, and the fact that we were able to join the cast backstage afterwards. The next morning, Sunday the 27th, I purchased a copy of *The New York Times* to read during the train ride back to Washington. The first few sentences of a very long article on the subject outlined the nature of the conspiracy:

"The diabolical plot to burn the City of New-York, published yesterday morning, proves to be far more extensive than was at first supposed. It has already proved to the entire satisfaction of the authorities, that the affair was planned by the rebels and has been in preparation for a long time past, the men selected to perform the work were sent to this City at various times and under various pretexts, and arriving here they formed themselves into a regularly organized band, had their various officers, including a treasurer, whom they could always find, and who was always ready to supply them with the money necessary to carry out their infernal work, and they proceeded deliberately to mature their plans for one of the most fiendish and inhuman acts known in modern times.

The plan was excellently well conceived, and evidently prepared with great care, and had it been executed with one-half the ability with which it was drawn up, no human power could have saved this city from utter destruction. It was evidently the intention of the conspirators to fire the city, at a given moment, at a great many different points, each as far remote from the other as possible, except through Broadway, and this thoroughfare they wished to see in a complete blaze, from one end to the other. To do this, they commenced at the St. James Hotel, corner of Broadway and Twenty-Fifth-street, next the Fifth-avenue Hotel, extending from Twenty-third to Twenty-fourth-street, then (missing the New-York Hotel, which it seems was not included in their list) The Lafarge House and Winter Garden Theatre, just below Amity-street; next followed the St. Nicholas, Metropolitan, Howard, Belmont, and others. In all thirteen of our principle hotels. About the same time several hay barges along the river were set on fire, and attempts were made to fire Barnum's Museum and other public buildings. Had all these hotels, hay barges, theatres, etc., been set on fire at the same moment, and each fire well kindled, the Fire Department would not have been strong enough to extinguish them all, and during the confusion the fire would probably have gained so great a headway that before assistance could have been obtained, the best portion of the city would have been laid in ashes. But fortunately, thanks to the Police, Fire Department, and the bungling manner in which the plan was executed by the conspirators, it proved a complete and miserable failure."

We never discussed the political aspects of this event, but Anna's body language told me that she regretted its failure. I might have suspected that she knew something in advance, but dismissed the thought when I realized that she would then have known that the Lafarge was one of the targets. I doubt she would have put herself that close to danger and hoped that she would have also been concerned for my safety. But I wasn't 100 percent certain of any of that and decided that it was probably best not to think about it.

Chapter 32

MARY COMES TO WASHINGTON

*M*ary moved into the townhouse on December 1 as planned and, for selfish reasons, I made certain I was there to offer my assistance. I continued to visit at least every few days over the course of the month, both to court Anna and to ward off other potential suitors. The older tenants didn't concern me, nor did female tenants like Nora Fitzpatrick[95]. But when younger men passed through, I couldn't resist making sure that I didn't have any competition. Louis Weichmann[96] fit that mold. He moved in at the beginning of November and was an old classmate of John Jr.'s from St. Charles College. Anna sensed my jealousy and pointed out that before the war broke out Louis had been studying to become a priest, thereby suggesting that I needn't worry. So had her brother, I didn't say out loud, and look at what he had become. Weichmann was now a clerk at

---

95 Honora "Nora" Fitzpatrick, born in 1844, was Mary Surratt's first female boarder. Coincidentally, Nora's older sister Anna's attendance at St. Mary's Institute in Bryantown briefly overlapped with that of Anna Surratt.

96 Louis J. Weichmann was born in Baltimore in 1842. He was at various times a clerk and schoolteacher, and he would become a witness for the prosecution in the trial of the Lincoln conspirators.

the Department of War, and, given his association with John, I had to wonder what secrets he might be passing along. After a time though, I satisfied myself that he had no interest in Anna, which was all I cared about. I would have other characters to worry about soon enough.

Around the middle of the month, the Union and Confederate armies clashed again in a major battle around Nashville, Tennessee. We didn't know it then, but this would be the last significant engagement of the war outside the coastal states. What we did know was that it was a resounding victory for the Union with Confederate General John Bell Hood's forces effectively eliminated as a functioning army. There were 85,000 men involved on both sides, with 9,000 killed, captured, or wounded. Two thirds of the latter were Confederates. A few days later, Sherman's March to the Sea campaign ended in Savannah on December 21 when that city surrendered. While the Union had of late been daring to sense that overall victory might be in the cards, these two events swayed public opinion even further in that direction. I was at the Surratt townhouse to celebrate the holidays on Christmas Eve, but the atmosphere was somewhat subdued because of these Union victories. While I pretended to share their sentiment, my mood turned genuinely dour when John Jr. dropped his own bombshell that afternoon. He reported that a family acquaintance, Dr. Samuel Mudd, had "just yesterday introduced him to that famous actor John Wilkes Booth." Anna lit up at the news but had the good sense not to blurt out that we had met with Booth in New York a month ago.

"You must bring him around here to meet us," she squealed. Nora Fitzpatrick, who was becoming increasingly friendly with Anna, enthusiastically agreed.

"He's staying in town to star in Romeo and Juliet next month," Surratt said. So I will certainly invite him. Anna shot me a glance that suggested "get us tickets". Given this foul news, Anna's enthusiasm to meet John Wilkes and the time of year, for a brief moment I contemplated proposing marriage to her. Although it seemed a sure way to stake my claim, I didn't. But, looking back, that seed was probably planted in my mind that day.

In early January, I procured tickets for Romeo and Juliet, and I strongly suggested to Anna that she discourage any visits by Booth to the Surratt townhouse before we attended. I was worried that he would recall meeting us in New York last November and would say as much, which would lead to some uncomfortable questions. She understood the problem and immediately set about asking John to hold off. We did see Booth's performance that month, which the *National Review* wrote was "the most satisfactory of all renderings of that fine character." Using one of my Brady Studio's carte de visites, I talked our way backstage afterwards. I figured if we saw him here before we met him at the townhouse, we could head off any mention of the Winter Garden Theatre in front of Mary and John.

"Oh, Mr. Booth, it's such a pleasure to meet you again," Anna gushed, once we got our turn with him. There was no shortage of well-wishers and hangers-on backstage, as had been the case in New York.

"Please call me John," he said with a wink at her that I found inappropriate.

"I thought your performance in Julius Caesar was wonderful, John, but your Romeo is simply divine." And on it went. Mercifully, at one point she excused herself to use the ladies' room, no doubt to ensure that her makeup was holding up. I took advantage of the opportunity to do my work, and Booth gave me the perfect opening.

"I am grateful to have this opportunity to thank you Mr. Bailey," he said. "Both for your support of me and for your generous donation toward the statue of William Shakespeare. Edwin showed me your letter in New York."

"It was the right thing to do," I lied. "And please call me Jack."

"Well then, Jack," he said, "Please do let me know if I can ever be of service to you."

You can stay the hell away from Anna, I thought, but instead said, "Actually, you could do me a small favor if you don't mind."

"Name it," he replied.

"I understand that you recently met Anna's brother John," I said.

"Ah," he responded. "Now I know why her last name sounded familiar. Yes, I did, through a mutual friend, Dr. Mudd."

"Well, you may soon get an invitation to visit John's town-house here in Washington so you can meet the family. I'd be very grateful if you didn't mention that Anna and I met you in New York. Of course, you can say that we met here tonight, but mention of the Winter Garden might prove awkward."

After a long moment he smiled and said, "Yes, of course. I understand completely." The sparkle in his eye told me that this favor wouldn't come without cost. Anna returned at that moment so I couldn't take things any further but, despite his Cheshire Cat-like expression, I felt confident that we had a deal. After more banter, I suggested we take our leave, at which point Booth looked deep into Anna's eyes and invited her to join him back-stage after any performance of his that she happened to attend. In normal circumstances I would have taken offense and called him on it, but he had something over me now and he knew it. And he knew that I knew it.

Before dropping Anna off at the townhouse, I suggested that we stop by the Round Robin for a nightcap. Once seated, Anna continued chattering on excitedly about the play we'd just seen, *Julius Caesar* at the Winter Garden, being backstage on both occasions and, much to my annoyance, the thrill of knowing John. As I listened to all this and thought about the steady stream of boarders that would no doubt be coming and going from the townhouse, I made a rash decision and proposed marriage.

"My goodness, Jack, this is so unexpected! I don't know what to say!"

"Well, I hope you say yes, of course," I replied. But she sat silently for a minute before proceeding.

"I'm so conflicted at the moment, Jack," she finally offered. I hadn't expected this hesitation but, to be fair, it was all very sudden for me as well. I hadn't planned this.

She continued, "It's just that, well, lately I have had my eyes open to all the possibilities out there in life. Moving into the city, meeting new people, experiencing travel." By new people, I had a feeling she meant Booth, but I asked, "Is this about the misunderstanding over Lincoln last fall?"

"Oh no," she said. "I realize that was my mistake. And I realize that I'm getting to that age where people will begin to wonder if there is something wrong with me, but ... I just don't know. Can you let me think about it? Can we discuss it another time?"

"Of course," I said, in shock. I had surprised myself by even asking and was now doubly surprised that she hadn't said yes. Travel, new people—it all added up to Booth in my mind.

"And can we please not tell anyone that we've had this discussion?" she asked. "That would mean a lot of pressure."

And it would make it easier to keep your options open as well, I thought, but agreed so I could stay in the game. On the way from the Willard to her townhouse she was cordial, but she seemed to put a little distance between us that worried me. It wasn't until I'd bid her goodnight and had a couple more drinks at the Star that I started to get angry. I had invested a lot of time and effort in this relationship, and she was apparently willing to walk away from it on the off chance that an actor, of all people, would be a better choice. With his looks and the way I saw women swoon over him at the three performances I'd now seen, I guarantee that he was more interested in grazing the buffet than settling on a single dish. She'd soon learn that, was my guess. Although I was not present for Booth's first visit to the townhouse, I heard that at least he had kept mum about the Winter Garden. If he was going to make a move, that would have been an easy way to have Mary ban me from seeing her daughter. As it turned out though, even more pressing matters required my attention late that month and into February.

While the March to the Sea had generally been fought south from Atlanta to Savannah, its successful conclusion in late December allowed Sherman to start to focus his attentions else-where. I normally wouldn't have paid much heed, but after being summoned to Pinkerton's office and briefed on the situation, I suddenly cared very deeply about where Sherman went next.

"He's waging total war, Jack," Pinkerton exclaimed in a voice that was an octave higher than usual. "Burning, pillaging, de-stroying everything in his path, with Lincoln egging him on. He and his men are drunk on success, convinced they can bring the South to its knees."

"I've read as much in the papers. Seems like it is working though," I said before I thought it through.

"Well, now that he's conquered Savannah, Jack, where do you guess he might go next?" I wasn't looking at a mirror but am sure my face became pale as the realization sunk in. "I'll save you guessing. Charleston, Orangeburg, Columbia—everywhere he hasn't set to the torch yet. And, yes, everywhere our cotton is."

At this moment I was glad to have Pinkerton as a partner and thinking of it as "our cotton". But I now shared his sense of panic. He hadn't said it, but we both knew that we didn't get paid until our product arrived in Atlanta.

"Surely you can order Sherman to spare our shipments Allan. They are going to benefit the Union after all!" I said.

"Two problems with that Bailey. Firstly, he's operating without supply lines and so there are not reliable communications. Telegraph cables have been cut and he's only reporting back to Grant through the occasional runner," Pinkerton reported. "Secondly, he is Grant's fair-haired boy and has carte blanche to do whatever he pleases. And I hear that Grant heartily approves of Sherman's methods."

"Then get to Grant," I said. "Better yet, ask Lincoln to do it. It was New England voters he was trying to appease with this whole plan."

"Do you think I haven't done that?" Pinkerton responded. "The communication problems are only slightly improved between Grant and Sherman. And the election is long over, so Lincoln is far less concerned about the New England mills than he was two or three months ago."

I was frustrated but couldn't see a way out. "I thought the trains we use are flying Union flags," I said, grasping at straws.

"Every thinking Southerner in Sherman's path is flying Union colors at the moment, Jack," Kate chimed in. Even if they see them, Sherman's men just assume it's a ruse.

"Welcome to the business world, Allan," I sighed. "We've had two or three shipments get through, so even if we lose the next couple, it's a relatively small loss if you consider the profits we've already made."

"Maybe small to you, Bailey. But I need you to get down there and have Sherman lay off our cotton. You know him. Tell him it's all meant for the North. I can't be seen to be directly involved," Pinkerton ordered.

I can imagine how that would be a problem if he knew you were invested, I thought. But instead I said, "I've only met Sherman a couple of times. On the first occasion he was holding a gun on me because I'd been accused of spying for the Confederacy."

The last thing I needed was another trip to South Carolina, so my instinct was to talk my way out of the possibility. But Pinkerton batted away my attempt at that with, "Then I'll send Kate with you to help your credibility. Kate, I'll draft you a letter to take to Sherman. I'll arrange transport for you both by sea down to Fort Fisher, North Carolina, and will have horses and provisions ready when you land. Our position is that this cotton must be left unmolested, and it must get north to fill commitments made by the President himself." Clearly he'd thought this through.

"Will you also alert the Confederate garrison there to provide us safe passage, Allan?" I asked sarcastically. Fort Fisher was on the coast, 30 miles south of Wilmington, North Carolina and, as far as I knew, both were still under rebel control.

"General Alfred Terry[97] and his men have taken care of that issue Bailey," he responded. "They will have the entire area secured by the time you arrive. I've already sent him word that you are coming. I didn't expect to be sending Kate, but him loaning us a second horse won't be an imposition. Get packed."

I could see that Kate was about as enthusiastic as I was for a 500-mile sail down south, a horseback ride through opposing armies, marauding raiders, hostile locals, and God knows what else. But she remained stoic, and we both spent the next five minutes listening to Pinkerton's instructions and advice about where

97 Alfred Howe Terry was born in Connecticut in 1827. He attended Yale Law School but ended up serving in the U.S. Army from 1861 to 1888. He saw action at Bull Run, Charleston Harbor, Petersburg, Fort Fisher, and Wilmington. After the Civil War he helped negotiate the Treaty of Fort Laramie in 1868 and served as the last military governor of the Third Military District in Atlanta, where he developed a hatred for the Ku Klux Klan. During the Great Sioux War of 1876, men under his command discovered the bodies of George Armstrong Custer's men. He was sent to Canada in 1877 to negotiate with Sitting Bull. Terry died in Connecticut in 1890.

and when to meet our boat, how to find Sherman and, yet again, what to say to him.

At least the schedule that Pinkerton dictated allowed me a day to check in with Brady and pack a few things for the trip. I also decided to visit Anna to let her know that I would be traveling south for a couple of weeks "to check in on my cotton business." I arrived at the townhouse unexpectedly and what I encountered there did nothing to reduce the anxiety I was feeling about her procrastination on my proposal. Seated around a table in the first-floor dining room I found John Jr., Booth, and three men I'd never met, all being served refreshments by Anna. The way that they abruptly stopped talking when I entered told me that they had no interest in my joining the conversation.

John filled the momentary silence with, "Jack, a pleasure to see you! I think you know Mr. Booth here. He mentioned that you and Anna met him at the theatre a few days ago. This is George Atzerodt, David Herold, and Lewis Powell[98]. Turning to them he said, "Gentlemen, this is Jack Bailey. Jack is a cotton trader from Charleston, a photographer with Mathew Brady and an occasional suitor of my sister." While I bristled a little at the last bit, I had to admit it was all true.

---

98 Atzerodt, Herold, and Powell were all hung along with Mary Surratt on July 7, 1865, for their part in the Lincoln conspiracy. Atzerodt was meant to assassinate Vice President Andrew Johnston as Booth shot Lincoln, but he lost his nerve and spent that night (April 14, 1865) drinking at the bar of the Kirkwood House hotel. Lewis Powell was to assassinate Secretary of State William H. Steward that same night and, while not successful, he did wound him and several members of Steward's household. Herold had accompanied Powell to Seward's house, then helped Booth flee to Surrattsville, Dr. Samuel Mudd's home and beyond, following Lincoln's assassination. Herold surrendered when he and Booth were surrounded by Union troops on April 26, 1865, on a farm south of Port Royal, Virginia. Booth was shot and died that day.

Another uncomfortable silence followed, which I broke with, "Speaking of Anna," I said, looking at her while she lingered near Booth, "I wonder if I might see you privately for a moment."

"Yes, just for a moment Jack," she said. "I'm in the middle of fixing our guests lunch." She steered me outside onto the street, which positioned her to ensure that it was indeed going to be just a moment.

"Booth is living here?" I asked, once we were outside.

"No, but the others are," she said.

I decided not to make things more uncomfortable than they already were, so I said, "I just wanted to let you know that I must travel back to South Carolina for a couple of weeks to deal with a few shipment issues. I'm not sure exactly when I will be back, but I was hoping that you might have had an opportunity to come to a decision."

"I'm sorry, Jack," she responded. "With all these new tenants I haven't had much time to think about anything else. Maybe the time that you will be away will surely give us both an opportunity to reflect on the future." Hearing that and, in the same moment, the sound of laughter coming from John's group inside, rekindled the anger I'd felt at the Star after she stalled me the first time.

"Perhaps it will," I said in a tone that I hoped would leave her guessing. "In any event, I will stop by upon my return." The moment I turned away to start back along H Street toward 10th, I again heard laughter coming from the townhouse dining room. While I knew it wasn't directed at me, I couldn't help but resent their camaraderie. I silently wished them all ill.

Chapter 33

A VOYAGE TO FORT FISHER[99]

he following morning, I met up with Kate at the Sixth
Street docks, but it took me a moment to recognize her as
she was dressed in a very masculine manner. Smart, I thought, given that she'd likely be the only female onboard the USS Acacia[100], our transport down the Potomac and out into Chesapeake Bay. The Acacia was a 125-foot-long steam powered tugboat that was loaded with supplies for Terry's troops. In addition to Kate, me, and the crew, there were a handful of men of various rank on board. At full steam, assuming no surprises or bad weather, I figured we'd be on the water for nearly two days.

In addition to what she was wearing, I noticed that Kate had packed efficiently. Everything she carried could easily be

---

99 Fort Fisher, located eight miles north of the mouth of Cape Fear River,
guarded the entrance to Wilmington, a key port for the Confederacy. Known
by the nicknames "Southern Gibraltar" and "Malakoff Tower of the South"
(a Crimean War reference), after many improvements in the early years of
the Civil War, Fort Fisher became the largest Fort in the Confederacy. Its
significance increased with the fall of Norfolk in 1862.
100 The Acacia was a 125-foot-long steam-powered tugboat first
launched in the fall of 1863. It carried two 20-pound and two 12-pound
guns and a crew of 58.

accommodated on a horse. I didn't see any weapons but would eat my hat if she wasn't carrying at least a derringer and a knife. Hopefully we wouldn't need them.

"Good morning, Kate," I offered when I came up alongside her.

"Good morning, Jack," she replied. "Hope you aren't the type to get seasick."

"I'm sick of traveling this route, that's for certain, but can assure you from the many times I have, that I don't seem to get bothered by the motion," I replied.

"Ah, right," she said. "I'd forgotten about Port Tobacco and Norfolk."

"And Cold Harbor, and my return from the Combahee, and the Peninsular Campaign to name a few more," I said.

"Sounds like you know this route well enough that you could take the helm then," she replied with a smile. "By the way," she continued, "I'd be grateful if you would address me as Kitty Warren on this trip any time that we are with anyone other than Sherman or Terry. It's an alias I use in the South. Unfortunately, my real name and my association with Allan has become known among the rebels."

"Kitty Warren doesn't sound all that different from Kate Warne. How about we use Livonia Chord instead?" I suggested playfully. She immediately got the reference to Antonia Ford, the ex-Confederate spy and now wife of Joseph Willard of Willard hotel fame.

"Glad to see that you haven't lost your sense of humor, Jack," she said. "We'll likely need it on this long shot mission."

"Long shot? I didn't hear you trying to talk any sense into Pinkerton when he demanded we try," I said. "Or offer any support when I did." Her assessment of our odds apparently matched my own, although hearing it out loud somehow made our prospects seem more bleak.

"I know him well enough to know it would have been pointless Jack, especially with him being personally invested." She continued. "But even if we get to Sherman, I doubt he could control his men to that degree even if he wanted to. They have been marauding about for months, plundering, smashing, or burning everything in their path and, as we know, with the enthusiastic support of both Sherman and Grant."

I offered her my flask and was surprised when she took a swig. Despite the early hour, I followed suit. We were soon invited on board, shown our separate quarters, and asked to present ourselves to the Captain in his quarters a half hour after we got underway. The Captain invited us to join him for a light meal, during which he went over the plan that we had already heard from Pinkerton. We'd sail down the coast past Wilmington, North Carolina to Fort Fisher, where "Kitty" and I would disembark. General Terry would supply horses and provisions for the next part of our journey. Clearly the Captain was unaware of any of our plans beyond his orders to hand us off to Terry, for which I was grateful. After the meal he declined my offer of a cheroot, so Kate and I took our leave and went topside where I lit up and we both enjoyed the scenery. We stood on the port side, and when we passed the inlet that led to Port Tobacco, I sensed she was remembering the role that town had played in Surratt's hijacking of my first sale of cotton to the north.

"How are things with Anna?" she asked.

She had no way of knowing, but it was when I escorted Anna from Surrattsville to Bryantown on my way to Port Tobacco four years ago that the seeds of our relationship were sown. "Complicated," I responded.

"I can relate," she replied in a tone meant to discourage any questions. Changing the topic, she recalled our first meeting in Baltimore when she and her fellow agents had accosted me on

North Calvert Street as I was walking from the station back to the Barnum Hotel. We shared a laugh and then fell silent for a moment.

"It's been quite the journey since then," she observed. "What were you really up to that day?"

"Just as I said at the time, I had read about Lincoln's intention to pass through there on his way to Washington and thought I would go have a look. If I had known what was in store over the next four years, I might have taken a train up to New York and sailed home instead of traveling back to Charleston." I replied.

"But think of all of the experiences you would have missed," she said. "Meeting Lincoln, hobnobbing at the White House, working with Brady."

"Bull Run, Gettysburg, Fredericksburg, the Combahee." I responded, catching myself before blurting out something about the two Union soldiers I'd had to put down. We leaned against the rail in silence again, immersed in our own thoughts. After briefly retiring to our quarters to freshen up, we joined the Captain, off-duty crew, and the other passengers for a surprisingly enjoyable dinner. As you'd expect, the introductions lacked much in the way of detail. I suspect some of the other passengers were, like us, on some assignment or other that they'd prefer not to discuss. The mood was jovial though, as we all seem to share the feeling that the end of this war might be in sight. When the Captain offered after dinner drinks, one of the passengers picked up a guitar and treated the group to a predictable collection of Union songs, including "Nelly Bly" and "John Brown's Body". He was a first-rate picker with a voice to match. We laughed when he played "Dixie" in a mocking manner. I thought of John Beam when he sang "My Old Kentucky Home", and we all sat in quiet reflection when he ended with "Home Sweet Home".

After breakfast the next morning, Kate and I were standing along the starboard rail when the Captain came by and said that we had just passed Norfolk. The memory of my unplanned swim there brought to mind how the water had washed away the ink on the safe passage letter that Lincoln had given me. I told the story to Kate and emphasized how the fact that the paper had been rendered blank likely saved my life.

"If you are worried about Allan's note to Sherman, Jack, I can assure you that it is in a place where it won't be found," she said with an exaggerated wink. Several clever retorts crossed my mind but, in a rare moment of restraint, I kept them to myself.

The remainder of the voyage was uneventful. At this point in the war, the Confederate Navy wasn't an issue, although I noticed that we were keeping sufficiently clear from shore to avoid any rebel artillery or sharpshooters that might be lurking. At dinner, the Captain announced that he expected to anchor off Fort Fisher at some point during the night and that we'd put into shore the next morning if conditions allowed. I assumed that by "conditions," he was suggesting that the area might not yet be completely in Union hands, which indeed proved to be the case.

Chapter 34

THE SEARCH FOR SHERMAN BEGINS

*J*ust after dawn, I joined Kate and several of our fellow passengers on deck. While all seemed quiet at Fort Fisher, we could hear the unmistakable sounds of battle off to our right, where Union troops were making their way north up the peninsula toward Wilmington. There were dozens of Union ships offshore, with some slowly following the troops northward to provide supporting bombardment. Our Captain approached Kate and me with the news that we were to accompany some of his crew in the first rowboat to go ashore. He was sending a few men to figure out how and where they could safely offload the supplies the Acacia was carrying and I'm sure he was keen to rid himself of his human cargo—us—as quickly as possible.

Upon landing, Kate and I walked toward the Fort, marveling at the destruction all around. The most recent battle had taken place only a couple of days before our arrival, but it had come on the heels of another major, but failed, Union assault that had taken place in late December. Once inside the seawall, I went up to the first officer we encountered and asked where we could find General Terry. He directed us to an area toward the northeast end of the Fort where, after being questioned by a couple of his officers, we were allowed to meet with him. Kate introduced us, then the two of them discussed what would come next. As they talked, I couldn't help but notice that there was far more than the usual carnage in this particular area of the Fort. Once Kate and Terry finished their conversation, I asked him about it.

"The magazine exploded[101]," he said. "Likely sabotage, but we'll know soon enough. What we do know is that it killed two hundred, including both Confederate prisoners and some of my men. We'll add to that grim tally with a hanging or two as soon as we find out who was responsible, no matter what side they are on."

"Jack, General Terry has arranged for a boat that will take us across the Cape Fear River and down to Fort Caswell[102] where he has horses and provisions waiting," Kate said, pointing to the southwest.

"How far is that?" I asked.

"About 8 miles across the water," responded Terry. "And, in addition to the supplies I have arranged for you over there, you are welcome to scavenge anything you find here. There are a few

101 Just after sunup on January 16, 1865, Fort Fisher's magazine exploded killing more than 200 men. Each side initially blamed the other, but a subsequent inquiry found that the likely cause was drunken Union revelers shooting off firearms and using torches to search for loot. Unlike the rest of the Fort, the main magazine had not been assigned guards the previous night.
102 Located at the mouth of the Cape Fear River, like Fort Fisher, Fort Caswell was meant to protect Wilmington, Carolina, which lay some twenty miles upriver. Fort Caswell was also impressively armed, with more than sixty-gun emplacements. Today it serves as a retreat for the North Carolina Baptist Assembly.

Spencer[103] carbines lying around that you might find useful, for one thing."

"We'll look around, but we won't take any of those," Kate said.

"Up to you," replied Terry, "Just be at the wharf on the river side in half an hour. I'll have Colonel John Wainwright[104] meet you there and accompany you to Fort Caswell. Please give my regards to General Grant and Allan Pinkerton when you see them next." That explains the first-rate treatment, the use of a colonel and offer of valuable repeating rifles, I thought. He knows the muckety-mucks. Once out of earshot of Terry and his men I asked Kate why on earth she wasn't interested in Spencers.

"If we run into trouble, it would be difficult to explain why an innocent Southern couple just trying to stay clear of the fighting would each be carrying one of the Union's finest repeating rifles," she said.

"Good point," I said. "So, we are a couple now?"

Ignoring the last remark, she said "Come on Jack, let's find some Confederate coats and hats that fit and stuff them into our luggage. They are likely to prove more useful than rifles." I still wouldn't have minded a carbine but saw the wisdom in the uniforms. My first choice would have been a Confederate Officer's

103 Some 200,000 Spencer rifles were manufactured between 1860 and 1869. It was a seven shot, .51 caliber weapon, and the first military rifle to use metal cartridges. Although used by some (Custer was a fan), the Union Department of Ordinance felt that too much ammunition would be wasted by soldiers using repeating rifles, and therefore no government contract was awarded and most of the troops continued to carry single shot long guns.
104 Colonel John Wainwright was born in New York in 1839. He was one of Lincoln's 75,000 volunteers and mustered in as a private in 1861. He saw action at Bull Run, Charleston Harbor, Cold Harbor, Petersburg, Fair Oaks and elsewhere, eventually climbing the ranks to Colonel. Wainwright died in 1915 and is buried at Arlington National Cemetery.

Cavalry hat, but we both settled for nondescript Kepi's. I must say that Kate looked quite fetching in hers and I made a mental note to see if Anna might be game to wear one during some amorous moment in the future. Satisfied with our finds, we made our way down to the wharf and presented ourselves to Colonel Wainwright, boarded the boat, and set off to the southwest.

I'm usually quick to strike up conversation in such circumstances, as one never knows what useful tidbit might be gained unexpectedly. We discovered that Wainwright had been promoted to Colonel only a few days ago and that he'd been one of Lincoln's 75,000 volunteers when he joined the army as a private shortly after the fall of Fort Sumter in 1861. He'd been wounded in the shoulder during the recent fight for Fort Fisher, although obviously not hurt badly enough to prevent him from escorting us to Fort Caswell. Once there, he hoped to get more sophisticated treatment for his wound than would have been possible from Terry's field medics. We were probably about halfway down to Fort Caswell when an enormous explosion there caught us all by surprise.

"They must be carrying out orders to spike the guns and detonate the magazine," explained Wainwright. "And good riddance too. Once we get to Wilmington, we'll have sealed off all the Southern ports. We'll see how long Lee can last after that!" I read somewhere later that the blast had been heard as far as a hundred miles away, so you can imagine what it sounded and felt like to us, just a few miles across the water.

"Seems like a needless waste," I observed. "Why doesn't the Union use the munitions?"

"There is far more there than we could move, I suspect," he said. "And no point in risking it falling back into rebel hands."

Once on shore we could see that an entire wall of the fort had been destroyed by the blast. Barracks and other buildings were also smoldering, but it seemed to me that some of those fires had been underway since before the explosion. Wainwright excused himself to find our horses and supplies, but not before I asked if he could make some discreet inquiries about Sherman's whereabouts. Kate scowled at me for revealing our objective, but I figured it was better to have him asking around than us, and we certainly needed some clue as to where to start. Wainwright returned about an hour later with two fine looking horses, provisions, and no information about where Sherman might be other than a rumor that his army was bearing down on Savannah, Georgia. He set off again in search of medical assistance, although promised to check in with us before he returned to Fort Fisher.

Kate and I found a quiet spot to settle in and then debated about what to do next. With no definite idea where Sherman might be, we faced a dilemma. Savannah lay 300 miles to our south and Atlanta more than 400 miles west. We could spend a week heading toward one or the other and, if we guessed incorrectly, it might be two or three weeks before we caught up with him.

When Wainwright returned, we thanked him again for the ride across the river and told him that we planned to camp here until we received more definitive word on Sherman's whereabouts. He promised to let us know if they heard anything over at Fort Fisher and said that he would ask the commanding officer here to do the same. In the end, we spent a week enjoying the hospitality of the Union troops guarding their newly captured, if partially destroyed, fort. For the most part though we kept our distance, and, for obvious reasons, Kate did her best to look like a male soldier.

Wainwright returned almost exactly a week later with news from Pinkerton. Allan had written us that Sherman was "heading toward Savannah, Georgia, after which he planned to move up into South Carolina." He went on to say that Sherman's earlier rampaging had disrupted the rail lines to the point that our cotton coming out of Charleston had continued north to Columbia instead of turning west through Augusta to Atlanta. Columbia lay about two hundred miles due west of Fort Caswell but, since the ultimate goal was to protect the cotton, we decided to go there even in the face of uncertainty around Sherman's plans.

After seeing the horses fed and watered, Kate and I initially set off toward the northwest to get away from the swampy lowlands near the ocean. We decided to avoid towns along the way and to travel mostly at night. While doing so would slow us down to about 30 miles a day, it seemed safer than the alternative. Using a map Terry had given us, our plan was to cross into South Carolina south of Tabor City and head due west toward Columbia on a course that would take us south of Marion, Florence, and other towns along our two-hundred-mile route. While there was plenty of time for talk once we found places to hide every morning before dawn, we rode mostly in silence at night. No point in eliminating the advantage of darkness by giving ourselves away with chatter. We also wore the Confederate jackets and hats we had retrieved from Fort Fisher, since the odds of encountering rebel troops were significantly higher than seeing Union men.

About four days inland we spent the day resting in an outbuilding on one of the many abandoned farms we had seen along the way. Before mounting up to set out again on a nighttime ride, I went around back to relieve myself and came face-to-face with an eleven or twelve-year-old girl.

"What are you doing on our farm?" she asked accusingly.

"Just stopped here for the day, Miss," I responded. "We are actually leaving right now."

"Are you with General Beauregard?" she asked.

"Not with the man himself, but part of one of his armies," I lied.

"My daddy and my brother are with him," she said. "But I haven't heard from them in a while."

"Is your mother around?" I asked.

She hesitated, teared up, and said, "Yellow fever." In my last communication with Dawson he had mentioned that they were experiencing a great deal of both yellow fever and smallpox in Charleston. "I am staying with a neighbor."

She looked emaciated, so I reached into my pocket and offered her the large piece of jerked beef I had been planning to eat on tonight's ride. She seemed hesitant to take it, but her eyes were as big as banjos, so I pressed it into her hand. She stepped back quickly but kept it. As I turned to leave she said, "I wrote letters to my daddy and my brother, but the mail isn't working. Can you take these envelopes to them?"

"I'm not sure I'll see your daddy and brother," I began, but her desperate look was hard to resist. "But how about I take them and give them to the first senior officer I see. He'll know what to do."

She stepped forward and thrust them into my hand then stepped back again and saluted. Then she turned and ran off toward the woods.

"So, there's a softer side to Jack Bailey," said Kate. I turned to see her peeking around the side of the building.

"I just don't want her to run to an adult and report us," I replied as I stuffed the letters in the back pocket of my pants.

"Right. Good thinking," she said with a wink. "No concerns for her at all. But let's get going right now anyway."

We figured we were southeast of Marion, South Carolina, at this point, and, according to the map, we had a crossing of the Great Pee Dee River to look forward to nine or ten miles ahead. I knew that river was a couple of hundred feet wide and that crossing one of its bridges probably wasn't a good idea even in the dead of night. What I didn't know anything about was depth, so we had some scouting to do in the darkness. We reached its eastern banks around midnight and spent the next hour or two looking for potential crossing points but found none. We decided to hunker down for the coming day in a stand of trees from which we could observe any river traffic that might happen by and get a better sense of our options. By the time evening approached neither of us had had any epiphanies, so we resigned ourselves to having to risk crossing one of the bridges in the middle of the night. If it was guarded, we'd have to talk or shoot our way across, but even that seemed less risky than having the horses swim us across. God knows how many snakes and other creatures lurked in those waters anyway. I'd rather deal with something I could actually see, like a sleepy rebel soldier.

Shortly after dark, Kate announced that she was going to go down river to a sandy shore we'd spotted earlier in the day and give herself a quick wash before we set off. I jokingly offered to help, but she instead 'respectfully asked that I do the same' after she was done. "And eyes front soldier," she said as she went off. When she got back about fifteen minutes later I shed down to just my pants and an undershirt, then made off back the way she had come. The weather had been warm over the past few days, and I had to admit that it felt good to be rid of all the sweat and trail dust. I had just gotten dressed again and was taking a last look across the river when a voice said, "Here's another one of them." I turned around to see three scrawny young men in Confederate uniforms. One of them was pointing a rifle at me. A British Pattern 1853 Enfield, if memory serves.

"Whoa, gentlemen," I said. "I'm just a cotton trader from Charleston on my way west to avoid Sherman." I started to reach for a carte de visites but realized that they were in the pocket of the coat I had left upriver with Kate and the horses.

"And I'm a New Orleans paddlewheel Captain," said the one with the rifle. "Trying to find a boat I lost here here on the Pee Dee."

"You alone?" another asked.

"Obviously," I lied.

"He doesn't appear to have anything other than the clothes on his back," said the one who had just finished searching me for weapons.

"Definitely from Florence," replied the one with the rifle at the ready. "Let's go then mister. It's back to camp for you. And keep the talk to a minimum. I'm tired of listening to you escapees coming up with one bullshit story after another." They shoved me up toward a path that led away from the river, and I dared not look back lest I give away Kate's presence. Hopefully she would figure out what had happened and make herself scarce.

After moving back a few hundred feet from the river we turned north until we came upon a road where we turned west and soon came to a bridge. We crossed and on the other side met up with a dozen more soldiers who were also herding a group of prisoners. We all fell in and began what was to be a hellish 15-mile walk, prisoners on foot, rebels on horseback. Sometime around midmorning the next day we came within sight of what I would soon learn was the infamous Florence Stockade[105].

---

105 The Florence Stockade was built as an alternative to Andersonville prison in Georgia. While only open for six months (from September 1864 to February 1865) at its peak, the Florence Stockade held 18,000 prisoners. Some 2,800 would die there.

Chapter 35

JAIL TIME

I had never heard of the Florence Stockade, but as we approached its walls, I received a brief tutorial from one of my fellow prisoners.

"It was opened last September," he said. "The rebels figured that Sherman was going to overrun Andersonville, so they built this place as an alternative."

Now I had heard of Andersonville Prison in Andersonville, Georgia (a.k.a. Camp Sumter), although it wasn't until after the war that its grim tally became known. Of the 45,000 prisoners that had passed through its gates, almost thirty percent died. The fact that it held four times as many men as it was designed to accommodate led to shortages of food and water, as well as abysmal sanitary conditions. Its commander, Captain Henry Wirz, would be executed after the war, having been convicted of war crimes for the part he played in the horror. To be fair, I'd also heard rumors of poor conditions at Union prisoner of war camps, including Camp Douglas in Chicago and Camp Chase in Columbus, Ohio. Neither side could take the high road on this issue.

"There are about 7,000 of us here now," he continued, "which is half of what it was a few months ago. They are in the process of moving us up to Greensboro or over to Wilmington since Sherman is coming our way." Given that he'd been a prisoner for months at Andersonville and now here, I was impressed with his knowledge of the current situation and told him so. He said that news filtered in with every newly captured Union soldier. He also reported that the rebels had far fewer guards here at Florence than they needed, especially with some escorting groups of transferees to Greensboro and the like. That explained the number of escapees, I thought. Our conversation ended abruptly with a rifle butt striking the back of my new friend, administered by one of the sentries at the main gate.

"Lieutenant Barrett[106] is going to have a private word with each of you," said the same guard, "so you can wait for your turn over here." Judging from the looks and groans coming from my fellow prisoners, I had to assume that Barrett wasn't in line for any humanitarian awards. The blood and bruises that appeared on of the men that came back from their interviews confirmed as much. When my turn came, I was marched into Barrett's office and more thoroughly searched as he watched. The letters I'd taken from the little girl were discovered in my back pocket and handed to Barrett.

"What's this?" he said looking at them, then me.

"Letters from a young friend that I was asked to deliver to her father and brother," I answered honestly. He ripped one open and read it in silence. When he'd finished, he carefully put it back in its envelope.

"And how would a Union soldier come to be entrusted with delivering such letters to Confederate officers?" he asked me.

"They probably wouldn't be," I replied in my best English

---

106 Lieutenant James Barrett of the 5th Georgia Infantry oversaw the actual stockade, while Lieutenant Colonel John Iverson commanded the entire operation.

accent. "I'm not a Union soldier. I'm a cotton trader from Charleston. The name's Jack Bailey." I offered a handshake but was ignored.

"Then how did you come to be picked up by my men?" asked Barrett.

"I was traveling north to find out what is happening to my shipments," I answered. "And frankly I was also keen to escape the smallpox and yellow fever that are running rampant through Charleston," I added. "Your men picked me up when I was bathing in the Pee Dee. They didn't give me much of an opportunity to introduce myself." As I've said on previous pages herein, the more truth you can inject into your story, the better your chances of selling it.

He chuckled at that but sent for the man that had held the rifle on me when I was arrested. After Barrett asked him a few questions, he turned back on me.

"So you'd have us believe that you walked all the way up from Charleston in an undershirt?" he asked.

"No sir," I replied. "As I said, when your men found me bathing they weren't all that interested in having a discussion. They marched me off before I could retrieve the rest of my clothes or my horse."

"We were in a hurry to rejoin the rest of the troop," my captor offered defensively, no doubt trying to head off Barrett's next couple of questions. Instead, Barrett dismissed him, then fixed a long gaze on me.

"Charleston you say," he finally said. "Easy enough to make up a story about being a cotton trader, but a lot tougher to fake what I know as fact. I spent some time in Charleston. Tell me where I would find the Custom House. In your alleged business, you surely must have been there many times."

I had indeed. "Broad Street at East Bay", I answered.

"If I continued south down East Bay Street, where would I soon find myself?" he continued.

"On East Battery Street," I replied.

"And what would I find to the east of both of those streets?" he asked.

"One dock after another, with Canal Wharf at the far north end and Southern Wharf at the other. Not to mention a dozen or so dangerous taverns and houses of ill repute scattered thereabouts. I can recommend one or two of the better ones if you like." Thank God he was asking me about the darker areas of town. And this was one situation when offering up more than asked could help establish credibility.

All this talk of Charleston's underbelly caused me to recall my old friend Stephen Lee, with whom I had frequented many of that city's watering holes and bordellos in the spring of 1861. Although he was a Captain in the South Carolina militia at that time, I'd read that Lee had been promoted all the way up to Lieutenant General in the C.S.A., so I offered his name as a reference.

Barrett didn't respond, but after another long pause he said, "You look fit enough Bailey, and since we are decidedly short-handed, I hereby draft you to serve as a guard here at Florence. You look like you have a few years on most of my men here, so I am also giving you the rank of Corporal. Welcome to the Confederate States Army, 5th Georgia Infantry."

I would normally have objected but, given the opportunity to pick which side of the wall to be on, the guard's side seemed a more prudent choice. So, for once I kept my mouth shut and within a few minutes had been kitted out with a Confederate jacket, Kepi, and a rifle, all of which had seen better days. One of Barrett's aides was instructed to take me to a sergeant in the guard unit, who in turn would show me around and assign me shifts.

As I walked out of Barrett's office, I avoided looking toward the men that I had just a short time ago been marched into camp alongside.

My new boss, an exhausted-looking Sergeant Johnson, took me up one of the guard towers from where he pointed out the layout of the Florence Stockade. Surrounded by upright timbers that had been driven several feet into the ground, the camp encompassed a little over 20 acres. Much of that area was covered with the stumps of trees that I assumed had either been used to build the walls or burned as firewood. A river ran through the grounds and seemed to be used for a variety purposes, including as a source of drinking water, a place to bathe and, toward the area where it exited camp, as a toilet. Earth had been built up outside the walls both to help support them and to discourage tunnelling. Johnson confirmed that the prisoner population was dwindling as they continued to transfer men to North Carolina and away from Sherman's advancing forces. My ears perked up when he said that I would be tasked with assisting in one of those transfers at some point soon. And so, in the span of a day I had gone from being Pinkerton's messenger to prisoner to armed guard at a Confederate States Army prison.

As it turned out, the living conditions for the minders at Florence were only a notch or two above what they were for inmates. While we guards had a little more in the way of food, clean water, and clothing, everyone faced the same harsh winter weather and lack of shelter. I suspect that more than a few keepers had also fled in recent weeks. Over the next few days, I did my best to look keenly engaged in my work, showing up early for shifts and volunteering for small extra assignments. During that time, I learned that Lieutenant James Barrett of the 5th Georgia was a brutal monster, capable of torture, murder and God knows what else. I did my best to avoid him and silently vowed to shoot him the first chance I got in the unlikely event that Sherman came knocking at our gates. I also remember thinking it a shame that Brady wasn't here to document the squalid conditions, although I wondered if the photographs might have been too gruesome even for the more sensational newspapers.

On February 2, we heard that Sherman had captured Savannah the previous day. A couple of days after that I was asked to lead a group of rebel soldiers tasked with moving prisoners about three miles north to the train station. Once there we would hand them off to a prison train bound for Greensboro, North Carolina. When the time came, I picked a dozen of the scrawniest, least intelligent rebel guards I could find, and we set out with a hundred and fifty or so Union prisoners. The weakened state of these Union prisoners, dehydrated and half-starved from lack of food, made herding them a slow and arduous task. Given their condition, though, none posed a threat, and I probably could have done the job with half the guards. Once we turned these men over to rebel troops at the station, we turned back south toward the Stockade, although I had no intention of completing that leg of the trip. About a mile into our return journey, I told the men that I knew someone operating a distillery in the woods nearby. I said that these moonshiners would be nervous and very likely to start shooting if approached by a group, but that I could manage it alone and would share whatever I bought from them with whomever was willing to contribute toward a purchase.

I didn't get much in terms of cash from this bedraggled group but didn't expect to. That wasn't the goal. What I really wanted was for them to buy into my story and continue their way back to the Stockade without asking any questions. That said, I did collect a small amount and made a good show of logging names and totals. As we separated, I rode east while they continued south. As soon as my men were out of sight, I turned back west toward

Columbia, which I knew to be about 85 miles away. Although Barrett couldn't really spare the men to come after me, and I hoped that my brief feint to the east would send any pursuers off in the wrong direction, I kept up an aggressive pace for the first hour. Based on some of the things I'd seen and heard that Barrett was capable of, I had no desire to be brought in front of him as a deserter. I stopped after a dozen or so miles when I came across a lake. I did keep the uniform on, however, as I knew from some of the officers at the Stockade that Confederate General William J. Hardee's[107] army was making its way north from Charleston on a path that would put them between me and Columbia. If stopped and questioned, I figured that I knew enough about the Florence Stockade to be able to concoct a story about scouting potential routes to move prisoners north. Happily, that was never necessary, though I did find that I needed to use the scouting ruse to procure some provisions from a small farm the next day. I had left Florence with water, but nothing in the way of food, so rode up to an older man working his land and, with feigned confidence, told him that I was a scout for General Hardee. I asked him if he would be able to supply me and, before he could respond, produced the coins that I had taken from my men. Although he outfitted me generously, I sensed he was relieved when I rode off.

107 William Joseph Hardee was born in Georgia in 1815. He graduated from the U.S. Military Academy in 1838 and remained in the U.S. Army until 1861 when he resigned to join the C.S.A. He saw action at the Battles of Shiloh, Perryville, Chattanooga, Peachtree Creek, and Atlanta, to name a few. Nicknamed "Old Reliable", Hardee died in Virginia in 1873.

Chapter 36

A REUNION

*A*fter securing supplies from the farmer, I decided to go back to riding only at night as Kate and I had done after leaving Fort Caswell. While that would slow my pace, I saw no reason to be in a hurry since I only had the vaguest notion of where Sherman might be. Better to take my time and be safe than to rush and get captured again. I had about seventy miles to travel before reaching Columbia, and if I averaged ten miles or so a night I could be there in a week. Between the darkness, the swampy conditions in these parts at this time of year, and a couple of cloudy nights that complicated navigation, even that slow pace proved a challenge. Nevertheless, by February 11 I reached a point west and north of Hopkins, about two miles east of the Congaree River. I figured that if Sherman was coming north from Savannah, he would almost certainly end up following the Congaree, which ran straight through Columbia. My guesswork paid off at dawn the next morning when the sound of skirmishing and the appearance of smoke to the west confirmed that at least some elements of his forces had indeed come up that way.

Confident that I had by now evaded Hardee's forces, I tied the Kepi and a rock inside the Confederate coat I had been wearing since Florence and threw the lot into a swamp. I probably should have tossed the rifle as well but just couldn't bring myself to do it. When the sun was fully up, I started riding toward the smoke while rehearsing a surrender story in my head. About a half hour later I came to the edge of the woods I had been using as cover. I stopped when I saw Union cavalry laying waste to a farm with the same vigor I'd seen applied to plantations down on the Combahee in 1863. One of the things I'd learned in this war was to avoid approaching men while they are in full rage, so I decided to hold back until things quieted down. I didn't have to wait long, however, as a half dozen Union cavalrymen came tearing out of the melee and rode straight toward me. I cursed myself for having ventured too far outside the woods, made a show of tossing my rifle to the ground, then raised my hands and prayed for the best.

"You are under arrest," said the lead man.

"Excellent," I replied with genuine relief since the alternative was likely a bullet. "I've come from Fort Fisher with a message from Allan Pinkerton for General Sherman."

The specifics probably caught them somewhat off guard, but the response was, "You'll need to deal with General Kilpatrick."[108]

"That's fine too, thank you," I said. "Can we see him straight away?"

---

108 Hugh Judson Kilpatrick was born in New Jersey in 1836. He graduated from the U.S. Military Academy in 1861 and was the first U.S. Army officer to be wounded in the Civil War (at the Battle of Big Bethel on June 10, 1861). Kilpatrick was mustered into the Army as a Second Lieutenant, but within three months was a Lieutenant Colonel. Jailed on several occasions for corruption, drunkenness and accepting bribes, he had amassed quite a reputation by late 1864 when Sherman said, "I know that Kilpatrick is a hell of a damned fool, but I want just that sort of man to command my calvary on this expedition." Kilpatrick died in Santiago, Chile, in 1881.

"Is your name Bailey?" the senior man among them asked. Now it was my turn to be surprised.

"It is," I said. "Jack Bailey."

"Follow us then. Another one of Pinkerton's men, er, I mean women, has been with Sherman for the past few days. We were asked to keep a lookout for you," he replied. "A good thing too, you should know. We'd normally shoot an armed man emerging from the woods."

So Kate had made it. And, more importantly, likely saved my skin. As we rode further west toward the Congaree I recalled hearing about General Hugh Kirkpatrick. At Gettysburg he'd earned the reputation of being reckless, a tendency that would show itself again when he'd taken 4,000 riders into Virginia to within a few miles of Richmond in a failed attempt to liberate Union prisoners. He'd come under Sherman's command a year ago and by all reports had embraced Sherman's scorched earth tactics with zeal. I now had no doubt that I had indeed been very fortunate to not be shot or hung by his men.

We caught up with Kilpatrick on the eastern side of the Congaree where he was receiving verbal reports and hurriedly giving orders as men came and went. There was no camp or headquarters per se, which confirmed that they were on the move and driving hard toward Columbia. The lieutenant that arrested me spoke to one of Kilpatrick's aides while the rest of us hung back. The aide then went over to Kilpatrick who listened, looked over at us and then strode toward me.

"Bailey?" he said.

"That's me," I answered.

"I was told that if we found you I was to send you over to General Sherman. I'll have my lieutenant here escort you. Along the way, please inform him of anything you might have seen or heard on your way from the coast that we might find useful.

Confederate troop movements, installations, whatever." With that brief exchange, he turned and strode back from when he'd come. All business, this one.

We crossed the river on a pontoon bridge that the Union troops had recently installed and found Sherman's camp a couple of miles to the southwest. As we approached, the lieutenant rode slightly ahead, spoke a few words to a sentry, then turned back toward Kilpatrick's position with only a tip of the cap. The sentry asked me to dismount, then directed me toward what I assumed to be Sherman's command tent. I was about twenty feet away from it when Kate came running over yelling "Jack, you made it!"

"So did you, I see," I answered as she gave me a hug that would have seemed excessive just a few days ago.

"I thought you'd been captured and taken into the Florence Stockade," she said excitedly. "I followed tracks from the Pee Dee, and it looked like you were heading that way. There were a lot of hoof marks, so I decided it would have been foolish to try and rescue you."

"It would have been. You did the right thing and probably saved my neck anyway by coming here and alerting Sherman. I could easily have been shot this morning by some of that lunatic Kilpatrick's men," I said.

"How on earth did you escape?" she asked.

"It wasn't too difficult. I got drafted as a Corporal in the Confederate Army, landed a job as a guard, and just rode away one day when I was escorting Union prisoners to the train station."

She stared at me for a few seconds and then threw back her head and laughed uproariously. "There's that sense of humor again Jack—even in the face of danger. But you can tell me what really happened later. Right now, we have other problems."

"Such as?" I asked.

"We will go see Sherman together, but you should know this. A few days back Rebel General Joseph Wheeler[109] sent a note to him under a flag of truce. In it he offered to stop burning the cotton in our path if Sherman agreed to stop torching every house we came to," she reported.

"I've just seen Kilpatrick's handywork, so 'Fighting Joe's' request isn't surprising," I said.

"Sherman's response was, though," she replied. "He said 'I hope you will burn all cotton and save us the trouble. All you don't burn, I will.'"

"Shit," I said. Then, "Sorry, pardon my foul language."

"It gets worse," she continued. "You'll hear it soon enough, but when the troops have been on the march the past couple of days, they chant 'Hail Columbia, happy land! If I don't burn you, I'll be damned.'"

I let that soak in and then asked, "Have they started torching the city?"

"We haven't taken it yet," she answered.

"I mean the rebels," I clarified.

"We don't know. And we don't know if our cotton is there in any case," she responded.

As I was considering all this one of Sherman's aides came to fetch us and we proceeded into his tent.

"Jack Bailey," he said as he extended his hand. "Good to see you, although unless you are here to take photographs, I fear I am going to disappoint you."

109 Joseph Wheeler was born in Augusta, Georgia in 1836. He graduated from the U.S. Military Academy in 1859. He resigned from the U.S. Army in 1861 to join the C.S.A. and saw action at the Battles of Shiloh and in several campaigns, including Kentucky, Chickamauga, Chattanooga, Knoxville, Atlanta, and Savannah. He would represent Alabama's 8th District in the U.S. House of Representatives from 1885 to 1900. Wheeler died in New York in 1906.

"No photographs today," I replied. "I'm here to try and salvage some cotton shipments that have been bought and paid for by the Union."

"So I understand," he said. "Miss Warne here passed along a letter from Allan Pinkerton. Unfortunately, my primary directive is to bring the Carolinas to their collective knees. I don't have time to ship cotton or to discourage my men from taking whatever action they feel necessary to get the job done."

"Including destroying everything in sight," I stated.

"Exactly," he said. "And, as you should well know, it's impossible to prosecute this kind of action while telling thousands of men, many of whom are avenging lost comrades, to burn that but spare this. This army is not a precision instrument."

I couldn't fault his logic, but decided to try another angle with, "Both you and Pinkerton report to General Grant."

"Who has mentioned none of this to me," Sherman responded. "The few messages I do receive from him contain nothing but encouragement to do whatever it takes. By the way, do you know for certain that this alleged Union cotton is sitting in Columbia?"

Thinking that a complete loss in this debate was imminent, I responded, "No, but I am willing to go there and confirm it." I could sense a wide-eyed look coming from Kate's direction but was hoping that Sherman would tell me to bugger off. But after a long silence he said, "I really don't give a damn about this cotton. But if you are dumb enough to go into Columbia for a look, and if you survive that and agree to bring back information about Confederate troop strength, gun positions and so on, I promise to at least consider a way to leave your shipment unmolested."

Not very definitive statements, but it was the best we had so far. "Agreed," I said, now convinced that Kate would talk me out of it. When she did, I'd still get credit from Pinkerton for the attempt, once she told him I'd suggested such a bold mission.

"Come back to me in the morning with your plan," he said. "You'll need help getting in there and I'll do what I can in that regard if it doesn't unnecessarily endanger any of my men. Dismissed."

Chapter 37

COLUMBIA

Much to my horror, as soon as we were clear of Sherman's tent and out of earshot of his staff, Kate expressed enthusiastic agreement.

"Great idea Jack," she said. "I still have those rebel coats and Kepis from Fort Fisher. If Sherman's men can get us close, we can slip into town for a peek. With the Union banging at the gates, I'm sure it is chaos in there. We should be able to look around in the confusion without attracting any attention. We'll confirm whether the cotton is there and take a few reconnaissance notes for Sherman."

"I don't recall saying 'we'," I said to give myself time to come up with another reason to kill this insane idea. Or, better yet, have someone else kill it for me.

"I've been in enemy territory more than once Jack," she said.

"In a town on the front lines?" I asked. "I can tell you from personal experience that it'll be worse than you think."

And back and forth we went for the next hour but, in the end, I had stupidly dug myself into a hole from which I couldn't escape without looking like a coward and a fool. The front-line campfires, camaraderie, and music we heard that night, which I would normally find comfort in, didn't work their usual magic. When I finally bedded down under the stars, I suffered a very restless sleep. The only consolation was the return of my Cooper and flask, which Kate had kindly brought with her from the Pee Dee. And the latter was the only reason I got any sleep at all.

My spirits recovered some the next day when Sherman refused to see us. "Too busy," his aide told us. Come back tomorrow. We spent that day relocating closer to Columbia along with Sherman's command and the rest of his troops. We received the same terse response the following day, February 13. I figured he was just biding his time hoping we would give up, but Sherman finally agreed to meet us again on the 14th, and he sat quietly while I outlined our strategy, glancing occasionally at Kate.

"Fine," he said when I'd finished. "I think you are both crazy, but in the off chance I can get some useful information out of this, I'm willing to try. You'll go tomorrow. Come here at dusk in your rebel uniforms and I'll have a few men get you close to the city. At 11:00 p.m. on Thursday the 16th, meet them where they dropped you on the 15th. That'll give you a full day in town and help ensure that you aren't shot coming back out. That said, shed the rebel uniforms before you rendezvous and wear these white scarves around your neck just to be sure you are properly identified. And, by the way, there is a good chance that we'll be shelling Columbia while you are there. Sorry, but I can't stop progress while you two are dithering around."

The notion of an escort and the added touch of the scarves raised my confidence level some, but I still found myself silently hoping that Beauregard's rebel troops would break out and force us all back downriver. Since that didn't happen, Kate and I presented ourselves back at Sherman's headquarters just before sundown on the 15th. We kept our rebel garb in a sack so as not to alarm any of the Union troops as we moved north through camp, only putting them on once we'd reached the outskirts of town. Sherman's men left us on our own just outside the city, and we stood up and walked in with confidence so as not to look suspicious. Kate had been careful to tuck her hair under her cap and she had smeared a little dirt on her face and hands so, at least in the poor light, she looked every inch the rebel private.

We had just entered town when all hell broke loose as rebel cannons started firing toward the Union lines. Looking off in their direction we could see that the Union idiots had lit scores of campfires in full view of Columbia. I'm sure that the Confederate artillerymen could hardly believe their luck, and nor could we. As predicted, the town was in complete disarray as residents and soldiers alike scurried around preparing for an evacuation. The cannon fire added to their sense of urgency and greatly diminished any chance that we'd be stopped and questioned. We were able to roughly identify the location of all the active rebel cannon and noted them on a map that Sherman had given us, thus completing that part of our mission almost straight away. When the Union started to return fire, we looked for shelter and, given that there were so many, had no problem finding an abandoned building in which to hunker down. We ended up staying in that building until the following morning.

Once the artillery exchange died down, the streets were all but abandoned, and we would have been very conspicuous wandering around in the early hours. With the help of my flask and some jerky, we got some sleep and didn't venture out until the streets were busy again the following morning. We didn't know it at the time, but Beauregard himself was still in town and planning to evacuate that evening in anticipation of being overrun by Union forces. It didn't take us long to find cotton, and lots of it. Bales of it lined many of the streets in the city, which I found extraordinary until I came across a copy of the previous day's newspapers.

In it, a Major Green had published an order demanding that all cotton be pulled from the warehouses and sheds and put in the streets to be burned. Normally it would have been taken out into the fields to be torched, but all available transportation was being used to move ammunition, government papers, cash, coin, and other valuables from town. Apparently the locals hadn't expected Sherman to come knocking so soon.

Having found the cotton, we continued to walk around to confirm the locations of the cannon we'd heard the following evening, although most of them were being readied for the retreat. Seeing that, I talked Kate into burning the map we'd marked up, since it would soon be worthless as intelligence. But it would most certainly earn us a date with the hangman if found in our possession. We needed something to take to Sherman though, so we made mental notes on troop strength, the type and quantity of materiel being moved and anything else we thought he might find interesting. By mid-afternoon we were confident that we had enough information to exchange for the sparing of our cotton. Although I ventured in and bought a bottle of bourbon, we resisted the temptation to settle in for a meal at one of several taverns that were still operating. We instead returned to our bolt hole from the previous night and planned to remain there until 10:00 p.m. or so, at which point we would move toward the rendezvous point. In part to pass the time, Kate finally demanded to know how I had escaped the Florence Stockade. She was amazed when I told the full story, and that it matched the brief explanation I had given her a few days ago. We shared a few laughs along with the occasional swig of whiskey and enjoyed a comradeship that only shared danger can bring.

When the time came, we emerged to find the streets still bustling with people frantic to salvage what they could on their way out of town. There were also roving bands of civilians in various stages of drunkenness. Apparently, this lot had decided to stay and have one last party before the Union rolled into town. We were forced to move against the flow as the evacuees were heading north and our destination was to the south, so we took to the side streets. Just as we cleared the edge of town, a Confederate officer rode up and said, "You two. Fall in. We have some work to do on the bridges tonight."

Outgunned and with no choice but to comply, we fell in with a couple of other officers and a dozen men carrying torches, barrels of gunpowder, and other items that told me that something was about to get destroyed. I whispered to Kate to stay close as we marched toward the river and set about following orders to burn several bridges across the Congaree. This work was harder than I would have expected and, unfortunately, the resulting fires lit up the area as if it was midday. Bolting under the cover of darkness was no longer an option. Adding to the risks was the fact that several Confederate snipers were about, armed with their deadly Whitworth rifles. I have no doubt that they would have turned those guns on any of their own had they thought someone might decide to flee prematurely. The net of it all was that we missed our date with Sherman's extraction team.

When our work was done, the officers galloped off toward town without comment and the enlisted men followed on foot. Once amongst the buildings, Kate and I were able to slip away unnoticed and into another abandoned dwelling. It felt as if the Confederates were completely abandoning the city, although we didn't feel confident enough to be rid of the rebel uniforms until we observed four men in a wagon flying a white flag and heading south toward the Union positions. It wasn't long before the bluecoats started appearing in town, led by General Oliver Otis Howard[110]. I recognized Howard from a couple of visits he had made to Brady's studio and suggested to Kate that we go out to meet him. She had transformed herself back to a rather fetching woman and she put her arm in mine as we approached Howard's parade "only to make us look harmless," she claimed. As Howard passed close I called out with congratulations. When he looked my way I boorishly yelled, "Remember me from Mathew Brady's studio?" I guess he did, as he immediately moved his horse in our direction.

"Well, now that I see you up close, I do indeed," he said. "Whatever are you doing here?"

"Miss Warne here of Allan Pinkerton's office and I are here doing some work for General Sherman. Do you know where we might find him?" I asked.

"I expect he'll be along this way shortly," Howard responded.

In a rare moment of forethought I said, "Could we trouble you for a couple of Union uniforms? It would be a shame if we couldn't get to him because of some confusion over our loyalties."

With that, Howard turned around and pointed to an aide that had heard the entire exchange. He moved his horse out of line and over to us where he dismounted, and we waited as horses and wagons passed us in droves. Eventually the aide waved over a wagon that was carrying wounded soldiers and, after spending a few moments looking for jackets of reasonable size and condition, Kate and I were in bluecoats and Union kepis. I'd have preferred a cavalry slouch hat, but beggars can't be choosers.

---

110 Oliver Otis Howard was born in Maine in 1830. He graduated from the U.S. Military Academy in 1854 and saw action at the Battles of Bull Run, Seven Pines, Antietam, Chancellorsville, Gettysburg, Chattanooga, and in Sherman's March to the Sea. He played a role in the founding of Howard University in Washington (where he served as President from 1869 to 1874) and Lincoln Memorial University in Harrogate, Tennessee. Howard died in Vermont in 1909.

We leaned back against a building to wait for Sherman and watched as Howard's men started to fan out and take control of the city, building by building. It is customary for the first troops in to take on the role of police and not uncommon for them to enjoy the fruits of victory in the local establishments. Despite our fatigue, I suggested to Kate that we had earned a night out on the town once we reported into Sherman, and she agreed. About midday, Sherman and his entourage entered town, and we called out and waved to him as he came abreast of our position. He yelled back to meet him at the courthouse in two hours. We knew from our reconnaissance that it was in the center of town, so we decided to join some of Howard's men in a tavern nearby to get some food. Kate warned me to take it easy on the drink, which was wise advice but difficult to follow given the quantity of alcohol being consumed all around us. We heard that great quantities of bourbon and other spirits had been transported here from Savannah to keep it away from Union forces bearing down on that city. With the rebel's hasty evacuation of Columbia, they had neglected to destroy or take it away again, just as they had failed to destroy the cotton bales that now lined many of the streets around us.

When the time came, we made our way over to the courthouse. It was a grand building, as one would expect in a state capitol. Sherman and his team had commandeered offices on the second floor, which offered access to a large balcony overlooking the street.

"Glad to see you are in the correct uniforms for a change," he chided. "Although you, Bailey, seem to have a penchant for switching sides dating back to our first meeting in Centreville before Bull Run." I started to defend myself, but he cut me off with a laugh and assured me he was just joking. I could tell from the look on Kate's face that I was going to be asked to tell another story later. Clearly Sherman was in a good mood as a result of this latest victory.

"You missed the rendezvous," he then said. "We thought you might have been captured, or worse."

"We were, in a way," Kate replied quickly. "Pressed into service by a Confederate cavalry officer helping to evacuate the city." Clearly, she didn't want me blurting out anything about burning bridges. "We couldn't break away until a few hours after the 11:00 p.m. meeting time."

"Some of it is a moot point now, but we do have information on the quantity of soldiers and materiel that were here. We had marked the rebel's cannon positions on your map but burned that when they started moving them out." I added.

"Smart," he said. "Get caught with that and, well," With that he offered us drinks and we sat down and went over the intelligence we had gathered. That done, Sherman stood up and said, "As you can see, the cotton was spared. I'd like to take credit for that, but it was just lucky circumstance. Is there anything else I can do for you two?"

I hadn't thought of it until just then, but I'd had enough of this campaign and felt a sudden urge to get back up north. "I can't speak for Kate, but I need to get back to Washington. Any suggestions on how I might best make that happen?" I asked.

"I am sending a messenger and escort over to General Schofield in Wilmington. They leave in the morning. It's a two-hundred-mile ride, but you are welcome to join them. From there you will have to arrange to get on a ship heading north," he answered.

"We will join them, thank you," answered Kate.

After he told us where and when to meet the soldiers going to Wilmington, we thanked him for his help over the past few days, shook hands, and then made our way back onto the street.

By this point the winds had picked up remarkably, but the victory party was in full swing all around us. The taverns were overflowing, slaves were coming out of houses and offering Union soldiers drinks from bottles that only yesterday belonged to their former masters. Although officially frowned upon by Howard and Sherman, looting proceeded apace. I steered Kate into one of the taverns, where we ordered some food and soon had enough drink onboard ourselves to join in the singing and celebrating. No melancholy tunes tonight though. Someone sat down at an old piano in the corner and guitars, banjos and a fiddle came out one after another. "When Johnny Comes Marching Home", "Tramp, Tramp, Tramp," "Marching Through Georgia," "Garyowen," "Battle Hymn of the Republic," and "Battle Cry of Freedom," all rang out loudly, as if in competition with other establishments up and down the street. Kate gave me a peck on the cheek and kept her arm around my waist when we all sang "The Girl I Left Behind." Given her show of affection, I was quick to pull off her kepi so that our fellow revelers could see she was a woman.

I could have gone all night, but eventually Kate reminded me that we had an early morning and long ride ahead. We decided to go back to the shed we had hidden in our first night in town. It seemed far enough off the main streets to get us clear of the unruly mob and modest enough to not attract attention from looters or anyone else that might come that way. I grabbed a lantern from outside the tavern and off we went. I must admit that we were both staggering a little, but we soon found the lane that led to our hideout. Cotton bales lined the street and, as we passed one, I laughed and pointed at the stencil on the side. "Bailey Importers" it said. So, Elkins, God rest his soul, had carried out my order to start doing that after my difficulty in identifying our cotton that ill-fated day in Norfolk. And obviously Dawson had continued the practice. I recounted the history for Kate, after which she demanded to hear the Centerville story that Sherman had referenced. We shared a good laugh at that one as well, and how my letter from Lincoln had played a part in both situations. Then without warning, she leaned in and gave me a long kiss. I had a brief thought about Anna but assuaged my guilt by recalling her refusal to accept my proposal. As I swung Kate up onto the cotton bale, she said, "Just a minute," then reached under her coat and pulled out a Colt Pocket Revolver and laid it on the bale. Even in my inebriated state, I recognized it as a Model 1855. George Armstrong Custer is pictured with one in his U.S. Military Academy cadet photo in case you'd care to see an example.

"And here I had you figured for a little pepperbox derringer," I observed.

"That's a lady's gun," she said. "And, as you're about to find out, I'm not always a lady." Maybe not a lady, but all woman I soon discovered.

There has been a great deal of speculation over the years about who was responsible for the burning of the city of Columbia, South Carolina. In the end, almost 70 percent of the city's blocks were destroyed. The Confederates blamed the Union, although Sherman was to claim, "I never ordered it and never wished it," but he continued, "I have never shed any tears over it, because I believe it hastened what we all fought for—the end of the war." The Union predictably blamed Confederate saboteurs. I just hope that the lantern Kate kicked over in the throes of ecstasy wasn't the cause, although it was only a short time after it toppled that we had to run from the raging, wind fanned flames around us.

Instead of going to the shed, which it seemed would soon be engulfed in flames anyway, we decided to proceed straight to the rendezvous point for the ride with Sherman's messenger troops to wait out the night. As we rode out of town the next morning, we both glanced back wide-eyed at the devastated capitol of South Carolina.

Chapter 38

BACK TO WASHINGTON

We covered ground much more quickly on our way back to the coast than Kate and I had coming west from Fort Caswell. With several heavily armed cavalrymen as escorts we could travel by day, and they pushed us hard. We covered the two hundred miles in four days, more or less retracing the route we had used on our way to Columbia. Based on my advice we steered well south of Florence and passed Tabor City to the north this time around. We arrived outside Wilmington late in the day on Wednesday, February 22, just as Schofield's army was mopping up. Confederate General Braxton Bragg[111] had pulled his troops out of Wilmington early that morning, and thus the last major rebel port was now closed to the Confederacy. In another signal that the end of the conflict may be near I read later that Tennessee had passed a new constitution that abolished slavery.

Smoke from Bragg's men torching cotton, tobacco, and other

111 Braxton Bragg was born in North Carolina in 1817. He graduated from the U.S. Military Academy in 1837. He resigned from the U.S. Army in 1856 to run a sugar plantation in Louisiana. Bragg joined the C.S.A. in 1861 and saw action at the Battles of Shiloh, Perryville, Chickamauga, Chattanooga, Fort Fisher, and Bentonville. Bragg died in Galveston, Texas, in 1876.

stores still hung over the city as we made our way in. Many of the bridges across the Cape Fear River had been burned, although Union troops had already constructed several temporary pontoon crossings. We accompanied our escorts to Schofield and were able to secure a note from him granting us passage on one of the Union supply ships heading back up the coast to Washington. As luck would have it, these vessels were leaving frequently, with many transporting wounded soldiers. Kate and I made our way over to port straight away, Schofield's order in hand. I was tired of this route and part of me would have preferred to take the horses back up to Washington, but the Confederate Capitol of Richmond and several battling armies lay directly in our path. And, assuming smooth sailing and no stopping, we'd be in Washington in three days by sea, versus more than twice that over land.

I wouldn't recommend the accommodations on a military transport ship during wartime, but we didn't have much choice and the price was right. There wasn't any privacy of course, but I sensed that Kate and I were both a little grateful for that. Although I didn't regret what had happened that last night in Columbia, I didn't see much future in it, and I sensed that Kate had similar thoughts. She remained polite and sociable, as did I, and I was relieved when it became clear during the journey that we would remain friends. Somewhere along the way my mind started turning again to Anna, with whom I could imagine a future. I vowed to myself that I would give it one last try with her as soon as we returned.

We pulled into the Sixth Street docks on February 25, about three weeks after we had departed. I offered to escort Kate back to her office, but she politely declined. We held out our hands to shake, but ended up in a brief embrace before I hailed a buggy to take me the three miles northwest to the Petersen House. I think I logged almost twelve hours of sleep that night, as my body tried to restore itself from the adventures of the past three weeks.

As much as I wanted to hurry over and see Anna the next morning, I felt I owed Brady a visit and went over to the studio first thing. He was all business at first and, after commenting on my recent three-week absence, sat me down for the talk I had been expecting for some time. With the war winding down and his staff more experienced and self-reliant, he suggested that the time had come to part ways. Never wanting to burn bridges (despite my recent experiences in Columbia), I let him off easy by saying that I would soon need to return to my cotton business full time anyway. I had already been thinking along these lines and planned to ask Pinkerton for his help in putting me in touch with the buyers in New England that we had been selling to through the army. Once the war was over, I could imagine both continuing that business along with resuming our pre-war flow back to Liverpool from Charleston. The combination of the two could make for very lucrative trade. Once through the difficult bits of the discussion I told Brady what I had seen in Florence, Columbia, Fort Fisher, and the like, and recommended that he send a team down there. He thanked me for the suggestion as well as for my service these past four years and gave me the rest of the day to pack up my effects, not that I kept much in the office.

Late that afternoon, I ventured over to the Surratt's townhouse fully intent on charming Anna and, at an appropriate time in the next few days, proposing to her again. When I arrived, I found John Jr. in a familiar huddle with Atzerodt, Herold, and Powell, all of whom I had met there on previous occasions. As usual, they immediately stopped the conversation they were having while John made a few awkward comments about it being nice to see me again. Mary came down the stairs and greeted me more warmly, at which point John and his friends left.

"So nice to see you too, Mary," I said, returning her greeting. "I've just returned from a business trip to South Carolina."

"I'm surprised that there is any business there at all, with that animal Sherman on the loose," she said.

"That's why I went," I offered. "I was hoping to find a way to ensure that my inventory was spared but, alas, it was not. A wasted journey, from that perspective. But enough about that. Have you settled into life here in Washington?"

"My preference would be to live in Surrattsville, but I am certainly enjoying the lease payments from the tavern and the rest," she replied. "An unfortunate set of circumstances courtesy of my deceased husband, as you know."

"But it is fortunate that you had this townhouse to fall back on," I said in an effort to say something positive. "Not everyone would have had that choice. I'm sure there will come a time when you are able to move back to Maryland."

"I guess that's true," she admitted. "It's difficult to see how anything will be the same again though. I still can't believe that Lincoln was re-elected."

I didn't want to start down that path and segued with, "Well, speaking selfishly, it's been nice to have you and your family so close by. And on that topic, I was wondering if Anna was home."

"She's not," Mary answered. "I thought you two must have fallen out. She's been spending time with Mr. Booth of late. In fact, she's out with him right now."

Trying not to sound rattled, I replied, "With all due respect, Mary, I find your daughter to be very charming. Unfortunately, my recent travels have prevented me from seeing her more often, but I was hoping to rectify that."

"I try not to interfere with my children's lives," she lied, "but I must say that you would seem a more stable partner for Anna. I like Mr. Booth but, well, he's an actor and..."

"Say no more," I interjected, trying to project that stability she apparently admired. "I am sure that things will work out as intended. I would be grateful, however, if you let her know that I called and was asking after her."

"I will, Jack," she promised with a wink. "And good luck to you."

My worst fears confirmed, I decided to retreat to the Star Saloon to gather my thoughts. While consuming several bourbons too many and some food that the Star's proprietor, Peter Taltavull, put in front of me (as a precautionary measure to counter the alcohol, no doubt), my emotions ran the gamut from deep despair to outright hostility and back. In the end, I decided I wasn't going to give up without a fight. I would keep calling on Anna, try to put my best self on display and hope she'd come around. I got the sense from Mary that I had an ally in her and I would try to get John's help again. Thus emboldened, I paid the bill and started back across the street to the Petersen. Outside, I ran into young Joseph Burroughs holding a flower arrangement and heading toward Ford's Theatre.

"Hello, Peanut," I said. "What are you doing out here?" Ten-year-old Joseph had earned the nickname "Peanut John" by selling peanuts at Ford's during shows. I was one of his regulars and bought from him both there and on this street when I wanted to take a handful into my lodgings.

"Taking some flowers to Mr. Booth inside Ford's," he responded. "He is giving his fiancée a tour and wanted to impress her."

"His fiancée!" I shouted. "That classless bitch!" Completely rejected twice in one day it seemed, first by Brady and now Anna. At least Brady had been gracious about it. I still had an unanswered proposal in front of Anna, for God's sake.

"You know Miss Hale then Mr. Bailey?" asked Peanut.

"What? Who is Miss Hale," I asked, suddenly even more confused.

"Mr. Booth's fiancée, but please, please don't tell him I told you. It's supposed to be a secret," he implored.

"Surely you don't mean Lucy Lambert Hale[112]," I asked. Lucy was a Washington socialite, whom I'd heard at various times had captured the attentions of Oliver Wendall Holmes, Lincoln's private secretary John Hay, and Robert Todd Lincoln, just to name a few.

"That's her. Senator Hale's daughter," Peanut answered.

Well, I'll be damned, I thought. The Lord taketh away and the Lord giveth, to paraphrase Job 1:21. I can't remember ever having a day so filled with swings in mood and fortune, but I hoped this was the last of it. I wondered if Anna knew. Probably not, was my guess, unless Booth had told her today. I decided to drop around the Surratt townhouse again tomorrow to try and figure out what was going on. If Anna didn't know now, I would make sure that she was fully informed by this time tomorrow. I just needed to figure out a way to make it happen without coming across as a complete cad.

"Your secret is safe with me, Peanut," I said over my shoulder as I practically skipped up the steps of the Petersen House. "Make sure you get a big tip from Booth. I'm sure he'll be in a generous mood!"

---

112 Lucy Lambert Hale was born in New Hampshire in 1841. On the afternoon of April 14, 1865, hours before Lincoln was assassinated, Hale was studying Spanish with Lincoln's son Robert and John Hay, one of Lincoln's secretaries. Her father had just been appointed the U.S. Ambassador to Spain. Hale's photograph was among the personal effects found on Booth's body on April 26, 1865. In 1874, Hale married William E. Chandler, who would also serve as U.S. Secretary of the Navy from 1882 to 1885. He would as a U.S. Senator from New Hampshire from 1887 to 1889. Hale died in 1915.

Chapter 39

BACK ON TRACK

*a*fter nursing a hangover for the better part of the morning I strolled over to Surratt's townhouse around lunchtime. There was no sign of John or his ragtag group of friends, but I did find Anna and Mary working in the kitchen, preparing a meal for the tenants. After a quick greeting, Mary excused herself and left me alone with Anna.

"I apologize for stopping by without notice," I began. "But I was in the neighborhood and thought I would take my chances. I was actually here yesterday as well."

"Yes, Mother told me," she responded. "I was out running some errands."

"Your mother mentioned that to me. I hope Mr. Booth was able to provide some useful assistance."

"Listen, Jack," she started, but I decided I should interrupt in case she was poised to break things off with me permanently.

"I'm just surprised he has the time to help you out given his upcoming nuptials," I said. "Such a good friend."

"Nuptials?" she repeated, wide eyed. "Surely you must be mistaken! I mean…"

"Yes, who would have thought that Lucy Hale would ever settle down. I know she's 24, but she seemed to be having so much fun being squired around town." I had planned to find a way to have Mary do this dirty work, but I saw an open door and decided I had better stick my foot in while I had the opportunity. I prattled on as if I thought this was all common knowledge and that I wasn't betraying any secrets. There is no way that Booth could trace the source back to Peanut in any case. I mentioned Hale's age because even though Anna was two years younger than Lucy, I knew that she was getting concerned about being too long on the shelf herself. Convoluted logic I'll admit, but anything to help my cause.

Anna put on a brave face and participated in a little more small talk before saying she had to focus on preparing lunch and then some cleaning. She suggested I call back again soon, and I could tell her mind was racing in a thousand different directions. I offered to return on Saturday to escort her to Lincoln's inaugural address, mostly because it was the first thing that popped into my head. In normal circumstances, I think she would have declined to see the "Illinois Ape" again but, in her haste to get rid of me and be alone with her thoughts, she agreed. That would also allow the news I'd just shared about a week to marinate.

On Saturday, March 4, I again darkened the door of the Surratt townhouse, where I found a very different Anna. I first saw Mary though and, after the usual greeting, she mumbled something about "knowing that something wasn't right with that actor" and imploring me to "be kind to Anna". "Of course," was my response. Along with saying I had never and would never be anything but. Always selling.

Anna came down the stairs looking as fetching as I had ever seen her. I hoped she had prettied herself up for me but suspected that she might have done so in case we ran across Booth at the inaugural. If the papers were to be believed there would be thousands in attendance, and she likely assumed that Booth would be among them. Given Booth's apparent dislike of Lincoln though, I had my doubts. Although it was unlikely that Anna would have named me as the source of her information on Booth's engagement, I reminded myself never to say anything to him that might make me a suspect. I truly hoped that our paths never crossed again anyway but, as it turned out, it wasn't long before I was to see him, albeit from a distance.

In their March 3rd edition, the *Daily National Republican* stated, "The city has begun to overflow with strangers who have come to witness the re-inauguration of President Lincoln tomorrow. The hotels are running over. In some of the leading ones the parlors were occupied by ladies and gentlemen, sitting up all night because no beds could be found for them." After reading this I decided to arrive a little early to pick up Anna. But when we saw the crowds that had gathered in front of the East Portico of the Capitol building, I thought that we had lost any chance to get close in any case. There were people milling about everywhere, but I fortunately spotted one of Brady's crews setting up thirty or so feet back from the stage and about the same distance off to Lincoln's right. They were kind enough to let us stand with them, otherwise we would have ended up well back with a lousy view and out of earshot. The day had started out overcast with a little rain, but by the time Lincoln began speaking the sun had broken through the clouds.

"There he is," hissed Anna at one point.

"You are only seeing him now?" I asked incredulously, thinking she meant Lincoln.

"I mean Booth," she clarified, then pointed. If you consider that now famous image of a hatless Lincoln speaking that day as a clock face with him at the center, you can see Booth on the balcony above him and slightly to the right at about 1:00. His is one of the highest heads visible in the photograph.

Lincoln's speech has become widely recognized as one of his best, but I was struck that he yet again referenced the fact that he hadn't been opposed to slavery in the South, he just hadn't wanted to see it expand. In his first inaugural address he had said, "I have no purpose, directly or indirectly, to interfere with the institution of slavery in the States where it exists. I believe I have no lawful right to do so, and I have no inclination to do so." This time, four years on but speaking about the days leading up to the war, he said "One-eighth of the whole population were colored slaves, not distributed generally over the Union, but localized in the southern part of it. These slaves constituted a peculiar and powerful interest. All knew that this interest was somehow the cause of the war. To strengthen, perpetuate, and extend this interest was the object for which the insurgents would rend the Union even by war, while the Government claimed no right to do more than to restrict the territorial enlargement of it."

I couldn't decide if this was a clumsy attempt at reconciliation with white Southerners or his way of saying to them "see, this war was unnecessary and all your fault." I also wondered how the now freed colored population felt hearing their President suggest that he would have allowed slavery to continue in Dixie absent the rebellion. But he ended with a bang by saying, "With malice toward none, with charity for all, with firmness in the right as God gives us to see the right, let us strive on to finish the work we are in, to bind up the nation's wounds, to care for him who shall have borne the battle and for his widow and his orphan, to do all which may achieve and cherish a just and lasting peace among ourselves and with all nations." I admit that my mind that day was less on the President's speech than it was on Anna and what I could do to win her back. I would have preferred to have done so because of my own virtues rather than as her way of getting revenge on Booth but was worried that in my current state I might accept her either way.

Although admired now, Lincoln's address did attract criticism at the time. On Monday, March 7, an article in the *Daily Constitutional Union* opined that, "The inaugural address of President Lincoln has one merit. It is short. In addition, there is no mistaking the obstinacy of purpose which he shows on the subject of war. Amidst the semi-spirit of mysticism which it has pleased him to throw around it, and which is a marked characteristic of the man, the stern, unyielding partisan fanaticism rings out clear and unmistakable. It is cold and hard. It exhibits neither the wisdom of the statesman or the humanity of the man."

Perhaps a more entertaining speech to have witnessed would have been the one Andrew Johnson gave as he took the oath of office for the Vice Presidency. I had figured that choosing a Democrat as his Vice President was a masterful component in the Republican President's plan to heal the country. But Johnson showed up drunk and gave a rambling address to the Senate after being sworn in. The press pulled no punches, least of all the *Providence Daily Post* which, on March 8 suggested that "…instead of the plodding but inoffensive Hamlin (Lincoln's first VP), they (the Republicans) got a—well, an animal that is restive, wild, uncertain, and dangerous. They got Andy Johnson, and in him, and through him, they and the country are become a bye word, a scorn, a laughingstock." It went on "… to the manners of a clown, he adds the imbecility of the sot…" Not a news clipping that you are likely to find in the Johnson family scrapbook, I'd wager.

As I said, I was probably too distracted and smitten to have fully appreciated Lincoln's address at the time, and the comedy in Johnson's would likely have been lost on me. As it was, I just appreciated the fact that I had been able to spend the better part of the day with Anna and was delighted when she accepted my suggestion that we meet again.

Chapter 40

RENEWED COURTSHIP

J spent as much time as Anna would allow courting her during the month of March 1865. As I came and went from Surratt's townhouse, I usually encountered various combinations of John Surratt, David Herold, George Atzerodt, Lewis Powell, and John Wilkes Booth. On a couple of occasions, Mary Surratt would be engaged in conversation with them. I thought it odd that Booth was still welcome in her home but didn't see any upside in asking her or Anna about it. While the group remained guarded whenever I was around, they became gradually less so over those weeks as they realized that my sole interest was Anna. Knowing what would soon transpire, it likely sounds like I am trying to establish my innocence, but I never did overhear anything that gave an indication of what they were up to. Their growing anger and agitation with the war was obvious, however, and it grew as the news rolled in. On Monday, March 13, the *Baltimore American* reported that they had "…received the files of the Richmond papers on Friday," and, based on that, "We presume that the question of employing negroes as soldiers is definitely settled." The notion of the Confederate States Army using colored troops outraged Booth especially, although John Junior wasn't far behind. I considered pointing out how they had performed with distinction for the Union for years, with the 54th Massachusetts Infantry Regiment's performance at Fort Wagner114 top of mind. But I held my tongue, in part because I couldn't fathom any former slaves willingly serving an army that was fighting in support of slavery in any case.

With the benefit of hindsight, March 18 proved to be a day of lasts. Booth was to give his last performance that Saturday at Ford's Theatre, when he played the part of Duke Pescara in "The Apostate." A few days earlier I had asked Anna if she cared to attend and was delighted when she said no. And said it emphatically, no less. That day also turned out to mark the final meeting of the Confederate Congress. Sunday March 19 was the first day of the Battle of Bentonville, about ninety miles north of Wilmington in North Carolina. Confederate Generals Joseph Johnson and Braxton Bragg attacked Sherman's forces and, being outnumbered three to one, the results a predictable rebel loss. Rather than pursue the defeated rebel forces, Sherman continued his march east towards Goldsboro, no doubt with the doggedness I had witnessed in him first-hand just a few weeks back.

A few days later, on March 25, and a little closer to home, Confederate General John B. Gordon launched an attack against Union General John G. Parke's forces at Fort Stedman[113]. Fort Stedman lay about 140 miles south of Washington and just east of Petersburg, Virginia. Gordon's effort was a desperate attempt to finally break the siege at Petersburg and, with the benefit of a very early start that morning and the element of surprise, his men enjoyed some initial success. But within a few hours the

---

113 The Battle of Fort Stedman (a.k.a. Battle of Hare's Hill) took place in the waning days of the Civil War on March 25, 1865. There were 72 Union soldiers killed and 450 wounded versus 600 Confederates killed and 2,400 wounded.

Union had turned the tables and inflicted heavy casualties on the Confederates in the process. I'm not certain about Brady, but I know that Tim O'Sullivan was at Fort Stedman taking photographs because I have since seen some of them. I also later read that Lincoln happened to be in the area meeting with Grant that day and that a Confederate prisoner was shocked to see them both so close to the action. He said they rode past him, "seemingly not the least concerned and as if nothing had happened." He and the other rebel prisoners around him reportedly took this as a sign of soaring self-confidence and they later "agreed that our cause was lost."

As Gordon retreated and moved east toward Confederate Generals A.P. Hill and Pickett, more fighting ensued at Lewis's Farm (March 29), White Oak Road and Dinwiddie Courthouse (both on March 31) and Five Forks (April 1). While the rebels enjoyed some tactical successes during these actions, they were again outnumbered, further weakened, and the stage was set for the Union to finally break their nearly 300-day siege of Petersburg.

Setting aside Booth's performance as Duke Pescara, each of these events over the preceding couple of weeks further darkened the moods of John Surratt and his fellow plotters. But I could not have cared less about any of it. Things were going very well with Anna, and I wasn't about to get thrown off track by the rabble hanging around the townhouse. On April 2, or Evacuation Sunday as it was called in recognition of the fact that Jeff Davis, his Cabinet, and most of the citizenry fled Richmond, the atmosphere at the Surratt Boarding House was particularly tense. While Surratt and his henchmen felt anger and disgrace, my mind went elsewhere. When a head of state flees his capitol on short notice, I figure that he surely must be carrying all he can from his Treasury. Cash, gold, silver, bonds—all manner of transportable wealth must surely be in play. I thought about mentioning this to John Jr. but reasoned that his loyalty to the disintegrating Confederacy would be stronger than any desire to enrich himself via another hijacking. Instead I decided to get Anna away from this depressing cabal and talked her into dinner at the Willard.

Given that it was a Sunday and the fact that Washington was sensing that victory might be near, Willard's dining room was packed. When I apologized to Anna and suggested we instead try the National Hotel, she insisted that we simply walk down the hall to the Round Robin Bar for old times' sake. Although the National was only six blocks away down Pennsylvania Avenue, I was relieved that she eliminated the need to make that trip. After our drinks arrived I nearly fainted when she said out of the blue, "Jack, I accept."

"Accept what?" I asked, hoping she meant what I wished she meant.

"Your marriage proposal. I've been a fool these past few months. Moving into the city, the war, John's fanatical friends hanging about, our financial difficulties," she said.

I cut her off with, "Forget all that Anna. Water under the bridge, as they say. Recent history has been difficult enough, let's just start talking about the future. I'll start by ordering some champagne."

Naturally, the topic soon turned to when we would get married and where we would live. When I suggested that the war would soon be over and that I should return to Charleston to get Bailey Importers back on its feet, Anna struggled with the notion of leaving Washington. Her mother needed her and would be devastated, she said. I countered that Mary would still have John Jr. around and that their brother Isaac would almost certainly be back from the war before too long. Both would have a lot more time on their hands when hostilities were over, I further reasoned. That seemed to strike a chord with her, although she asked that we not tell her family until she devised a plan. Remembering the last time she made this request I agreed but insisted that we give ourselves a week—until next Sunday, April 9. At that point we'd break the news, come hell or high water.

Of course as luck would have it, April 9 was the day that Lee surrendered to Grant at Appomattox Courthouse[114], some 90 miles west of Richmond. "Surrender of Lee's Army! Grant Dictates the Terms. Jeff Davis at Danville with Some of His Cabinet" the *Daily National Republican* would crow on April 10th. "PEACE! PEACE!" was the headline of the lead article in Washington's *Daily Constitutional Union* that same day. Of course rumors had already reached Washington by April 9, and thus caused a delay in Anna and I making any announcements to her mother. When I was leaving Surratt's Boarding House after dinner that night, John followed me outside and asked if we could talk. I handed him a cheroot, then lit his and the one I had just put in my own mouth. Right then Booth happened along, although I didn't offer him one.

"A sad day, Jack," Surratt began.

"Indeed," I agreed, although I was referring to the postponed announcement about my marriage to Anna and not the Confederacy.

"I don't think it's too late to strike a blow, however, and wondered if you wanted to play a part in our plans," he continued, while pointing to Booth and himself.

"I don't know what your plans are this time, John, but on prior

---

114 Using a white linen dishcloth as a flag of truce, one of Longstreet's staff rode into General George Armstrong Custer's lines and started the process. Custer then met Longstreet, although they agreed that terms would be up to Lee and Grant, who would soon meet at the home of Wilmer McLean in the village of Appomattox Courthouse. Ironically, McLean had moved there just after the First Battle of Bull Run to escape the war, the end of which would now be settled in his living room.

occasions when I've agreed to help you I've ended up in the waters off Norfolk in the middle of winter, getting shot at by hundreds of Union soldiers near Fort Stevens, and fleeing Soldier's Cottage for fear of being charged with murder," I replied.

"You see, I told you he was a decent sort," Surratt said to Booth.

"Thanks for saying so, John, but I think I'll pass this time. You'll understand why in a day or two," I added.

"You don't even know what we are suggesting," Booth chimed in.

"Nor do I want to," I replied. I'd already heard enough to think that I should take this all to Pinkerton, but I knew that doing so would scotch my chances with Anna. Hearing their actual plan would obligate me to do so.

"I'll tell you what," pressed Surratt. "Spend a day or two thinking about whether you want to go down in history as a hero to the South, or if you'd rather be known as a second-rate cotton trader and one time photographer's helper. We can talk again in a day or two."

Given how emotionally distraught these two obviously were, I decided to ignore the insults. I could see this easily coming to blows, although I would have put a quick halt to that with my Cooper. Which, of course, would have also ruined my chances with his sister. Instead I said "Fair enough" over my shoulder as I strode away west on H Street toward 10th and the Petersen House.

When we'd had a quiet moment the previous night before my altercation with her brother, Anna and I agreed to have lunch on Monday, April 10 at the National Hotel[115], at Pennsylvania

---

115 The National was built in 1826. During the Civil War Confederate sympathizers were known to meet there and John Wilkes Booth would stay in Room 228 the night before he assassinated Lincoln. The hotel was demolished in 1942.

and 6th and a stone's throw from Brady's studio. During the meal I expressed my frustration about how there never seemed to be a good time to make our announcement to her mother and, much to my surprise, Anna agreed. I suspect she was dreading the thought of telling Mary, as well as the drama that would surely follow. Thinking on my feet, I suggested that we elope this coming Friday, April 14. I tried to sell the idea using the fact that it happened to be Good Friday, which would give us luck. It was nonsense of course, but I knew people who believed that eggs laid on Good Friday would never go bad, and that bread baked on that day would never go moldy. "And thus nor will our relationship ever go bad or moldy," I concluded in a desperate leap of logic. And think what you will, she agreed.

We spent the remainder of lunch planning logistics. We'd meet late that evening here at the National, catch a buggy to the train station the next morning, and make our way south to Charleston. I had no doubt that the effects of the war—and Sherman—would mean that there would be gaps in the train tracks and other obstacles along the way, but I felt I knew that route well enough to manage. If I could get in and out of Fort Sumter and the Florence Stockade, and change sides several times within 48 hours along the Combahee, what was 600 miles through a demilitarized Dixie? I'd have my "King Cotton" Cooper and his twin brother along for the ride and would pick up a pepperbox derringer for

Anna before Friday. A Remington Zigzag[116] would do nicely if I could find one.

When I suggested that we take a room upstairs after lunch to seal the deal, Anna reminded me that, as far as her mother knew, she was out buying provisions for their tenants' meals, and she was already overdue to be back. So I helped her into a buggy, sent her north up 6th toward H Street, then started walking up Pennsylvania Avenue toward 10th Street. That route took me past Brady's studio and I couldn't resist going in to have a look around. I was glad when I ran into the man himself.

"How are you Jack?" he asked.

"Never better," I replied. "Especially with this war over."

"Amen to that," Brady replied. "Although there is still plenty of work to do for us. I am taking some men down to Richmond where I hear the devastation is something to behold."

"Having seen Columbia shortly after it was torched, I can well imagine," I said.

"I also hope to convince Lee to sit for me there," he continued. "You should come along. I recall the first time we met you told me you knew him. That might help me get him to agree."

"Ah," I responded, suddenly remembering what had transpired. "I do recall telling you that I knew Lee, but I meant General Stephen D. Lee not General Robert E. Lee. I apologize for the

---

116 The Remington Zig Zag Derringer (a.k.a. Elliot's Pocket Revolver) was designed by Eliphalet Remington, founder of Remington Arms. It was a six barreled six-shot, .22 caliber revolver manufactured in 1861 and 1862. About 1,000 were made. Remington Arms was started in 1816. It filed for bankruptcy in 2018 and again in 2020 but reemerged in 2022. The company has made many gun models over the years and its customers have included Annie Oakley, George Custer, and Buffalo Bill. The iconic Model 870 shotgun, which debuted in 1950, is still produced today and, with 11 million built, it ranks as the most popular shotgun of all time.

confusion." The twinkle in his eye told me he knew that the mis-understanding had been intentional, but he let it go.

In mid-afternoon on Tuesday, April 11, I went to the Surratt Boarding House unannounced. While I wanted to see Anna, I'd also decided I should redouble my efforts to ingratiate myself with Mary. She wouldn't be pleased about our elopement, but I figured that the more she liked me, the quicker she would get over it. I arrived to find that Anna was out shopping, and I remember hoping that she was doing so in preparation for our trip to Charleston. But Mary was home, which suited my needs perfectly. I helped her clean up the lunch she'd just served and asked all the right questions about how she was getting on. My questions about Isaac brought a tear to her eye, as she hadn't heard from him for several weeks. I took the opportunity to give her a hug and promised to make some inquiries. John appeared at one point looking agitated, and after Mary excused herself and went upstairs, he asked if I had come to any decisions.

"How can I make a decision on something I know nothing about?" I asked.

"Fair enough," he replied. "I tell you what. Some of us are meeting in front of the White House tonight to hear Lincoln's victory speech. We'll get a drink afterwards and will tell you what we are thinking. I believe that you'll be interested."

I couldn't resist confusing him a little and said, "Is this about the Confederate treasury?"

"What?" he replied.

"Gold, cash, silver. It must be on the move somewhere," I said.

"I have no idea what you are talking about, Jack. Just meet me in front of the White House tonight before 8:00 p.m. I'll be with Booth, Powell, and some of the other gentlemen you've met here before."

I wanted to point out that calling them "gentlemen" was being a little generous, but instead agreed. I'd planned to go anyway, not just to hear Lincoln, but also to enjoy the revelry that was sweeping Washington at that moment. It was reminiscent of the joyous atmosphere in Columbia after the Union had taken the town, but hopefully we'd skip the fires this time. I left word with Mary that I would drop around to see Anna again tomorrow and then I walked over to the Star Saloon for some dinner and refreshments. It was a little over a half mile from the Star to the White House, and I figured I would walk that as well, despite the muddy streets that were a hallmark of Washington in the spring.

Chapter 41

BAD TIMING

The festival-like mood in Washington extended into the Star, which was as crowded as I'd ever seen it. Fortunately my friendship with proprietor Peter Taltavull meant that there was always room for me somewhere, although today it would be standing at the bar. I chatted with him intermittently while he hurried about serving patrons and as I scarfed down the dinner and several drinks I'd ordered. Peter had treated me well over the past four years and because of that and the charitable mood I found myself in, I tipped him heavily before leaving for the White House.

The President was due to speak from the north portico, so I made my way there cursing as I slogged through the mud. As had been the case last month at the inauguration, there was an impressive crowd waiting to hear words from their President, just two days after Lee's surrender. While looking around for Surratt I noticed a group of people fawning over Booth. As distasteful as the thought was, I figured that if Surratt wasn't with him, he soon would be, so made my way over to him. Surratt wasn't there, but Lewis Powell was, and he gave me a perfunctory nod as I came up alongside them both. While the ladies loved looking at Booth, it seemed they thought Powell cut a fine figure himself. I thought he always had that look in his eyes that suggested he was just a comment or glance away from a donnybrook but, again, you'll just think I am saying that with the benefit of hindsight. You'll see what I mean if you look at the photographs of him in irons after his forthcoming arrest.

I asked about Surratt, and Booth said they expected him to be along at any moment. Before we could talk much more, a great cheer went up as Lincoln appeared. The bands that had been playing patriotic songs quickly petered out and all one could hear for some time was sustained applause. Looking around I noticed that neither Booth nor Powell had joined in the clapping, so I put my hands in my pockets. I could see Mary Todd Lincoln and a gaggle of her friends at a window near the President, and son Tad bustling around his legs.

"We meet this evening, not in sorrow, but in gladness of heart," the President began after the cheers subsided. "The evacuation of Petersburg and Richmond, and the surrender of the principal insurgent army, give hope of a righteous and speedy peace whose joyous expression cannot be restrained,"

Anyone expecting him to dwell upon, or take credit for, the Union's victory over the Confederacy was soon disappointed. After crediting Grant and the Union army, he quickly moved on to talk about reconstruction. To my mind he spent an inordinate amount of time discussing Louisiana, which had recently adopted a constitution that abolished slavery. As he prattled on, I scanned the crowd to try and gauge what sort of reaction he was getting. That's when I spotted Pinkerton staring at me. As soon as our eyes met he nodded his head in a way that suggested he wanted to meet a little farther back in the crowd. With Booth and Powell fuming and cursing Lincoln at every turn, I welcomed the opportunity to leave. I said to them both, "I'm going to have a quick look around for Surratt. When I find him, I'll bring him back here." Booth dismissed me with a wave of his hand and neither of them took their eyes off Lincoln.

"Changing careers again Jack?" Pinkerton asked when we met about 50 feet back of Booth.

"What do you mean?" I replied.

"Befriending Booth," he responded. "I thought you might be getting ready to try your hand at acting."

"He's certainly not a friend, I can tell you that. And no career changes for me. I met him a couple times when he sat for Brady," I lied. "I plan to return to Charleston soon to get Bailey Importers back on track."

"I guess with the war over there is less chance of losing more shipments and more money," he said.

"Listen Allan, about that. I feel terrible, even though we all knew the risks and we all took a loss. And you know as well as I do that if

Lincoln's Second Inauguration, Courtesy of the Library of Congress, LC-DIG-npcc-29803

you subtract that loss from the successful sales we made previously, you about broke even. But I was wondering – if you can help get me in touch with those buyers in New England, we'll cut you in on future business. I guarantee you'll be happy you tried again."

"Good money after bad," he said like a true Scot.

"I'll front you the money Allan. No risk to you. Just get us connected to those buyers," I said. Better to have him in the tent than not, I figured. And this would be a genuine help.

"I'm not doing anything unethical," he said, at which point I knew I had him leaning in the right direction.

"That's good," I replied, "Because neither am I."

"I'll think about it. On another topic, I assume you know that Booth is a rebel sympathizer," he said.

"One of several reasons we aren't friends," I replied.

"Watch yourself, Jack. This war isn't over in the minds of some," he warned as he strode off.

"I'll be in touch regarding New England," I yelled after him.

At this point Lincoln had just finished his speech. Had Pinkerton not called me away, it's very likely that I would still have been with Booth. If so, I would have heard him say the words that others would report he said that night, including "That is the last speech he will ever make," and "Now, by God, I will put him through.[117]"

Had I heard all that, I would have gladly reported it to Pinkerton. I owed Booth a nasty turn for his flirting with Anna and, with Surratt not present, I could have done so without im-plicating him and, by extension, putting my relationship with

---

117 Lincoln's speech that night was also witnessed by Charles Augustus Leale, a Union Army surgeon that had graduated from medical school less than two months earlier. He was the first doctor to treat Lincoln the night of his assassination. Leale was born in New York in 1842. He died in 1932 at the age of 90.

Anna at risk. If I had done so, would Lincoln have lived? It's a good question.

Unaware of the significance of that chat with Allan and still euphoric about my planned elopement, I walked back to the Petersen House and made a list of things to do before I retired for the night.

Chapter 42

ANOTHER CHANCE ENCOUNTER

J spent April 12 and 13 quietly making arrangements for my move back south. I wrote to my father to say that I would be back in Charleston by the end of the month. I settled up with the Petersen's and paid for my room through the 14th. I saw Anna on a couple of occasions and convinced her to sneak some of her belongings out of the house so I could ship them and some of my own possessions down to Charleston. Better that we travel light, especially Anna, since she could only leave the house on Friday night with what she could carry. We agreed that she would wait until Mary fell asleep, which meant she would be leaving their boarding house around 11:00 p.m. I offered to come and pick her up, but she would have no part of that in case her mother or anyone else from the household spotted us. She pointed out that the National Hotel was only six blocks south of the townhouse, straight down 6th Street. She also said that her friend Nora Fitzpatrick had agreed to escort her and reminded me that she would be carrying the derringer I had given her a few days earlier.

"So, Nora knows," I said.

"I trust her, Jack," she replied. "And I just had to tell someone!"

Frankly, I was relieved that she had because it confirmed her commitment. Not that I doubted her, but there had just been too many twists and turns along the path of our relationship for me to be completely at ease.

On the morning of April 14, I went over to Pinkerton's office to ask him again if he would be interested in remaining a minority partner in Bailey Importer's domestic business, but neither he nor Kate were around. I had read that Lincoln was signing legislation to create the U.S. Secret Service that morning, so assumed they might be there to witness that. In any event, I scribbled "LET ME KNOW" on one of my carte de visites and asked one of the clerks to pass it on to Pinkerton. From there I went to the train station and purchased tickets for Anna and myself on a train leaving first thing the next day.

That afternoon, I went to the National, checked in, and dropped off my luggage. As I was leaving I ran into Al Waud in the lobby, so I stopped to have a drink or two and do a little reminiscing with him. An hour or so later I left and, since I was in the neighborhood, stopped by Brady's studio, but was told that he had set off for Richmond to get photographs of that city and, with any luck, Robert E. Lee[118]. Maybe it was the drink, but I was feeling a little nostalgic and so I decided to wander around the city some to kill time. I eventually went back to Pinkerton's offices, thinking that I would prefer to have our partnership discussion face-to-face, but he was still out. Frankly, I was also hoping to say goodbye to Kate, but she hadn't returned either.

Eventually I found myself back at the Star, thinking I would have dinner before going back to clear out the last of the few things remaining at the Petersen House. Once again, the Star was busy, as was Ford's Theatre next door, where "My American

---

118 Brady did get permission to take that photograph and did so on April 16, 1864. Lee posed on his back porch in the uniform he wore for the surrender at Appomattox Courthouse. It would be Brady's last Civil War photograph.

Cousin" was on offer that evening. Peter Taltavull saw me come in and pointed me to the back where a barmaid was just cleaning up my usual table as its current occupants were picking up to leave. Peter came over and sat for a while and we chatted about the end of the war, reconstruction, Jeff Davis's whereabouts and other news of the day. After a while Booth came in, spotted me, and sat down at my table.

"What are you doing here Bailey?" he asked.

"I live across the street," I replied. And that was still technically true, at least for the next several hours.

"Hmm. Never quite trusted you Jack. I don't know why. I guess you never found John Surratt on Tuesday night," he said.

"Tuesday night? Oh, at the White House. No, I didn't. When the speech ended I'd decided I'd had enough slogging around in the mud, and I went back to my rooms," I answered, suddenly wary. He had that "I'm ready to brawl" look in his eye that Powell seemed to always have on display.

"I could have had her you know," he said, looking around the room.

"The barmaid? I don't know her, but I'm sure she knows you. You're probably right," I said, trying to lead him off in another direction.

"Anna Surratt," he replied, looking me right in the eye.

Again attempting to change the topic I said, "By the way, what are you doing here John?"

He ordered another double, then said, "I work next door."

"Right," I said. "Should have been obvious."

"And I have my grand finale this very night," he continued.

"I think the play has already started," I said. "Shouldn't you be over there?" As if on cue, at that moment we both noticed some of the stagehands straggling in, so intermission must have been underway.

"Plenty of time," replied Booth. Then, going back to his taunts, "Lucky for you that Lucy came along."

I shifted in my chair in such a way as to make my Cooper more accessible, stood up and said, "Sod off Booth. You are just the kind of ass that gives your profession a bad name."

He threw back his head and laughed. "We'll see about my name tomorrow," he hissed over his shoulder as he rose and moved to join the stagehands who had assembled at the bar. Not wanting any trouble during my last few hours in Washington, especially the kind of trouble that might lead to the use of firearms, I paid up and headed for the door. I figured I would gather up my things from across the street, walk over to 6th Street and wait for Anna to come along so I could escort her the last two or three blocks down to the National.

Chapter 43

LAST

J decided to relieve myself in Baptist Alley behind the Star before going back across the street to my room at the Petersen. I heard a horse snorting by the back of Ford's Theatre and, walking over to investigate, found Joseph Burroughs holding the reins of a mare.

"Hello, Peanut," I said. "What the Sam Hill are you doing out here at this hour?"

"Ned Spangler asked me to hold her here for Mr. Booth," he responded, pointing a thumb at the horse. "He had been doing it himself but then he had to go in and help change sets for the next Act."

"Well, you shouldn't have long to wait, son. I just left Booth in the Star finishing up a nightcap. He's drunk, which means there might be a good tip in the cards.[119]" With that, I patted Peanut on the head, walked around the building, crossed 10th Street, and went upstairs to finish packing for my rendezvous with Anna.

---

119 As it turned out, the only tip that Peanut John received that night was the tip of the handle of Booth's knife, which sent him sprawling to the ground bleeding.

Mary Surratt, Lewis Powell, David Herold, and George Atzerodt post hanging, Courtesy of the Library of Congress, LC-DIG-cwpb-04230

www.ingramcontent.com/pod-product-compliance
Lightning Source LLC
Jackson TN
JSHW020142200325
80913JS00004B/83